D0495523

# SINS OF OMISSION

## Gemma O'Connor

## BANTAM BOOKS
LONDON · NEW YORK · TORONTO · SYDNEY · AUCKLAND

SINS OF OMISSION
A BANTAM BOOK : 0553 81263 7

Originally published by Poolbeg Press Ltd, Dublin, Ireland

PRINTING HISTORY
Poolbeg edition published 1995
Bantam Books edition published 1999

1 3 5 7 9 10 8 6 4 2

*Visit the author at*
*www.gemmaoconnor.com*

Set in 11 pt Sabon by
Deltatype Ltd, Birkenhead, Merseyside

Bantam Books are published by Transworld Publishers Ltd,
61–63 Uxbridge Road, London W5 5SA,
in Australia by Transworld Publishers, c/o Random House
Australia (Pty) Ltd, 20 Alfred Street, Milsons Point, NSW 2061,
in New Zealand by Transworld Publishers, c/o Random House
New Zealand, 18 Poland Road, Glenfield, Auckland,
in South Africa by Transworld Publishers, c/o Random House (Pty) Ltd,
Endulini, 5a Jubilee Road, Parktown 2193.

Reproduced, printed and bound in Great Britain by
Cox & Wyman Ltd, Reading, Berks.

## Acknowledgements

This book has had a protracted incubation. I am extremely grateful to my family for their unwavering and good-natured support throughout: John and Emily for stylistic (and general) good advice, Oscar for unravelling the PC, Simon and Frances for professional medical advice, which, if I've got it wrong, is my fault not theirs.

My warm thanks also to: Orla Murphy, Jon Stallworthy and Úna O'Connor for letting me talk (at length) through the plot; Sarah Frost for producing the final typescript so accurately and so quickly, Richie Gill for keeping me calm when the screen went blank; Mary Campbell, my encyclopaedic guide to Clerkenwell; my sister Pauline Fitzpatrick for providing me with a Dublin base, Toon and Edith Huson in Holland, Patricia Scanlan and Ruth McCarthy for being so enthusiastic about the final draft.

Christine Green has believed in and supported me ab initio, I would like to thank her and my editor at Poolbeg, Kate Cruise O'Brien, for thoughtful and sensitive editing and finally, my publishers for their stirring support.

*The Grand Canal is no longer as neglected as I described. I hope the army of volunteers who, over the past few years, have cleaned and cleared it so successfully, will forgive me for seeming to ignore their transforming work.*

*And again, for John, of course.*

# PROLOGUE

... the point is, if he had not been speaking Dutch the first time they met, she would not have assumed him to be Dutch. And had she not assumed that, she might not have made other assumptions nor taken so much on trust. She might have expected to know more about him, his family, his birthplace. She might have questioned more and thus learnt more. Or at least learnt that there were large gaps in her knowledge of him and, moreover, gaps she didn't even bother to consider.

Someone from nearer home would have been questioned more closely. A neighbour, failing to comply to expectation, would, oddly enough, have given rise to more disquiet. Her curiosity once aroused might have lent more urgency to her probing for information. So that if, in those circumstances, the accumulated knowledge had not shown coherence she might have attempted to find out why not. As it was, because she believed he was from Holland, a country she had never even visited, she hardly perceived how little she knew about him. Any facts about him which did not fit with others she attributed to his foreignness and set aside as of no consequence. The totality of her ignorance of the people, their way of life and their language masked the detail of her ignorance of the individual. She took everything on trust from a seeming stranger. She would not have been so naïve about a local.

*Of course, Bid was in love. Passionately, completely and I believe Cas was also in love, at least at the end. Nobody I spoke to appeared to question that. They said anyone with half an eye could see it. It wasn't just their similar colouring which made them look like parts of the same whole, but because their happiness in each other glowed. Yet strangely the glow did not spread to include those around them, rather it formed a barrier between them and the world. To be admired but not shared.*

*Not that they were much in company. Almost from the beginning they were content with each other, so that as they got to know each other as a couple, friends did not. Of course the fact that he wasn't free – already married – would have contributed in any case to the air of secrecy; but somehow there was more to it than that. As the relationship deepened, their preoccupation with each other grew. They created their own private world, own private rules and reality was not allowed to intrude. But alas, reality has an insidious way about it and even the most perfect relationships cannot remain static. As they loved more they got to know each other a little more. Random questions must have yielded random snippets of information. Perhaps at the end her questions became more directed; curiosity would not be stilled. Bit by bit the pieces slipped into place and the story unfolded. But by then it was all too late. Half-truths and secrecy had become a way of life; unpalatable facts set aside or ignored so they got out of the habit of facing reality especially if it threatened their relationship. Until the end that was the important thing and nothing, absolutely nothing, was allowed to interfere with it.*

*Fatally, they had both, individually, a history of skirting around issues they did not like. Perhaps it was inherited, certainly it was part and parcel of her background – I am prone to it myself – and if her axiom was 'forget it and it will go away' she was not unusual in that. As long as no-one reminded her of her lover's family she could pretend they did not exist. Both to herself and to her mother.*

*It had been ever thus, as those who knew them have attested. Even while Bid was growing up her mother avoided intimacy. Embarrassing questions might form but were never voiced. Discussion was simply not part of their agenda; things had to be nice and if they weren't nice then they could pretend. Except that as time went on it was slightly more than pretence. So, faced with something as important as a married lover, neither mother nor daughter could discuss it. But above everything they could not bear to admit, discuss or cope with, any significance it might have on Bid's future.*

*That was serious enough, but then as time went by Bid developed a wilful tendency to still any disquiet she had about her own ignorance of Cas's background. Whatever could not be explained was, she insisted to herself, because of his foreignness. This was a mistake. But her major mistake was that first assumption, about his nationality, and had she not made that assumption four people would not have died.*

Grace Hartfield,
Ballymahon.
Sunday, 29th October 1990.

Friday, 13th April 1990


**STOP PRESS:** A man's body, retrieved from the Grand Canal, has been identified as a missing tourist. His name is being withheld until his family has been informed.

*(Extract from Dublin Evening Herald, late edition.)*

# CHAPTER ONE

'Hey, Mister! Did ya see tha'?'

Two scruffy urchins ran along the canal bank towards the old man who was standing about fifty yards from the lock, intent on a funeral cortège which had halted outside the middle house of the terrace directly opposite. Cap in hand, he stood mumbling softly to himself while he squinted short-sightedly at the seven or eight cars idling behind the sleek black hearse; then, as the procession moved ponderously forward, he crossed himself piously and muttered something about it not being much of a show. Obsequies observed, he turned towards the water and took a small white paper bag from his pocket. Still maundering and scolding, he sprinkled crumbs while at his feet the ducks screamed and cackled for more.

'Away with ye all now! Away with ye!' He waved his arms feebly at the birds; but not being satisfied, they paid no need, flapping greedily from the murky water, ever more insistent.

'Hey, Mister! Mister, did ya see tha' man? Mister?' Small filthy hands grabbed at his jacket.

He pushed them off angrily.

'What? What do youse want?' His hand cupped his ear as he bent over and glared at the two small boys. Hail, rain or shine, for days now they had been fishing by the lock and he did not approve.

15

'Dirty little gurriers!' He pushed them away. 'Youse should be at school. What's this country coming to at all? Too much television, that's what. And videos. Get away outa tha'!'

For an instant the children fell back, but driven by some more urgent impulse tried again: 'Mister! He went in the water . . .'

'What? What did you say?' The old man glowered down at them. Frantic with impatience, they answered, in unison, at the tops of their voices.

'One at a time and quietly. Ya don't have to shout my head off!' he roared.

The taller of the two bounced up and down with frustration.

'But, Mister. Mister, tha' man. He's in the canal. The man tha' was sitting on the seat. Next minit,' the boy's voice rose shrilly, 'he was gone.'

The boy gulped back a sob. The old man gawped at them for a moment before waving them away.

'Gone where? Are ya joking me or what?' He started off down the towpath leaving the children chorusing a last desperate appeal:

'No, Mister, honest. In the water . . . the man . . . Honest.' They were wide-eyed with distress.

It was no use. They turned disconsolately away, vainly searching for some more sympathetic audience. There was nobody else in sight except those sitting unheedful, in the passing cars, but they'd been warned to stay away from the road. The boys walked indecisively back along the towpath; as they got towards the bridge Billy grabbed his pal.

'Ya saw it, didn't ya, Wayne? Ya saw him going

16

in, didn't ya? Ya must have. Wayne?' He shook the other child's shoulder.

'Aw, leave off, Billy. I wanta go home. I want me mammy. Come on, Billy. Please, Billy, I want to go to the lav.'

The smaller boy began to cry. Billy put his arm around his friend's shoulder and pulled him towards the lock.

'No, Billy. No! I don't want t'go there no more. Billeee . . .' His voice rose in a piercing yowl as rivulets of urine ran down his leg.

'Oh jaysus, Billy, look wha' you made me do. Me ma'll kill me. Ow, Billy, wha'll we do?'

They edged uncertainly towards the water and peered in. Apart from some bubbles rising to the surface there was no movement and no sign at all of the man. Wayne began to howl again.

At that moment, a woman who had been watching the funeral on the other side of the road, crossed over and walked up on to the bridge. She was leading a reluctant small dog and, while he marked out his familiar territory, she glanced carelessly over the parapet.

'What's all the commotion about?' she called to the children. 'Have you pair lost something?' she asked and backed down to the bank.

The children exchanged glances, then she was almost thrown off her feet by the younger boy who broke away and hurled himself into her arms, sobbing. She held him, absently stroking his stale and matted hair, her nose twitching with repugnance. The other child stared at her suspiciously, streaks of dirt outlining his reddened eyes. His

17

mouth opened and shut as he swayed back and forth.

'Is something wrong?' she asked politely and held her hand out to him.

'Please, Missis ... please ... the oul' fella wouldn' believe us. Missis ... aw, Missis ...' The boy began to shake violently. He rubbed his filthy hand across his nose.

Holding on to the smaller boy, the woman sank down on the damp grass and held out her free hand.

Cora Farrell had been wondering for some days now how it was the two children were not at school. They'd been glued to the lock for at least a week. Indeed, she'd seen them quite often over the past fortnight as she walked her dog. Did their mammies know, she asked herself, or did they care? They were awful young to be out on their own.

She smiled at the taller of the two.

'Now, quietly, tell me what ails you and let's see if we can do something about it. What's your name?'

'Billy, Missis. Tha's Wayne,' he said impatiently.

She supposed it could be worse, a few years younger and he'd probably be called JR. She smiled encouragingly.

Billy bit his lip with frustration. He looked dazed. Reality had been squashed out of him by the effort of getting some attention which he already suspected was much too late. He turned slowly and pointed at the bench outside the pub on the opposite bank of the canal. He spoke very slowly, as if he was beginning to doubt his own story.

'Missis, there was a man . . . he was sitting there for a long time, looking at Wayne and me . . .'

Miss Farrell's heart skipped a beat.

'Did he do something to you? Touch you? Tell me, what did he do?'

'Nothing . . . jus' watched Wayne and me fishing. He was there yesterday as well. Jus' sitting there; drinkin' out of a bottle. He didn't eat or nuthin'. Then he went . . .' Billy's voice died away. He cast his eyes downwards and began to kick the dirt with the tip of his shoe, all the time biting his lower lip and sniffing. The child on her lap snivelled noisily.

'He jus' went in the water, Missis,' he whispered. 'He jus' went in the water. One minit he was there and then there was a little splash. He went in the water.' The voice thinned with awe.

'Missis, I think he drownded.'

He dropped to the ground and began to sob in great heaving gulps. The tears running down his cheeks made black streaks all over his face. He kept his head down.

Cora looked at him in stunned amazement. Was the boy telling her that he'd just witnessed a man drown? A *little* splash? She clutched at the straw the child had inadvertently held out. Surely the man would have called for help? Or at least made a *big* splash?

'Billy, think carefully now. Did he shout for help?'

'Naw, Missis, he said nuthin'.' The child's voice rose in a despairing wail. 'He made no noise, Missis . . . jus' a little splash and then no noise at all. He didn't shout or nuthin'.' The big wet eyes pleaded to her. She swallowed her rising panic. The dog beside her began to whimper softly.

'Did you see him fall?'

'No,' they both mumbled, then Wayne added, 'we had a knot in our line. When we looked up he wasn't there no more . . .' His voice trailed off.

'Did you try to get help?'

'Oh yeah, Missis!' Billy came to life with a shout of fury. 'But the oul fella wouldn' listen. He said we was telling lies. But we saw it.'

'Had you ever seen the man before?' Cora wondered what on earth she was going to do.

Billy was glaring at her mutinously, clearly expecting his story to be dismissed.

'Yeah.' Wayne pursed his mouth then wiped his snotty nose with the end of his sleeve. 'Like Billy said. He was here yesterday.'

'Was he drinking then as well?'

The children looked at each other and pointed to the uneven ground beneath the bench where an overturned bottle dribbled away the last of its amber fluid. Another, empty, lay a little further off. Cora Farrell took in the scene and drew her own conclusions.

'Did he speak to you?' she asked, uncertain as to what to do next.

'Naw. Like we told you, he was jus' sittin' there. We told him he could have one of our samwiches but he wouldn'. He kep' starin' at them houses over there.' The child turned and pointed across the road at the terrace opposite.

'And he didn't go near you?' Still she delayed. 'Did he say anything at all?'

They shrugged guiltily.

'We asked him did he want to borrow our rod. He said no thanks. Tha's all. Honest.'

Wayne looked at her for approval.

'Nothing else?'

'No, Missis. Honest to God.'

Miss Cora Farrell stood up and took each child tightly by the hand. She walked gingerly forward and peered into the lock basin. It was then that she recalled noticing some slight movement when she'd first looked over the bridge. Nothing stirred now. Wedged behind the lock gates was the accumulated detritus of years. The sight appalled and disgusted her but there was no movement in the grey-green water.

Anyone falling in there, she concluded, would be poisoned long before he drowned. Why hadn't the man struggled? Or would his drunken state account for that?

'God between us and all harm,' muttered Miss Farrell, piously fingering the Pioneer pin on her lapel. Then, as the boys' small sticky hands tightened around hers, her heart lurched and she began to panic in earnest.

What on earth was she to do? How was she to convince anyone that the children were speaking, as she now believed they were, the truth? And what good would it do anyway? If indeed the man had gone into the water, even five minutes before the children told her, then he would be well and truly dead. Her stomach sickened at the thought of what filth might be lying below the surface.

When first she saw the bedraggled pair she'd thought innocently that the poor little miseries had lost a few pence and with a small glow of goodwill

21

hoped she might be able to put things right. Something about them appealed to her. She wished now she'd walked by and cursed the curiosity that had led her down to them.

This will teach me to mind my own business, she thought resignedly, knowing it wouldn't. She rose to her feet.

'We'll go and get help, boys,' she said grimly. 'There's a police station just down the road. Pull up the rods and lay them on the bank, Billy, they'll be quite safe. We'll leave Bunch to mind them.' She tied the dog's leash to a bar of the lock gate.

'Will the guard put us in jail?' Wayne snivelled.

'Will they get us for mitchin' school?' Billy asked more circumspectly.

'Indeed they will not then. They'll say you're two fine brave boys!' she said confidently.

'Touch wood,' she muttered to herself as she led them away.

# Grace

*April to late July 1990*

**BUSH, J:** *HIBERNIA CURIOSA, A letter from a Gentleman in Dublin ... a view of the manners, customs, dispositions, etc. of the inhabitants ... London, Flexney 1764. 8 vols with plates, disbound and in severe need of refurbishment.*

## CHAPTER TWO

The milk float whined its way along the long suburban street, stopping every now and then for the milkman to sprint, head bent against the rain. Up and down the wet garden paths he ran, ducking to avoid the water cascading from the overhanging trees. The street was deserted except for a solitary woman, outlined in her doorway, who watched as he approached her house. Every now and then she turned and peered out anxiously as if expecting someone. The milkman eyed her furtively each time he stopped. He knew her slightly. She was an early riser, occasionally waving at him as she drove off in her ancient green Mini. Good-looking dame, well-preserved, tasty figure. Hadn't let herself go like some he could mention. Friendly; always a cheery wave.

Now, alerted by her pale face, he wondered if she needed help. He almost expected her to call out but she did not, nor did she appear to even notice him. As he came nearer he sensed that her desperation was resigned rather than urgent. She might have been standing there for ever, leaning against the doorpost like a marble statue, looking as if she hadn't slept for a week. Her white towelling robe was belted tightly and she held the collar closely around her neck. Her shoulder-length hair was uncombed and pushed roughly behind her ears. A sprinkling of freckles across the bridge of her nose stood out like blotches, accentuating the unnaturally white skin stretched across her wide cheek bones. He was surprised at how much older she looked close up; tired, gaunt and middle-aged.

'Did you want some milk, Missis?'

'What?' Startled, she turned then smiled apologetically. For a moment her face was transformed, the pale, dark-fringed eyes, crinkling up as if smiling was more habitual than the white anxiety she quickly resumed.

'I said, did you want some milk?'

'Oh no. Sorry. I was looking out for the postman. Have you seen him?' Her hands fluttered incessantly as she spoke, one plunging into her pocket, the other tugging and fixing the collar of her dressing-gown.

'But there's a strike on, there is no post.' The milkman paused in the action of lifting a box from the back of the float, and looked at her curiously.

'Yes. No. It's over. They said so. On last night's news.' She turned away as if suddenly aware of her undress and the extraordinary impression she was making.

'But I don't suppose there'll be any delivery for a few days,' she murmured and gave him a feeble smile. 'While they get sorted out.' She shrank back into her hallway at the sound of the next door opening.

'That'll be the day!' boomed her neighbour,

Jason Pepperstock, half catching her last remark. 'That lot need locking up.' He rolled the words with relish then pulled the door shut with a loud bang. 'Morning, Grace!' he roared as he turned abruptly and kicked aside a small brightly coloured tractor lying in his pathway and careered straight into the milkman. Three milk bottles crashed to the ground.

'Why don't you look where you're going, my man?' Pepperstock growled imperiously and, without apology, stalked off. The milkman stared furiously at the debris, then met Grace's eyes over the fence.

'If Mr High-and-Mighty wants his milk loose, he can have it!' he announced and added 'bastard' under his breath.

'The rain seems to be getting worse,' Grace murmured distractedly as she went inside. 'That should help to clean it up.'

'All the same to me,' the milkman replied and charged back to his float.

Shuffling disconsolately into her kitchen, Grace Hartfield poured yet another cup of tea and tried to remember if the news bulletin had said when the postal delivery would be resumed. It could only be a matter of days now before . . . before what? Panic rose like bile.

God. Oh help. How was she to manage? She had no idea where he was or what he intended. The unthinkable had happened. Cast adrift now without means, he held her at his disposal more thoroughly than if he'd locked her away. She was outraged at her helplessness. How could she have been so trusting, so stupid? He must write. He must.

But even as she clung to the hope that the postal service could, in some miraculous way, restore order to her life, she acknowledged that there were other ways her absent husband might have arranged their finances. Like coming to see her. Like talking things over. Like telephoning. How dare he walk off with their joint initiative, leaving her totally at his whim with no way and no means of ordering her own life?

Three weeks since the night he left her. Things were getting very tight and the end of the month loomed ominously. How could she pay the bills? If only she could stop this incessant worry and settle down to work. Proper work. The urgent business of getting a new catalogue printed, for instance. Unless she sold some books her income would dry completely. Then where would she be?

Would bookselling alone support her now? Even as she asked herself the question, her lip curled sardonically. She knew the answer was not unless she could up the ante. Investment, better stock, more frequent sales as her crony George had pointed out more than once. Sick joke. Who the hell would loan her money now? The banks would talk, but would they listen? She should never, ever have bought that confounded collection, on a subject about which she knew nothing and with which she'd been messing since he'd left. It all needed time and care, instead of which, trying to cut her losses, she panicked into selling too hastily. She was sure to lose money. Damn, damn, damn. What on earth had induced her to buy such junk? On the off-chance of making a quick killing too, when experience alone should have warned her against such folly. Who was she trying to impress?

Did the days ever pass so slowly?

She was up and waiting for the postman each dreary morning for almost a week, avoiding the milkman's concern by hiding behind the door until the letters fell on the mat, but as five, then six, days passed, desperation had driven her to wait on the doorstep. Waiting for news, her stomach churning. Waiting for Reggie. Bolting indoors whenever contact with any of her neighbours threatened, for she couldn't bear to face their questions no matter how kindly meant.

Later, whenever she recalled the moment when the postman pushed what she afterwards thought of as THE LETTER into her hand, Grace Hartfield felt ill. Expecting one kind of trouble, she had suddenly found herself swamped by something much worse.

The postman handed her a large bundle tied roughly with white string. It was mainly circulars, a few letters and, unbelievably, only a couple of enigmatic cards from Reggie. She was on the point of snapping that most of it was junk anyway when he thrust an important-looking brown envelope into her hand and asked her to sign for it. Then with a brief nod he shuffled off down the path mumbling under his breath.

She held the envelope while she watched him go, her fingers nervously playing over the smooth legal manilla, then laying it with her other letters on the doorstep, she dropped the rest of the bundle into the dustbin. Afterwards she wished she'd dumped the lot.

She'd thought as she opened it that it boded ill.

29

And she'd been right, for the act of reading it had, with a stroke, wiped away the certainties of the past. As the word solicitor leapt from the heading, she thought she was going to faint. Divorce, divorce flashed on and off like a neon sign in her head; her heart pumped painfully. Divorce? Is this how it was done? Mercilessly, without human contact? Her eye swept the few short lines. Then she sat down abruptly and tried to unjumble the words into coherence enough to re-read the letter.

At first she could make no sense of it as she scanned it for Reggie's name, or divorce, or settlement or any single word which matched the questions in her pounding head.

The letter was short. Addressed to her from a firm of London solicitors,

> *We have been instructed by Messrs Quinlan and Bradshaw of Dublin . . . Next of kin . . . Following the recent deaths of your sister, Mrs Eileen Ann Lacey and her daughter, Bridget Lacey . . .*

Her first reaction was complete disbelief. She re-read the letter, slowly this time, forcing herself to concentrate on what it said. She rushed to the phone. It was all a mistake. They'd got hold of the wrong person. Listen, listen to me, she cried, my sister's dead.

'Yes, Mrs Hartfield, that is why we were instructed . . .' the measured tone never faltered.

'No. You don't understand! My sister's dead. She disappeared years, thirty years, ago. Her name was Sullivan, Eileen Sullivan.'

'Yes, Eileen Ann Lacey née Sullivan. You say disappeared . . . ?'

'No, no! Dead. I said she's dead.'

'Yes. That is why we wrote to you.'

'Please. Listen to me. You've made a mistake. My sister's been dead for years. Thirty years.' She almost spat the words. There was a long pause before he spoke again. No, he did not think there was a mistake. Then a long silence into which her fearful question dropped. How had he found her? Oh, no mystery to that, came the calm unnerving reply. One of the executors of her sister's will had known where in England her parents had settled. It was not difficult, there was a procedure . . . a formula. Quite easy. It took a little time, that was all. Time.

'Who?' she whispered.

'Let me see.' There was a sound of rustling paper. 'Mrs Hartfield? Does the name Crowley mean anything to you?'

'No.'

'Father Seamus Crowley?'

She almost put down the phone then, afraid she was going to be sick. Her flesh crawled. *The admonitory hand outstretched.* She pushed the memory away.

'No.' She could hardly form the words. 'No, I know no priests.'

He began to explain again, as if to a child, ponderously insisting that it was she who was mistaken. As he spoke, disbelief gave way to anger and then confusion. What he implied was impossible to take in while the anxiety of her crumbling marriage played relentlessly on her jangling nerves.

She could not tell whether past or present was the

more threatening, nor admit that the one might have some bearing on the other.

The future she had been pushing away, afraid of the solitude, afraid of blame, afraid of the unknown. Now, as this new fear rose to choke her, she had a sudden vivid flash of her mother's tired face and, as the image recurred, she began to plunder the past for explanations of her present failure.

Every menacing disclosure from the solicitor reduced her ability to cope on either front, yet confirmed how cautiously she had peered back and how little she had shared or even spoken about her childhood. Slowly she conceded how thoroughly she had censored what she allowed herself to remember. She read the letter over and over, crumpled it up, tossed it aside then retrieved it and smoothed it carefully, to read it compulsively yet again.

For the next two days she swept through the house in a frenzy of cleaning, refusing to dwell on what she could not comprehend. Then, fearful of vengeful leisure, she returned to the safety of her world of books. Three days later the solicitor rang.

'Just to clear up a point or two. Mrs Hartfield, are you listening?'

She would be quite well off, there was quite a lot of property: her sister's house in Dublin, her niece's flat in London. Taken together, a tidy sum. Was there malice in his use of the words? Sister, niece? With brutal simplicity he disposed of their lives, drawing from her a combination of outrage and disgust that the two women should be so neatly shelved. Tidied away to set her free. Become her disposable income.

She fell silent then, contemplating her anxieties of the previous weeks, the unpaid bills, her absent spouse. Then came the scurrilous thought: her position vis-à-vis Reggie had strengthened. A split second of elation before her churning stomach heralded a new terror. Was she allowing herself to be talked into committing a crime by claiming property to which she had no right? She'd almost blurted out the words when he'd startled her by suggesting that she should ring the Dublin solicitor.

'There are some things he'd like to discuss with you.'

It took some time but when she finally worked up courage to do so, the relaxed Irish voice quickly lulled her disquiet by encouraging her to talk. He asked no awkward questions, but spoke inconsequentially about nothing in particular, like an old and valued friend. Over two or three phone calls she allowed him to tease information from her that she had forgotten or suppressed.

Had she any memory of the place she was born? When had her family removed to Birmingham? How could it be that she knew so little about her dead sister? Think back, think back. Instructions arrived daily. Then quite casually, as she was about to ring off at the end of their third or fourth conversation, he said:

'I think we can clear everything up now, Mrs Hartfield, if you could just drop into the office.' He said it as if it were just down the street and she'd agreed before she had time to stop herself. He did not seem to think it necessary to ask if she could afford the fare and she couldn't bring herself to inquire if he might make some advance against what he kept calling 'her expectations.'

She stared down at the phone, absently drumming her fingers on the table, contemplating her cash flow. It did not add up to much: fifty-six pounds and forty-two pence in cash. Not enough to cover her fare to Dublin. Her credit card had, by now, reached its limit and soon she would have the first (polite) request to pay up or else. Twelve days to the end of the month. Phone bill due on the twenty-second. For starters.

Could she approach the solicitor? Should she? Tempting though it was, the thought of baring her soul and admitting that she was almost on skid row did not appeal. Bad enough that she knew how things stood, she could manage without his prurient sympathy.

A detailed search of her clothes yielded, from various pockets, only four pounds and ten pence. It was while she searched through Reggie's wardrobe that she came upon a veritable bonanza in the form of a Marks and Spencer bag containing an assortment of shirts, underwear and socks, all unopened and complete with labels. She was astonished. A reluctant shopper, Reggie usually left the acquisition of his smalls to his wife and Grace had very definitely not bought this lot. Who then? There was no receipt and so no indication as to how long the bag had been there. But why look a gift horse?

With a gleam in her eye and the plastic bag clutched beneath her arm, Grace made her way to Ealing Broadway. The young woman at the accounts desk sifted through the goods and counted out a wadge of cash vouchers. No receipt, no cash. Composing her face into what she hoped was a fair approximation of recent bereavement, the Widow Hartfield leaned over and murmured in her ear. The girl called the supervisor. They conferred in whispers, glancing sideways at Grace, who was staring sadly into the middle distance. Then with sudden resolution and expressions of sympathy at her loss they handed over a neat pile of crisp notes to the value of one hundred and thirty-four pounds.

Slaking off her mournful air, resourceful Grace hurried off to the travel agent. The ticket, a day return, cost one hundred and eighteen pounds. Grace went to call on Dee Pepperstock.

'How much do you need?' Dee was surprisingly finicky about discussing the whys and wherefores. Her pen was poised over her cheque book. Grace cleared her throat and grimaced.

'Hundred quid?' Grace mumbled. 'It's only for, er, a couple of weeks.' She bit her lip. 'Cash?'

'Cash? Crumbs. I haven't got anything like that here. Will it do tomorrow?'

Grace cleared her throat. 'Better today, if you can?'

'I'll go to the bank.' Dee shrugged and got to her feet. 'You'll have to look after the kids. Mind if I do a few errands at the same time? I'll be back before five.'

Grace met her eye. 'Take your time,' she said languidly. 'I haven't got anything else to do.'

She flew to Dublin at the crack of dawn the following morning. She had journeyed fearfully and was surprised at how kindly she was dealt with.

Bartley Quinlan was expansive and plump with a whiskery red face. Grace was completely disarmed on finding, when he rose to greet her, that at five foot seven, she towered over him. He didn't seem either to notice or mind but went on treating her like a valued, or perhaps more accurately, a dependent relative.

At first Grace took the Pickwickian manner at face value but became uncomfortable when she realized how skilfully he was manoeuvring her into disclosure. At the end of the long interview, while he was fussing over what sort of biscuit she must have with her tea, he slyly asked if she would like to meet Seamus Crowley? The noise his spoon made against the bottom of his teacup was the only sound in the room.

As she balked, he didn't attempt to hide his surprise, but watched, his plump hand playing over his lips while he listened to her demur. In the ensuing silence she had a sudden desperate urge to throw herself across the desk and bury her face against that solid, manly, pin-striped shoulder.

Her confusion puzzled and touched Quinlan. Watching her, he wondered how so apparently sophisticated a woman could have so little confidence. Her vulnerability had a disarming youthfulness somehow. He had been expecting someone older, more the sister's age. There seemed to be ten or twelve years between them, perhaps even more, they could almost be mother and daughter. The quick nervy movements reminded him of the older woman when she'd come to sign that fateful will. When was it? Two or more years before. A handsome woman, but when she came back to

check something a few months back, Eileen Lacey
had been ravaged by disease, and he'd been
shocked at her wretched appearance. She too had
the same preoccupied air. They resembled each
other in that, and their unnerving quality of silence.
Eileen never said a word about a sister. A private
woman, formidable in her way, he harrumphed
softly to himself. She'd certainly led poor old Fergus
a merry dance.

This one had a hint of that as well but was much
more uncertain of herself. Not uncertain enough to
give anything away. No mention of family, for
instance. Strange, most women referred to husband
or family but Grace Hartfield did not. Lack of
reference to children wasn't so strange since she had
none. But she had a husband, had had him for over
twenty years: Reginald Staveley Hartfield, copywriter. Just been made redundant from a big
London agency. Oh he knew quite a bit about the
Hartfields, one way and another. Bit of marital
trouble there, he deduced from her fidgety anxiety.
To her childlessness, he sentimentally attributed her
indefinable sadness, and less sentimentally her slim
and youthful figure. But, whatever her worries, she
didn't mention them.

Come to that, she didn't say anything about
herself either. Quite a distinguished antiquarian
bookseller in her way, as he knew because his
London colleague knew someone who bought from
her regularly. George something or other. And
apparently, George had said, Hartfield Regional
Books was the biz.

Striking-looking women both of them. Mysterious. Those calm pale eyes gave so little away, and

yet so much. If he were to guess, he'd say that all this was giving Mrs Grace Hartfield a bit of a nervous breakdown. She was only barely under control and obviously realized the impression she was making and hated it. Too private, too intelligent not to resent the intrusion.

His unblinking eyes held hers. Something he'd said had touched a raw nerve. What was it? The mention of the priest. Probably nothing more than the understandable revulsion of the lapsed Catholic. Amen to that, he thought piously, though she could do worse than old Seamus Crowley.

'I'm flying back tonight.' She broke in on his thoughts. 'Some other time, perhaps.'

'Tonight, eh?' Bartley Quinlan leaned backwards, pulled his antiquated watch from his self-consciously old-fashioned waistcoat pocket and, in a burst of avuncular *bonhomie*, suggested lunch. She nodded agreement dubiously.

'Take your ease,' he said, patting her hand as she slipped on her jacket. 'Seamus can wait. He has all the time in the world. Hasn't he just retired? Isn't it well for some?' He paused then, the sharp eyes twinkling conspiratorially, but Grace looked away and muttered something about the future and felt the familiar cramps turn her insides to jelly. He hadn't the heart to press her.

'I'll just get my clerk to get cracking then we'll go to the Burlington. It's hard by. They keep a reasonable table and the stroll will do us good.'

Over lunch he described the Dublin house and London flat which would be hers. He furnished her with names and addresses and then, almost without pausing for breath, his eyes never leaving her face, he starkly described the bleak outline of how violently her sudden wealth had come to her.

'I don't understand . . . I assumed they died together . . . in an accident . . . car.'

'But my letter said,' the solicitor's eyes narrowed, 'your sister's only child. She killed herself. They died within a week.' He paused for several minutes before he retold the story patiently, now half-familiar to her unaccepting mind.

Afterwards they walked back along the canal which they'd crossed to get to the hotel. They'd passed two locks before he touched her arm and pointed across the road to a tall shabby house in the middle of a terrace.

'There it is, over there. That's where the Laceys lived.'

The house by the canal – hers now or would be, as well as the London flat, he explained, as soon as probate was cleared. Would she like to see inside? She hated that probing look. They stood in silence while he fumbled with the key, but just as they were about to enter she turned away and said in a small voice that she would like to go home, she wasn't ready.

It was like coming out of a dream. He cajoled playfully until her hesitant protestations grew emphatic and she began to sob in loud uncontrollable gasps. He took her arm firmly and led her to the pub across the bridge and pushed a huge drink into her hand.

'It's only shock,' he said, 'delayed shock, Mrs Hartfield. You'll be fine now.' He sounded so kind, so concerned, so fatherly. Her friend. He knew so much more about her than anyone. Her head began to swim.

Suddenly she couldn't stop talking. She had to know. She had to know something about this woman – she could not yet say sister – before she could accept ... accept everything ... she ... the ... she owned. Everything: house, money, letters, clothes, secrets.

'Secrets?' He looked at her with interest, but his interruption was drowned by the flood of her worries as she reiterated her stubborn belief that, despite his protestations and the evidence he had laid before her, she knew, absolutely knew, that the dead women were not related to her. How could they be? You were supposed to know sisters, even nieces. She knew neither. He patted her hand and hushed her protestations as he might have quieted a tiresome child. She fell silent then. He's made a mistake, she told herself, and vowed she would, must, prove him wrong.

He patted her hand but she snatched it away. She would have to prepare herself, for if she accepted what he said, then her life had indeed been turned upside down. All the simple facts of her history that she believed no longer held true. Who was she? What was she? She would have to understand and adjust before she could explain.

It was too momentous. She could not start here, for who could she turn to in this town where she knew no-one, save only a solicitor who claimed to know more about her life than she did herself? He terrified her with his carefully modulated certainties, peeling away the fragile layers that Reggie had left intact. What would be left when she had been quietly stripped of the only identity she knew?

When at last she fell silent, he suggested she come back to his office to rest while he sorted her business.

'Thank you, but I think I'll stay here for a bit. What time will you be ready?'

'Five? Half-past? Come about then. I'll arrange for a car to take you to the airport.'

When she made to protest he held up his hand. 'I'll take care of it, Mrs Hartfield. It will cost you nothing,' he said blandly and swept out.

She tramped around the city for three exhausting hours, not seeing anyone, hardly speaking, wondering why she did not feel some sense of familiarity. But she did not. She froze into her own misery, walking in ever decreasing circles through the broad streets. Though she did not realize it, she never wandered far from either Fitzwilliam Square where Quinlan had his lair, or the edges of Rathmines and *The House*. It was only when she found herself, inevitably, winding up on the bench in front of the pub on the canal bank, that she began to work out how closed the circle was.

She had a crazy notion that she was being watched, manipulated in some way towards the house. She was certain that if she went inside, someone would be there, in possession, and would pounce on her and then the nightmare would spin out of the last vestiges of her control. The thought transfixed her. Everything seemed to be slipping away, the fixed points in her life had gone. Cast adrift.

Mesmerized and unable to tear herself away, she

sat staring at the house, trying to imagine a life within, forcing herself to concentrate on the small family. Few people came by. Some children fishing who watched her curiously and shouted to each other in a rough glottal accent she could not understand. An irritable-looking old man fed the ducks, pulling stale bread from his pockets, scolding and coaxing as he walked along. A short, spry woman walked her snuffling dog, which pawed at a withered bunch of flowers lying on the edge of the lock-gate. She hauled at the straining lead and hurriedly crossed herself before stopping to greet a passer-by. Once or twice while they talked, the woman looked as if she might accost Grace but instead turned away as if embarrassed by her impulse. She half-raised her hand as she crossed the bridge and stared back, then shook her head and passed on.

The terrace opposite had nine houses. She studied it obsessively, forcing herself to concentrate on the shabby house rather than its late inhabitants, trying to guess its age. She had by now absently taken in that the local architecture hardly changed from one century to another, so that individual houses were hard to date. The central three of the terrace were a storey higher than the rest, making for the pleasing symmetry so particular to Georgian and Victorian Dublin. Her eye slid past the one which fascinated and repelled. There was a plaque on the house next door. She recalled pointing it out while the solicitor stood with the key poised. The words had stuck in her mind.

JOHN MITCHEL
JOURNALIST, SOLICITOR, PATRIOT.
1815–75

Before she could stop herself she'd said to him, 'They forgot his telephone number.'

And he'd smiled and retorted wryly that it might have pleased Mitchel better had the order of his preoccupations been reversed, but had looked apprehensive, then alarmed, when she'd overexcitedly begun to babble about the relative values of his professions and avocation.

'He'd have done better to stick to the professions,' Quinlan remarked drily, 'he was deported for his patriotic duty.'

Three or four of the houses had already been retrieved into newly renovated smartness, though the communal piece of ground in front had, so far, escaped attempts at cultivation. Few people came or went into any but the house on the end, to her left as she looked across. The Transcendental Meditation Centre alone attracted the young, and, as she watched the comings and goings, she began to wonder about the sister and her child. What did they look like? She tried to conjure up the girl, wondering vaguely if they might have resembled each other. Thirty, almost thirty-one. Was she at her peak or had she been one who flowered early? Short or tall? Dark like Grace or fair? Fat or thin? Bridget Kate. Pretty name. Unusual. Not Katherine apparently, just Kate. She imagined her walking in and out, strolling by the canal bank, growing from girl to woman. Did she have friends here, or lovers?

Inexorably, Grace's focus shifted to the daughter who somehow presented less threat than the mother. Some time during those endless hours, while she waited for the documents which she was told would give her access to the girl's property in London, she began to allow herself to think about her dead, unknown niece. Dead mother, dead child. She could not give herself the intimacy of naming them, but from nowhere came a furious desire to understand, to avenge, what had so calamitously destroyed them both and left her, Grace, exposed and confused. Would knowledge make sense of it?

Where and how was she to start? The younger woman, she'd been told, had lived in London for nearly ten years. London, the consolation of naming it was almost tangible. Safe familiar London. Home and family. Where all her happiest days had been spent. Had Bridget Kate Lacey felt that too? Had she known the pleasure of Sunday mornings at half-empty museums? Of every amusement in the world being within reach? Of stolid, solid citizens sitting like zombies on overcrowded trains? Of nights out, walking through the bustling streets? Had she ever felt the dread terror of being alone while the rest of the world paired off?

Clerkenwell. All those years when they might have passed each other in the street, might have met at some party, or at a theatre, or shopping for hats. Both of them Londoners, probably with shared preoccupations, even perhaps shared interests. Would a flicker of recognition have passed between them? An instant rapport? Londoners. Alone, in the nightmare, that common ground consoled, could be explored. The girl had lived and died not ten miles from the aunt she never knew. All those years of longing for children, traipsing in and out of one gynaecological humiliation after another, when all the while a sort of surrogate child was so close by.

The shame of it; they might have been friends.

Allies even. The idea formed and took shape, the girl would help her unravel the peculiarities of her family's past. Grace's resolve began to grow: the mother could wait. She could not, would not, go near that awful house. As soon as she got back to London she would start at the other end.

**BINYON, Laurence:** *DREAM-COME-TRUE, London, Eragny Press 1905. A rare copy of this slim vol. designed by Lucien Pisarro. Board edges distressed, spine defective, still elegant. Rare.*

## CHAPTER THREE

It was well past midnight when she got home, numb with exhaustion. She could hear the phone shrilling as she fumbled with her key. Reggie, drunk and befuddled, demanded to know where she'd been and, when she refused to tell him, announced he was 'coming round'.

'Round from where?' she demanded coldly.

And for what? To save her from the gas oven? Had he forgotten that she had no idea where he was living? His permission for her comings and goings was not required. She could manage. Let him take his damned desire for privacy and go to hell.

But he was in full garrulous, unstoppable flow. He clearly expected protestations of undying affection and dependence and seemed stunned at her coolness. She felt a jab of elation at how the balance between them had subtly shifted; the illusion of his strength was almost gone, though at some level she still clung to it tenaciously. She was not charmed by his maudlin sentimentality.

Redundancy has destroyed his life, his pride, his self-esteem, she thought, and whether he means it or not, he is making me redundant too. She laid the receiver quietly on the table, went into the kitchen and shut the door against the low rumble of his voice. He's awash with self-pity, destroying everything in sight. Something bigger than this has happened to me, she wanted to shout, more momentous even than redundancy or absconding husbands. Wasn't it ironic, she thought bitterly as she poured a nightcap, that what he took to be independence and lack of interest achieved in a moment what all her weeks of pleading could not?

Too late. She was not going to be messed about by his whims any more. The happenings of the previous days had blunted her sympathy and for the first time it was disgust rather than terror she felt with his insistence on time off. She might well develop a taste for it herself, she told herself loftily. Now she had the means. The sneaky brutality of the guilty thought startled her.

She would not tell him. None of it. He would take it over: instruct, bully, arrange. She would disappear under his manful smoothing of the way. Nothing would be faced or resolved. Eased. The inconvenience of her resurrected family would be eased away out of her control, out of existence. As she wearily climbed the stairs, she realized with absolute certainty that she wanted to journey into her past alone, to digest without distraction whatever might unfold. And, if she were honest, to edit the story she would choose to share. The hell with sharing. How could she ever trust him again? The doormat stirred; she too needed time. She ran back down the stairs.

'Why don't you just bugger off and sort yourself out?' she shouted into the still cackling phone.

'What?' He sounded so absolutely amazed and

47

affronted that she almost burst out laughing with the realization that this hadn't come into his reckoning and, in a sense, had taken some of the glamour off his bid for freedom. As he started to cajole, she wondered if it was uncertainty or respect which made him suddenly more willing to talk. When at last he said good night, he did so nervously, and with promises of an early meeting. She was elated that she could say goodbye without caving in to his charm.

Her relief lasted only until the dead relations once again took up residence in her head. For several days she did not stir from the house. She read and re-read the pile of documents she had brought back from Dublin. One day a set of keys was delivered by special messenger. She held them, her fingers caressing the worn leather label BKL. It sounded like an upmarket car. *Vorsprung durch technik.*

Still clutching the keys in her hand, she climbed and searched the attic for the bits and pieces she had saved from her childhood home and tried, as she sat in the gloom, to remember if it was she who had been so thorough in discarding what she now sought so avidly. She eventually found a little brown attaché case, dusty and battered, propping up a broken armchair. It was stuffed full of old school reports and other useless bits and pieces but held no clues about the sister who had disappeared from her life when she was eight. Disappeared. That word again. She sat in the dusty armchair forcing her mind back, conjuring the past. Blank. When had anyone said dead?

*Dark-clad woman called, they stood murmuring*

*in the narrow hallway. Then the priest. She pressed against the wall unnoticed till Mammy whispered her to the other room. Where was Dada?*

*Had her parents gone away? She rocked to and fro but couldn't remember. Everything blank . . . she was lying on the big bed . . . Eily's been taken from us . . . the whispered words . . . a tragedy . . . the child's hand tracing a pattern of spittle on the blue counterpane . . . closing her eyes, pretending sleep. The mother fumbling at the chest of drawers, pulling something black away . . . bending over the child and tiptoeing out. Now she's putting on the black clothes and soon the carriage will take them away. Nonie in the kitchen wearing Mammy's overall. When would the funeral be? A day off school. Nonie gave her sweets and said how she must be good, for her Mammy and Dada . . . people coming to the house . . . Dada standing against the window . . . Dada roaring . . .*

For a day or two she'd been made a fuss of in the little school when she'd sobbed, as children do, that it was all her fault. Fault? Her stomach suddenly contracted with remembered fear, but rack her brain as she might, everything else was a blank.

She had no impression of falsehood, just something too painful to dwell on. Her parents had hardly spoken of the past and they were spared memories and the importunings of neighbours because they'd emigrated to Birmingham soon after it happened. Why Birmingham? Were they following some lead or had they chosen it at random? Was it simply the anonymity of a big city they craved?

Why should she have questioned what she was

told? She had accepted it because it never occurred to her that it could be otherwise. Parents did not speak untruly. They could not speak of it, they said. That seemed reasonable enough; the death of a beloved daughter, barely eighteen.

Wrong. They had not said death. She's been taken from us was all they said. Now, Grace wondered that she'd been so incurious, could know so little about the circumstances. Were they ever described? Or did she protect herself with selective deafness? The dim memory she had of her grown-up sister had faded for want of nurturing. Every younger child's dream come true. An only child now. Their treasure. The only one. When, once or twice, she had fearfully asked, her gentle, frail mother had said that she preferred not to be reminded, it made her too sad.

Had it made Grace sad? As she came down from the attic she remembered only fear. It gripped her in its memory as if it had been with her always, vicious and terrifying. When had she pushed it away? She'd grown up thinking of herself and accepted as an only child, how could she come to terms with the information that this had not been the case?

Someone, somewhere had made a dreadful mistake. When had she turned the word tragedy to accident? Was it lying on the bed that day listening to the murmuring in the front room, the noise spilling into the hall? She could almost see the dusky blue satin with the dark spittle forming the smiling face. Lying sleepily with her face against the smooth softness, the words floating singly into the gloom.

*Desperate ... accident ... blaze ... disgrace ...*
*miles ... poor innocent ... tragedy ... so young*
*... blackguard ... sorry ... sorry for your trouble*
*... the shouting and banging of doors.*

There must have been a body. Had her parents
identified it? Had it been so damaged that they'd
made a mistake? But if that were so, then why did
her sister disappear so completely that she was lost
sight of for more than thirty years? Could she have
been so badly injured that she'd lost her memory?
Grace's horrified mind could not bring itself to
dwell on another possibility: that her sister had not
died but recovered. For if this were the case then she
would have had to have made a deliberate decision
... to what?

No, lost memory was infinitely preferable, she
would not have treated her parents so cruelly. How
could she? Yet she could have ... must have. The
thought filled Grace with repugnance.

But that did not stop her mulling the problem
over and over. Could it have been the old, old story
of pregnant girl spurned by cruel parents? But her
parents had not been like that. Or had they?
Besides, it did not fit the facts. Because of course,
she now knew there had been a child. Thirty. The
sister had disappeared when? Thirty-three or four
years ago. If she'd gone because she was pregnant,
there would have to be another child. Yet Quinlan
had insisted that there was just the one and she did
not challenge him. According to him, who claimed
to know the family, the Laceys had been married
for more than thirty years, he described them as
close, very close.

The whole thing was bizarre. Like some ghastly

51

joke. A dead sister turns out not to be dead only when she dies. Her only child dies within a week. Addition and subtraction in one fell swoop. Now you see them, now you don't. Set it to music, thought Grace macabrely, it would make a fortune. But who would believe it?

She was sleeping badly, prowling around the house fretting about Reggie. Missing his warmth beside her, she'd get up and drink tea or lace some hot milk with whisky, hoping for rest but unable to stop her thoughts racing from one set of problems to the other. With the unleashing of her dormant memory, she began to have nightmares. At first a faceless, voiceless presence invaded her sleep. Then one night she dreamed she was a child again back in the little house by the stream. In the pitch darkness she could hear the water rushing over the stones. The eaves of the roof made a tent over her head. The window creaking in the wind. She could hear voices hissing in the dark. The rain lashing on the windowsill.

*And then the scream. Who screamed? Who screamed? Her father standing beside the bed, a light in his hand.*

She woke up sweating and found to her shame she'd wet herself. She'd had the dream before. As she changed the sheets, the memory almost came back, elusive, half remembered, tantalizingly just out of reach. She lay in the bath whimpering with humiliation and frustration. And nameless, unknown fear.

So many fears. She longed then for the warmth of Reggie's arms. The pain of loss seared through her like a physical blow, leaving her gasping. How dare he go? His defection was the more brutal for having left the way open to these invading women, complicating her already shattered life. Unlooked-for relations altering her story as if it were their own. How dare they say they belonged to her? She would prove them wrong.

She examined her pale face in the mirror. There should be some vast outward sign of all this pain, but there was not. No added lines, just a slight darkening under the pale grey eyes, the dead-white face thin and drawn. She peered closer. Was her dark hair more liberally sprinkled with grey? She dropped the towel and turned slowly around. Only the puckering of the scars on her barren stomach and slight droop of her unused breasts betrayed her age, the blue-black marks on her long, still slender legs, the downward drift of her backside. Those ugly livid scars, the daily reminder of her futile dogged persistence. How could she display those intimacies to some unknown stranger? How does one start again at forty-one? She was not con-ditioned for change, nor had she looked for it while the rough and tumble of their life held together. So little changed in twenty-two years.

And so much. It took so long to build a life. Eight weeks to pull it down. Three weeks without him before the thunderclap of the undear departed unhinged her completely. She huddled on the cold bathroom floor and wept for the time of innocence when she'd thought that all she had to worry about was contained by her tiny world; Reggie and Grace and the poor lifeless blobs she continued to produce long after she'd been warned to stop. She tossed and turned until dawn, then, abandoning the struggle for elusive sleep, drove to Clerkenwell. She stood outside the girl's flat, willing some solution, some flash of remembrance. But looking up at the blank windows she knew she had not the courage to enter alone for fear of being challenged. She tried to convince herself that it was because she did not want to intrude until she learned more than the stark facts the lawyer had intoned. She was filled with repugnance at the thought of pawing over the girl's belongings without knowing what she would have valued. She needed to learn things about her niece that only those who knew her and loved her would know. Not dead, but alive. She would seek her through her friends. A life could not be so easily dismissed. Surely she must have friends? She would go to the girl's place of work, and try to find them. Someone there might help.

She walked about until she found a workmen's café and sat moodily shovelling sugar into a mug of bitter, black coffee, stirring her memory, fighting down the sickening fear again, forcing herself to think about it.

Why fear? Why not pity, longing, sadness? It was none of these things. Grace now timidly admitted what the sharp-eyed solicitor had recognized and remarked on:

'There was nothing you could do, Mrs Hartfield, why are you so afraid?'

Not upset, distraught, amazed, angry, puzzled. *Afraid.* He'd chosen the word with care and said it twice.

'Tell me, why are you so afraid?'

'Responsible.'

The word was out before she could swallow it.

Her hand shot to her mouth. With his chin on his hand, he paused for a long moment before asking very casually:

'That's a strange thing to say. What do you mean?'

Her face was burning then, the nerves in her stomach fluttering uncontrollably so that she could hardly force the words out.

'I don't know. Something. I don't know.'

'Something?'

She shook her head slowly and looked past him. 'Something I can't remember.'

**PARR, Louisa:** *THE FOLLIES OF FASHION. A bound selection of prints . . . used to illustrate the outrageous fashion designs and bizarre hair-styles of the Georgian period. Wanting title page, provenance unknown, otherwise interesting. Unique?*

## CHAPTER FOUR

Once she steeled herself to make enquiries of Quinlan, it did not take long to track down Bridget Kate Lacey's place of employment. Her job had drifted across conversations with the solicitor from the beginning with qualifying words like ironic, sad. Now Grace was readily provided with the name of the magazine for which Bridget Kate had been the agony aunt. Given the circumstances, the job did indeed sound ironic and sad. Grace rang the editor of *Diva* and hesitantly asked if she might see where the girl worked.

There was a long silence before the crisp voice grudgingly agreed. She sounded bemused yet much too polite to inquire why and, out of nervousness, Grace found herself giving a very confused account of reasons which sounded more limp with explanation, nevertheless she could not rid herself of a need to acquaint herself with her late niece's place of work.

'Niece?'

The word cut her short and there was an awkward pause before the editor said that she believed there were still some of Bid's things stored in the office and perhaps Grace could collect them?

Bid. It was the first time she'd heard the name and it conjured youth and softness in a way that the more formal appellation had not. As if the girl might be there, waiting for her, just that short journey away.

Grace took the tube to Oxford Street early next afternoon, and it was some indication of her state of mind that she got lost several times as she prowled around, anxiously searching for the address. She couldn't remember when she'd last wandered through Soho during the day. Usually she and Reggie went there at night after concert or theatre, pausing outside three or four restaurants before deciding which to try.

They? Who was she kidding? There wasn't a 'they' any more. No Reggie 'n Grace. Just Reggie. Just Grace. She wondered when she would be able to think of him with fondness and not with a furious growl at his betrayal of their long affection. Or when she would be able to believe, or accept the possibility, that good old, nice old, Reggie had scarpered for good.

Goodbye for ever? Who would break the news to his aged mum, still hoping against hope for the grandchild they'd promised so often? They'd snarled at each other over that, each wishing the other the burden of responsibility, then decided lamely to wait for a time, until the moment seemed right or, as she still allowed herself to hope, when Reggie's enchantment with freedom had faded.

She turned into Argyll Street, past the crowd queuing for the matinée at the Palladium, until a sudden downpour sent her scurrying across the street to shelter under Liberty's awning which stretched along the length of the shop. The window display mocked her sombre thoughts – gaily costumed punting parties filled the entire façade, every detail carefully attended and conjuring, for one heart-stopping instant, the river at Richmond, that summer she and Reggie met, three months after her mother's death. He dwarfed her, took her over, made her feel safe. Tall, good-looking, sexy, comforting Reggie. Sodding bastard.

The shower turned off as abruptly as it started. She cut rapidly through Carnaby Street into Broadwick and towards Poland Street, stopping several times to check the address against her *A to Z*. She stepped off the pavement and walked quickly past a huge vegetable van, manoeuvring itself into an already overcrowded Berwick Street, and did not notice the motorbike coming too close behind her.

'You'll get yourself killed, girlie!'

She whirled around, startled by her own stupidity and leaned against a shop window to recover. Girlie. Her father's voice. The sad remembered eyes. When had he said that? Thirteen or fourteen? Before, surely before, for he had died when she was barely fourteen. Girlie. She'd almost forgotten.

More carefully now, she edged sombrely past the market stalls still dripping from the recent rain, customers bustling about, costers shouting their wares. Then she turned the corner into Jule Street and looked with surprise at the offices facing her. She'd expected the magazine to be housed in something modern and imposing, glamorous. Instead the short, creaking terrace of eighteenth-century houses looked harmless and inviting, dwarfed at either end by two soaring glass towers and opposite by a crumbling fifties ruin which must have been the very latest thing in its day. She checked the address again and then, drawing a deep breath, crossed the street, climbed the steps and, pulling open the door, stepped into the hall where the porter directed her to the first floor reception.

DIVA MAGAZINE:

PROP. & MGR. DIR: ED HAMPSHIRE

shouted the notice at the foot of the stairs. Proprietor; no wonder the woman sounded so terrifying on the phone. Beneath it, sharply engraved into the steel plate, were the names of the staff. Grace ran her eye down the list. Editors, sub-editors, design, marketing. Then:

BK LACEY: PROBLEMS PAGE

The building had been recently renovated. As she climbed the stairs, she passed a beautiful carved fireplace sitting forlorn and eccentric in the wall at the first landing. Little else remained of the original interior. When she reached the top, she could see the receptionist through heavy glass doors.

'The editor?' The girl smiled and directed her upwards to where a short, stern, grey-haired woman stood staring down on her.

'Mrs Hartfield?' She stood back to allow Grace to precede her and then ushered her towards a pair of low armchairs on the half-landing.

There was a short awkward pause as each waited for the other to speak.

'Mrs Hampshire?'

'Miss,' she said firmly, as if waiting for some recalcitrant schoolgirl to explain herself.

'You said I might take my . . . er . . . Bridget Kate's things away?'

'Bridget Kate? Bridget?' She spoke impatiently and stared at Grace for a moment and then passed her hand over her eyes.

'I'm sorry, Mrs Hartfield, I do not mean to be rude. You mean Bid. I've never called her anything but Bid.' She managed to imply both a kind of proprietorial affection and some failure in Grace, who mutely wondered which of them had more right to give or seek condolence.

'Oh. I did not know . . . her.' She could not bring herself to say niece, my niece, or Bid, all were too intrusive, too intimate. There was another interminable pause.

'Then who are you? You said . . . you live in London? I thought you said you were her aunt?' Miss Hampshire accused. How dare Grace not know her own niece?

'Yes. Unfortunately we never met,' Grace answered grimly. Why the hell should she explain what she did not understand herself? After a moment she added: 'It must have been a dreadful shock for . . . her friends.'

'I still cannot believe it. Such a failure . . . in all of us . . . Are you her mother's sister?' she asked abruptly, either not noticing or ignoring the impact of her next remarks on Grace. 'I met her once or twice.'

She looked intently into Grace's startled face, her lips pursed. 'You look a little like her. Taller.'

Grace turned scarlet. Like whom? Mother or daughter? But the moment passed as the older woman lapsed into silence, then, seeing the

60

receptionist hovering on the stair, she rose abruptly and shook Grace's hand, blocking her way to further inquiry.

'Amanda will take you to Bid's office. Ingrid will show you around. When you're ready I will arrange for the porter to fetch the boxes.'

Thus dismissed, Grace followed the girl through to the general office of the magazine. It was huge, bustling and crowded and seemed to run the length of the terrace. Its floor area was divided into ten or twelve units, each of which was subdivided by desk space, two, or in a couple of cases, three. The overall impression was of a chaotic jumble of electronic equipment, papers, books, dirty coffee cups, umbrellas, raincoats and all the paraphernalia there weren't enough cupboards to hold. From the entrance it looked like a mixture of bookshop and garden centre; trailing greenery coaxed over unlikely surfaces subverted the would-be high-tech ambitions of the recent conversion.

They walked almost the full length of the room. Small notices identified each cubicle, heads sometimes turned to look as they hurried past, then as quickly turned away. Did she imagine the furtive murmuring? Grace had the unnerving feeling that she was watched, known for who she was, then shunned. She wondered that they did not recognize that she shared their revulsion. Yet how could they know anything of her?

Shamed by her fantasies, she closed her eyes for an instant and almost ran into Amanda who had stopped and with a wave of her hand indicated their destination, then, smiling cheerily, called a greeting to a friend and bounded away. The cubicle was set apart, as if it had been fashioned from a small room in the return of the old house. Grace was now standing in a little space, obscured on the one hand from the bustling main office and not quite in sight of what had been BK Lacey's work space, the entrance of which appeared to be around to her right. A neatly printed notice at eye level on the corner read:

## PROBLEMS
## HEALTH & BEAUTY

Hesitating for a moment before plunging in, Grace became aware of a low murmur on the other side and was just going to announce herself when a voice said:

'Some relation?' Silence, then: 'Gawd. What'll I say?'

As if the question had been directed at her, Grace also realized that she didn't know what to say or even what she was doing. She stepped backwards to try to gather her courage and still her pumping heart. After a moment or two, swallowing deeply, she stepped quietly through the opening in the partition.

A tiny, emaciated young woman cradled the telephone and half rose to greet her. She had a rather discontented appearance. Extremely elegant. Huge unnaturally violet eyes, a beaky nose, a wide slightly crooked mouth. She was beautifully made-up. Her fine blond hair cut in a neat page-boy. It was a face straight out of the twenties and she was dressed to match in a short straight black tunic dress with her thin legs encased in black tights. She stared at Grace without smiling. As the interview went on, Grace surmised that this was habitual rather than contrived. It was, nonetheless, extremely intimidating.

'I've come to collect Bridget Lacey's things,' she said and held out her hand. 'I'm Grace Hartfield.'

'Ingrid Marsh. Hi.' She offered a slim white hand as the phone began to ring. 'Health and Beauty,' she warbled, as she picked up the receiver, leaving Grace still standing at the doorway, wryly acknowledging the style but wondering if Health could be entirely accurate.

She looked about her. The room was a reasonable size and had good light but the area to her left looked forlorn and dusty. There were a couple of cardboard boxes on the floor under the large grey desk and an unsteady-looking pyramid of files added to the air of disarray. Wherever the current Problems editor was functioning, she was not functioning here. The dreary space looked as if it had been abandoned since the day its occupant had last sat answering letters.

So this was where BK Lacey worked for eight years. Answered her letters. Sorted out problems she couldn't sort out for herself. Made enemies and friends. The ghost began to assume flesh and character.

Shelves had been emptied and the desk had an unused, uncared for look. There were several dead plants still scattered about, even, she realized with a start, items of wardrobe belonging to the late agony aunt. Some brightly coloured scarves lay at the top of one of the cartons and what appeared to be a rather beautiful suit, still encased in a dry-cleaner's plastic bag, hung from a picture hook behind the desk. She wondered that the formidable Miss Hampshire had not, long since, commanded the detritus to some more obscure corner. Surely they needed the space?

She noted with interest that both desk and filing cabinet had been pushed against the wall leaving the room divided roughly, an extra third in Ingrid Marsh's favour. Here everything was neatly arranged with a large bunch of fresh and powerfully smelling lilies on the desk. She took the twenties theme seriously, did Ingrid. There were three highly stylized black and white fashion prints on the wall behind her and, at her right hand, a characteristic art deco figure of a dancer in a sequinned cat-suit. They might have been twins.

Ingrid cradled the receiver and, looking up at Grace, indicated the chair on the other side of her desk. She was poised and smooth and unyielding and Grace, already uncomfortable, became more so. At no point did Ingrid look directly at her.

'It's good of you to see me. Miss Hampshire said you worked with em . . . Bid for some time. That you were . . . er . . . friends,' Grace improvised. Ingrid stared at her scornfully.

'We worked together.' Her tone was cool and emphatic. 'I was her assistant for a while. Part-time. She shared me with the Beauty editor.' A short awkward pause as she shrugged: 'What can I tell you?'

Everything you know, Grace willed her, silently casting about for some suitable prompt, but before she could reply Ingrid spoke again.

'Edy, I mean Miss Hampshire, said you were related.'

'Remotely,' Grace lied smoothly. 'We never met.'

'Oh, I thought she said . . . You don't know why . . . ?' Her voice trailed off.

'No.' Grace swallowed. 'But I'd like to try to understand. So if there's anything, anything at all you think might help?' Her voice died away under the baleful stare. She tried another tack. 'Tell me about your work.'

The girl was obviously relieved to concentrate on the magazine. She talked quickly and with some slight animation about her present job, but did not respond to any attempt to get her back to her time on the Problems page. Instead she grumbled about not having any help. The editor no longer saw any need. She did not say so, but subtly implied that it was only Bid Lacey's inadequacy or some real or imagined favouritism on Edy's part which provided her, and her alone, with an assistant. It was her sole reference to the dead girl.

'She was lucky to have you around,' Grace ventured insincerely, already partisan. 'Have you had your present job long?'

'I only got promoted after she left,' Ingrid replied shortly.

'Left?' Funny how some people couldn't mention the word.

'Died.' The word was whispered. 'Died.'

It sounded so benign. The lawyer had been more brutal. Suicide. The solitary act which sent waves of guilt far and wide. And shock. Did that explain the animosity? Even given that she was in an unenviable position, Grace had a powerful urge to shoot the messenger or, in this case, the erstwhile assistant. She blushed with mortification at her impulse.

'It must have been awful for you,' she said and meant it.

'I don't understand,' Ingrid burst out bitterly. 'Everyone was such pals with her but they won't come near this place now. Like I had the plague or something. Not one of them helped, I had to do everything. That's her stuff in those boxes.' She jumped up, pulled them out from under the desk and tore open the tops, standing aside for Grace to examine the contents. Looking into the first box she decided that the contents must just have been swept straight off the desk without any attempt at sorting. Grace firmly re-closed it. It would keep until she got it home.

She leaned across and picked up the bundle of brightly coloured scarves from the second box. Underneath, an extremely green cardigan was revealed. Acrylic, with hideous knobbly embroidery across the shoulders. A gift from St Michael, size 16/18. She had not pictured her so large. She lifted it gingerly. It was not too clean, not from dust but from too much wear, it smelled stale and human and much too intimate. There was a pair of scuffed black pumps on the bottom beside a pile of matching plastic hair combs, peacock, yellow and pink. Long hair then. She must have worn it up. The vividness of the picture made her start. She returned the items one by one, her hand lingering on the scruffy bundle of scarves. Large, untidy and florid. Something was out of kilter. Her gaze drifted back towards the cleaner's bag hanging on the wall.

'Gorgeous. Isn't it?' Ingrid pulled down the bag and shook out the suit. The soft pale banana-coloured silk slid across the desk. Nicole Farhi. Expensive and beautiful.

Small size. Slim then. Long skirt. Slim and tall. Or tallish. Stylish.

'Yours?'

Ingrid shook her head regretfully. 'Hers.'

Surprised, Grace wordlessly compared the contents of the jumbled box with the shimmering silk. Exit large beefy lady.

'I don't know how she could afford it.' Ingrid's discontented voice broke in on her thoughts.

'One-off perhaps. A treat?'

'No. Everything she wore was like that. Designer stuff. Mega labels.' The voice caressed it. The butterfly ghost fluttered dangerously.

Strange, thought Grace. The bank account didn't warrant designer labels. Nor had there been much evidence of conspicuous spending. Nor earning for that matter. So who bought the clothes? And what about the other stuff?

'The cardigan hers as well?'

'Oh no. She wouldn't be seen dead in junk like that.' Her startled eyes met Grace's. 'Oops,' she murmured sibilantly and picked up the sweater disdainfully. 'It was just lying around. Probably not hers at all. Well, I mean to say.' She shrugged.

Of course not. The image in Grace's head adjusted itself. That carton could be safely disposed of, the contents of the desk would bear longer and leisured investigation. In private. Ingrid marked it with Grace's name. She was now openly anxious to draw the interview to a close but Grace still lingered, vainly trying to think of some way of gaining access to the life of her mysterious niece.

As yet she could form no picture of what kind of woman she was, nor what she looked like. The suit, still draped on the desk, looked elegant and beautiful but try as she might she could get no further than picturing it, in her mind's eye, on some faceless mannequin. The large unruly lady kept trying to escape; the suit definitely did not fit with the scruffiness Bid had otherwise left behind.

They had run out of things to say. Ingrid had become sullen and non-committal again and Grace was wondering if it were worth asking about Bid's friends when she noticed Ingrid's hand snaking covetously over the pale shimmering silk. She waited for a moment then casually folded up the suit and laid it on top of the discarded box.

'Could you dispose of this for me? Would you mind?' she asked. Ingrid laid her hand on the pale silk but did not lift it, nor did she look up.

'You've been very kind.' Grace waved her hands vaguely around. 'Doing all this, and agreeing to talk to me.'

They were on a see-saw of mistrust and suspicion, yet there was no denying that Ingrid had done her best in an unenviable position. If only she'd shown some affection or even the slightest grief. Grace now realized how much she'd wanted to like Bridget Lacey and that Ingrid's obvious if unspoken dislike had augmented her own distaste for prying.

After a bit Ingrid moved to the other side of her desk and the two regarded each other levelly and silently.

'I'm sorry,' Ingrid said at last, 'I can't help my feelings. Everyone acts like I'm responsible . . .'

She spoke bitterly for a few minutes, hardly

making sense, about how she felt her colleagues blamed her in some way for Bid's death. It sounded as though she'd bottled her resentments and anger and was shaking them out randomly and spitefully.

'Didn't she have any close friends then?'

Ingrid abruptly pulled open the bottom drawer of the desk before replying. The drawer was full of small toys. Grace looked questioningly at her.

'She had a friend who used to come in some-times, I think she was helping Bid . . . with the letters and stuff. Unpaid I bet.' She gave a knowing little sniff. 'She sometimes brought her kid . . . proper little pest. She played with those . . .' She nodded towards the toys obviously moved by some memory for the first time, then she turned to gather her own things.

'A friend?' Grace spoke so urgently that Ingrid turned in surprise, but her gaze shifted beyond Grace.

'Sarah Roberts.' ED Hampshire's voice startled them. She came towards Grace, her face tired and drawn. Nodding a brief goodbye, Ingrid melted away to join the general exodus from the office.

'I came to apologize,' the editor said gruffly, 'and to say how sad I am about Bid's death.'

Grace waited.

'You were asking Ingrid about Bid's friends?' She looked bleakly around and, catching sight of the brightly coloured jumble in the open carton, sat down abruptly.

'Poor Bid. She was so . . . so festive.' She sighed.

'Those were hers?' Grace almost shouted the words.

'Oh yes. Those were Bid's.' The firm voice had

become tender. 'Before she started that silly business of changing her image. Dieting. Her beautiful hair.' But whatever her regrets about the beautiful hair, she did not explain.

Two conflicting images drifted through the room. The svelte and the . . . the festive? Grace suddenly felt so weary she almost missed the information she had been trying to get all afternoon.

'Sarah Roberts was her closest friend. I can give you her address. If you'll come to my office.' She indicated the cartons. 'I've asked the porter to arrange to send those on. Oh? Only one? You can give him your address on the way out.' She stood back courteously to allow Grace to precede her.

'I hope Sarah will see you,' she said thoughtfully. 'I will ring her and ask, if you like? She is very troubled I believe. It may help her of course . . . to talk.' She looked up. 'It may help you both,' she added penetratingly.

In her cool spacious office she added a phone number to the address she'd already written down, then walked Grace towards the stairs and stood waiting until she reached the hall.

Grace handed her card to the porter as he held open the door.

'Miss Hampshire said . . .'

'Yes. I'll get it done in the morning.' He had a gravelly voice and sharp inquisitive eyes. 'That Ingrid has a tongue in her head. Relation was she, Bid?' He paused before adding enigmatically, 'She seemed to have a lot on her mind.' He watched her carefully and, when she didn't respond, he shuffled away.

DE BOS, Guy: *FABRICATION DE LA DEN-TELLE EN BRUXELLES. illus. 41pp. Slim vol. Edges frayed, incomplete, lacking frontispiece. Otherwise fine.*

## CHAPTER FIVE

The day Grace tried to make contact with Sarah Roberts, the telephone answering machine declared her unavailable. Grace left a short message explaining who she was, requesting that they meet. A few days later came a note to say that Sarah was away for a couple of weeks but would be in touch as soon as she returned.

With the initiative taken from her, Grace tried dispiritedly to restore some normality to her disrupted life and resuscitate her neglected bookselling business. Apart from the still urgent need of ready cash, the hiatus had been no real disaster since it was in the nature of things for busy times to coincide only with the issuing of catalogues and dispatching of books. Accumulating stock was a more measured affair and there were often long periods of slack while the items for a collection were gathered. Being a one-woman band gave her a precious flexibility, albeit with an attendant drop of income during pauses; but this hadn't, until very recently, mattered a great deal either way. However, Grace now reflected, if her single state were to become permanent, as it looked only too likely to be, then all that would have to change.

The first week of June had come and gone without any amelioration of her sagging finances. True the bank had agreed to honour what they were pleased to call the absolute necessities, which didn't, she realized, when a cheque to the local off-licence bounced, include spiritual aid. Her humiliation was acute when the manager slyly asked if Mr Hartfield was ill, then?

A mere two months ago, yet another lifetime. Those weeks were sharply etched on Grace's mind, that day especially – the day he left, the beginning of chaos. The end of innocence.

It had started like any other, she remembered every tiny detail: the alarm clock went off a few minutes too late, she'd forgotten to buy any marmalade and the plunger in the coffee-maker broke in her hand while she was pressing Reggie for some decisions about their summer holiday. He, unaccountably grumpy, had stormed out saying he'd have breakfast in the city. After he left, she'd sat drinking her solitary tea, enjoying the newspaper – all of it – not just the centrefold tossed reluctantly across the table.

The sun was shining, which was remarkable, since the weather had been atrocious for weeks. The grass needed cutting, it was long enough to hold sparkling droplets of overnight rain and she noticed it while contemplating the likelihood of getting her laundry dry before the next downpour, but by the time she'd loaded the washing-machine the rain was coming down in torrents. Ordinary, ordinary day. Like a thousand others.

The threat of the postal strike for the following week was announced at the end of the news. She paused, hand on the knob, to hear the item out before switching off. The kitchen fell silent except for the ticking of the clock. She wondered idly how long the strike would last and if it would affect her. She was soon to find out. Did she imagine the sense of foreboding she afterwards recalled as she turned the pages of the paper? Strange how that tiny news item caught her eye, for she'd read it without any premonition of its significance to her, yet when the solicitor pushed the cutting across the desk, weeks later, she could almost have recited it from memory. *Inquest on journalist. Lonely death in Scottish hotel. Verdict unequivocal: death by suicide while the balance of her mind etc. Thirty.*

The stark shorthand gave no clue to the turmoil which led to the tragedy. She'd switched the radio back on to the ten o'clock news as she washed the dishes. The implications of the forthcoming postal strike were elaborated upon briefly, otherwise the bulletin was, she recalled, full of disaster: a boat-load missing off the Cornish coast, a dreadful pile-up on the M25 and a London property dealer fished out of a canal somewhere. She didn't catch the place because the phone rang: a bookseller friend reminding her to get her skates on. They had arranged to meet at a sale in Oxford. Wanting to impress, she'd dawdled too long getting dressed and chose a too-light suit in which she'd shivered all day.

Just as she was leaving the house the two Pepperstock children from next door arrived in

73

anoraks and gumboots, all smiles and chubby dimples, with a bucket to collect frog spawn from the garden pond. Clucking with impatience, she led them around to the back garden where their mother was squeezing her way through a broken part of the fence. Grace hadn't seen her for some days.

'Luke! Jamie! Come back inside at . . .' Deirdre Pepperstock's voice died away as she noticed Grace and took in her glad rags. 'Oh! Grace, sorry about this. Going somewhere nice? I, er, thought I'd scrounge a cup of coffee,' she added, over-brightly.

'I have to get to a sale in Oxford,' Grace said. 'Sorry, Dee. Tomorrow maybe?'

Pepperstock minor waded into the pond to screams of protest from his ma. Grace went back towards the house.

'Can't make tomorrow,' Deirdre called after her.

There was a sharp scream followed by a loud splash as the younger child plunged bodily forth. The pond wasn't deep; he sat up and began to splash his older brother. Chuckling maliciously at the sight of Dee Pepperstock's beautifully shod foot delicately poised over the muddy water, Grace quietly locked the back door, relieved to escape the probability of a half-hour litany of Jason Pepperstock's too familiar shortcomings from his wife. Though she was fond of the younger woman who was sharp and witty, it was Grace's private opinion that the Pepperstocks were something of a pair; both of them competing like anything professionally and utterly bored with the trials of family life. Which, she acknowledged guiltily, was probably why Deirdre was getting up her nose just then. As far as Grace was concerned, the children were the best of the bunch, especially the little one. But then, Grace was perhaps over-romantic about children, not having any herself.

The traffic on the M40 was relentless and the almost continual roadworks made the drive much longer than she expected. Even where it was clear, the Mini, flat out, could barely hold to fifty mph, so the sale was almost over by the time she arrived at the tall, shabby, gothic pile on the Winchester Road, about half-a-mile from the city centre. Her friend was standing guard over a couple of ancient, striped, hat boxes.

'Very nice, George,' she whispered. 'Hats?'

'No, take a look. Absolute find, my dear.'

The boxes were stuffed to the brim with a jumbled assortment of folders, pamphlets, leather-bound books, pattern samplers, and, done up in a dark blue tissue, in still excellent condition, small exquisite samples of lace. Grace fingered through them. A few she could readily identify as Brussels, Nottingham, Chantilly, Honiton, and a couple which stirred some vague childhood memory: Limerick, Carrickmacross. There were at least a hundred others. She looked at George quizzically. Someone was going to have to work very hard indeed.

'Bit outside my usual. What on earth would I do with that lot?'

'Too regional for Hartfield Regional Books?' George tutted ironically.

'No. I know nothing about lace that's all. Anyway who'd buy it?'

'I could give you a lead or two. Come on, you could do a gorgeous catalogue. Stylish. Give yourself a treat.'

'Some treat,' she laughed. 'What do you want for them?'

They worked out a deal over lunch, moaned about falling prices, lack of nice books, profits and fun. Then they went and spent too much on a few bargains in the Turl bookshop and George held her hand through *Kind Hearts and Coronets* at the Penultimate Picture Palace. By the time she got back to the car Grace was in high old humour; even the two parking tickets clinging limply to the wet windscreen didn't unduly bother her.

She planned her new catalogue on the way home. It could be pretty. George had suggested that she might display the collection in his Hampstead shop – when she finished working on it of course. A doddle. Everything handed to her on a plate. She sketched the cover design in her mind's eye – printed on lavender – lavender and old lace. She grinned to herself, probably have a bit of trouble cajoling some amusing copy out of Reggie on lace, the old chauvinist. She could already hear his snorts of derision.

Thus she drove back to London: relaxed, pleased and enjoying the John Dunn show despite the heavy traffic. She was within a mile of home, on the Ealing Road, when she edged to the left to take an avoiding shortcut through Occupation Lane. As she turned, a man staggered from the corner pub and straight on to the road. With her heart in her mouth, she slammed on the brakes and the Mini spun twice before miraculously stopping a few yards from where the drunk stood looking at her with a broad puzzled grin.

Her heart was pounding. He sauntered over to the car and with exaggerated *politesse* leaned through her window.

'That,' he slurred nonchalantly, 'was a spec ... spec ... spectacular purr-uu-ette, Madame!'

Grace stared at him, unable to speak. A huge white Mercedes turned the corner behind her and the driver immediately began to blow his horn. A look in her rear-view mirror showed a red face and a furiously waving arm. She turned to the drunk who grinned again and bowed.

'Forgive me, Duchess,' he said gallantly. 'My lift has arrived.'

And with that he sauntered back to the Mercedes while a fascinated Grace watched through her mirror. The driver turned around, his face apoplectic with rage and amazement, as the drunk climbed amiably into the passenger seat and sank back.

Surreal. Grace, shaken but laughing hysterically, started forward, already embellishing the incident for retelling. God! but she could murder a drink! She gave a little shudder. Murder a drunk. She counted herself lucky that she hadn't been going too fast. Her thoughts drifted to what she would cook for supper, back to the lace collection and inconsequentially to the children next door. She reminded herself to buy something for young Jamie's birthday. She hoped Reggie had recovered his equanimity; she was looking forward to a quiet, relaxed evening. Like any other. Funny old day. As she parked the car she had absolutely no presentiment that her entire world was about to collapse.

Out of habit she flicked on the kitchen radio. The weather forecast promised more rain, then *The Archers* came on. She took some veal from the fridge and was just pouring a stiff Scotch when Reggie burst in. She poured a second and held it out to him. He looked past her and grabbed angrily at the glass. It fell and shattered on the floor as he stood swaying above it before collapsing at the table.

'Murdoched!' His voice was slurred and angry. 'Murdoched!' Well, he was a copywriter.

'What?'

'R-E-D-U-N-D-A-N-T,' he spelled out laboriously.

'On a Wednesday?'

It was all she could think of, Wednesday, it didn't seem right somehow. Odd. Surely people were paid off at the end of a week or a month? More appropriate. She clung to the detail, unable to absorb the enormity of what he said, her inconsequential train of thought keeping panic at bay. Reggie glared at her and shrugged.

'A week ago, Friday,' he said roughly.

Her turn to stare. 'Ten days?' she whispered, 'ten days? For God's sake, why didn't you say? Ten days?' She knew then that she'd stepped on the escalator, and it was travelling downwards.

Ten days. She was appalled that he had kept it so long to himself. Ten days? Her heart began to pound.

'Say? What was there to say? It's only my life for fuck's sake.'

And mine. She was too numbed, she could not say it. How could her life collapse in so few minutes? Where were the warnings? It was too important not to have a fanfare. They stood shouting at each other with the hideous Ambridge burr providing a ludicrous chorus. It didn't occur to either of them to switch the radio off. A fifteen-minute story of ordinary folk.

When she'd finally made sense of what Reggie was saying, she pleaded that a man of his talent would find something else very quickly, but he just laughed at her bitterly and asked what the hell she knew about it?

'But you're only forty-seven! There's always the books!'

'The books?' She almost bit her tongue off at the sight of his snarling face.

'Fuck the books! Fuck the sodding books!'

'Please Reggie, please . . .'

He started to roar at her then, floundering around the kitchen, scattering everything his shaking hands touched while she stood rooted in the middle of his vortex, white and speechless. Suddenly he stopped and passed his hand wearily over his eyes.

'You're out of touch, Gracie, wrapped in your tidy cocoon!' he said hoarsely. 'Men of my age are unemployable. Didn't you know?'

He sat staring at her moodily then suddenly announced he was off.

'Off? But you usually just go,' her voice was dead. 'Why are you telling me now?'

He looked too drunk to go anywhere, but he stood up with surprising dignity, took her face tenderly in his hands and said sadly:

'Poor little Blackbird, I'm not strong any more,

I've lost my way.' Oh! that rueful grin of apology. 'I'm sorry, I need some time.'

Beloved man. She was too paralysed to say anything. Twenty-two years. My God, she screamed silently, why can't I stop him?

He turned at the door as *The Archers* signature jingle burst forth.

'Christ! I hate that frigging programme!' he shouted. A few minutes later the front door slammed. She'd drunk half the bottle of whisky before she found his note on the newel post in the hall. It simply said he'd be in touch. The casual cruelty of it floored her.

Somehow she got through those first weeks, plunging herself into work, willing herself out of the miasma of pain. By the time he contacted her she had moved from her catatonic state and begun a slow burn of anger and she might have been able to cope then but for THE LETTER. The unknown, unlooked-for relatives. That had really put the boot in. Between them, they had comprehensively scuppered her life.

QUEEN VICTORIA'S Favourite: *A short description of Her Majesty's lace items in Torchon, Honiton, Buckinghamshire and Bedfordshire lace, by a Lady of the Royal Household, with many examples mounted by Her Majesty's own hand.*

*A curious item: original Turkey binding with gold-tooled dentelle lozenge on front cover, no attribution, no chronology. A worrying if charming hotchpotch. Mint.*

## CHAPTER SIX

When her mind began to split, Grace did not recall. Two trapdoors just appeared, one labelled Lacey, the other Despair. Between them, addled and emotional, she swung wildly. With whatever was left of her will, she was obsessively determined to keep both terrors contained and apart, lest together they might engulf her. Some previous version of herself might have been able to cope, but now her connective and analytical skills were subsumed into passivity. As each day passed she became more deeply depressed, paralysed by tears and anxiety. She was too afraid and too numbed, as yet, to be angry.

The only peace lay in the bookroom. She had only to step over the threshold for her competence, which elsewhere eluded her, to snap into place. The books were like old friends; she knew each one. She moved around the shelves taking them down randomly, carefully, her finger placed confidently on the upper edge taking care not to pull or injure fragile spines.

She would stand turning the leaves with butterfly fingers, her hand running the length of the page. She knew her books and revered them. Could tell exactly where each was bought and for how much. What had charmed her about content or appearance. She did not collect for herself and had never wanted to but she knew intimately the wants of every one of her rather select group of customers. She enjoyed sharing their triumphs when she presented them with a coveted prize. This defined her; she was a collector's collector. The care and attention she gave her books and her clients was well known and, amongst that selected group, cherished. They respected her instinct and her knowledge and in time she had come to appreciate it herself. It would not make her rich but it made her content. For Grace, books were not dry old things but beautiful, sensuous and carefully nurtured friends. The bookroom was her haven.

The rest of the house was too full of memory and served only to remind her of what she'd lost and what threatened. Her head ached with the constant effort of trying to grapple with the unknown. All around lay hidden snares. Every brown envelope developed a clenched fist; every phone call the potential for disaster. In unavoidable meetings with neighbour or friend, she discovered a minor skill at dissembling, but no skill at all at stopping the awful aching hurt. She functioned in a haze, barely on the right side of sanity with a constant and at times almost irresistible desire to close her eyes and opt out completely.

Frustration followed the visit to the magazine and the continued absence of Sarah Roberts. Frustration, confusion and irritation. Bridget Kate Lacey was a complete enigma now. Before, she'd been a vaguely sympathetic shadow. Now, the overblown garish figure kept dissolving into a pale shimmering wraith. Ingrid, having outlined a selfish fashion-plate, had tantalizingly introduced the possibility of something completely different. Then Miss Hampshire had hinted at a more likeable character which for some reason had been evoked by the bright colours tumbling out of the box. It was this image that Grace irrationally fixed on.

The promised delivery of the girl's property was unaccountably delayed. It did not take long for Grace to begin to revise her opinion of Ingrid's claim that the rest of the workforce had isolated and even, in some vague way, collectively blamed her for what had happened to Bid. Whatever that was. Delicacy – or was it concealment? – did little for understanding. As she impatiently waited for the box to appear she began to wonder if Ingrid had been so fanciful after all. The porter answered her increasingly terse enquiries with complaints about his painful hip, his wife's latest illness, lack of assistance. It was perfectly clear that nothing short of a boot up the backside would compel him up to the office. A brief note to Miss Hampshire eventually concentrated his mind.

It was, after all, a pathetic little hoard; random and inconsequential, giving little clue to the girl's character or way of life. There were few personal items except for some snapshots and a small bundle of closely filled notebooks. These read like unfulfilled ambitions: snippets of stories; articles on a bewildering range of subjects, attempted then abandoned; a few lines of uneven verse. Grace examined the photographs compulsively. Which of the four or five young women was her niece? Whose were the children? The list of questions for Sarah Roberts grew and grew, but had to wait for the time being since she still appeared to be away. Then, out of the blue, came a brief note which suggested a meeting for the following week.

But by the same post Grace had a briefer and altogether more threatening letter from the bank about her continuing lack of finance which smartly jolted her into a different reality and she was forced to delay the proposed meeting a little longer.

By now the problems attendant on Reggie's bunk had reached crisis point and, as domestic chaos engulfed her, Grace found herself unable to touch, much less examine, the dead girl's things. Her mood swings became more violent and unpredictable, the crippling, destructive emotional turmoil leeched her strength and spirits.

He had taken to phoning late at night, to berate or plead, it was never clear which. Often the calls came when she had drunk too much to talk and could not make sense of his ramblings. Sometimes, just when she had dropped off to sleep, the insistent ringing would insure yet another night of restless tossing and turning, leaving her lethargic and drained. Decisions were not addressed much less solved, they both seemed to have been cast into limbo, each sealed in a separate directionless vacuum. They could not let go, yet neither had the will nor the ability to pull back. Most of all they could not talk. There's something I've got to tell you, Bird, he'd say. But he never said what.

The days passed slowly. All Grace's effort was concentrated on generating some income for herself.

By now the joint account had been unilaterally closed and the bank was being extremely coy about issuing her with replacement bits of plastic. No matter how often she tersely fumed about the impossibility of even existing without, she was met with the same bland assurance that things were being sorted out. It was quite a shock to realize that Mammon appeared to have an even more vested interest in keeping the family unit together than God.

With a flash of inspiration, prompted by the threat of finding herself with no source of income at all, she had, rather dubiously, divided the lace collection in two, the first of which could be offloaded without delay. Fortunately one of the boxes contained several invaluable *catalogues raisonnées* of their magnificent lace holdings from the Bruges Gruuthuse Museum but even with those to hand it took many precious days to resift the material, rewriting copy, seeking out appropriate illustrations, setting aside items whose value was in doubt. But in the end part one and the putative part two divided neatly enough into historical descriptions (with mounted examples) of lace-making in (i) continental Europe and (ii) the British Isles. The latter was by far the greater and more unwieldy; to such an extent indeed that she now decided to sell it on, untouched, to someone with more expertise than herself. She then issued the catalogue of part one and held her breath waiting for a nibble. She had something of a wait.

Her lack of feel for the subject made her uneasy. She suspected she hadn't done it justice and that left her feeling vulnerable. A feature of her professional survival was that she usually went out of her way to make her bookselling as little of a gamble as possible, having learnt how easy it was to dribble away a fortune in small sums in often foolish and vain attempts at forming collections unique enough to tempt and inspire the opening of fat cheque books. Now, as she sat biting her nails, she realized sourly that her job was very like her marriage, with the same ups and downs and this one blunder into relatively unknown territory might be enough to topple the careful reputation. Part of her had always hated that necessary imposed restraint and there had been times when she'd felt an almost irresistible urge to break out and throw caution to the winds. But this, clearly, was not the time.

She was acutely aware that, in her present predicament, buying two large boxes of serendipity was about the riskiest thing she could have done. Risky, or to be more accurate, a silly attempt at flirtatious bravado. George had issued a challenge and she had responded without remembering that he was rich enough not to have to worry about loans sitting idly gathering 16.25% interest and rising. What had appeared to be, under George's influence, a harmless enough sum, was rapidly accumulating into something approaching the national debt.

Grace reminded herself that she'd got where she was, as a bookseller, by a judicial and, occasionally lucky knack of being able to build collections around subjects which interested her. And what interested her was finding the best, the most coveted, even in the obscure fields she sometimes found herself rummaging. Fastidious about presentation, she had also over the years developed many of the skills more usually associated with the restorers she could seldom afford to employ. She had a good nose for a bargain and, better still, was able to recall and connect one title with another over long periods of time. But perhaps her real skill was in limiting her interests very strictly to literature and literary figures in a geographic context – hence 'regional'. Her reputation, like many another, had been built slowly and carefully; profits from her first collection financing her second and so on until this, her thirty-second. Though profits, as she knew, was rather overstating the case.

What better reason for not venturing into un-charted waters? She recognized that her knowledge of lace and its history was sketchy; but as she handled and sorted the material, researched it, cleaned, mounted, indexed and wrote it up, she became ever more tantalized with the realization that given enough time, care and attention, then she truly might have something very special on her hands. Or might have had, by taking time to search out a, or better still, *the* buyer. But she had no time; not while the pressure to present herself at the bank's cash dispenser was growing with each passing day. Nothing short of a rocket would have sent her, begging bowl in hand, bankwards, or, even more unthinkable, Reggie-wards, for the purpose of wheedling an advance on vague promises of quite a considerable inheritance. She still would not think of this as a possibility. It was, as she'd been insisting to herself all along, a deadly mistake.

Impatiently waiting for offers to roll in, she did not notice that her answering machine was on the blink. To avoid explaining Reggie's continued absence to the alert enquiries of friends and neighbours, she spent rather a lot of time either shut away in her bookroom or driving aimlessly from bookshop to bookshop. So it was that she did not receive a single call about the new collection for almost a week.

Grace was not herself. She wasn't eating properly but was getting through the remains of the drinks cupboard at a rate, if not yet spectacular, then certainly resolute. Reggie's hoarded wine stock was more often than not her only sustenance of an evening. Grace was slowly disintegrating, pinning her last vestiges of self-esteem on the hope that she would be able to give herself a temporary reprieve with a successful sale.

The fat American, whose loud ringing at the door woke her one morning at nine-thirty, obviously meant business. Holding her splitting head with both hands, Grace peered through her bedroom window and spotted the woman nobbling Deirdre Pepperstock over the garden fence with enquiries as to the whereabouts of Hartfield Books. The harsh voice must have enthralled the entire street. Grace flung on her clothes and damped her unwashed hair before she threw open the door with a smile which went a fair way to cracking open her face.

The woman was vaguely familiar. Bookseller. New York? No, Boston somewhere. An *aficionado* of the antiquarian book fairs. Loud, aggressive and driver of legendary bargains. Piggy something. Piggy, no, Peggy Hippsley. A tough cookie. Grace's heart sank, she did not like selling on to other dealers.

'This stuff sold?' The catalogue was thrust under her nose and, before she considered, Grace shook her head. Announcing her intention of looking over the collection, Mrs Hippsley moved down the hall like a flotilla. Grace travelled limply in her wake.

Round one to the Combine Harvester she thought sourly.

'Can I see it? Right away. I haven't much time. Lucky you're near the M4, I got to get to Bristol. You don't answer your phone,' she accused harshly over her shoulder. 'You been away? That's no way to run a business. Issuing catalogues, then going away.' She didn't so much speak, as cascade.

She turned to run an appraising eye over Grace who was checking the machine. The jack-point was half out of its socket. Pushing it home, Grace mumbled something about a death in the family and offered her a cup of coffee. Her remark had some effect for the woman was silent for long enough for Grace to gather her wits and fill herself with a half-pint of her strongest and blackest brew. Her insides felt as though they'd been rubbed down with sandpaper. Silently resolving to eat rather than drink in the future, she led her guest upstairs and into the bookroom. The small black eyes darted about as if she were making an inventory of the entire household. Everything was rapidly and thoroughly scrutinized – rugs (good if threadbare), curtains (in need of cleaning), pictures (so-so) and the entire stock of books (no comment). The beady eyes swept the room like a laser. Grace, biting back a pathetic urge to apologize for its deficiencies, drew the woman's attention to the collection laid out on the octagonal library table, where even the dimmest items looked splendid against the gleaming rosewood.

With much fluttering and wheezing and jabbing of her plump white fingers, Mrs Hippsley sorted

through the display, picking this and that for dispar-
aging assessment or, more tellingly, silent and satisfied appraisal. All the while, Grace watched her like a
fisherman his line, planning how best to haul in her
catch. After a half-hour or so, the American woman
began checking each item laboriously against the
catalogue. For all the world, thought Grace, as if she
expected me to hold on to the choicest items. The
accuracy of this thought caused her wild, if suppressed, amusement. The American's attempt to cut
the price ludicrously did not.

'Rather eclectic,' the harsh voice drawled. 'I can see
you're not used to this kind of material, are you?' The
studied nonchalance, as she stood idly turning over
delicate lace, stiffened Grace's resolve.

'So of course the price is much too high,' she
finished.

'On the contrary,' Grace replied stoutly, 'it is very
reasonable. As you will know.'

'Hmm. And incomplete of course . . .'

'The price reflects that,' Grace parried. Sheer
bloody-mindedness prevented her from mentioning
that the remainder of the collection would be offered
for sale at some future date. Future. That was the
problem. She knew so little about it. The threat of
being left with unsaleable material niggled uncomfortably, suggesting caution.

'Very few people are interested in the history of
lace-making . . .' Mrs Hippsley left the words hanging in the air and wagged her massive head sadly.

'As a matter of fact there are several interested
parties coming later in the week,' Grace interjected
fluently and mendaciously, hanging grimly on to her
nerve.

There was a moment's expectant pause before Mrs Hippsley continued, '. . . but I have such a weakness for beauty . . . Say, twenty-five per cent off?'

She handles her bounty with admirable restraint, thought Grace laconically.

'Ten,' Grace countered firmly and immediately felt she had pushed too far. Much as she disliked her, she had no doubts about Mrs Hippsley's scholarship and knew she had shrewdly surmised that the illustrated history (two centuries worth) of European lace-making was strictly outside Grace's competence. Nor was she going to be too subtle about putting her thumping great finger on the vulnerable spot.

'Fifteen. Final.' She lumbered around the room, pulling this book and that from the shelves, then pushing them back without comment, while Grace stood like an unconsidered guest in her own room.

She should never have said the stuff was available, she should have sent the blasted woman off for a few hours while she prepared herself to do battle. Her head was cracking open. If only the bloody woman would go.

'I don't suppose you'll need these?' Mrs Hippsley picked up a package of catalogues and laid them on top of her haul.

'I'm afraid they're bespoke.'

To her credit she laughed at Grace's stiff refusal then disarmed her by confessing that she saved all the Hartfield 'bro-shuures.'

'I have them all. Every one. Thirty-one in all. You know, Gracie, you have a nice little feel for print.' Gracie winced.

'You're very kind,' she replied wryly.

'You British are so inventive! But you all got that

91

cottage industry mentality.' The light of victory had appeared in her eyes. 'Too restrained.' She means retentive, thought Grace, her smile becoming ever more fixed.

'You gotta think on a more cosmic scale, Gracie, you could make money out of those bro-shuures.' With the skill of a card-sharp, Miss Peggy slipped a dozen or so catalogues into her bag, then smiled insouciantly.

Thanks a bundle, thought Grace grimly, her temper rising dangerously. Bro-shuures indeed! If she says that word once more I'll crown her. What the hell does she think I am? A dusty little travel agent?

She looked up. Peggy Hippsley was looking at her speculatively. Grace felt like thumping her. Alarmed that her expression might echo her thoughts, she bent her pulsating head and was horrified by a large stain on her blouse. Oh Lord. Not a new stain, a faded old stain. As she casually moved her hand to cover it, she was mortified to notice her tormentor watching with interest and, was she mistaken? Sympathy? She flushed.

'Will you excuse me for a moment?' she said, as casually as she could, melting out of the room. She rifled through her wardrobe and quickly slipped on a sweater and brushed her hair. Mrs Hippsley was busy studying her new acquisition and did not look up on Grace's return.

'Any idea who collected this?' The dealer's tone implied little hope of a sensible reply.

'Yes,' Grace said quietly. 'A woman called Hannah Deutsch. I have a couple of photographs of her. Apparently a group of German Jewish refugees settled in Oxford in 1938 – academics, a publisher, couple of doctors and their families. A very distinguished group, but they had a pretty lean time of it at first. Some of them, including Hannah, were interned during the war. On the Isle of Man, I believe. Dreadful irony, they escaped the German camps then we locked them up,' Grace said ruefully. 'She brought the lace collection with her from Berlin, in a beautiful old hat box. Someone must have looked after it for her during her internment.'

Mrs Hippsley slipped her hand into her bag and drew out a massive wadge of banknotes. Grace's heart leapt. No cheques: no trouble with the bank. She struggled to remain impassive.

'Cash. You agree to fifteen per cent reduction then?' She waited for Grace's assenting nod, then, in merciful silence, began to count the notes into a neat pile. When she finished she looked up slyly and slowly retrieved two of them.

'We'll split the tax,' she drawled. The *coup de grâce*. One irritating ploy too many.

'There is no tax,' snapped Grace and defiantly pushed the notes back across the table. 'I prefer not to haggle,' she added firmly.

One note fluttered downwards, the second was returned to the bag. After a moment's hesitation, Grace picked up the bundle and flicked the notes quickly through her fingers before slipping them into the table drawer.

'You got something on your mind?' The American's voice had lost its edge. 'You got to take yourself seriously in this business.' When Grace didn't reply she lumbered to her feet.

Don't let yourself go. She wasn't quite rude enough

to say it. Grace was damned if she was going to respond to the invitation to unburden herself. After all, she hadn't been quite overwhelmed, had she? She'd got what she craved; a financial respite. Relief flooded through her and with it, resolution. Suddenly she made up her mind what she would do with the rest of the collection; she could afford to be magnanimous.

'Would you care to have the hat box?'

'Sure. And the photographs.' Never one to miss a trick, was Peggy.

'Certainly.' Grace laughed and handed them over. Mrs Hippsley examined them and looked at her suspiciously.

'What age was she when she settled in Oxford?'

'Oh, quite young I think. She inherited all this from her grandmother and mother.' She eased her visitor towards the door.

'So she didn't collect it herself?' Mrs Hippsley's eyes narrowed.

'No.'

'None of it?'

Grace didn't reply. She helped lift the box into the car boot. Then stood on the pavement while Mrs Hippsley squeezed herself into the inadequate front seat. As she was starting up the engine, the American rolled down the window. She looked puzzled. 'When did she die?'

'Who? Mrs Deutsch? The late seventies I believe.' Grace replied, waiting for the explosion. It followed very swiftly. The engine was turned off.

'Hey. What are you playing at? If she didn't die till the seventies, where's the rest of the stuff?'

'There is no "rest". I catalogued the entire contents

of the box. There are no other items from Continental Europe. What you have is exactly as it was brought out of Germany in 1938. It is, I believe, unique. And complete.' She turned to go.

'But, there must be more . . .'

'Mrs Hippsley,' Grace said evenly, 'you have precisely what was offered in my catalogue. All of it, plus the photographs, some letters and the original box with Hannah's signature. You asked and got fifteen per cent discount plus a further fifty pounds. And you know better than I that the price was already low. So, if you have a problem, let me return your money and you may return what you've bought.' She quelled her butterflying insides and held Mrs Hippsley's furious gaze until she said sarcastically:

'OK, OK. Cool down. I guess she turned her attention to British lace? Eh? You think I couldn't work that out? Why be so damned secretive? Not my stuff anyway. So what's your problem? I did just fine.' She laughed up at Grace's flushed face, turned the engine and roared off, her panache implying that, whoever got the worst of the bargain, it was not P Hippsley.

It was not the way Grace usually treated her clients and she was appalled at her own rudeness. She climbed the stairs heavily and ran the bath. Then she undressed quickly and lay back in the steamy perfumed foam and calmly planned how best she could sell the remainder of Hannah Deutsch's collection.

She dressed herself carefully in fresh grey linen slacks and white shirt, then, glancing at her watch, dialled the string of digits which got her through to Max Lindquist, curator of the most comprehensive library on the Arts and Crafts Movement in the United States.

'My dear Grace, I've been trying to get hold of you for days.'

He expressed mild regret when she told him she'd already made a sale.

'Hell, Grace, how much did you say?' He sounded appalled. 'Peggy Hippsley, eh? Ah well! Few of us get the better of that old harridan! I don't doubt she'll be on my doorstep next week. Oh Lordy, Lordy.'

There had been a few items he would have liked, he said, but never mind, his compatriot would, no doubt, line them up (with the price suitably jacked up) for his delectation. He laughed.

'As a matter of fact, I am very much more interested in the second part of the collection. When will it be ready?'

'That, Max, is what I wanted to talk about.'

They were old friends and he was far away and so it seemed easier to be frank with him. He listened without comment until she'd talked herself out. She spoke a little about her marriage breakup and less openly about the Laceys. There was so much to sort out, she did not see how she was going to be able to give enough time and attention to the work. She needed a few months free. She let her last remark hang in the air for a moment before touching on her worries about her compatibility with lace and the time it would take her to mug up on the subject. She outlined her hastily devised scheme. He copped on at once and countered with some questions. Then, becoming all business-like, he suggested a neat solution:

'One of our curators is in London on compassionate leave – mother dying, very protracted – he's just the person. As a matter of fact I think it would be a relief for him to have something to do.'

So it was arranged. The exiled curator would look at the collection and, if it was as she described, if they could reach an agreement on the price, then the museum, that is to say he, Max, would buy it – with all faults – in other words, as it was. Would she be willing for him to look it over and then, if the deal went through, to let him work on it while he was in England? In her home?

A day or two later he presented himself. He must have walked from the station because the shoulders of his Burberry were soaking wet and his fair hair was plastered to his scalp. She thought, when she opened the door, that he was a Mormon because he had that super-clean-cut look that only mid-western Americans seem to be able to achieve. About five ten. Mid to late thirties. He held out one hand and took off his steamed-up glasses with the other. Mmm. Mormons don't have knowing eyes like that. Or was he just myopic?

'Murray Magraw.' He had a strong jaw and a huge crooked smile. 'Can I come in? It's awfully wet out here!' She stood back to let him pass.

'I'll get some towels.' She grinned. 'It's a bit chilly for paddling.'

She watched as he rubbed vigorously at his hair. Not fair. Greying blond. Too long. Thinning. She revised his age upwards. Nearer forty than thirty. He bent to take off his shoes and socks, both soaking. Carrying a little weight around the middle. Long bony feet. She picked up the shoes, both had holes in the soles. Single? She offered him coffee.

'For coffee I would kill.' He'd put on the glasses. Sea eyes, surprisingly dark lashes.

'That's better, I can see you now.' Myopic then. 'Shall we start again?' He smiled disarmingly. 'Grace?' Her spirits began to rise.

That day was like an oasis. A healing respite, fenced before and after with the trauma of pain, too much emotion and stress. For those brief hours she set her grief aside and gave herself to the healing pleasure of concentrating fully on her work, and the rarer pleasure of sharing with someone whose enjoyment was equal to hers.

They spent the afternoon making a careful inventory before he declared his interest in acquiring the remaining stock. He went through the catalogue of part one to make sure she hadn't unwittingly let any treasures escape. She raised her eyebrow at that, quick to take offence. He wasn't fazed.

'You want me to convince Max, don't you? You know what he's like. Careful.'

He grinned conspiratorially as she nodded, then he laughed. 'I'm only trying to keep the price down. But it's no use, you knew we'd want it.'

'Hoped. Guessed.'

'Guessed?' he exploded. 'But it's good. Really good. I thought you said all this was new to you, Grace? It's a terrific find. Ma'am, you certainly know your stuff.'

She could have hugged him for that. Could have hugged him, full stop. Instead she broke open a bottle of Reggie's best Mersault. An hour or so later Murray went away in a glow of triumph and alcohol, clutching a sheaf of papers and promising an early return.

'It depends on how my mother is, of course, some days are easier than others.'

'Why is she . . . ?'

'In London? Oh, she married an Englishman about twenty years ago. He died last year. There's no-one else to look after her.' He sounded unenthusiastic.

'I'm sorry.'

She stood watching as he walked down the garden. They would buy the collection. Murray itched to get hold of it. Even before he said so, she had known, just by looking at his hands. His reaction was very like her own. Tactile. The Hippsley cash would clear her most pressing bills and if this deal went through she would be free to sort out . . . what? One thing at a time.

Reggie? No. She surprised herself by acknowledging that this time there would be no short-term solutions with Reggie. Instead she opened the other trapdoor: Laceys. She'd bought herself more time.

As Murray Magraw turned to wave goodbye she felt a sharp pang of regret that she couldn't forget everything else and instead continue working with him. Or was it just a reluctance to reopen the past? She had made the way clear, yet all she felt was the return of anxiety and the awful ennui of fear.

Deirdre Pepperstock passed Murray Magraw just outside the gate. She turned to appraise him before noticing Grace. She waved sheepishly, walked on a few steps, then stopped uncertainly. She'd recently had her hair bobbed. It looked fabulous.

'Who's that, Grace? He's awfully handsome!' She laughed roguishly.

Grace sighed and invited her in. It was about time

she repaid the borrowed hundred quid and explained her situation to Dee. She'd been avoiding her friend for too long. She hadn't spoken to her properly for weeks. Not since Reggie's departure in fact.

Anyone less preoccupied than Grace might have observed that Deirdre Pepperstock had been, for an equal time, assiduously and successfully, avoiding her.

**QUINN, H:** *DIARY OF A VAGRANT HEART.* *Pentagon Press, presentation copy, lurid cloth binding, worn. Endpapers foxed. Dust jacket in good condition.*

## CHAPTER SEVEN

When Murray Magraw arrived to start cataloguing a couple of days later, Grace was free at last to turn her mind fully to what she now euphemistically dubbed the family business. She went to call on Sarah Roberts.

It turned out that Sarah Roberts lived only a couple of streets away from her friend Bridget Lacey. The house was situated in a pretty square about seven minutes walk from King's Cross Station. Both the square and the streets leading to it were all part of the old Lloyd Baker estate. It comprised not more than a hundred or so houses, contained within Amwell Street to the east and King's Cross Road to the west, bounded on the north and south by Percy Street and Lloyd Baker Square. Campbell's guide provided Grace with the information that building started around 1820 when similar developments were popping up all over London. By 1830, the market garden, which the new estate replaced, had been entirely absorbed to house the newly affluent legals and clericals. Mr Pooter might have done worse: the leases were long; the houses generous, central and retained some memory of the gardens upon which they were built.

Small businesses gradually grew up in the surrounding streets. An occasional mews provided livery for horses. A colony of clockmakers flourished off Wharton Street. Mr Cruikshank, from the comfort of Amwell Street, self-consciously cartooned 'The March of the Bricks'; the new housing estates not yet being quite respectable. Soon other, more up-to-date, more desirable crescents and terraces would be developed further out, with more trees, more space and without the unsettling distractions of the boarding houses opened to accommodate the players from the nearby Sadler's Wells Theatre. Prosperity ebbed and flowed with the passing years, sometimes up, more often down. Gradually the small estate settled into sleepy decline, until the early nineteen eighties when the leaseholds began to be sold off and prosperity edged in once more.

The area, completely unknown to Grace until recent events, and a nice surprise when she found it, was a charming enclave whose nineteenth-century streets were almost unchanged except for some recent renovation. It was quiet and secret and unexpectedly small-townish. There was something soothing about the order and sameness of the houses, built in pairs, meandering up the incline of Wharton Street. That Bridget Lacey was astute enough to have found such an agreeable place to live, Grace silently applauded, the more so because she must have found it long before prices began to rise. Could it have been the similarity of these quiet streets to her native Dublin which made her so prescient? As Grace mused on how often her niece might have walked that way she only half noted that she had begun to think of the girl as her niece.

But even so, she still did not allow herself to dwell on the circumstances of her death, always shying away whenever her regretful thoughts turned towards her.

Work was going on in four or five of the houses on the north side of the street as she dawdled past, killing the quarter hour before her appointment. One, a mirror image of the house which held the Lacey flat, was covered in scaffolding and its open door tempted her curiosity. She peered into the hall but could go no farther because the floorboards had been taken up. The staircase too was gone and soon the wide hallway with its beautiful ceiling rose would be altered to accommodate another entrance, but for the moment it was still intact and through the open door she glimpsed the remnants of old decency in the preserved moulded plaster-work of the sitting-room. A romantic place to live. Was Bridget romantic? Bridget, Bid or Biddy perhaps? Grace wondered what she called herself.

So far, she had been disinclined to enter the girl's flat. At first it was simply fear of trespass and the hope that Bartley Quinlan would call one day to tell her that there had been, as she suspected all along, a mistake. But he had not. Though, rather unnerv-ingly, he had recently telephoned several times, ostensibly to talk about some detail or other but really to air his curiosity about what she intended to do with 'her' property in Dublin. He was, he said, somewhat worried about it lying idle, there were so many vandals about.

Her mind didn't seem to be able to make any reality of the property being hers, or being in danger. He might have been describing some remote outpost the other side of the world for all she could make of it.

'Well, Mrs Hartfield, as soon as you've sorted out the London flat . . .'

She almost flared at him for that. Did he think she was running in and out of the Everard Street flat every day, she wondered angrily? Ransacking the contents? Stamping out Bridget Lacey's life?

'. . . perhaps you could come over.' He sidled to the point. 'I have a client who may be interested in the Rathmines house. We'd get a good price. A cash buyer.'

He mentioned a large sum. That shabby old pile? Surely he was mistaken? Cash. So temptingly offered after she'd spent weeks in a fever of anxiety about a fraction of the amount he mentioned. The temptation to grab and run lasted only a split second. The two parts of her life were entirely separate and had to be kept so. There was no way of applying solutions crossways. Grace held tenaciously to her cockeyed logic without being able to explain it to herself, much less to someone as sharp as Bartley Quinlan.

'I'm . . . er . . . very tied up at the moment. A few weeks perhaps?'

'Fine, fine. When you're ready.'

Then just as she was about to put down the receiver:

'Oh, by the way, Father Crowley was asking about you. He's anxious to meet you.'

The door in her mind slammed shut.

'I'm afraid it's not possible just now,' she said tersely. 'I'll be in touch when I've made a decision.'

As she walked slowly up the street her courage

faltered with every step. She forced herself to concentrate on the girl, but other images kept intruding. Up to now she had been able to close the Pandora's box. By opening it a little further would she lose all hope of being able to do so again? Bridget, Bid.

She'd been up at dawn, prowling around unable to settle, drinking endless cups of coffee, steeling herself for the meeting with Sarah. By the time she left the house she'd changed from slacks to skirt to suit and back again to slacks before settling on a sombre grey skirt and jacket which hadn't seen daylight for several years. In some previous existence Reggie had laughingly dubbed it her 'wake suit'. Glimpsing her image reflected in the shining surface of a parked taxi, Grace owned that she might indeed have been on her way to a funeral.

She plodded resolutely on but the aptness of that sudden thought almost made her turn tail and fly for cover. Back to the safety of her own house, to the agreeable company of that nice laconic American who had arrived just as she left the house and was probably now happily ensconced with her books while she set out on her dismal pilgrimage. Alone. When she could more comfortably have taken up Murray's urging to work jointly on the collection. No doubt Deirdre was already plying him with coffee. She could never resist anyone so good-looking.

Which sparked the thought that Deirdre had been singularly unhelpful when Grace had told her the previous afternoon about Reggie's departure. Laughing it off nervously as another temporary bout of AWOL, she had appeared much more interested in the American and slagging off both her husband and the new au pair. She'd launched into the attack on Jason the moment she entered the kitchen and hardly paused for breath until the kids came hammering at the back door. Grace had paid back her loan but otherwise hadn't really managed to get a word in, nor after the first few minutes did she want to, for Deirdre had seemed terribly edgy and anxious to get away as quickly as possible. Which was, when she thought about it, quite unlike her.

Somewhere off at the edge of Grace's sensibilities Reggie shuffled softly. Blackbird bye, bye. Blackbird. He hadn't called her that for ages. Hadn't called her anything. Hadn't phoned for several days either. Someone, somewhere must be looking after him. If only, if only . . .

The Roberts's house had been gentrified, lovingly and carefully but the work was much too fresh and it matched uncomfortably with its more mellow twin in the middle of the south side of the small square. On three sides of the central garden the terraces were complete; eight houses, four pairs. The fourth side of the square had been long since demolished, the crumbling walls sprouted brilliant purple buddleia at every level.

No-one answered the echoing doorbell. Still a little early, Grace leaned wearily against the railing surround of the basement area and waited some minutes before trying again. Still no reply. Puzzled, she checked her watch for the time. Perhaps Sarah had changed her mind at the last moment? With a shaming charge of relief at her unexpected reprieve,

Grace scribbled a note and pushed it through the letterbox.

They must have approached silently because when she turned mother and child were standing on the step below her, looking for all the world like refugees from a Victorian painting, the wan-faced adult seeming to draw strength from the sturdy little girl by her side. They were an arresting pair. Sarah was much the same height as Grace, painfully slight, frail and incredibly young-looking. Perhaps it was exhaustion which gave such translucence to the pale olive skin and accentuated the delicate structure of her face. She certainly didn't look as if she'd just been on holiday. Her colouring should have made her look vivid and striking but the dark rings around her clear hazel eyes dominated and made her look sad, haunted almost. She had an unruly mop of curly brown hair which fell to her shoulders from what looked suspiciously like a paper-clip perched on the top of her head. The effect was charming and perhaps gave a better clue to her more normal self.

Her clothes too emphasized her youthful appearance and were greatly at odds with her solemnity. She wore a skimpy tangerine skirt which was topped by a little plum-coloured jacket made of some soft fabric which clung to her slender frame, a striped shirt collar peeped out at the neck. Her legs were bare, feet thrust into flat black sandals. She was not at all what Grace had expected.

The little girl appeared to be about three or four. Her hair, straighter and darker than her mother's, was cut short and clipped back from her eyes by a tiny pair of lurid green sunglasses which she kept fingering with her free hand. She was tanned, with plump red cheeks and huge eyes almost as dark as her hair. She was clearly in a foul temper, her mouth turned down in a stubborn sulk. She must have been plucked from a garden because her broad-striped blue and white dungarees had grass stains at the knees and her bright red sandals had been squeezed on to a pair of extremely grubby feet. She struggled irritably with one strap of a small knapsack on her back and, when she turned to look up at her mother, Grace could see that it was in the shape of a brown bear. As Grace watched, the child broke free and stomped up to the door and began to kick crossly at the boot-scraper. Sarah Roberts held out her hand.

'I'm sorry I'm late, I had to collect Alice. She didn't want to leave.' She stared at Grace momentarily then dropped her eyes.

'You must be Mrs Lacey's sister,' she said disconcertingly as she fumbled in her pocket for the latchkey.

They trooped silently into the house. The child immediately headed off up the stairs while Sarah led Grace into the front room where she stood awkwardly biting her lip before suggesting tea. Then, without waiting for Grace's reply, she gathered up the few toys scattered on the sofa and dived out of the room, closing the door firmly behind her.

She went upstairs. The old house creaked and groaned with every step. First into the front bedroom. There was a murmur of voices, a squeal of protest, a shout, then two pairs of feet came running down the stairs. The sounds died as they moved to the back of the house. Shortly afterwards the front door opened and closed and a heavier step walked through the hall. A man's voice called out and was answered. A baby cried. Then silence again.

Grace glanced around the room. An elaborate hi-fi system. Several austere architectural drawings framed in steel. Three Anthony Gross etchings, one above the other, on the left of the fireplace. She straightened the middle one. On the other side a chunk of carved stone – part of a broken column? – squatted on a wooden wall-bracket. Over the fine marble fireplace a framed print of a glorious beefy nude by Matthew Smith. A smallish bookcase of blue-covered Penguins. A pile of Lego in a basket, My, or perhaps Alice's, Little Pony tucked under the hearthrug. Two or three beautiful pieces of antique furniture and two vast battered sofas covered with old red and gold bedcovers. Under a perspex cover on the coffee table, a small model of a row of rather bleak little houses, with a flamboyantly signed label.

Grace wondered what Thomas Roberts, B.Arch. RIBA looked like, and whether the light baritone she had just heard was his. Shortly afterwards he obliged as, to an accompaniment of shrill chatter, father and daughter exited through the front door. She spied them on the steps outside. He held the little girl's hand in his and a sleeping baby in a harness on his back. He was extremely tall and looked rather older than his wife, late thirties perhaps; his face was also haggard and weary looking. Grace wondered idly where the baby had been when they came in.

She was still standing at the window when Sarah

returned, carrying a tea tray. She stood for a moment at the doorway and smiled shyly and fleetingly. She looked more vulnerable but her smile was without warmth or engagement. The awkwardness between them became almost tangible, their silence over-filling the room and it was now, as in her mind Grace juxtaposed friend and niece, that the full horror of that youthful suicide began to take on reality. Until that moment, with the girl unknown and remote, it was the dead/alive/dead mother she'd most feared, selfishly thinking of both deaths in terms of the consequences to herself. But now she understood that the effects were much more far-reaching. She was just one victim; suicide sucked everyone in its wake. Sarah's almost palpable distress was witness to that. Concern for the dead began to fade, it was the living who were being brutalized and destroyed with hopeless remorse.

As she busied herself with the tea tray, Sarah's eyes flicked surreptitiously over Grace's face as if comparing her with someone.

'You look like Bid's mother,' she announced abruptly, pushing her hair back from her eyes. 'But I expect you know that.'

'No,' Grace said softly. Sarah stared at her sullenly.

'Yes, you do,' she contradicted flatly.

'I'm sorry. I mean I didn't know we looked alike. We were separated as children. I last saw her when I was seven or eight. I thought . . . I was told . . . I understood she was dead. You will find it very strange, but I never met her daughter. I knew nothing whatever about her. About either of them.

110

Until they died, that is. It was a horrible shock. Awful.' She faltered before Sarah's wide-eyed and obvious disbelief. 'Look. Please believe me. I had no idea I had a niece. If only I had known ... how much I longed ... all those years.' Again silence descended until Sarah's scorn challenged Grace to blunder on.

'Her death must be much more shattering for you. Being so close. I should not have troubled you. But I desperately wanted to find out something, anything, about her. Can you understand? It's all so meaningless. That's why I came to you, because I know nothing whatever about her.'

It was no use. Even if Grace had been tempted to embark on her muddled family history, there was simply no way she could make it understandable to herself, much less to Sarah. Nor would she find it easy or even plausible to explain why she'd come. She was no longer sure why it was so desperately important to learn something about her niece, the child she could not have. The visit, clearly, was a stupid, unforgivable blunder.

Without warning, Grace began to tremble, the cup rattled softly against the saucer, then more violently, as her right leg began to jump uncontrollably. Sarah looked acutely uncomfortable – frightened almost – but she still said nothing.

Why oh why had her sister cut herself off? What had caused that drastic flight, that life-time's unforgiving silence? And, the question kept edging in and no matter how Grace tried to ignore it, would not go away, *what part had she, Grace, played in that unrelenting alienation?* For surely this was at the root of it: why had she been content to go through three-quarters of her life without any curiosity about her dead sister? It would have to be faced. But not yet.

Deep at the back of her mind, too deep for her to own, lay fear. Whenever her thoughts slid backwards she felt that same sickening lurch of nausea. The mention of her sister's name brought nameless, unbearable dread. Was this why she was concentrating on the niece? She hardly understood what dim instinct had led her towards her sister's child. Had she instinctively hoped that by focusing on her she might find a way of edging backwards?

Now it appeared that Sarah knew them both. Would she have agreed to see Grace had she not, even unconsciously, also wanted to talk her own grief and pain away? What would touch her? Allay her suspicion? More urgently, how could Grace describe the happenings of the past weeks or explain the ignorance and duplicity of a life-time?

Or was it too absurd to expect someone so young, preoccupied with a young family, to understand or sympathize with the emotional inadequacies of the middle-aged, when she herself was so obviously in need of consolation?

Somehow, as Grace sat gloomily searching for words, the Lacey tragedy and Reggie's defection once more merged and gelled into one, the pain of each overlapping and fusing.

Sarah, sad, withdrawn and silent, sat nervously pulling on and off her wedding ring, like a child waiting to be chastised. She looked up and, as their eyes met, Grace, who had sought consolation, became the consoler. Suicide. That was what mattered here. Suicide. Desolation was etched into

112

the girl's face. Her exact contemporary, her closest friend had gone to some anonymous hotel room and without calling for help had killed herself. No room for doubt, no hope of mistake: total brutal rejection. How could she ever have thought anything else important?

'I . . . we quarrelled . . .' Sarah whispered.

'Ah.' Like a sigh.

'I feel it's my fault.'

'Oh my dear,' Grace said softly, 'it was her family who failed her, not you. Do you hear me? It was her family.'

'She always said she had no relations,' Sarah accused in a bleak monotone.

'Yes. She didn't know.' *The stupid waste.* 'Obviously, nobody thought of telling her.' *Or me.*

Grace's bitter words touched some chord in Sarah. Something about the way she spoke, sat, and the strain on her face laid bare the older woman's deep unhappiness. She looked vulnerable, as if her privacy had been invaded. Her rapidly blinking eyes held back tears. Sarah suddenly thought she'd never seen anyone look so sad and wondered, since she claimed not to know Bid, why Grace Hartfield cared so much?

Embarrassed by Sarah's silent scrutiny, Grace got up and began to fiddle with the ornaments on the mantlepiece. In her restlessness, her resemblance to Bid's mother was unsettling, yet as Sarah looked at her more closely the likeness to Mrs Lacey became fugitive and suddenly, as Grace turned her head slightly, there was a hint of Bid in her tired features. That vague familiarity invited confidence.

Poor old Biddy. Without warning, Sarah's anger

with her friend evaporated, releasing her grief and pent emotions about the suicide. She longed for explanation, peace, forgiveness for her failure to help her friend. Tom wouldn't listen, he kept urging her to let it rest, to stop blaming herself and concentrate instead on how they were going to manage now that the bulk of his contracts had collapsed. And the baby never stopped crying. But how could she bury so many years of friendship in silence?

She wanted to dump her remorse, pour it away, but the words wouldn't come. Even so, the silence between them imperceptibly lightened and became less fraught.

Hesitantly, Grace sat on the sofa beside Sarah and, taking a bundle from her handbag, silently laid it between them. Without speaking, they began to sift through the small pile which had come from the magazine office, stuffed into a pocket file at the bottom of the wretched cardboard box. Most of it was personal; letters, one or two clippings yellowed with age whose interest was no longer decipherable, and photographs. Grace had already poured over the sparse collection, unsuccessfully trying to match the conflicting descriptions she'd had of her niece. She held out a small colour print of an overweight young woman holding a baby. Until she met her, she'd assumed it to be Sarah. A large floppy hat sat uncertainly on the gathered-up hair, partly obscuring the face which was bent towards the howling child. The woman was dressed in a brightly patterned skirt and overblouse. Perhaps it was the unfortunate get-up which made her appear heavier than she probably was? The other people in the picture were also hatted and stood in what looked like the porch of an ancient church. Now she recognized Sarah among them.

'Alice's christening. Biddy was her godmother,' Sarah said ruefully and set the picture to one side.

So that was her niece, proprietor of the box of tat. The svelte mannequin bowed out. Grace picked up the snapshop and examined it greedily.

'What age was she then?'

'Alice is just four. She was twenty-six, nearly twenty-seven when that was taken.'

She looked too old for her age. Frumpy. It was hard to make anything of her except that she was large and untidy and cheerful. Festive was probably too far-fetched. No discernible family resemblance. Grace felt slightly let down.

'And this?'

'Oh. That's odd. I've never seen this.' Sarah turned over the magazine page. 'We don't take the *Telegraph*,' she said dismissively. 'That's Van Rijn.' She dropped it back on the pile. 'She was going to marry him.'

'Van Rin?'

Sarah smiled fleetingly. 'That's how it's pronounced here. Rin. The Dutch say it a little differently, more like rein. It's spelt R-I-J-N.'

'Ah. Rembrandt's name? It's Dutch for Rhine, isn't it?'

'That's right. Cas Van Rijn. He was her . . . er, boyfriend.'

Boyfriend? He looked too old, in his forties. Good-looking if a little predatory.

'Boyfriend?' Grace felt unaccountable dislike, which was immediately and uncannily echoed by her companion.

'Fiancé.' Sarah sounded as if she resented him. 'Did you not know about the . . . ?' About the what? But Sarah didn't finish whatever it was she was going to say, nor add to it. Instead, she picked up the cutting again and sat dreamily fidgeting, turning it over and over. Whatever it was about it, or the man it portrayed, seemed to act as a catalyst because quite quietly, and without raising her head, Sarah Roberts began at last to talk about her dead friend.

**DU MAURIER, George:** *TRILBY, the tragic story of Trilby and Svengali. Limited edition, wood engraved illustrations and border, original holland backed boards, corners rubbed, unopened.*

# CHAPTER EIGHT

'It was all our fault in a way. That's what I keep coming back to. She'd never have met Cas Van Rijn if we hadn't introduced them. Here. In this room, on her twenty-ninth birthday. The end of June. Two years ago.' Sarah made a slight moue of either regret or displeasure before resuming in the same flat expressionless tone.

'The idea of a birthday party started because a friend of Tom's was home from the States and we wanted Bid to meet him. Tom's partner, Stephen Rawlings, and his wife, Prue, came. We hadn't intended inviting Van Rijn at all, but the partnership had signed a huge contract with his company that same day and somehow he just came along. Another couple of friends cried off at the last minute so at the time we were quite glad to have him, and fools enough to think it might be useful.' She snorted derisively.

'We were all a bit high, or at least Tom and I and the Rawlings were, because they'd been trying to get that contract tied up for months, but we were also a bit edgy in case anything went wrong. But everything seemed fine and Bid got on really well with Tom's friend, Richard, which was what I hoped would happen. I can't remember Van Rijn addressing a single word to her all evening.' Sarah looked at Grace thoughtfully.

'But that's when she fell in love with him?' Grace asked quietly.

'If she did, she didn't say a word to me about it. She can't have. She seemed terribly interested in Richard, and they started going out – next day in fact. I understood, she gave me to understand, that they were together for months and months but after she died Richard told me it had been very on and off and only lasted a matter of weeks. He said she chucked him that September. I couldn't believe it.' Sarah's voice rose querulously.

'So, when did she meet Van Rin again?' Grace persisted.

'Rijn,' Sarah corrected pedantically. 'I've no idea when or where,' she added through clenched teeth. 'She told me nothing.'

She drew her forefinger and thumb together and held them up. 'For years we were as close as that. We saw each other three or four times a week. She used to drop in all the time. We were like sisters.' She glared at Grace and added pointedly, 'Better than sisters! Then he took over and I was simply tossed aside. She didn't seem to care how I felt.'

'Had you been friends long?' Grace interrupted, smoothly guiding her companion towards less troubled times. Sarah brightened immediately.

'About eight years or so. We started at *Diva* on the same day, as a matter of fact. She'd just come over from Ireland. I was in the design department, she was a sort of secretary/assistant. When she found the flat in Everard Street we moved in together.'

'She found the flat?' Grace felt unaccountably pleased.

'Yes. Bit of a fluke really,' Sarah said carelessly, taking all virtue from the find. 'Some Irish friend of hers who was returning to Dublin put her on to it. It was in lousy condition but the rent was very low. On our sort of salary, mortgages were out of the question but when the estate was broken up and sold sitting tenants got a fantastic deal. We bought this at the same time.'

'Did you share for long?'

'About five years. We were very close. Both of us were only children, so that was a bond from the very beginning. Strange when you think about it, we were very different.' As Sarah's thoughts drifted backwards her voice lost some of its tension and lightened, though an underlying hostility surfaced now and then.

'We hit it off at once. She was a bit scatty but she was such fun; friendly and easygoing, you know? People thought she was very open but it was all on the surface; apart from me she had very few close friends. Never made much effort. Dead lazy.' As she said the word Sarah's head jerked back and her hand shot to her mouth, only half-stifling a high-pitched giggle. 'Poor old Biddy.'

'Is that what she was called, Biddy?' Grace asked. 'Did everyone call her that?'

'No, that was Alice's name for her. When I first met her she used her full name – Bridget – but Edy started calling her Bid and it stuck somehow. Actually it suited her and she liked it.

119

Her parents always called her Bridget. Or Bridget Kate.'

'ED? That's Miss Hampshire? Was she happy at *Diva*?'

'Who, Bid? Sort of. It hasn't a huge circulation, so it's a bit of a dead end. After she got the agony-aunting job she was happy for a while, but it didn't last. The job was more demanding than you'd think. I used to go in sometimes and help her when she got behind. The sad thing is that she was quite good at the letters – sympathetic – when she took the trouble. But she got very discontented, always trying to get into what she called proper journalism. It wouldn't have worked; she hadn't the talent.' Sarah's dismissive verdict was not made more attractive by its casual certainty. She picked up the christening photo and stared at it intently before passing it to Grace.

'That's how I want to remember her. Before he came on the scene and changed everything. Fun and comfortable and happy.'

'And fat?' Grace could not contain herself. Had her niece been no more than a foil for Sarah's slender beauty?

Sarah smiled ruefully. 'She wasn't that fat you know. Her weight fluctuated wildly and she had a bit of a thing about it, always covering up. The clothes she wore made her look bigger than she was, ghastly splashy prints which didn't suit her. But, of course, she'd never take advice. She hadn't a clue really. Lord, you should have seen the thing she turned up in that night for her birthday dinner. She got caught in a shower and arrived soaking wet. Too late to go and change of course, after she'd promised to come early and help with Alice. That was typical as well.' She shrugged.

'I lent her a dress that night. A silk caftan thing my mother brought back from India, it was the only thing I had that would fit her. It was a kind of terracotta colour and it looked amazing against her hair. I wonder what happened to it? I can't remember her giving it back.

'Her hair was red, that really bright colour the Irish have. She had a great mass of it, absolutely gorgeous. Tinker's hair she called it but you could see she was actually quite proud of it.'

She held out her hand for the photo and stared at it sadly. An odd little shudder ran through her body. She drew in a long deep breath and suddenly began to talk more openly, as if the reservations she had been wrestling with had been resolved. And because Grace sensed that she'd faded from Sarah's consciousness, she asked few further questions but listened intently, determined to hold every detail in her memory. The room became preternaturally still, the house no longer creaking and in the fading afternoon, time and space quite simply ceased to exist. Even the street sounds seemed hushed.

'She was quite tall. Did you know?' Sarah said softly. 'I remember how surprised I was at how tall she looked when she lost all that weight. So slim and pale with that shining cap of copper hair. He'd persuaded her to have it cut and hennaed. It was really clever actually because the darker hair made her very pale skin look rather beautiful. She began to dress better too, more upmarket.' Sarah's voice speeded up with remembrance.

'I hadn't realized how wonderful her eyes were either. They were a sort of light brown, almost orange. I don't suppose I ever really looked at them properly. I mean you don't, do you, with friends? I suppose they looked bigger somehow when her face thinned down. It was such a surprise, she was really striking. I was gob-smacked. Van Rijn transformed her. All those changes were down to him. She did everything he said.'

She lapsed briefly into silence before continuing. 'She always had that effect on men. All her boyfriends were exactly the same. For a while she lived with a real geek called Colin. He also tried smartening her up, though he never managed it. Honestly, she could be so naïve. She let him walk all over her. They met just after her father died, around the time I got married and moved out of the flat. I'd never have let him near the place. He was a complete pain. Bid was forever jollying him along. It was so humiliating.' The memory obviously still rankled. 'She was like that with her mother as well.'

At last the girl was edging in the direction Grace wanted her to take.

'Did you know them, Sarah? Her parents I mean?' she interjected quickly.

'Oh yes. Quite well. They came over a few times when we shared and once Bid brought me to stay with them in Dublin. I got on really well with her dad. Her mother was much more reserved, polite but rather remote. The sort of woman you could never quite manage to call by her first name, you know? Never completely relaxed. It rained the whole weekend,' she added inconsequentially.

'After Fergus died – that's Bid father – Mrs Lacey

went off the rails a bit, got religion. She was keen to have Bid back home and Bid's reaction was to run like hell. Her mother could be quite demanding and I expect she was afraid of being swamped, of losing her independence. They didn't really get on. They were so utterly different: Bid all over the place; Mrs Lacey so neat and self-contained and always immaculately turned out. You could see that Bid's clothes used to irritate the hell out of her but she'd never come out and say so, she kind of took side swipes at her.' Sarah's pretty nose wrinkled in distaste.

'The amazing thing was that she seemed to be able to do it almost without saying anything, you know, with a withering look. She wasn't easy to like. She rather dared you to like her. Very offputting. I wonder if she was as sure of herself as she pretended? When I first knew her, Bid made out she didn't notice; as if her mother's jibes didn't affect her. But they did. She just didn't allow herself to react. Fergus was the same. Sweet, absent-minded, amiable old pushover. Cigarette ash all over him. Gentle as could be. Bid adored him and he adored her right back. Anything she did was all right by him.' She stopped and pondered again.

'Come to think of it, I'm fairly certain the difficulties with her ma only really started after Fergus died. I expect she was lonely. She desperately wanted Bid to go back to live with her. Bid was surprisingly tough about it and Mrs Lacey couldn't quite come out and ask. Maybe if she had, Bid would have caved in? I don't know. But once Cas Van Rijn came on the scene there was no budging her.

'The trouble between them got going in earnest when Bid began to talk about getting married. It must have been about November or December, five or six months before she died. Funny that, because I don't believe Mrs Lacey had met him by then, so it wasn't a personal vendetta but I suppose she must have realized that Bid was serious about him. Apparently she kept banging on about seeing her "properly settled" – married. I suppose I think she meant in a church. Specifically an Irish Catholic one. I suppose all mothers worry about their daughters, don't they?' Sarah stopped short, grabbed Grace's arm and looked intently into her eyes.

'But you know, it was more peculiar than that. I mean, I might have been dreaming, but I had the impression that it was the *ceremony* Mrs Lacey was harping on about. She had a real thing about civil marriages. Of course, Catholics can't get married in register offices, can they? I expect that was it. Bid wasn't too fussy either way. Anyway it was all a bit premature. He wasn't in a hurry. He didn't even show much interest. It was all on Bid's side as far as I could see.' Sarah moved restlessly about the room, fluffing pillows and rearranging the objects strewn on tables and bookcases. Her face had become flushed and excited.

'I'm afraid it was me who let slip he was married. There was the most dreadful barney. I shall never forget it. Mrs Lacey blew up completely and after that she refused to stay with Bid. A fornicator's flat, she called it. If it wasn't so stupid, you'd laugh, I mean, give me a break. It wasn't as if he was the first man Bid slept with, was he? In any case they were never there, he had his own fornicating pad.' Sarah giggled, then abruptly her mood darkened. 'Oh Bid was nobody's fool, she kept them well apart while there was so much uncertainty about the divorce. Mrs Lacey would have rumbled him in a flash, unless of course he set out to charm her – which he was quite capable of . . .'

'He didn't charm you,' Grace interjected flatly. Sarah looked at her with dawning respect.

'No. But then my husband was dependent on him, we both were. He was the biggest client the partnership ever had, so Tom was practically an employee if you like. I was quite nervous of him and besides,' she added with the residual surprise of a pretty woman overlooked, 'I'm not sure that Cas Van Rijn even noticed I existed.' She sounded venomous.

They fell silent then, each lost in their own thoughts until Sarah burst out:

'I don't remember when I began to figure out what a dreadful liar Bid was. She strung us along for ages, leading us up the garden path for months and months. How could she do that? Why? It was so underhand. I was really, really upset. When I told Tom he was furious. I mean he worked for Van Rijn, who was a bit of a tricky customer anyway, and it didn't help to have my best friend messing around with him. We had such a row about it. Which, I thought, was a bit thick. After all, who brought that bloody man into our house in the first place? Not me.

'But when I look back, I can see that things were

125

never the same between Bid and me after that party, though I didn't really cop on for ages.' Sarah's shoulders sagged, she ran her hand over her tired eyes.

'Honestly, the man was a complete shit! All that delay about the divorce – if he ever got one! I suppose his wife dug her heels in, who knows? Maybe he didn't want one either? To be honest, I was certain he was having Bid on, but of course she never said a word either way. She was besotted by him. He just took her over. Completely. I never saw anyone so mesmerized.' Her voice quivered with venom.

'She was like a toy for him. He was very proprietorial. He made her over; she completely changed after she met him, became a different person. Would you believe they flew off to Paris to have her hair cut? Pretentious git. And the clothes! They must have cost a fortune, there was no way she could afford them. I hated the way she completely lost her independence and self-respect. I couldn't get used to all the changes. I hardly knew her any more. She sort of faded away from me. And Alice. Before she met him she was really good with Alice, then she just lost interest, couldn't be bothered.' Sarah jumped up, rummaged frantically at the chest of drawers and pulled out a bundle of photographs. She shuffled frenziedly to get at the one she sought and when she found it held it out in her shaking hand.

A slim elegant young woman smiled serenely at the camera.

'That's Bid?' Grace asked in astonishment. Sarah nodded and picked up the christening photo.

'Look,' she cried, thrusting it under Grace's nose. 'Look!'

It was uncanny. There seemed not to be the slightest resemblance between the images. They were like two different women. Grace began to understand Sarah's dismay, her mistrust of the Dutchman. He had taken her friend away. Erased her into a walking fashion-plate. Made her over. The old Svengali act. No matter that she looked more beautiful, there was something vaguely unpleasant about it. Sinister almost. And the girl at the office had transmitted that same unease. A thin line of sweat trickled down Grace's back.

'Where was his wife while all this was going on?' Grace asked curiously.

'I've no idea. I only met her once or twice. Livy, she's called, lived in Amsterdam. There were children, you know. Two boys. Grown-up, I think. Mrs Lacey really freaked when she found that out. A married man was bad enough, but a married man with children. That's what she called him. That married man! The way she said it was like a badge of identity. A married man. Or a big man. Or a bad man. Bid got really fed up with the way she kept banging on about it. And I suppose I was just as bad. I really wanted to be pleased for her, but I couldn't. Now, I hate myself for being so mean.' Sarah's voice fell away to a whisper. 'She never faltered about him, at least not to me. I wish I hadn't held back, been so judgemental. I should have been happy for her.' She looked at Grace piteously.

'I don't know if she meant to get pregnant. It's an awful thing to say, but now I wonder if she was just

127

trying to pin him down? I mean, if she'd been really sure of him she'd have given up the job, wouldn't she? She didn't like it and he had all kinds of money and he wanted her at his beck and call. Or so she claimed, but they never actually set up house together, did they?

'She had ghastly morning sickness, I really don't know how she managed to work, but she clung on in there, which surprised me. But now I feel she must have had doubts from the start. I can't think why she fell so hard for him. OK, he was rich and sophisticated and good-looking, in a way. Actually, they looked very good together, they had much the same colouring, which is probably why he knew exactly what would suit her. He was always very careful about how he looked; expensive clothes, Italian shoes, you know the type of thing? And after a while she began to dress like that too. Bit flash I thought. Always taking her to trendy restaurants and places like Covent Garden, never mind that she knew nothing about opera. Jazz or pop was much more her line. He knew a lot about paintings though. That was genuine. He was forever going to sales and I believe he had a marvellous collection.

'I was in the hospital having Laurence when she told me she was pregnant. She was ecstatic. She wanted that child so badly. She said they both wanted it. That was in early March. She said they were to be married by the end of the month and she wanted Tom and me to be witnesses. Somewhere quiet, she said, it was all arranged. It wasn't, of course, but at the time I almost believed her, she looked so happy. I thought it odd that she didn't say anything about the divorce but I didn't have the heart to ask. I had the most horrible feeling that she was trying to convince herself it would work out.

'Then everything fell to pieces. A month or so later, Mrs Lacey died and Bid flew over to Dublin. She rang me two or three times, I kept offering to go over to help her but she didn't seem to want me to. She rang several times, last time on Sunday. Tom took the call. I was out. Then she disappeared.' She bit her lip.

'She fetched up in Edinburgh. I've never understood why. It was so weird. I thought she was still in Ireland, we all did.' Sarah plucked nervously at the hem of her skirt and held her stricken face away from Grace.

'She killed her baby.' The horrified whisper was almost inaudible and, losing her balance, Sarah toppled forward, crying in great heaving gulps.

'The letter must have come in the second post, otherwise I would have noticed it when I took Alice to nursery school, wouldn't I? But I didn't, so it can't have been there. If only I hadn't gone shopping. I kicked it as I came into the hall at lunch-time. When I opened it, Biddy's gold cross and chain fell out. The minute I saw it, I knew something dreadful had happened. She always wore it, never took it off.

'She'd written on hotel paper. I tried to phone but my hands were shaking so much I kept getting the wrong number. It took ages to get through. The receptionist said Bid wasn't to be disturbed. "She specifically said," the woman on the phone kept saying it . . . "specifically" . . . stupid cow. I asked until when? "When what?" she said. Time? What time? What time could I wake her? She must have thought I was barking. She had a really strong Scottish accent. I began to cry. She kept talking but I couldn't understand . . .

'I rang Tom. I must have read the letter, mustn't I? He kept asking questions very slowly. Questions, questions as if I was an idiot. He didn't come home for ages. But what did it matter?' She spread out her arms despairingly. 'She'd been dead for hours.

'The police came. I suppose Tom must have sent for them. They read my letter. I shouted and shouted – "Biddy's in Dublin!" "Oh no," they said, we checked. Edinburgh. Edinburgh? They said the hotel manager had found her. She was dead.' Sarah clutched Grace's hand and whispered: 'They asked me to identify her. No! I kept crying, No, no! she wouldn't do that. Not Bid. Tom said I couldn't, it was too soon to leave Laurence. I began to shout at him. He had no right. He'd been so awful about her. He kept saying he would go. Bullying me. I hit him. I screamed and screamed. I didn't want him to come. He kept saying I wasn't strong enough. The policewoman made horrid sticky tea. She said she'd take me up there.

'I asked for the letter back . . . such a small bit of paper . . . the awful words just scribbled. Sal Sal Sal. Over and over. I began to laugh. Sal the Pal she called me. What sort of pal was I? It was like a nightmare, a mad joke! I just laughed and laughed. I couldn't stop. Someone hit me . . .

'I don't remember the journey. I just remember seeing Bid. She was so white and still and there was such a peculiar smell. She had a little smile on her face. I thought she was going to jump up and say she was only fooling. Her hair was all red and frizzy, I remember that specially. The henna was washed out, like she'd been caught in the rain. She was in her old nightie, one she had when we shared the flat. It didn't seem right, the frilly pink nightie; it was much too big. She looked like a little girl, so frail and sad. The room was so bare and cold; it smelt of sick. Someone took us out and gave us more tea. There were clergymen hovering about. Priests? Probably not, how would they know that she was Catholic? She had no-one to tell them, no relatives at all. There was only me.'

She had no relatives. The accusation pounded at Grace's head as she held the girl while her choking sobs died away.

'I wanted to help but she wouldn't let me go over there. We were getting on all right. We were. We were.' Sarah's voice had become a hoarse whisper. 'The last time I spoke to her was the night of her mother's funeral. After that, I never got through again. The phone was always busy, off the hook . . . or ringing, ringing . . . so loud. I wake up at night sometimes and hear that empty sound. Now they're all dead. I can't bear it. All of them. They're all dead.'

She started at the sound of a key turning in the front door, bent down distractedly, placed the teacups on the tray.

'Why didn't they ask her fiancé to identify her?' Grace touched her arm, but Sarah made no reply. She passed her hand over her tired red eyes, then she took a wrinkled envelope from her pocket and held it out. Grace's hand closed over it.

131

'Is this what you came for? I'm sorry. I've been talking too much. You've been very patient, listening to me.' She pushed her hair back nervously. 'I'm sorry, what did you say?' She sounded half dead.

'Why didn't the police call her fiancé?' Grace blurted as the door burst open and Alice rushed in to pick up her discarded toys. She was followed by her father who waited at the doorway, holding a sleeping baby in his arms. Sarah appeared not to notice him; she took the little girl by the hand and walked slowly out of the room. Ignoring her husband, she disappeared down the hall. Tom Roberts stood silently watching Grace from the doorway for a long moment before answering her question.

'They couldn't. How could they? He'd disappeared. Did you not know? They pulled him out of the canal, he wasn't identified until the day after she died,' he said gruffly.

*A seat by the water's edge, a dog sniffing a bunch of withered flowers.*

'Where?' she whispered, knowing.

'Near where she lived. Dublin.'

'Did he . . . did he?'

'The verdict was open. But it's hard to imagine he couldn't swim.' She couldn't tell if his dislike was directed at the dead man or at her. 'He was something of a perfectionist,' he added sourly. She stared at him blankly.

'Oh for heaven's sake,' he said impatiently, 'who else but a Dutchman would choose a canal?'

'Jesus.' She drew back as if he'd struck her.

He held her horrified gaze for a moment. 'Read the letter,' he instructed harshly. The infant stirred and whimpered as the father laid it down on the sofa, lit a cigarette and drew on it deeply.

Dropping her eyes she opened the envelope. A beautiful rose gold cross and chain slipped through her fingers and lay gleaming on the dark carpet. It looked old and valuable, the chain a complicated rope of three or four interlocking strands, the Celtic cross, an inch or so in length, was delicately engraved.

Under the stylishly printed hotel crest and address, the scribbled unpunctuated writing looked incongruous. The liberally sprinkled capital letters only served to underline the horror buried in the prosaic words.

*I don't know what else to do I found the pills by her bed Ironic really when I've had enough gin I'll swallow the lot and sleep and Sleep don't be upset I feel calm there is no other way Sal I want you to have the cross and chain it's the only thing that's really mine remember when we bought it in Camden Market and the bank nearly bounced the Cheque? Oh Sal I was so happy then everything went wrong I can't bear it for the Baby my poor little soft little Baby I don't know what else to do.*

*Oh Sal Sal Sal it was all lies everything I believed in was Lies.*

'What did she mean by that?' Grace whispered, half to herself. He advanced towards her and took the letter.

'How would I know? Something must have happened in Dublin,' he said impatiently as he stuffed it in his pocket.

133

'Besides her boyfriend's death?' she ventured timidly.

'Boyfriend? Is that what you'd call him?' he snorted. 'It's not clear if she knew anything about that. Perhaps,' he added pointedly, 'she was having family problems, but I expect you know something about those?' His hostility grew with every word and the infant, perhaps sensing it, began to howl. Suddenly the door burst open and Alice rushed back into the room and began fussing over him.

'Daddy, Daddy, Laurence is hungry!' She pounded her fists against his legs.

All Grace's pent-up emotion burst on her in a blinding flash of rage. She could barely restrain herself from grabbing and shaking the child senseless, her dislike so violent as to be barely controllable.

'I'm sorry. I should not have come.' She bent her head to hide her emotion. 'I'm so sorry for upsetting you both.' As she turned to go he stepped in front of her.

'Look. Bid was Sarah's closest friend, almost part of our family in a way. I've known, knew her, as long as I've known my wife. She was a silly cow and I didn't much like what she was up to but that doesn't matter now, the only thing I care about is Sarah. She is eaten up with remorse; our lives are being destroyed by it. Look at me for heaven's sake. My business is folding and I'm tied up at home baby-sitting.' He sighed deeply.

'When Van Rijn died his partner pulled out of all our contracts, leaving us high and dry. You see how things are. Sarah blames me for . . . I don't know . . . for not coping with her pal's death better, for throwing my weight about, perhaps, for calling in the police? I don't suppose I managed it very well and now she won't touch the baby. And she won't talk to me about it. About anything.'

'Listen,' his anger rose again as he ground the words out, 'Edy Hampshire told me who you are. Why the hell didn't *you* look after your niece? Don't you think you had some responsibility?' He jiggled the baby up and down to quieten him and looked at her angrily. 'I'm at my wit's end. You've no right to be here, dredging it all up again. I told that old trout it was a lousy idea. I don't believe in all this "talking it through" rubbish. We're not responsible. I just wish we'd never met any of you.'

The child's cries became a thin whimper as his voice quietened. The flash of anger passed, leaving him haggard and depressed.

'I am sorry. I should not have come,' Grace repeated, aghast at how she'd blundered into simplifying something as momentous as suicide, by thinking only of an ancient tragedy and how it threatened her own peace of mind.

As she stumbled down the steps Tom Roberts caught her arm.

'Look,' he sounded contrite, 'I shouldn't have attacked you. Perhaps talking has been a release, helped my wife?' he added plaintively. 'Who knows?'

'I hope so, Mr Roberts. I hope I haven't done more damage.'

Lies, the letter said. Lies. She knew about lies. Or was Bid only referring to the mysterious fiancé? Who or what had killed him? And where did she, Grace, come in? Because there was a connection, her stomach cramping with swallowed bile was witness to that. Sarah's words still echoed with all their conflicting images and hints of fear and something not quite right. The force which had engulfed the Roberts family threatened her own uneasy hold on reason. Lies. Lies. Lies. Suddenly the image of the dark clad priest flashed through her mind again.

It was well after seven when she got home. Murray Magraw, who had been hanging about waiting for her, had just given up and was leaving the house when she staggered up to the door and bashed straight into him. He put out a hand to help her up the steps as her legs buckled.

She looked completely drained, catatonic almost, and didn't reply when he spoke but allowed him to lead her upstairs. When she got to her bedroom, she pulled away silently and crawled like a child into the unmade bed.

He opened the window to air the musty room, then drew the curtains and tiptoed out pulling the door closed behind him. As he went downstairs he wondered if she'd been meeting the absent husband and if so what the hell had he done to her?

The fridge was empty. It contained two half-empty bottles of wine, something congealing on a plate and a stinking lump of mouldy cheese. No wonder she looked half-starved. Murray walked briskly to the local supermarket to restock supplies. Grace was still sleeping when he got back.

He poured himself a dry martini, switched on the concert on Radio 3, and began to prepare supper. He heard the first scream while he was dropping the pasta into boiling water. He was already on the stairs when the second bloodcurdling cry rang out.

*The window creaked in the wind . . . burst open. The pale curtain flew into the room . . . something beating in the darkness. Whispers. A face. Someone at the window. Then the scream. Who screamed? Who screamed? Someone coming. Someone coming in the darkness.*

Murray pushed open the bedroom door cautiously. Grace was huddled on the bed, facing him. Though her eyes were open and bloodshot, he realized she was still asleep. She held the cover stuffed against her mouth, muffling the low whimper.

'Grace?' he spoke softly, afraid of waking her too suddenly.

The curtain flapped against the open window. She half screamed then burrowed down into the bed. Murray tiptoed across the room to close the window, then, turning the shade away from the bed, switched on the bedside light.

'Grace, wake up. Grace?' he whispered softly. She lay still. He went to the bathroom and ran warm water over the corner of a towel. She struggled up as he approached the bed, still half asleep. She was shaking. He gently wiped her face with the towel, then rubbed each clammy hand, talking her awake.

# Bid

*27 June 1988 – July 1989*

*Dear Daisy:* Ever since my father died my mother has been interfering in my love-life. I know she wants me to be married, but she's always finding fault with my boyfriends and trying to put me off them. Even though I'm in my late twenties I find it hard to stand up to her...

*Dear Confused:* Late twenties-going-on-sixteen. Sounds to me like you need some assertiveness training...


# CHAPTER NINE


'One thing's certain, you won't get it if you don't try,' Mrs Lacey said. 'I can't believe you haven't applied yet!'

'The bag is really beautiful, Mam, must have cost a fortune, love the colour...' Bid wedged the receiver between shoulder and ear and began to swop the contents of her old bag into her mother's birthday gift.

'You're not listening to me, Bridget!'

'I'm delighted with it, it's just what I needed.'

Silence.

'Did you hear what I said?'

Bid steeled herself. She had determined, during her mother's latest, fortnight-old campaign, to tell her to back off but for a moment longer hesitated; dissembling came easier to her.

'I told you, Mam, I wouldn't get it. I haven't the right experience.'

'What are you talking about? Haven't you been

141

working on that magazine for seven years. What's that if it isn't the right experience? Sometimes, Bridget, you astonish me. Where's your ambition, girl?'

'Yes, but . . .'

'But what? It's a great job. It's what you want, isn't it? To come back to Dublin?'

*What you want*, Bid thought mutinously.

'Look, Mam, I can't break my contract.'

'Contract? That's new! You've never mentioned any contract!'

*Only because I never thought of it before!*

'There's a penalty clause.' Pleased with her invention, Bid elaborated gleefully.

'What sort of penalty? Is that usual?' Mrs Lacey sounded incredulous, as well she might be.

'ED's idea.' Bid was now in free flight. 'And you know what she's like – a law unto herself.'

'In that case, no need for you to pander to her,' Mrs Lacey said briskly. 'Is there? You can always plead family commitments, I doubt she could stop you.'

'I really don't feel up to any more changes just now.'

'You're twenty-nine. If you don't move soon you'll be stuck. You work in a young people's profession.'

'Yes, Mam, I'm aware of that.' Bid sighed resignedly. No use admitting that seven years with an obscure, small circulation monthly would fail to ignite any interest in Dublin's glossiest; specially when promotion had been strictly under the patronage of a highly partisan editor. Bid had an unnecessarily poor opinion both of her competence

142

and prospects and was certain that, if she applied for other jobs, she would be rumbled.

'Don't get uppity with me, Bridget Lacey. Isn't Dublin good enough for you?'

'Why do you say things like that?' Bid asked coldly.

'I'm only thinking of your own good.'

Bid counted silently and furiously to nineteen before caving in and coming clean.

'Look, Mam, I am not applying for the job. I don't think the time is right. One upheaval is enough. I don't want to move just now, not job, not flat. I just don't feel like making the effort.'

'Well you should make the effort. I'm very surprised at the way you're letting yourself go. You need to smarten yourself up, go on a diet or something.'

'Sorry, I have to go.' Bid was close to tears. 'I don't want to talk about it.'

'I'm only saying it for your own good. No man is worth it. You'd be better off over here, where you have friends.'

'What friends? Everyone I know seems to have emigrated. I know more people here than in Dublin.'

'What about your friend Mairead? She's got a lovely place on the coast. You could have your own flat in this house, God knows it's big enough. I'm rattling around like a pea in a tin can. What's to keep you in London now that fellow's pushed off?'

'My job keeps me here, my flat . . .' Bid interjected. *My life.*

'Not that he was ever thinking of settling down.' Mrs Lacey ignored the interruption.

'Well, as a matter of fact, he was.'

'What? You're not sitting there telling me that fellow was planning to marry you? I don't believe it!'

'Not me. *He* got married three months ago.' Bid felt a wild surge of pain in admitting her humiliation.

'But he's only gone what? Four, five months? He must have been two-timing you! He's like the rest of them over there!'

'Six. Six months. Almost. Do you mean the whole of the UK or just London?' Bid asked tersely.

'You're much too gullible, Bridget. Even your Dad, God rest him, had that Colin's number, the minute he set eyes on him.'

'My Dad?' Bid exploded. 'How could he, they hardly met! Anyway Dad wasn't like that!' – *rubbishing people.*

'I'm only telling you what he thought.' Mrs Lacey sniffed. 'Anyway, I never trusted that fellow an inch.'

So there we have it, Bid thought despairingly. Up to her usual, putting her prejudices across as Dad's. When did she ever notice what he said or thought? Or what either of us wanted? Dad would be on my side; comforting me, not heaving on the guilt.

'Yeah. I expect you're right.' *Aren't you always.* There seemed little point in battling on. Bid fell resignedly into placatory mode.

'Listen, Mam, I have to go. I'm going to be late. I want to get home and change for Sarah's party. Smarten myself up,' she said bitterly, then pulled back again. 'It's sweltering here, really humid, the office is like an oven.'

144

'Yes, it's been like that over here as well. There's an awful stink coming from that old canal . . .'

'I don't know how you can bear living next to it. Why not move to something more comfortable. Like my flat. You could easily get a job over here,' Bid answered insouciantly. Mrs Lacey had the grace to laugh.

'You mean stop trying to run your life?'

'Something like that.' This time, they both laughed. And then, as was normal with them, they spent a couple of minutes making the most conventionally affectionate goodbyes, as if the manipulation and resistance hadn't taken place. This had the curious effect, long practised, of hurt being meted out for precisely no result. After which a thoroughly dispirited Bid cradled the phone and, bracing herself for the horrors of the journey home, hurried out of the office.

It was indeed one of those steamy days that London produces, randomly, each summer when temperatures rise and the fury quotient in already hard-pressed commuters stops just short of outright madness. All along Oxford Street the traffic was bumper to bumper. Drivers honking and glaring their frustration while on either pavement a slowly moving conveyor belt of massed and sweating humanity pushed forward mindlessly but urgently. Rain threatened, the sky lowered and darkened, but the dull rumbling of thunder was drowned in the growling mêleé. Rounding the corner from Poland Street at a brisk lick, Bid pulled up short, glanced at her watch, then stood on tiptoes staring in moody consternation at the solid wall of humanity grumbling past. Her mother's untimely phone call had kept her even later than she'd realized. No hope now of getting home in time to change. She glanced down at her limp and sticky clothes and hunched her shoulders in acceptance of the inevitable.

There she remained, caught in the instant, poised indecisively as she searched for the best direction to take; left towards the tube at Oxford Circus, or straight ahead to the long line of immobile buses on the other side of the solidly packed street. Neither possibility attracted, nor did either hold any hope of getting her to Clerkenwell on time. She was tempted to return to her office to sit out the rush hour, or while it away more congenially in the pub where no doubt half the magazine staff would be still propping up the bar. She half turned, then chiding herself for faintheartedness, she braced herself and pushed forward.

Even in that hostile setting, heads turned at the sight of her splendid hair. It was the most striking thing about her; abundant, beautiful and the colour of autumnal beech. Pale and unfreckled skin. Nice light-brown eyes. After that it was more or less downhill, nature's bounty seemed more inhibition than incentive to improvement, or perhaps it was simply that she didn't try. The too-ample flesh made her look rather shorter than her medium height. Make-up sketchy, heavily patterned over-blouse straining around the wadge of material of the matching gathered skirt intended to obscure the excess weight on her hips. The pity was that, dressed more simply, she would have looked only slightly overweight and more subdued colours would have enhanced the vivacity of her colouring and the startling beauty of her hair.

146

By the time she crossed the road the number 63 bus had closed its doors and was inching its way eastward. Though she could see it was already full, she pounded on the door. The driver waved her aside, mouthing impatiently 'full' or something more explicit.

She pulled a face, stepped back and stood balanced precipitously on the edge of the pavement as if contemplating lying down in front of the next bus. The idea appealed, for the thought of the evening ahead appalled her; never had a birthday been so unwelcome. She had stupidly given into her friend Sarah, while churlishly and unfairly resenting the good-natured gesture. To make matters worse, she was pretty certain that some dreary candidate would be rolled out for her delectation over dinner; a well meant but pointless exercise; Bid was definitely off men. And while she despised herself for being weak-kneed and ungrateful, she wished she was strong enough or brutal enough to follow her own instinct of healing solitude. Yet she knew she would doggedly yank on the glad rags and end up smiling and nodding in some boozy attempt at sociability when she'd much rather stay quietly home nursing her misery in a cool scented bath with an endless icy, lemony, gin and tonic at her elbow. In solitude. She hated the thought of being star turn for the evening. Twinkling was definitely out.

Bridget Kate Lacey was unhappy; not just disgruntled because she was late. No. She was tired, cross and flustered and utterly fed up with the raw deal life had dealt her. Six months before, her boyfriend of two years' standing, whom she'd fully intended marrying had, without warning, walked out of her life and it seemed the only person who had neither expected it nor welcomed it was herself. Predictably, Sarah had been unrestrained with her 'I told you so's' and had thus robbed Bid of any incentive to confide the more unsavoury elements of the relationship. Instead, Bid had turned to her neighbour in the flat below who, perforce, having witnessed the ructions going on above, alone knew how definitely and brutally she'd been demolished.

Before, she had been open and easy-going and friendly. Now, a growing determination not to be made a fool of, to make somebody pay, hardened. Bid hid her anger well, she was much too well-mannered not to. To outward appearances she was much the same, uncharacteristically low-key perhaps, but inside vulnerability sneakily fermented into destructive resentment.

She turned and plodded wearily along the edge of the pavement until at last at Rathbone Street she spotted a cab dropping a fare. She charged towards it.

'Percy Square please. As quick as you can.'

The driver laughed. 'I'm not the bloomin' Concorde, Miss. It's going to take a bit, the traffic's brutal. Must be an accident somewhere.'

She climbed aboard, sank back, closed her eyes and tried to figure out what exactly her mother was going on about. The most recent battle was just one in a long line in, not so much a campaign, more a flurry of trial skirmishes which had started shortly after her father's death a couple of years before. It was all such a pain and so completely unexpected. Her mother was normally reserved, rather secretive

148

in fact and decidedly independent. If asked, Bid might have predicted that, after the initial grieving, she would have responded well to widowhood, but she had not. From the first she had been very anxious, cold and more silent than usual. Cold? No, confused, neither sharing her grief nor seeking to comfort her daughter. The remembered hurt was like a body blow and fuelled her resentment. Her mother's horrified reaction to Bid's casual (and as it turned out premature) mention that, if she and Colin married, it would be in a civil ceremony and in London, came as a complete shock.

'What? Not in a church?'

Up to then, she had thought of her mother as fairly relaxed about religion, yet the mention of a civil ceremony had her striking attitudes of a generation older and with all the passion of a religious bigot.

Agony-aunting had taught Bid that even the most modern mothers often harboured extraordinarily romantic hopes for tradition when it came to weddings, but she had not put her own mother into that category and was dismayed by the strength of her opposition to anything less than the full church do: nuptial mass, Mendelssohn, top hats, raw silk and, for all she knew, papal blessing as well. Her mother's attempts to get her to return to the old home front seemed to be linked in some mysterious way to her hopes for a traditional wedding and her fear of a solitary old age.

Perhaps up to then they had both assumed that, some time in the nebulous and far distant future, when her mother was older or in need of care, Bid would be on hand. But now the reality of that vague drift imposed itself; if Bid were to settle down – have a family in London or elsewhere, what then? But wasn't it all too melodramatic? After all, her mother was still relatively young, only fifty, fit and reasonably well-provided for. Besides she had a job and even if it was only part-time she always claimed to enjoy it. It didn't make sense. Was she just lonely? True, she had no family except her only daughter but she had her job, her friends. Not too many of those, came the disquieting thought, hasn't she always kept herself to herself? Neighbours? These too, alas, had been steadily dwindling as the area around their house was gradually re-zoned for business.

Thinking about it, Bid regretted her intransigence. Would she truly miss London? Her friends? What friends? Perhaps she should think about it again? She liked Dublin. Left to herself she would probably have leapt at the chance of returning but the plain fact was, she acknowledged with shame and some slight contrition, she simply did not want to fade back into her mother's control.

She sighed and drawing open her bag set about repairing her make-up. It was now almost half past seven. As she idly fingered the gold cross and chain at her neck, Bid eyed the meter warily. It was clocking up the pounds at an alarming rate of knots. With sinking heart she grabbed her bag and pulled out her wallet. Empty. Oh lord! she'd forgotten to go to the bank. She scrambled among the contents as the car turned into Great Ormond Street and found three pound coins. Her purse yielded a further two pounds and eighty-five pence.

At the corner of Gray's Inn Road the meter hit five pounds and forty pence and rising.

'Excuse me.' Bid banged on the glass panel. 'I forgot I had to drop something off at the . . . the . . .' She looked around frantically. 'Over there!' She pointed vaguely. The driver pulled over.

'Five sixty-five,' he said.

'Keep the change.' Bid smiled graciously. He glanced down.

'Keep it? I'll be able to retire on it!'

She picked up her carrier bag defiantly, swung her new leather satchel over her shoulder, and set off at a smart jog just as the first huge drops of rain hit the pavement. Head down, she charged on hoping it would pass. The sky darkened ominously. She made it to Wharton Street before the rain started in earnest. It beat onto the warm pavement in huge cups, swirling and dancing as the wind caught it. So near. Just up to the top of the hill and now she was going to get soaked. One hell of a way to start an evening. She bent down and took off the new red shoes she'd treated herself to at lunch-time and sprinted barefoot up into Percy Square.

*Dear Daisy:* I don't seem to have much luck with men but recently I met two blokes the same night and I felt attracted to both of them. One of them asked me out but I think I prefer the other one because I can't get him out of my mind . . .

*Dear Confused:* Ever hear the saying 'A bird in the hand . . . ?'


# CHAPTER TEN


Bid picked up her glass of wine and wandered over towards the window. After a quick shower and change of clothes, she felt and looked altogether transformed. At Sarah's insistence, her rain-soaked two-piece had been abandoned to drip its dye into the bath above. Instead she wore a rich terracotta Indian silk shift which, apart from a narrow black border at the neck and hem, was simply cut and unadorned. Her long, heavy (and still damp) hair was folded into a severe bunch on top of her head. She looked good, and, after a couple of glasses of wine and a short romp with her god-daughter, a deal more cheerful and lively than when she arrived.

She watched with interest as an old and beautiful dark green Daimler was skilfully manoeuvred into a very tight space a little way to her left. She could not see who was driving but her host, Tom Roberts, was standing in the middle of the road waving his arms about. She turned away, idly picked out a record and put it on the turntable. Franck's Sonata for Violin poured into the room as, at the sound of footsteps, she turned to face the door.

The man who came into the room was accompanied by Tom's senior partner and close friend, Stephen Rawlings and they were chatting amiably in what sounded like German. Or more likely Dutch, surmised Bid, at the familiar sound of Stephen showing off, going through his (extremely brief) war-time experiences on the run in Holland, a recital she could reel off (in English, of course) chapter and verse if asked. She particularly relished the marvellous exaggerated sounds he made at the back of his throat thereby drowning his unfortunate listener in a thin shower of spray.

They paused just inside the door, absorbed in their conversation. Bid moved shyly back where, screened by a huge pot of lilac, she could observe without being too obvious about it.

Although the Dutchman was both considerably younger and a couple of inches shorter than Stephen's six foot, he somehow managed to convey authority and presence as if he were used to being noticed. Early forties, perhaps, athletic, well-off, she summed up. He was beautifully dressed, his light grey suit hung flawlessly from his broad shoulders, the pale lemon shirt was of the finest cotton, perhaps even silk, the tie a discreet silvery blue. As he moved his left hand, a heavy gold Rolex showed briefly. To anyone more discerning than Bid this might have signalled excess but Bid was impressed. She thought he looked rather like the actor Charles Dance. His skin was lightly and evenly tanned. The hair was expensively cut and might once have been gold or light brown but was now tinged with grey, or perhaps – oh surely not? – had it been highlighted? In the fading light it was hard to be certain but however it was achieved she liked it. She leaned forward to check that the perfection lasted to his shoes and as she did so the movement caught Stephen's attention.

'My very dear Bid, I didn't see you hiding there! You look quite regal. Do come and meet our Dutch colleague, Cas Van Rijn.'

If this is a set-up, thought Bid cheerfully, I'm in favour.

Things were definitely looking up. But as she stepped forward to shake hands, Tom came through leading Stephen's wife, Prue, and a thickset man. Prue made a beeline for Bid and hugged her.

'Luvvy!' she said. 'We haven't seen you for ages. I don't need to ask if you're well!'

'Bid.' Smiling an apology at Prue, Tom pointedly drew Bid towards his companion. 'I'd like you to meet Richard Grey. We were at university together.'

Damn! thought Bid resignedly. His mission accomplished, Tom smiled expansively at the Dutchman then at Bid.

'Has anyone introduced you two? We're working with Cas on the new dockland project.'

'Isn't Livy with you?' Prue broke in. Van Rijn inclined his head and smiled icily at her. Oops, thought Bid, amused, there goes good old Prue putting her foot in it as usual. Whoever Livy is. Friend? Partner? Probably the wife. Weren't the best ones always married?

'I'm afraid not,' he replied curtly and, without offering any further explanation, turned to greet Sarah who had slipped in and was standing just inside the door, avidly watching for Bid's reaction to Richard Grey. Bid carefully avoided her eye but was distracted enough not to understand a word he was saying. Smiling vacantly, she now looked at him properly for the first time. If he'd been at university with Tom he must be around thirty-five but as he was stocky he seemed older, more settled. Fresh complexion and prematurely grey hair. Clothes more comfortable than stylish. Passable but not really her type. Whatever that was. From behind the tortoiseshell glasses a pair of sharp amused blue eyes returned her scrutiny. Then surprisingly, for she had summed him up as rather dull, he winked at her and laughed.

'OK?' His accent had a slight overlay of American.

Not bad she supposed, grinning back at him, not bad. But given the choice, she'd have gone for the Dutchman.

The dinner was excellent. Sarah had packaged small slices of turbot in thin envelopes of filo pastry and served it with a pale frothy sauce tasting delicately of fennel. While Tom was carving the saddle of lamb, Bid, mellowed by the perfection of the food and a steady flow of wine, was ashamed of her earlier churlishness. Turning her considerable charm on Richard Grey, she found to her surprise that she was soon enjoying herself. He was, he told her, newly returned to London after ten years working as a research chemist for Du Pont in Delaware and was trying to find somewhere decent to live. His adventures at the hands of whimsical estate agents kept them going for long enough to break the ice. He was also quite amusing about his efforts to re-establish some sort of social life. In spite of herself, for she was intrigued by the Dutchman, she found him excellent company and before long had been recruited to help flat-hunt. Halfway through the main course, they arranged to go to the cinema the following day.

As the evening went on, Bid relaxed. Moping and mourning the loss of a steady partner had left her feeling that she'd lost the knack of making new contacts. Six months' solitude had shaken her confidence. It was a relief to meet someone with such a nice line in deadpan humour, capable of reminding her of her previous more optimistic self.

Within a short time, as the wine began to have an effect, they were slyly egging each other on, mildly exhilarated at finding common ground as they recounted the demands of their widowed mothers. He had a fund of stories that he rolled out effortlessly, responding to her easy laughter but she was not too absorbed not to notice the Dutchman's bemused glances. He looked as if he were trying to place her.

Richard had brought a couple of bottles of Napa Valley Mumm. Tom popped the corks as Sarah served dessert. She'd upended the top of a shiny red apple in the centre of the flan to hold a birthday candle and a tiny sprig of blossom. She'd just struck a match when a loud and lengthy peal on the doorbell startled them to attention. Exchanging glances with Tom, Sarah signalled ignorance as, in the hiatus of silence, Tom went to answer it.

Murmured greetings were followed by loud guffaws of laughter from the hall. As the eyes of the diners turned curiously, two unlikely revellers entered, followed by an obviously disconcerted Tom. Sarah was on her feet to greet them but the elderly inebriates neatly side-stepped her and sailed blithely towards their quarry, waving two small packages and attempting a harmonized rendition of Happy Birthday.

Both were in evening dress but the results achieved were a tribute to their individuality: the elder and more grizzled of the two looked as if the suit, undoubtedly inherited from a long-dead and somewhat larger relative, had flung itself approximately at his shambling frame, whereas his companion was as neat and dapper as if he'd just that moment stepped out of Moss Bros. They were entirely and amiably drunk, beaming their delight unreservedly around the table and not the least put out by Tom's nonplussed reaction.

'Bradley, Roy! You said you couldn't come!' Sarah sounded a tiny bit miffed.

Bid jumped up, grinned an embarrassed apology at Sarah, put her arms protectively around her friends and hugged them. Ill-advisedly as it happened, because they at once swept her into a wild essay at the tango. She joined in for a moment or two before pushing them sternly away.

'Enough. I thought you two said you had to go to some college do?'

'It finished early.' Professor Bradley Moffat twinkled at her triumphantly. 'We just thought, we just thought . . . what did we just thought, Angel?'

'We just thought we'd like to greet you on the occasion of your birthday,' Roy Angel intoned with earnest dignity. 'But you didn't come home. We had a bottle of fizzie all ready. We got tired waiting.' He hiccupped. 'I'm rather afraid we had to drink it.' He gave the assembled company a satisfied grin.

'I also wanted to give you . . .' started Bradley, then eyeing Sarah, collected himself rapidly. 'My dear Sarah, I do most abjectly apologize for intruding on your party. We . . . em . . . we . . . For myself and my friend.' He waved his arm expansively around the table. 'Carry on, carry on, Roy! Homewards Angel.' He pointed dramatically at the door, then rather spoilt the effect by toppling sidewards. Roy caught him and together they backed out of the room. The dignity of their exit was only slightly marred by a shrill peal of giggles as they achieved their goal. Bid hurried out to see them safely down the front steps.

To her relief, when she got back she found the party greatly enlivened by her friends' antics. There was a good deal more laughter. The level of chat rose as the talk became more general. Stephen leaned down the table to tell an anecdote which spun off from one to another. Imperceptibly the individuals coalesced into a relaxed group.

The cheese board sat almost untouched. Richard turned to talk to Prue. Stephen sauntered over to the piano and began to play softly. Bid, momentarily left alone, cut a piece of Stilton then absent-mindedly reached out to pull a small bunch of grapes from a glass dish, upsetting her glass as she did so. A thin trickle of wine rolled across the table. Cas Van Rijn picked up the glass and stared straight across at her with an intensity which held her glance for a long moment as she took note, with mild surprise, that his eyes were very nearly the same light-brown as her own. Not bad, she thought, lowering her glance, not half bad. As she began to mumble her apologies he put his fingers to his lips and moved the cheese plate to cover the stain.

'I think you need topping up,' he murmured conspiratorially and picked up the wine bottle to refill her glass.

'Aren't you going to open your friends' presents?' he asked. 'They went to a great deal of trouble to give them to you.'

Bid giggled and tore open the smaller package. Inside, Roy had pinned a rather beautiful art nouveau silver brooch to a birthday card which simply said: *Darling Bid, a better year. All love, Roy.* The other was an envelope which contained a slim book, dedicated in careful pencil: *Bid – to fill a small gap in her collection – BM.* She held out the book, he glanced at the cover, then at her.

'You collect military history?' he asked in surprise.

'No.' She laughed again. 'It's the author I'm interested in – it's Sean O'Casey's first book. You've heard of him?'

'Of course.' He inclined his head mockingly. 'But I thought he wrote plays.'

'And other things.'

'You read about *Citizen's Armies*?' He read the title incredulously.

'Why not?' she asked, stung, then slipped with agility from her high horse and grinned. 'It's not exactly for reading, it's for collecting.'

'You are a collector of old books? How very surprising.'

'I don't see why!' she flared.

'The old professor, yes. You, no,' he said firmly.

'Not a woman's pursuit, huh?'

'Nothing to do with women.' His accent was undetectable except for a slight difficulty with his 'th' sound she noted distractedly.

'Then what?'

'To do with age, perhaps. Besides, you don't seem the type.' He was quite unapologetic and entirely sure of himself. Bid's irritation was not made the less by his perspicacity. She pursed her lips.

'I inherited a collection from my father, I just add to it when I can afford to. Professor Moffat is very knowledgeable, and kind, he searches out things for me. Perhaps you can tell me what "type" collects?' she finished acidly.

'My type, I suppose. You have to be both greedy and very determined. Not very attractive characteristics, I'm afraid.' He chuckled softly in self-mockery.

'Oh.' Bid turned away in embarrassment.

'No, you misunderstand me. You wouldn't do at all, as a collector, much too kind hearted. You are very protective of your friends, I notice.'

Oh did you now, she thought and stared at him in surprise. He held her gaze for a moment.

'I did not intend to insult you,' he said softly.

She blushed as he smiled across at her.

'You're from Ireland?'

'Is it that obvious?' she asked touchily.

'Obvious? No, Stephen told me. Are you also an architect?'

'No, I'm a sort of journalist.'

'Sort of?'

'Actually,' she replied defensively, 'I edit a letters page. I'm an agony aunt.'

'That is an unexpected profession for one so young.' For an instant he both looked and sounded rather Germanic. Bid almost expected him to click his heels, but instead he grinned like a schoolboy and she had the distinct feeling that he was pulling her leg. Her newly-fanned irritation cooled again.

Tom stood up. 'Coffee at the table or shall we move to the front?'

'Oh do let's stay, it's far too comfortable here . . .' started Sarah but the guests had already risen and were moving, glasses in hand, from the table. Bid held back to chat to Sarah.

'Outmanoeuvred,' moaned Sarah, getting to her feet. 'I feel really drunk. Like your pals. What the hell were they up to? Honestly they were pissed as newts. I did ask them you know! They always refuse,' she grumbled. Bid giggled and to avoid answering began to pile the dishes.

'Hey! stop that, we're doing them in the morning, remember?' Sarah said. 'Well? What do you think of him?' she added, thinking of Richard.

'Smashing,' said Bid absently, thinking of Van Rijn. They grinned conspiratorially.

'Good. I'm glad. You go and get some coffee, I'll put on the kettle again, be a few minutes.'

'Lovely party, Sal.' Bid smiled. 'Richard's OK,' she added over her shoulder as she went out.

She already said that, Sarah wagged her head as if she'd misheard. Perhaps if she had taken more notice, she might have been able to warn Bid off then. But feeling light-headed she slipped upstairs to freshen up and check her baby daughter.

The front room was at its best: the soft light disguised the faded furnishings, here and there catching the deep glow of old mahogany and oak. Coffee was being served from a beautiful Pembroke table Tom had inherited the previous year from his grandmother. The men formed a group and were talking about the proposed dock development. Prue rummaged through the record collection and kept up an incessant chatter to no-one in particular while at her side a bemused Richard was contemplating the brandy decanter with longing. Bid sauntered over to her favourite perch on an ancient wooden chest in the window which was made more comfortable with a tattered Turkish rug. Beside it stood an elaborate modern lamp which curved in an arc from its chunky marble base, giving off a subdued light which caught the glinting red of her hair as she sat down.

I've certainly had too much to drink, she thought contentedly. At that moment Prue found what she was looking for and Wynton Marsalis's trumpet sang softly through the room.

Bid closed her eyes and Cas Van Rijn, who was standing near the doorway, turned so that he had her comfortably in his line of vision. He gave Stephen not the slightest indication that he had not his full attention as he nodded seriously and agreeably to each point as it was made. In truth he was miles away. Something about the girl was vaguely and disturbingly familiar. He watched intrigued as she leaned lazily against the window-sill, her eyes closed. The oriental dress, and the hair, and the pose reminded him of someone or something half-buried. As she leaned further back, the light shone directly on her hair revealing its bright-ness, which was further enhanced by the earthy red of the dress. As she shifted position, he thought he recognized her familiarity. The colouring was wrong but every odalisque Matisse had ever painted lounged sensuously before him. Something else tickled at the back of his mind but for the life of him he could not make out what it was.

Bid had never looked better. The way she'd pulled her hair into that austere topknot suited her and the shadows cast by the light playing on her face created an illusion of perfection which in reality she did not have. Whatever misgivings Bid had about it, Sarah had made an inspired and generous choice in the dress. Its deep rich colour flattered the pale creamy skin. She looked strikingly sensual, even sexy, it was quite unmistakable. Richard had felt it at dinner and now, Van Rijn, a connoisseur of these things, was aware of it also. He crossed the room.

'You look comfortable.' Bid opened her eyes to find the Dutchman standing alongside her. She moved to make room for him and ran her hand over her hair. It was now almost dry and trying to escape.

'I'm afraid I'd almost dropped off,' she said ruefully.

'Bored?'

'Far from it. Too much good food and wine I expect.' She eyed him brazenly.

It was absurd but she could not deny, even to herself, that having made a date with the excellent Richard, she was now perilously close to lusting after this rather alarming man with her earlier conquest not six feet away. She blushed as she tried to hide her confusion. Her head was full of questions: Are you free? Who is – what did Prue call her? Have you a wife? she wanted to blurt. Instead, she asked prosaically:

'Have you lived in London long, Mr Van . . . er?'

'*Mister?* Oh, please.' He laughed. 'Call me Cas.' His eyes mocked her. 'Cas Van Rijn.'

'Van Rin? Difficult. You'll have to spell it.'

'Rin is fine. Some people say Rhine. That's what it means – R-I-J-N Dutch for Rhine. Rijn.'

'Rhein,' she mimicked and laughed. 'As in Rembrandt?'

'Yes, exactly. You like his pictures?'

'Oh yes indeed – the few I've seen.'

'Good. I have some nice watercolours you might like to see some time. And one tiny etching from Rembrandt.' He laughed his easy slightly mocking laugh. 'It is about the size of my thumb! Your name is Bid?'

'No. It's really Bridget. Bridget Kate Lacey.'

'I like it. Bridget Kate. Not Katherine?'

'Try Bid. That's what my friends call me.' She blushed as he leaned over her.

'I would be honoured.' He inclined his head. She pulled nervously at a lock of her hair which had worked loose from the collapsing topknot. The lamp beside them caught the burnished glints, if anything the disarray was even more attractive than the severity of the damp arrangement. He smiled. For a moment she thought he was going to put out his hand and touch it. She badly wanted him to, but he didn't move. She sat barely breathing.

'I'll fetch you another coffee,' he said abruptly. She looked up to see Richard Grey watching them with interest.

By the time he returned, Sarah had rejoined the party and nabbed Richard. Stephen was holding forth to Tom and now Prue was sensibly engrossed with the brandy bottle.

'Are you also an architect?'

'No. I'm a builder.'

'Oh really? You don't look like a builder!'

'No? And what does a builder look like?'

'Well, for one thing, he'd look er . . .'

'Rougher? Stronger?'

'Perhaps. Poorer maybe.'

He pulled out his wallet and handed her his card. *Cas Van Rijn, Director*, she read, *Hanning-Van Rijn b.v. Amsterdam – London – Boston*.

'Cas? Is that short for something?' she asked to hide her confusion.

'It's more a nickname. I don't use my full name.' He looked faintly amused but made no attempt to explain further. Bid eyed him uncertainly, not sure whether she liked the continual challenge her every remark seemed to provoke.

'If I tell you,' he relented, 'you must promise to keep it to yourself. I really hate it.' He leaned over her again and whispered: 'Cornelius.' He grimaced.

'Mmmm,' she said and grinned conspiratorially. 'Cas it is then. You're working for Tom and Stephen?'

He gave her a look of astonishment.

'No. Of course not. The Rawlings Partnership works for my company – we are international developers.' He spoke stiffly as if regretting the moment of intimacy. Bid coloured and neither spoke for a moment.

'We're doing something quite big in the dock-lands project, er, together,' he said, as if to make amends. 'It is quite interesting I think. Perhaps you'd like to see it some time?'

'That would be nice.' She was cool; he made her uneasy. She dropped her eyes to her empty cup and to her surprise he touched her gently on the arm. As she looked up, he held her glance.

'Tell me about your job, Bridget Kate. Do you like dealing with people's problems?'

Really, she thought, this man has a very uncomfortable way of looking at you.

'Well yes, I do quite like it, though perhaps it's time for a change. People think it's such an odd thing to do,' she said ruefully. 'They expect agony aunts to ... to be rather different, older,' she finished lamely, then looked at him sideways. He turned slightly and their eyes locked again. Bid's face flamed.

'Well, I'll tell you one thing,' he said after an uncomfortable pause. 'You're a hell of a lot better-looking than Claire Rayner.'

His English is very colloquial, she thought distractedly as Richard Grey walked across the room to join them.

*Dear Daisy: I have been going out with a man who is becoming very serious about me, but he doesn't turn me on and anyway, I prefer to keep things cool. I sometimes panic at the prospect of never getting married, but at the moment, I prefer to remain single ...*
*Dear Confused: Single, or available for somebody else?*


## CHAPTER ELEVEN


The day after the party Richard and Bid went to the cinema and for a short time fell into the habit of seeing each other two or three times a week. At first it looked as though their easy companionship might develop into love, but from the start there was an imbalance between them which gradually increased – as Richard became more involved, Bid became more elusive. Perhaps if he had pressed his claim at once things might have turned out differently but, assuring himself that given time she would come round, he held back. This was a pity because they got on well, shared interests and even discovered acquaintances in common. The age-gap of five or six years was more or less perfect and each was on the lookout for permanence. So why didn't it work?

Had it just been a matter of bad timing that birthday evening? A half an hour might have done it, even less: a miserable quarter-hour might have been enough. But the fates had conspired against

Richard Grey that night. If he had not been caught by a traffic accident at Holborn he might have turned up, as Sarah intended, early enough for him to join his friends in the kitchen to break the ice before the weightier members of the party arrived. Had he not delayed to buy the wine he would certainly have got there before the Rawlings and Van Rijn showed up. He was, in effect, hoist by his own generosity.

Even so, at some level they both wanted it to work. Or perhaps it would be fairer to say that he was the more whole-hearted about it. Things started well enough. As he got to know Bid, Richard realized how much he wanted her and how well they were suited. Everything about her delighted him; her warmth, her uncertainties, her ready laughter, good nature, even, so besotted was he becoming, her indolence.

Had he moved more quickly at the very beginning they might have had a chance, romance was in the early summer air and anything might have precipitated that first difficult move. Except that it didn't happen and Bid soon realized that, for her, it never would. He offered love, companionship and equality but alarmed by his seriousness of intent she shied away, unable to value what he offered so willingly. Had he been more grudging, he might have succeeded. He should have tantalized; made her supplicate. She was unused to a system of weights and balances being in her favour. She thought him dull because he provided no *frisson* of insecurity. It wasn't that Richard wasn't attractive, he just didn't attract her. He was good-looking, urbane, amusing but somehow it just wasn't enough. It was all too suitable; the spark was missing.

At times she tried to talk herself around, make herself interested. She knew quite well that she wanted to settle down, to have children, permanency, a home. Most of all, perhaps, she wanted some reassurance that she was capable of maintaining an adult relationship. Yet when it was offered she wilfully turned away, her thoughts and desires elsewhere.

Following Sarah's dinner party in June, and parallel with her growing friendship with Richard, Bid was speculating about Cas Van Rijn. Against all reason she felt drawn to him as metal to a magnet. His face swam into her consciousness increasingly and once or twice she'd found herself repeating his name like a mantra. His unavailability was a powerful draw. In idle moments she wondered what her feeling for Richard might have been if he'd been the first to walk into the Roberts's front room that night. Was it the unaccustomed champagne, or Sarah's vagueness, or simply her own desire to fall in love that contrived to make her susceptible to the person she had thought was the set-up?

Regretting what might have been, she drugged herself with fantasy in those first weeks, expecting him to get in touch. Hadn't he asked her to see the dock development? Not to mention that hoary old chestnut – the etching. When he didn't, she found herself looking out for mention of either his company or himself in the papers. When that failed, she asked sly questions of her jounalist contacts. From them she learned that Hanning-Van Rijn was

169

heavily involved in dockland projects all over the world. Then one day a friend sent her a copy of a survey, in a back copy of the *Telegraph* business section, of global dock development and this pinpointed their work in Boston, Baltimore and Rotterdam. But, apart from a blurred photograph, there was nothing on Cas Van Rijn. It didn't matter, she just kept searching; for despite her good intentions she kept him firmly in her sights.

She discovered his office was listed in Green Street, off Park Lane and an easy lunch-time stroll from her office. She took to sauntering non-chalantly past hoping to run into Cas – he had acquired a sort of intimacy in her imagination. In a regression to adolescence, the unavailability of the desired object strengthened the force of her attraction. But since she never once ran into him, she was forced to think about the absurdity of her daydreams and resolved to forget the Dutchman and concentrate on her available man.

The ensuing brief respite was the best time in their relationship. Richard was delighted – for about a fortnight – then without warning she backed off again. His reaction ranged from bewilderment to distress and finally annoyance but he found it hard to justify his expectations. It wasn't as if Bid had given him much cause to hope for permanence. Somehow they'd got stuck after the first glittering promise and he feared it wouldn't last.

Bid too was afraid. Selfishly, though she wouldn't admit it, she was fearful of being on her own again. She almost persuaded herself that she clung on because she enjoyed and respected Richard and didn't want to stop seeing him. But she didn't want it to go any further either. Each time Bid asked herself what held her back, she wondered at her folly in being intent on destroying what was so obviously suitable in favour of something which did not even exist. Life would have been so much easier had she fallen for Richard.

Meantime the dismal summer proceeded with no more sightings of the Dutchman. Bid longed to probe Sarah for information, and did not know whether to feel ashamed or proud that she never once mentioned his name to her friend. Was she merely protecting herself, she wondered, or deluding herself that some time, somehow, they would meet again and that Sarah and Tom might not like it? She, whose guilelessness had been her most endearing quality, inexorably added small deceits and their concomitant guilt to the uneasiness that began to grow in her dealings with her dearest friend. She was not happy but she didn't seem to be able to help herself.

In late August she took a promised holiday in the west of Ireland with her mother. She hadn't looked forward to it, only going out of a sense of duty; but it turned out well enough. They borrowed a friend's cottage beside the sea in Donegal which they'd been going to since Bid's childhood, and the combination of unexpectedly balmy weather and familiar sights and sounds almost managed to erase the Dutchman from her mind.

So she was more pleased than she expected to find Richard waiting for her at the airport. They greeted each other warmly, but, though neither was yet aware of it, they were entering the last stage of their relationship.

The flight was a few minutes late. Richard greeted her as she came through the customs hall.

'I've cooked us a meal, Bid, you won't recognize the flat – the painters have finished!' He put his arms around her. 'You look terrific, I've missed you.' She was surprised to find, as they walked arm in arm out of the terminal towards the carpark, how pleased she was to be with him.

The evening was warm, Bid tossed her jacket onto the back seat as Richard wound back the sun-roof. They chatted amiably during the drive to Richard's flat in Gloucester Terrace and were content and at ease, as if an unspoken pact had been made to start again from the beginning.

They'd parked the car and were rummaging around in the boot so did not notice the green Daimler when it purred to a halt at the traffic lights behind them. The driver, glancing idly through his side window, watched as Richard took Bid's arm, then as the lights changed, the car surged forward. Cas Van Rijn drove up the ramp to the M40, sped into the fast lane and, as the car shot away, he allowed his thoughts to dwell on the red-head. He was mildly disturbed that he found her attractive; she was not remotely his type. She was too heavy, too frumpily dressed, hair all over the place. Not for him, he thought. Nevertheless, he was surprisingly put out at the sight of her being touched in public by another man. It set his adrenaline pumping. He vividly recalled her charming smile, her uncertainty, the night they'd met. But what really intrigued him, he now realized, was that she had apparently not the slightest idea of how damn sexy she was. He felt a tinge of irritation that such an endowment could be so quixotically bestowed on someone so careless of its impact. He put his foot down on the accelerator impatiently.

The truth was that he had been wondering about her intermittently since their first meeting, though not with any great urgency. He'd vaguely intended to follow up that dinner party but had to go to the States first and then back and forth to Holland. As time passed without contacting her the edge went off his curiosity and he lost interest. Until he glimpsed her strolling along outside his office in early August, dressed as for a garden party. His immediate thought was that manufacturers of hectic prints would never go out of business while she had a say, but he had to admit she was hard to miss. He'd been standing at the window talking on the telephone as he watched her move out of sight. His eyes followed the shock of red hair as she strode away, fearlessly, with her back straight and her head thrown back, loose-limbed and very attractive. Now, seeing her again, the dying spark revived. Though, as it turned out, not quite enough for him to do anything about it.

In the end it was Bid's initiative which started the affair. Shortly after she returned from holiday, she took her courage in both hands and rang the Hanning-Van Rijn office. His secretary was not encouraging.

'Mr Van Rijn does not give interviews.'

'That's not true. I have one here from the *Telegraph*. With a photograph . . .'

'One, that was published several years ago. Two,

it is a general article about developers. It says nothing about the managing director of this company and three, that photograph was taken without permission. Mr Van Rijn was not pleased. Which magazine did you say you represent?'

'*Diva.*'

'*Diva?* You can't be serious! I don't imagine your readers would be interested in our work.' She sounded unmoveable.

'If you'd let me explain,' Bid was surprisingly persistent. 'I am interested in doing an article about Mr Van Rijn's picture collection. He invited me to see them,' she finished triumphantly.

'Oh. Really? Knowing you were a journalist?' The dragon voice had lost some of its certainty. 'You'd better leave your name and number. I'll pass it on to him but I doubt he'll oblige.'

Cas Van Rijn leaned across his secretary's desk and glanced at what she'd written.

'What's the magazine like?' he asked. In reply she magicked a recent copy from her bag and handed it to him.

'An unhappy cross between *The Lady* and *Bella*,' she answered uncomfortably. 'Middle-aged trendy. I cannot imagine why they'd want an interview with you.'

'Oh?' His eyebrows shot to his hairline. 'Then what?' he asked archly, 'is the redoubtable Mrs Petrie doing with a rag like that?'

'Weeell,' she dragged on the word. 'Would you believe because it has an interview with Kiri Te Kanawa? Quite good actually.' She sniffed.

'Tell me more.'

'I believe it started life as an opera magazine and

it still features interviews like this one, but over the years they've begun to beef it up. Trying to get a wider circulation I expect.' She shrugged and pushed it across her desk. Cas flicked through it, pausing on this page or that. He glanced over the Te Kanawa article. Something on the letters page made him laugh out loud. Before handing it back, he turned for some moments to the banner page.

'You're quite right, Mrs Petrie. Ring her back in a couple of days,' he instructed, 'and tell her there will be no interviews.' Then unaccountably he burst out laughing. Mrs Petrie looked up at him inquiringly but he just waved his hand and sauntered off. Whatever the joke was, he was keeping it to himself.

Cas Van Rijn tracked Bid Lacey down a couple of weeks later, on the last Thursday of September. He chose his time and venue with care; early evening and a public place. A public house in fact. The Immortal Fox was across the street from the *Diva* building where the staff, or a representative number of them, gathered after filing their monthly copy. Bid turned up as usual at about seven with her boss. Over the years it had become habitual for them to go out together for a meal afterwards or to the cinema. They weren't exactly close friends, there was too much disparity in age for that, and Edy had never been quite able to bridge the boss/employee gap. But she was pleased to keep an interested but vaguely superior eye on her protégée and Bid was good-natured enough not to resent it too much.

As usual, the pub was packed to the gunnels, with the overflow spilling on to the pavement. The editor stopped to chat to a group of the magazine staff while Bid pushed her way inside to order drinks. The crush at the bar had reached danger point, everyone was shouting at once, arms waving frantically. The barman caught her signal and with an imperceptible nod poured a couple of gin and tonics. A sea of hands reached but he delivered the brimming glasses with a flourish and took the proffered coins in one skilful motion. As she drew away from the bar a hand touched her shoulder and she turned to find herself eyeball to eyeball with Cas Van Rijn. He was the last person on earth she expected to see and, having almost succeeded in putting him out of her mind, he was not welcome. Specially after his refusal to respond to her initiative. She jerked backwards in surprise, sloshing half the drinks on the floor. She glared at him irritably, he smiled blandly.

'I'm just over here.' He pointed and she allowed herself to be edged towards a table, protected from the worst of the crush by a heavy pillar. She looked down at the bottle of Moët and two glasses and raised her eyebrows at him. Who did the bloody man think he was? Sauntering into her life after three long months? Or rather, three months of longing. Cheek. She was determined to keep her cool.

'Bit flash, isn't it?' she said rudely and nodded towards the extra glass. 'I see you're expecting someone.'

'I thought I might run into you.' He stared straight at her but made no apology. The memory of him ticking her off at the party popped into her mind. The curtness of his rather superior secretary still rankled. Two could play that game.

'Won't you join me?' again the conciliatory smile, but she was enough in command of herself to reply shortly:

'I'm sorry but I'm already with someone. I have to go.' She smiled coldly and was just turning away when Edy came towards her.

'Oh Bid, there you are. I must get back, that call has come in from Japan at last. Forgive me? I'll be back if I can.' She hurried away, then almost immediately paused and called over her shoulder:

'On second thoughts, dearie, probably best not to wait. See you tomorrow.'

Bid's face was a picture of indecision as she stood helplessly looking at the two gins, now half empty from continuous jostling.

'You're free now,' he said softly. She didn't reply but remained rooted in front of him. Their eyes locked. He would come and go as he pleased, she could feel it in her bones. She strove to control her pumping heart as the old familiar excitement rose in her. Poor Richard. For almost the first time in her life she had a man who treated her like an intelligent woman and not a scatty schoolgirl and here she was, standing like a lemon, waiting for this sod to crook his little finger. He would not mistake the signal she'd sent. She'd made a huge gaff in ringing him. Asking for trouble. She clamped her teeth shut and raised her head to dismiss him.

He looked the picture of confidence, a half smile playing around his lips and made no move to persuade her to stay. She found her gaze held while he challenged her to speak and she was uncomfortably aware that whatever she was thinking was probably written all over her face though, for the life of her, she couldn't determine exactly what she *was* feeling.

Fury at being taken for granted? Certainly. For he was taking her for granted, she was sure of that. Elation at the memory of the *frisson* which had passed between them on her birthday? It was in the air again. Distress that he was in danger of ruining her relationship with Richard? She instinctively knew that he wouldn't bother himself with the likes of Richard Grey. Save me from being used, she prayed silently. Oh Lord, I'm so stupid. Save me from being swept away.

Consternation was what she conveyed to him. His taunting look subtly changed as he slowly put out his hand towards the two tumblers she was holding and set them on the table. Her hands were shaking as he took them in his.

'Please sit down,' he said softly. 'It's taken me a long time to find you.' He made it sound as if he'd been hunting non-stop for the two months and twenty-three days since their first meeting. If asked, she could probably have specified the number of hours as well. His eyes didn't move from hers, it was as if they were alone in that crowded place for all the notice either of them took of the bustle and noise around them. Her heart began to race but for a moment longer she held to her resolve to go, to escape while she could, then he smiled directly at her for the first time. A slow sweet smile which, for an instant, made him look strong, sincere, straight. Her anger evaporated, she sat down abruptly. He said nothing until he'd filled her glass.

'Miss Lacey?' he asked formally, 'would you care to be my guest for dinner?'

She inclined her head and knew in that fearful moment that she'd surrendered herself.

179

## CHAPTER TWELVE

Her confidence seeped away with every step from the familiarity of the pub. As she walked beside him she became uncomfortably aware of her end-of-day appearance and its contrast to his more careful turn-out, and in the resultant silence, felt or imagined she felt that he already regretted his impulse.

They ate at a modest Italian place in a little alley off Poland Street. Bid had eaten there several times with Edy and as they passed she startled herself and him by suggesting it, then almost bit her tongue off with the realization that it was certainly more to her taste than his: candles stuck in Chianti bottles, red and white checked tablecloths and soft syrupy music. But he chatted affably enough while they chose a table and she'd almost relaxed when, with a passing glance at the menu, he waved it away and engaged a gradually more interested waiter in apparently flawless Italian. Whatever he said coaxed an unusually good meal out of a passable kitchen and his choice of wine earned the beaming approval of the now effusive waiter. Her embarrassment was mixed with grudging admiration, for he managed it all with considerable charm and she was definitely impressed.

'How many languages do you speak?'

'Some Italian, a little German, less French. You?' Bid had to admit that wherever else her talents lay, they did not rise to languages. He laughed at that.

'You don't need to, with your beautiful voice.' He raised his glass in tribute as the waiter appeared with their main course.

Their talk was desultory while they were served, after which he set out to charm her. They went through the usual preliminaries: work, origins and how long they'd been in London. When she told him she'd lived in London for almost eight years, he indicated that he'd been there longer. How much longer she asked?

'Oh practically all my life off and on. But of course I spend a good deal of time in Holland.'

'Oh. You mean you came here as a child? So that's why your English is so good.' She could just see him, golden-haired, wide-eyed, laughing mouth.

He smiled. 'Why did you come here?'

'Oh. Job. I applied to *Diva* from Dublin. I didn't want to finish the course I was doing. Stupid really, it makes it difficult to move on.'

'You wanted to interview me I believe?' He laughed at her confusion, but not unkindly.

'I really don't give interviews,' he said. 'That was not a brush-off. As you can see.' He looked at her levelly. *We understand each other.* She met and held his gaze.

'Tell me about your job. Bid. I can call you Bid?' He settled comfortably back in his chair. As she got to know him better, the phrase became habitual but this was the first time he used it and it became interlocked with her feelings for him. Cas. Tell me a story. Tell me about it, Bid. The way he said her name. She began to fall in love.

She told him everything, or almost everything: holidays, life as a child, leaving home, the death of her father. She hardly noticed how long she talked or how few his interruptions. He was a good listener and with such encouragement she was a natural raconteuse. It made for an easy and curiously intimate evening. Yet intimacy of an unexpected kind, for she knew as little about him at the end as at the beginning. She only half noticed how seldom he answered a direct question. More oddly, she did not consider it of any great significance. Instead she was struck by their mutual ease.

I've misjudged this man. The wine mellowed Bid's thoughts. I was sure he'd make a pass before the first course was finished, then what would I have done?

He didn't make a pass all evening or anything remotely like one. Even as she talked, her thoughts rampaged wildly. And why the hell hadn't he made a pass? He wanted to, didn't he? Surely she couldn't be mistaken about that? Could she? Not the way their eyes kept meeting. Wasn't he a bit old for her? While his apparent absorption in what she said was flattering and unexpected, she was rather overwhelmed by his sophistication and elegance. She wished she was wearing something smarter, more flattering. Something black and dashing. A hat with a veil. And red, red lipstick. Tomorrow the diet. He smiled conspiratorially as if he'd read her thoughts.

'You're very elusive you know, I had a hard time tracking you down.' He implied a long and frustrating hunt.

'You mean the meeting in the pub was intended?' she asked incredulously.

'Oh yes. I knew you'd be there.'

'You knew? How?'

He laughed and shook his head and touched the tips of her fingers with his.

'You seem surprised?'

She felt a great leap of excitement at the thought of his planning to meet her, seeking her out, then the question of whether he had a wife passed unkindly through her mind.

'Yes,' she said and blushed.

'You rang. I'm good at signals.' He grinned. 'And I wanted to see you again.' His fingers played on hers, tracing their length slowly, tantalizingly until he clasped both her hands between his own. She tried half-heartedly to pull away but soon gave up as his grip tightened.

'I see,' she said inanely.

'Are you upset?'

'Nooo,' she said slowly as she released his grasp.

Not upset. A bit apprehensive maybe, she thought to herself. *What am I doing?* She drained her wine, her eyes steady on his over the edge of the glass. He smiled and she was bowled over by a sudden surge of desire for him. It was not going the way she intended. She assumed he'd arrived at the pub intent on a mild flirtation. She was in control, she told herself, and was determined not to be taken in by him. But by the end of the meal he'd completely disarmed her. From the moment they sat down he seemed, well, he seemed genuinely interested in her. As if she'd done him a favour. How could he fake that?

He was so damn easy to talk to, to be with, she felt as if she'd known him for ever. An hour with him had shown her just how little she cared for Richard, yet she only felt mildly regretful. And very apprehensive. Also hot and bothered.

Cas Van Rijn. Even his name was exciting. What would someone so attractive want with her? Was he playing with her? Every time he looked at her he must see lust written all over her. She wanted him to make love to her, but he'd hardly touched her hand. As she looked up, he caught her gaze and held it.

He was attracted to her, she told herself breathlessly, his eyes betrayed him. She felt like throwing herself across the table to kiss his smiling mouth; to touch his eyelids with her lips. Lazily, he reached out his hand and wound her hair around it as if he were going to pull her towards him and kiss her, but he released her so quickly she wondered if she'd imagined it. Then he smiled again.

Oh, oh, oh. This must be what wooing means, thought Bid. Is he attracted to me? Oh, please let him be attracted. If I put out my little finger very casually, I could touch the golden hairs on the back of his hands. Would he notice? Such beautiful, capable hands. Nice the way the tips of his nails bend over like that. Stop staring. Will I see him again? If I'd said it, if I'd mentioned his wife he'd have thought ... What? What would he have thought? That I was ... that he was wanting to ...? He's probably separated. Must be. Ask him. No, no, for God's sake, don't. Is this just a fluke? How did he come to be in that pub? Not his style at all. Do I believe him when he says he wanted to see me? He waited three months. I had to push it. He's having me on. Must be.

She thought then, for almost the last time, about Richard, whose intentions were only too obvious. The pressure here was of a different, more intriguing, more dangerous kind. What did he want of her? A quick lay? A bit on the side? Then why on earth was he taking so much care? He didn't have to, surely he could see she was his for the asking.

The evening passed too quickly and, almost as if she'd spoken aloud, Van Rijn spent the rest of it allaying Bid's fears, making her feel comfortable. If he did not talk about himself, he talked about his interests, as if offering her the future to share them. He made it easy to push uncomfortable thoughts away. He spoke about his passion for watercolours, for opera. His addiction to his work, the excitement of big cities, art, life and an occasional flutter. She had a sudden hilarious vision of horses zipping through canals on water skis.

'You like racing? Is that a Dutch ... treat?' She grinned.

'Not especially. England is the place for racing. My father was very keen. We trailed around after him, here, there and everywhere.' That odd attractive secret smile again. Oh, let him love me.

'You still go with him?'

'No. My people are dead.' He was already signalling the waiter, he ordered more wine and for

185

an hour or so skilfully teased her interests from her and probed her background, her family. But in truth what they were saying was not really the point. The words were their music, any random set would do, as he circled around her like a dancer until her desire was at fever pitch.

When they left the restaurant at midnight she was already head over heels with love and wine. He hailed a passing cab and, as he handed her into it, kissed her lightly on the forehead.

'Soon, my dear.' He raised his hand in greeting as it pulled away. What did he mean by soon she wondered? How could he get in touch with her when he hadn't even asked for her phone number?

'Nor my address,' she muttered as she called it out to the driver. It didn't, in her woozled state, seem to matter very much.

A few days later, as she sat in the launderette idly watching the dye of a black sock leech into her entire stock of underwear, Bid at last acknowledged that Richard's hopes and hers did not coincide. When she got home she wrote to him, sealing the letter before she could change her mind. She hesitated just once, as she slipped the envelope into the postbox, but only for an instant. So near and yet so hopeless. Her head insisted that she was throwing away something good and fine for uncertainty and excitement, that nothing but trouble would come of it, that she shouldn't chuck him yet. But no matter how sternly she argued, she didn't seem able to help herself. She sighed, remembering their last carefree evening when it had briefly seemed everything would work out and then, without warning, how it all slipped away again.

*Dear Daisy: I met a man at a party, and we've been out together a few times, and I like him a lot. The trouble is, I'm not sure whether he's married or not, and I haven't been able to pluck up the courage to ask him. What do you think I should do?*
*Dear Confused: I think you know what you should do – stop fooling yourself.*

## CHAPTER THIRTEEN

Friday passed with no contact, then Saturday, Sunday. He'll ring on Monday, she thought, if he knew about the pub, he knows where I work. But Monday too slipped by without so much as a word. To make matters worse, her post bag appeared to be entirely composed of the outpourings of discarded 'other women' all demanding more reasoned replies than she felt able to come up with. As Dear Daisy's usual good sense bowed out, Bid took refuge in barbed irony.

By Wednesday morning her confidence was fading and she was beginning to regret her precipitous chucking of Richard. She comforted herself that at least she hadn't rhapsodized about Van Rijn to the Roberts over the weekend. She'd been sorely tempted, he was all she could think of, but somehow she couldn't face their disapproval or reminders that he might have other commitments. Which left her relieved that she could wipe the egg off her face and nurse her disappointment in private.

But even as she sternly told herself that she was a

complete fool, she could not prevent her sneaky memory rehearsing their meeting in minute and ever-enhanced detail. With pathological optimism she grabbed the phone whenever it rang. Ingrid, her unwilling and recalcitrant assistant, assumed a knowing and superior look. Bid determinedly ignored her.

When Richard rang for the umpteenth time she bit his head off. Then immediately contrite, she claimed she was working late after which she spent ten irritating minutes wriggling out of his insistence that she explain herself. By the time she put down the phone, without agreeing to a definite meeting, she felt like a heel.

She was also alarmed at her folly at having burnt her boats on a vague, and growing ever vaguer, promise of 'Soon, my dear,' which was beginning to assume the same threat as *don't call me etc*. As the day dragged interminably on, her confidence drooped and more than once she stretched out her hand to call Sarah for a comforting chat, but some inner voice warned her off and thus insidiously her life of subterfuge began.

Then, just as she had resigned herself to nursing her humiliation in private, an enormous bunch of flowers was dumped on her desk. They looked a trifle wilted. The porter stood shamefaced before her.

'What's this, Arthur? They look like somebody sat on them.'

'Not my fault, label come off,' he muttered crossly. 'How was I to know who they was for?' He handed over a small grubby envelope. 'Must've come in late Monday, I left early to go round the hospital like. The wife took bad again,' he whined.

'What about yesterday?' she asked as she examined the envelope. Pencilled in a cramped hand across the top, and partially obscuring her misspelt name, was the instruction that flowers and note were to be handed to Ms Leesy. It was hard enough for her to decipher, let alone Arthur, who had difficulty at the best of times. He'd probably been hoping that someone would claim the bouquet before now and save him the bother. She eyed the dead flowers and remarked that he might have put them in water at least. She tore open the envelope and pulled out a small card with a theatre ticket pinned to it. She giggled nervously at the cost. Covent Garden. The accompanying card was printed: compliments of Cas Van Rijn and underneath a short line in barely legible script: *I hope you can use this. Wear your beautiful red dress.*

What red dress? Could he be thinking of someone else? It took a minute or two for her to remember the borrowed dress. Her heart began to pump. She checked the date and saw it was for that evening. The horrendous cost of the ticket left little option but to go. Would he be there? If so why send the ticket? She felt a familiar surge of insecurity. Why didn't he use the phone like everyone else and ask her properly, instead of flinging it at her? Had he been called away and just sent on his own ticket – understandable considering the king's ransom he'd paid? Probably thought it'd be a treat for poor little her. On her own? Some treat.

It was a mad dash from the moment she sneaked away from the office at five to collect the red dress from Sarah. Then a wild flurry of irons, hair-dryers and a futile wait for the bath water to heat. As she left the house she was uncomfortably aware that her check blazer did little for the dress and that her hair, screwed hurriedly into an excruciating knot, was probably going to flop at the first opportunity.

*Soignée* and sophisticated she was not, but what matter since he probably wouldn't even be there? For ten precious minutes she waited for a bus before grabbing a cab which dumped her at the deserted theatre entrance with exactly three minutes to curtain up. As she hurried through the foyer a rather superior young man thrust a programme at her and, without pausing to think, she handed him the remaining contents of her purse just as another usher strode purposefully towards her and, clucking that she was very nearly too late, led her smartly into the auditorium.

The curtain was already rising. A hot, bothered and breathless Bid followed the usher to the front of the stalls, nervously folding her jacket as she went. Too late for cloakrooms. She slid into her seat to clicking sounds of disapproval from the row behind. The house was packed, but the seat beside her was as empty as her purse. As she feared, she was on her own.

The first act was well advanced before she relaxed enough to either listen or hear but by the time the applause broke out and the curtain fell she was so enraptured she didn't move until the general surge towards the bar brought her out of her reverie. Joining it, she sauntered up the aisle and allowed herself to be swept towards the foyer, up the stairs to watch enviously as parties chatted and drank and hailed their friends. She jostled her way along the length of the huge bar, purposefully, as if looking for someone. She was standing at the top of the staircase, in apparent amused contemplation of the painted ceiling, but in reality longing desperately for even the smallest glass of wine, when a hand touched her shoulder.

'Cas.' She turned with a delighted start and took the chilled glass of wine he held out to her. She sipped it slowly, then smiled at him over the brim.

He'd snaffled a corner shelf for the wine and oh, heaven bless him, a heaped plate of tiny sandwiches.

'I don't suppose you'd time to eat before coming?' He watched with amusement while she ate. 'Sorry I'm late. My flight was delayed. You look lovely.'

'Is that why you keep picking me up in bars?' she asked coyly.

'Why, so I do.' He laughed. 'You don't mind, do you?' The three-minute bell sounded before she could reply.

As they left the theatre he took her arm.

'I hope you like Indonesian food.' It was more statement than question. He led her round the corner and into a small restaurant, all soft lights, starched pink linen and the low buzz of discreet chatter. It was full, but because the tables were widely spaced, did not appear so. One had been reserved for them in a small alcove lit only by flickering candles. She compared it ruefully with the Italian place while admiring the aplomb with which Cas engaged the waiter. They spoke Dutch.

'You won't mind if I order?' he asked and waved away the menus. She felt mildly irritated then, catching him grinning at her discomfort, she shrugged and settled back. When he smiled, he was gorgeous. She melted.

He knew what he was at – the food was delicious. They drank a bottle of crisp Chablis, he ordered another. She wondered when she'd wake up to cool reality. She had no cab fare home and if they finished that second bottle she'd be too legless to walk. Still, she was damned if she was going to mention anything so mundane.

'You seem to be well known here.' *Do you bring your wife?*

He shrugged and put out his hand and touched her brow.

'I like your hair like that.'

'Do you? It won't stay up properly.'

'You could cut it.' He laughed. 'I believe it would suit you short. But I like it tied up like that. Tell me about your family?'

'I haven't any. I don't even have any cousins. I'd have liked a brother or sister. What about you?'

'I think I prefer to be alone. Tell me, Bid, did you enjoy Rigoletto?'

*Tell me, Bid, tell me.* After a couple of hours or so the restaurant had emptied, the waiters were ostentatiously yawning but they chatted on, or at least Bid chatted while Cas primed her with questions. She noticed again – did he notice she noticed? – how skilfully he deflected attention from himself. Each time she skirted delicately towards the question of his marriage, he veered away into some anecdote until she felt afraid to ask, then

192

suddenly he seemed to change his mind and for the first time referred directly to his wife. She learned that there were two sons, both abroad. He didn't say where, nor did she ask. He told her his wife was a businesswoman who also bred Arab horses. He seemed to indicate that they lived fairly separate lives but when she tried in the following days to recall what exactly he'd said, she could not.

She was not particularly surprised. Her years of agony-aunting had taught her that the direct question yielded pretty limited information and was sure she would eventually learn what was important. She caught herself up on that. Eventually? The man was, as she now knew, married, out of bounds. Or should be, the still quiet voice in her head warned; but she stifled it and listened instead while he told her about his work.

About that he was quite forthcoming. He made it sound exciting and, perhaps more surprising, entertaining. He was a remarkable mimic, she hadn't quite reckoned on a Dutch sense of humour but he did a fearsomely accurate imitation of Stephen's far back normal voice then broke her up with an astonishing rendition of him speaking his excruciating Dutch, spits and all. After that he slyly began to tell stories of a group of marauding Irish builders and sub-contractors who had been trying to hold him to ransom since they'd started on the Isle of Dogs development.

'Perhaps I should employ you, Bid, to hold them in check,' he joked.

'You seem to be managing very well. Anyway they'd never take orders from a woman.' Nor, she thought suddenly, would you.

Eventually he got up and excused himself. She watched as he spoke briefly to the head waiter then bent over the desk. Paying the enormous bill no doubt. She was much too content to feel guilty. She admired his courtesy, the cool unfussy way he went about things, his attention to detail which added so much to her enjoyment. Wealth, she thought wryly, was very, very seductive and much too easy to get used to and she recognized that she'd have no difficulty being educated out of more simple enjoyments. Like worrying about taxi fares, for instance. Thinking about the walk home, she slipped back on the shoes she'd kicked off her swollen feet. Now the waiter was hurrying away and Cas disappeared towards the gents. Bid, glancing in her pocket mirror, noted her too-bright eyes and gormless grin. He was smiling as he returned to the table and stood beside her for a moment, resting his hand lightly on her head.

'You look happy,' he bent and spoke softly in her ear. She looked up at him and for a split second they both saluted their desire.

'I've arranged for a car to take you home, my dear. I have a flight in an hour. I'm afraid I must return to Amsterdam.'

'You mean you only flew in for the evening?'

'Yes. I must go back now for a couple more days.'

'Business or pleasure?' she asked flippantly as she got up from the table. The waiter was holding out her jacket so she didn't notice Cas start, then recover quickly.

'Oh business of course. Our head office is there. My partner runs it.'

The waiter signalled that the cars had arrived. She walked out of the restaurant into the cold evening still holding her jacket over her arm. Cas opened the door of the green Daimler. A cab waited behind it.

'Sam, take Miss Lacey to Everard Street.'

And how in hell did he know that? Bid wondered. She lay back and closed her eyes. She was feeling very, very smug that she'd managed not to make a show of herself jabbering on about having no taxi fare. Mmmm.

She sat bolt upright. He hadn't mentioned another meeting though, had he? He seemed to be making a habit of drifting in and out unannounced.

*Dear Daisy:* I *am very worried because my friend is having an affair with a married man, she says they are very happy together and what they do is their own business, that they aren't hurting anyone . . .*

## CHAPTER FOURTEEN

From that evening, Bid was utterly enthralled by Cas Van Rijn and her enchantment grew with each meeting. Everything about him intrigued, even, or perhaps most of all, his reserve. The more he remained disengaged, the more she wanted him. He always left her without arranging another date and so she was forever on the qui vive, awaiting his call, unsure enough not to make arrangements which might possibly conflict with some yet undisclosed plan. Niggling worries about his wife were kept firmly at the back of her mind and never allowed to surface. All her previous rigidly held views of marriage-wreckers bowed swiftly out. If Dear Daisy had been allowed a say, she might have advised caution, but she was not. Bid pretended deafness.

All through October and November, in those very first weeks of her infatuation, Bid insidiously became isolated in her no-man's land of seemingly unrequited passion while her other friendships were ruthlessly sacrificed so that she might remain available.

She stayed at home more and perforce reacquainted herself with the book collection she'd inherited from her father which had lain virtually unattended for over a year, but now became for her yet another bond with the beloved. Cas collected pictures; she collected books. Strangely perhaps, she did not resent this enforced seclusion for she'd been more disturbed than she let on about Colin's defection and in addition she was thoroughly ashamed of how badly she'd treated Richard. Now in the solitary weeks while Cas travelled, and when often their only contact was by phone, she had more time to spend on herself. She began to take more care of her health and looks and she seriously began to lose weight. She swam once or twice a week and uncharacteristically enrolled in aerobic classes. When Cas sent her a beautiful cashmere pullover just a shade too tight, she went on a crash diet and was delighted to find that she was beginning to look positively slim. She dismissed the fleeting anxiety that he'd intended she should, for she was already aware of his admiration of well-turned-out women. But she didn't resent this, how could she, when she had the same idea herself? She simply wanted to look good. No big deal.

When he was around they were always on the move. Even while she was losing her head over him, Bid realized guiltily that they were probably avoiding those places where he might be known. Though it's got to be said that when she thought about her at all, she lazily assumed his wife to be safely tucked away in some unknown part of Holland, tending her horses. The sons? – what age were they? – in some upbeat school or college? Abroad, he'd said and that was all. Cas was quite unforthcoming about his domestic life or The Netherlands, though he spent half his time there, coming and going in much the same way as she took the tube to and from work. She rather took it for granted that the bulk of his acquaintance would be over there, safely out of prying sight.

For whatever reason, during that first couple of months they met nobody either of them knew, and this good – or had she known it, ill fortune – set the tenor of their behaviour for the future and made it easy for her to slip into the comfortable fiction of being in a world apart.

Most tantalizing of all, their relationship remained completely chaste. She therefore assumed, with electrifying logic, that his interest was, for want of a better word, serious. In spite of her twenty-nine years, Bid was neither experienced nor blasé enough to know the rituals and detail of subterfuge so necessary in a relationship like theirs. Naïvely, she underestimated the care he took to protect them and so was lulled by the seeming respectability of it all. For if they were not sleeping together how could they attract opprobrium? Her simplistic reasoning was breathtaking: theirs was no sleazy affair, she told herself, as countless others had told themselves before. It was special, unique.

Had anyone been watching the couple closely, they might have noticed that even as he groomed her, he was being slowly sucked into her myth-making and was teetering on the edge of falling in love with his creation. As the weeks slipped by it slowly became apparent that they were both savouring the ritual of courtship and illusion, teasingly holding out for the perfect moment, giving themselves time to adjust to the situation they were inventing.

He had spoken just once about Livy, implying a mutual tolerance, skilfully stilling Bid's doubts. She was not breaking up a happy marriage, theirs was a more adult, more casual arrangement which had held for a good many years and would not be damaged, but rather enhanced, by his new happiness. He and Livy could come and go as they pleased, they were not interdependent. In other words, his wife understood him.

Bid quickly appreciated that he did not invite, nor would he engage in, any prolonged soul-searching. But at this stage she was already too much in love to go in for it herself, at least in relation to him. What he said made perfect sense, why should anyone get hurt? Weren't they, all three, adults? Sharing him, if that was what was on offer, was a small price to pay, for, from the very beginning she couldn't bear the thought of losing him.

By the time they got to the bedroom she was in a frenzy of desire. He rang just before lunch one Wednesday in late November, two months to the day since their meeting in the pub and almost six since her birthday. He'd been abroad for four or five days.

'I've got something fine for you. A surprise. Come and have lunch?'

'Where?' She quickly gathered her roughs for the weekly editorial meeting. Ingrid would have to do it. She scribbled a note.

'I'll pick you up in half an hour.'

The surprise turned out to be a new flat. She was overwhelmed and embarrassed. He watched for her reaction as he led her up the stairs of a newly renovated pretty stable-like building close to Portland Place. Tucked behind a high regency terrace, Weymouth Mews was in a secluded cobbled laneway and comprised two or three dwellings only one of which appeared to be completed. It was protected from the street and the sound of traffic by a huge gateway which opened automatically as the car approached. Building equipment was stacked in one corner of the courtyard beside a half-filled skip, but there was nobody about. When she asked, Cas said that he hadn't yet decided what to do with the rest of the small enclave, the builder had defaulted without finishing the job.

'There'll be no-one to disturb us.' He touched the back of her neck with his lips.

The preamble was over, Bid felt a tingle of fear at the thought that there was no going back and as she looked around she floundered between elation and doubt. The flat was expensively but sparsely furnished. Everything looked brand new: curtains, carpets and gleaming paintwork. Some pictures stood against a wall waiting to be hung. He'd set out lunch for two on a small circular table by a window which overlooked a tiny enclosed yard at the rear. They drank cold Pilsener beer and ate sour-sweet marinaded herrings which he'd brought from Scheveningen. She liked neither but said nothing. She wasn't sure whether it was the fish or apprehension which made her feel ill. She pushed her plate away after a couple of mouthfuls and he silently took it away. He came back with a pot of coffee and they drank it sitting on the huge pale sofa while Bid queasily fought her guilt at not returning to the office. He walked her around the flat and discussed how they might furnish it. She was mildly perturbed by the opulence of what he proposed yet she nodded acceptance, her mind racing ahead, delighted that he was including her in *this* future at least. The air was electric with expectation yet he teased her with more coffee and talked amusingly about his recent trip while watching her apprehension grow. Or anticipation, she was not quite sure which. At three o'clock she rang the office to fib her excuses.

When she came back from the phone he had already cleared the table and was opening a bottle of champagne. She felt a mild sensation of stepping into a thirties movie set when he nodded towards a froth of tissue paper which had appeared on the sofa. *Me Celia, you Leslie*. The light was already beginning to fade and while she opened the parcel he drew the curtains. A soft creamy silk kimono slithered through her fingers. Oh help. He's making me his mistress, she thought, and almost fled.

'It's beautiful, Cas,' she capitulated, holding the silk against her burning cheek. He came over and took it from her and laying it on the sofa, drew her towards him and kissed her tenderly. He undid her jacket, skirt, unbuttoned her blouse, touched her shoulders and, pushing her gently away from him, looked at her. Then he knelt to undo her shoes, slowly rolled down her tights, his fingers hardly touched her yet each slight contact filled her with a desire for him so impatient she felt dizzy. She was incapable of anything more than compliance and made no move to undress him for he had concentrated their desire in his slow disclosure of her body. He put his arms around her to unhook her bra and touched her breasts with his tongue so lightly that she strained towards him as he knelt back to admire her for a long silent moment, then very gently he wrapped the gown loosely around her shoulders and as she watched, he stood up and slowly began to undress for her.

The silk wrap fell open, revealing her naked body.

She could feel the creaminess of it flattering her and, luxuriating in it, she hugged herself with the pleasure of her own sensuousness.

'Watch me, Bid. Look at me.' For a moment he stood over her like a conqueror, triumphant, lean, erect. He smiled down, his eyes latched on to hers, then teasingly, but with infinite and deliberate care, stretched himself along her body; shoulder to shoulder, knee to knee, belly to belly, tongue to tongue. They lazily explored their nakedness before exploding into a frenzy of love-making.

She could not believe the pleasure of it, the sexiness, the mutuality. It was unlike any past experience; different, new. They slept, woke and moved in unison towards the bedroom to start over again: the same sinuous excitement, holding back until they could not contain themselves, then the riotous plunge towards ecstasy, perfectly matched.

'Oh love me, Cas, again, again.'

His tongue lapped her excitement, his fingers moved around her compliant body, gorged with pleasure. She was amazed by her own responses; his almost absent-minded explorations maddened her with longing; there seemed no bounds to her desire to please him, or his to excite her. Never before had love-making seemed so right, so joyous. He anticipated her avidity and played her with a touch so deft that it seemed they would never want anything else in the world save this. They were like two parts of a whole; entirely and enthusiastically natural.

They lay back and smiled delightedly at each other and did not need to ask how good it was, instead they drank a glass or two of wine, bathed and then impatiently went back to bed again.

During those first heady weeks as they gave themselves wholeheartedly to the affair, Bid fell tumultuously in love and there began to grow in him a possessiveness which thrilled her. It sometimes seemed to her that he wanted to mould and arrange every incident of her life for their mutual pleasure. He insisted on overhauling her wardrobe, make-up. His attention to detail staggered her. He forgot nothing, every whim was indulged, every irritation erased.

When he was in London she hardly went near her own flat. The huge downy bed in the mews became their world, they rarely went out. He'd show up with hampers of her favourite foods and, with an instinct for what she'd like best, kept the fridge topped up with champagne. How could she help being dazzled?

Bid looked wonderful, glowing, happy and hugely in love. Her appearance was changing; she looked trimmer, more kempt. He showered her with gifts, clothes mostly. She began to discard her scruffy wardrobe. She had time for her friends only when he was out of town. Sarah, assuming Richard to be the cause, started dropping hints about weddings and Bid did nothing to disabuse her. As long as her friends thought they knew who her partner was, they would not interfere. From the beginning of her relationship with Cas she had been less than honest with Sarah. Now she hugged her happiness to herself and set aside her disquiet, persuading herself that discretion was her motive. Her sporadic visits to the square got briefer and briefer. What was there to say to Sarah when she could say everything to Cas?

When they went out at all they rushed back at breakneck speed. Even his touch was enough to release that breathless desire that simply engulfed her.

He teased her affectionately, called her wanton, and shamelessly gloried in her lust for him. The mews became a shrine to their love-making, everything arranged to the luxury of it. He would come to her, touch her shoulder then, sliding his hand into hers, draw her to him. They could hardly distinguish their separate pleasure when he entered her, and she would strain towards him willing herself to be part of him:

'Cas, Cas.'

Each time they came together they made love, twice, three times.

'Luscious girl. Primavera.' His tongue explored her greedily, they could not get enough of each other; he was as vigorous as a young boy.

By using only the new flat for their dalliance, they managed to keep their affair secret. Bid used her lover's constant absences to have periodic blitzes at work and to keep up with Sarah, who continued to attribute her euphoria to her burgeoning relationship with Richard, though she was puzzled, not to say a little upset, that Bid having taken over their friend, he appeared to have dropped them. Once or twice Sarah suggested making up a foursome and Bid, dissembling, would nod and promise to arrange it, then make yet another and increasingly fanciful excuse. Hurt, Sarah stopped trying.

Thus it went on until one night the following March, when by chance Sarah spotted Bid with Van Rijn in a restaurant. Their table was some way away and Cas had his back to the Roberts' so that at first she didn't realize who it was. She was about to go over when they stood up to go. They walked out hand in hand, looking to neither right nor left. Tom kicked her gently.

'Darling, you're miles away. What are you staring at?'

'I've just seen Bid, she was . . .' Tom swivelled around.

'Where?'

'Tom. She was with your developer chap – whatsisname – the Dutchman.'

'You don't mean Cas Van Rijn?' he asked incredulously. 'Does she know him? How could she? You've made a mistake.'

'Of course she knows him. Don't you remember he came for dinner last summer. On her birthday. You know, when we introduced her to Richard.'

'Maybe she's doing an article or something – for the magazine?'

'You're joking. She was holding hands with him.'

'Don't be daft! You've made a mistake, must have.'

'I have not!' Sarah was getting het up. 'Why didn't she tell me?'

'Tell you what, for pity's sake?'

'That she's having it off . . .'

'Hey! Aren't you rather jumping to conclusions?'

'You didn't see them. If that pair aren't going to bed I'll eat my hat . . .'

'Oh my darling, why not just eat your very, very expensive dinner and sort it out with your chum tomorrow? If there's anything to sort out. Why would she be interested in him anyway? He's married for one thing and he's well over forty . . .'

'So what? You're thirty-six, and you're hardly past it, are you?'

'Oh for God's sake, he's easily ten years older than me.'

'Rubbish,' she protested hotly. 'He's never. He

doesn't look anything like that. Anyway I bet you . . .'

'I hope you're wrong, my love.' Tom was suddenly serious. 'It could be damned awkward. Prue and his wife are old friends, you know, that's how we made the contact.'

'I didn't know that. How come?'

'Oh, you know old Prue and her horses. Apparently Livy Van Rijn is also a breeder. Small world. Known each other for years. And of course, she's also a partner in the business.' He pursed his lips. 'Come on, you're having me on. It's preposterous. Isn't it?'

Suddenly Tom didn't look so sure. He remembered his secretary's first reaction to Cas. Hadn't she practically laid down on the floor for him? And that French designer he'd shown up with one day. Neither had questioned his availability, they'd been all over him. Tom's ill-defined but persistent reservations about Stephen's enthusiasm for Cas Van Rijn began to take shape and with them came a vague discomfort at the partnership's increasing dependence on the Hanning-Van Rijn project.

The Roberts were saved further speculation by the waiter's timely appearance with the dessert menu and so their talk drifted to Tom's departure for America next morning. So the problem of Bid and her possible involvement with Cas faded, for the moment at least, into the background.

While Tom was away, Sarah took Alice to stay with her parents in Norwich and by the time they returned to London Bid had gone to Dublin. While she was there she rang for a chat and mentioned that Eileen wasn't terribly well and added that she was taking an extra week's holiday; Sarah assumed she

206

was staying on in Ireland. But three or four days later a card arrived for Alice from Paris and another for Sarah and Tom reminding them to keep the twenty-fifth of April free, as usual.

'I hope she doesn't bring her pal to my birthday, that's all!' Sarah said *sotto voce*.

As it happened, Tom had to rush up to Liverpool that day, so the girls pushed out the boat by themselves. They went to an old Soho favourite – The Amalfi – an Italian restaurant around the corner from the French pub. They hadn't seen each other for about six weeks and Sarah was blown sideways by Bid's appearance. She'd already vaguely noted her friend had been losing weight but now the change was startling. Her hair was newly cut and hennaed and she was dressed in a simple banana-coloured dress with a neat black jacket. The darker hair suited her glowing skin and Sarah, who had easily been the prettier of the two, recognized that she was now outclassed and, to her chagrin, minded dreadfully. They were both slightly on edge as they ordered, but by dessert they'd recovered something of their old intimacy.

'It's like old times.' Bid raised her glass.

'Not quite like old times. Look at you, Bid Lacey. I hardly knew you, you look absolutely sensational. And you've been avoiding me. I want to know why? Come on Biddy, give.'

Bid sighed. 'Honestly I haven't been avoiding you. Really. It's just that . . . it's just that . . . Oh Lord. Look you're going to have to keep this to yourself, Sal. Not even Tom. Promise?'

And then the whole story poured out: her depression over how she'd allowed Colin to punish and humiliate her, fear that she was incapable of any sustained relationship, the loneliness. Then her troubles with Richard. Meeting Cas. Falling in love. Worrying what people might think . . .

'People? Us, you mean?'

'Well, my Ma and well yes, of course, you and Tom.'

After all they knew him first, he was their friend.

'Not really, Bid,' Sarah protested. 'We hardly know him, not as friends. Tom works with him, that's all.' Sarah twitched with discomfort knowing what Tom would say. 'What about his family, Bid?' she asked quietly.

What indeed? It quickly became apparent to Sarah that they had no reality for Bid, that, if she'd thought about his wife or family at all, it couldn't have been more than superficially. All she wanted was to talk, talk, talk about Cas. Wonderful, desirable, amazing Cas!

A walking bloody miracle, thought Sarah sourly.

He was so intuitive. He could almost read Bid's thoughts, anticipate her wishes. Dead sexy. Amazing in bed. Honestly. She smirked like the proverbial cat over a tub of cream.

In other words, a lush bit of trouser, thought Sarah crudely, she certainly looks well fucked. Her eyes glazed over as Bid burbled on.

They spent every moment they could together. Cas had this fabulous new flat, private, nothing to do with his family she added hastily, it was just for them.

Struth! thought Sarah, bring on the bloody violins.

Well no, they hadn't discussed divorce. That wasn't what they were into anyway, there wasn't any need; they'd practically moved in together. The flat was gorgeous.

She didn't offer a guided tour though, did she? Was this silly twit really Bid Lacey? Amiable, easy-going, obliging Bid?

'What about his wife? Does she know about this?' Sarah cruelly determined that one of them would keep her feet on the ground.

Bid waved her hands airily.

'No, I'm not sure. Look, stop worrying. The Van Rijns have this . . . this very understanding arrangement . . .'

Oh yeah? Any minute now she's going to say adult. If she does, I'll throw up. Sarah was amazed at the rot her friend was mouthing. And shocked. Some romance. What price women's rights? Bid sounded like something out of a nineteenth-century bodice-ripper. Sarah hardly knew what to think of it all, but Bid could be very persuasive and despite her misgivings, it seemed churlish to continue her resistance. Only when she got home did she realize that she'd voiced hardly any of her considerable anxiety. No, more than anxiety, the knot in her stomach signalled fear. She wondered if, after all, the world didn't fear, rather than love, lovers and wished with all her heart that Richard had been the hero of Bid's story.

Mindful of her promise, she kept Bid's confidence for a few weeks but then she spotted them together again and, unable to contain herself, she told Tom.

'You're not serious? Really, I hate this sort of mess. We should never have introduced them. I just hope Prue Rawlings doesn't get wind of it. There'll be ructions if she spills the beans. Oh, why the hell can't your chum steer clear of my working life?'

'And what makes you think I've any control over them? They're adults, for heaven's sake. Don't be so pompous . . . anyway what business is it of the Rawlings?'

'Friends, you know, friends. And Prue can't keep her mouth shut.'

'So?'

'Oh, I don't know, I just hate the gossip, the awkwardness . . . the effect on our business.'

'Maybe she knows already? Bid was wittering on about an open marriage.'

'Oh yeah? How many of those do you know?'

They tossed the problem to and fro. Sarah told herself she was only anxious that her friend might get hurt, but Tom was more upset about his contracts getting scuppered by a messy affair which he persisted in feeling they had instigated, however innocently, and somehow felt responsible for. They were united on one thing at least: the fear that it might go wrong.

As it would. Tom had been worried for some time that the partnership had become over-dependent on the developer, that they had drifted into a position where their carefully nurtured business could be ruined by the outsider. What if he pulled out of their extensive agreements? They would be left high and dry, that's what. He and Stephen had stupidly allowed most of their bread and butter work to slip away under Cas Van Rijn's mega-projects and Sarah's bombshell had introduced an element of risk he hadn't foreseen and didn't welcome. Still, no use meeting trouble halfway. He put his arm around his wife.

'Sorry. I didn't mean to shout at you, love. I was upset.'

'Me too. Maybe I'm mean-minded, but I've an awful feeling it's all going to end badly,' Sarah began regretfully, then her barely suppressed anger surfaced:

'I can't forgive her! She's been so devious, it's been going on for months. I couldn't believe it . . . sly bitch didn't say a word . . .'

'Why the hell should she?'

'I'm supposed to be her best friend, that's why!'

'Do stop fretting, Sarah. It's really none of our business.'

'It bloody well is my business when I see my best friend acting so . . . so . . . so compulsively,' she said huffily.

'That's an odd way to put it.'

'Mmmm. Well, there was something about them, standing in the middle of Piccadilly, looking so, looking as if they were part of each other . . .'

'But isn't that how people in love are supposed to look? What's odd about that?'

Sarah eyed him thoughtfully. 'I don't know,' she said slowly. 'I suppose it was my reaction that was peculiar. I don't think it was jealousy or anything. I mean I don't really like him somehow, don't trust him. I honestly wanted to be happy for Bid but my heart began pounding. I felt threatened in some way . . .' Her voice trailed off.

'Nothing strange in that,' said Tom briskly. 'They'll be well threatened if his wife finds out!'

'Do you know,' said Sarah slowly, 'the thought of her never entered my head.' What was even more peculiar, and what she didn't tell Tom, was that she turned, and without greeting them, had walked the other way.

*Dear Confused: It would be best if you discuss all the alternatives with your mother and encourage her to see that returning home is not what you want. Perhaps you might get on better if you were a bit more honest with her, about your boyfriend for instance?*

## CHAPTER FIFTEEN

As Spring turned to Summer the rapture continued undisturbed. Gradually Bid learned how easily she could meet other less agreeable commitments during her lover's frequent absences, leaving her available to give herself wholly to him when he was around. She saw no irony in calling it freedom.

If Sarah still had misgivings, she was more careful about voicing them. During the summer months they resumed a reasonable facsimile of intimacy, seeing each other whenever Bid was at home in Everard Street. From time to time Sarah and Alice dropped in to help out at *Diva* and in return Bid obliged with baby-sitting.

Bid's two or three annual visits to her mother were never interrupted and continued as usual, except that she felt strong enough to ignore whatever tensions flared between them. She was circumspect too about appearing in too many new outfits, but her mother had a keen eye and while Bid's newfound care over her appearance was noted, the new haircut was greeted with vigorous dismay. She fielded her mother's probing about her life with amused tolerance or, if it got too close to the bone, by simply walking away. But careful as she was to conceal how very different her life had become, she could not contain all reference to her lover. As time went by and the strength of her feeling for him increased, her impatience with even the briefest interruptions of their time together grew. Even so, she was remarkably careful about keeping her guard up and, if she mentioned outings or theatre visits or anything to do with her life in London, she was always careful to suppress all reference to Cas Van Rijn by name. To all intents and purposes, as far as her Irish existence was concerned, he did not exist. Even her mother's harping on getting her to return home permanently did not touch her; she had become too wrapped up in herself.

It was not until late the following September, when Mrs Lacey was on a rare visit to Everard Street that Bid fully noticed for the first time how unwell her mother had become. With it came the dawning realization that, over the preceding months, she had become pale and lethargic. In reply to probing her mother simply said that she was thinking of giving up her job in the shoe shop because she found it tiring to be on her feet all day. Bid, alert to threats to her own freedom, almost persuaded herself that her mother's talk of tiredness was just another ploy in the campaign to get her back to Dublin. But with her departure the anxieties returned and she became restless and fretful. Cas became impatient.

'What you need, Bidissima, is a little sunshine,' he said firmly.

'Oh. Do I? Where?'

'Florence.' He grinned. 'I want to show you some pictures.'

'That would be nice,' she replied half-heartedly.

'Fine. We shall go next week. The weather will be glorious.'

'I'll have to see if I can arrange leave.'

'See? What's there to see?' He raised his eyebrows. 'Just tell your friend Edy. If she doesn't like it, give her your notice. I'll arrange the rest.'

Ten days later found them driving up a mountain road from Pistoia. They'd hired a car at the airport and, to avoid the lunchtime traffic in Pisa, had bundled themselves into it and hurried away. Two or three miles down the road, Cas shifted uneasily in his seat, pulled the contents from his back pocket and threw them carelessly on the dashboard.

The car was very hot in the afternoon sun, Bid lay back in her seat and dozed. When she woke Cas was preoccupied in trying to overtake a series of cement trucks which were depositing a thin layer of opaque grey dust on the windscreen. Unthinkingly, Bid leaned forwards to wipe it away and as she did so her hand strayed over his slim leather passport holder. She picked it up absently, opened it. and stared doubtfully. She had just turned to say something to him when his hand snaked out casually and took it swiftly from her. He slipped it, without remark into his pocket. The incident was over in a second. She could almost persuade herself that she was seeing things but her face flamed. He stroked her cheek gently and pointed into the haze.

'If you look over that way, you'll just see

Florence,' he said smoothly. 'It's about fifteen miles away.' He turned his head to smile at her. 'We're almost there, my darling.'

Bid did not respond. She opened her bag and began to repair her make-up; she was puzzled and uncomfortable and wouldn't look at him.

'There's the house,' he cajoled. 'You can see it through the trees.'

They turned another hairpin bend and just as the road became a dusty track he pulled into a gateway which led off into an olive grove. Through the trees she saw that an old farmhouse nestled comfortably into the side of the hill, the bright blue of a swimming-pool a garish contrast to the mellow stone and pink roof tiles. The place was utterly still with only the faint hum of a generator and the rumble of a distant tractor as counterpoint to the chirruping of the cicadas.

'Wonderful, isn't it?' He opened back the shutters and unlocked the door.

'You've been before?'

'Oh yes. Many times.'

'Is it yours?' she asked sulkily. He looked away.

'No. It belongs to my partner. We won't be disturbed. I'll unpack the car. Look about.'

She moved from room to room opening shutters. The house was spacious and uncluttered, the soft terracotta tiles cool under her bare feet, the white-washed walls mostly bare. The main room must have been fashioned from the entire original ground floor for it was huge, with windows opening to the east and west. There were several splendid pieces of furniture, their dark surfaces gleaming with the patina of age and elbow grease. The tiled floor was scattered with rich dark oriental rugs. Three stern black-framed, unmistakably Dutch, portraits stared balefully at her above their white lace ruffles. Cas joined her as she made a mock curtsy in front of them.

'Appeasing the ancestors I see!' he laughed.

She swung around. 'Yours?'

'No, no my partner's family. Three generations of Hannings,' he added hurriedly, again avoiding her eye.

'Does he use it much?'

'Who?'

'Your partner,' she said impatiently. There was a short uncomfortable pause.

'Livy is my partner.' He busied himself with the shutters before turning around. 'Surely I told you?'

She desperately wanted to scream her revulsion and fury. Swallowing her bile she turned to him as casually as she could.

'Your partner *and* your wife?' she spoke carefully. 'No, Cas, you did not.'

Niggling disquiet turned to anger. First that odd business about his passport, now this sledgehammer thrown casually at her. Fury turned to panic and panic to guilt. How little she knew about him. Always so close, so secretive.

His partner, his wife. How many times had he mentioned her? *My partner thinks this or that, I do not agree. No problem. It'll work out, always does.* The nameless partner, running the show in Amsterdam. And she, poor sap, had never once questioned him, never thought to ask for a name, a description. Twit.

A chastened Bid wandered silently through the

216

open door at one side of the vast fireplace. It led directly to what appeared to be the only bedroom and beyond that, on a lower level, the bathroom. The bath was large and luxurious and sunk into the floor. She turned on the water; it was warm. Someone unseen had prepared for their coming. So he'd been here many times, had he? When had he last shared this bed, any bed with his wife? She eyed the generous double bed stonily and knew she would not ask what Mevrouw Hanning Van Rijn looked like.

Bid battened down the disappointed fury and wandered through the rest of the house. The kitchen was back by the entrance and at the same level as the bathroom, with the windows set high in the walls; and, though it was cool, Bid, no longer so willing to be pleased by all things Van Rijn, decided it was hideously gloomy. She idly pulled open the fridge. It was full of fresh provisions. She touched an earthenware casserole sitting on the table and found to her surprise that it was warm. A mouth-watering smell of rosemary and chicken rose as she lifted the lid.

'There must be a maid somewhere,' she murmured half to herself.

'No,' Cas answered from the doorway, 'just the caretaker, Marcellina. She won't disturb us but she'll clear up when we've gone. The rest we'll manage for ourselves. Will you mind?'

Bid made no reply. She kept her back to him while she attempted to regain her composure but she was aware of him moving towards her and then of his arms resting on her shoulders. He turned her to him and drew her into the salon and held her

217

close until her body relaxed against him. He tilted her head up and looked at her earnestly.

'I have not been here with Livy for at least three years. That is what you want to know, isn't it?' He kissed her tenderly. No, she wanted to scream, when did you last sleep with her? But she said nothing, she could not resist him. Moreover she did not want to. He was hers.

'Bid, my love, do you believe me? I want you to myself. Just us. I want to love you, bellissima. Now.'

They made love lying on one of the beautiful rugs until the evening sun filled the room with warm pink light.

'Shall we go out for dinner or have it here?' he asked then.

'Here. Can we swim?'

He took her hand and they padded, naked, to the pool and made love again in the clear still water. Then in a passion he lifted her onto the edge and with her legs dangling in the water stood before her and entered her, urgently, greedily. She wound her legs around him, her darting tongue urging him to come again and again, her anger converting to ferocious demand that she, and she alone should possess him.

'Was she as good as me?' Not is, was. Past tense.

He pulled her into the water and jerked her towards him and entered her roughly, his mouth clamped on hers.

'Nobody has ever been as good as you,' he said roughly. 'I want you. You're mine.'

She laughed and swam slowly round until he pulled himself out of the water. He sat watching her for a few moments then went off into the house. He returned almost immediately holding a large glass of pale straw-coloured wine.

'Want some?' he called as she swam towards him.

He drank from the glass, then as she held up her hand for it, he knelt down and looping her neck with his free hand, pressed his mouth to hers and released the wine. She pulled him in and, wrapping her legs around him, once more taunted him to more frenzied coupling. Afterwards he floated away exhausted, then joined her as she lay and dozed in the dying sun.

'Perhaps we should stay here for ever? Would you like that, prima?'

She buried her head in the towel and smiled secretly, relishing the power of silence. He rolled over and watched as she slowly stood up and stretched, then relenting, bent down and ran her tongue gently along his lips.

'I'll go and unpack.' She laughed softly, knowing he wanted her to stay.

The year of their love-making had taken all lingering inhibitions from Bid and now, in sudden inspiration, it came to her that in suppressing her rage, she had, unaccountably, gained power. She smiled secretly to herself and revelling in her own sensuality, she strolled from the darkened terrace, through the tall open windows, into the big room. In some indefinable way, she sensed that fear of losing her had entered his mind for the first time and that it had increased her attraction for him in a way that all her protestations of devotion could not. A tiny glow of triumph coursed through her. Knowing he watched, she switched on a lamp before she moved around collecting their randomly scattered clothing. She bent and straightened, turning this way and that, no trace of self-consciousness disturbing the placid fluidity of her movements. As she walked through the bedroom, she paused before the mirror and ran her hands down her sides. She had become so lithe, she turned and admired herself. Sex relaxed her, made her glow. Now it was mutual, their lust, she leaned backwards and closed her eyes at the memory of it.

She turned down the bedclothes. What the hell did absent partners/wives matter? Who cared about the Mevrouw? He desired her, he loved her, nobody could fake such passion – could they? She would have him, she would not let him get away. He wanted her. She chortled with satisfaction at the thought of his vigour, then glared at the bed. He loved her, he was softer now, more thoughtful, gentle. Except in bed. There he was insatiable, animal. They both were. The more they made love, the more they wanted it. Thoughts of their exuberant love-making flashed into her mind as she ran the bath and suddenly she wanted him again.

She turned off the taps and ran towards him, smiling triumphantly at his tumescence, her hand touching the gold chain at her neck. He sat up and stared.

'Stand there for a moment,' he said, 'my Botticelli girl. My own primavera.' He drew in his breath as his hand reached up to pull her towards him.

'My lovely primavera,' he whispered softly, 'tomorrow I'll show you why I brought you here. We'll go to Florence and I'll show you how beautiful you are. I love you. I want you, for myself, for always.'

For a long moment she just stood looking down at him, and then she said quietly:

'I know. That's the best thing, Cas. I know.' But inside, she was still angry and unsure.

# Grace

*August – September 1990*

**APULEIUS, Lucius:** *DE CUPIDINIS ET PSY-CHES AMORIBUS, limited edition, fine engravings, original holland-backed boards. Origin obscure but finely presented.*

## CHAPTER SIXTEEN

The immediate aftermath of Grace's collapse was a low-grade fever and a three-day skulk. This was punctuated by increasingly confiding phone calls from Sarah Roberts and boozy visits from a concerned, though ebullient, Murray Magraw. It proved her nadir. By the time she pulled herself together she'd devised a plan of action.

She was at once thwarted by Murray who kept her almost hostage in the library in a kindly, if patently determined attempt, to keep her occupied. He had, she knew not where, got it into his head that she was at risk from a violent, if invisible, husband. He blandly insisted that without her know-how it would take him far too long to finish the work alone. Since she was still anxious to provide herself with a more secure cushion against penury, she judged it best to go along with him. So, once again pushing the dead and the absent from her mind, she allowed herself the calming presence of the sympathetic American. He was excellent company and it proved to be a soothing and restorative week, reinforcing her determination to get to grips with her situation. It was therefore something of an anticlimax when he disappeared.

And a surprising relief. For now at last she was able to return to her private preoccupations without need of explanation. She'd already begun to feel that his sympathy was in danger of edging towards the proprietorial. A small worm of uneasiness about how much she might have revealed in her cups wriggled uncomfortably at the back of Grace's mind, but she'd recovered enough to know that if she allowed her vague mistrust to surface she would again fall into a lethargy of inactivity, or worse, allow herself to get sucked into a spiral of suspicion. With a tremendous effort of will, she pushed discomfort aside and wrote to Reggie demanding a meeting, then rang Bartley Quinlan.

'The canal house, Mr Quinlan. I shall come over at the end of the month. I could meet your client then – the person who wants to buy it.'

Quinlan's reaction to her firm tone was almost comical.

'I am talking to Mrs Hartfield, am I?' He was playfully incredulous.

She laughed obligingly. 'You are, Mr Quinlan. As soon as I arrange one or two things this end, I shall give you a date.'

'Very well so. Is there anything else I can do?' He was wary but at the same time clearly anxious to prolong the conversation.

'I'm not sure.'

'The other executor would . . .'

'The priest?'

'Yes. He's retiring. Going back to his home town. He's asked about you several times, as you know. I wondered when you'd be ready to talk to him? He seems quite anxious to meet you.' Quinlan

226

made it sound as if the favour was in Grace's gift.

'I'll think about it, Mr Quinlan. I'll be in touch in a few days.'

She sat for a moment waiting for the shakes to start. The fear the priest's name had brought before flickered for a moment, then subsided. She leaned back in relief, breathing deeply and slowly, as the phone began to ring.

It was Murray to say that his mother had died a couple of days before. He'd be back as soon as he could to finish work on the collection.

'Unless you feel well enough to do a final check before sending it off? Max Lindquist is becoming restive, he's called several times.'

She was touched that with his own preoccupations he was still trying to keep her busy, even if he inadvertently made her sound like an incompetent. She wondered again how much she'd confided in him and felt a mixture of resentment and relief at how peculiarly comforting it had been to deposit her troubles with a comparative stranger who would soon go away and leave no lasting witness to her humiliation. On the other hand, it would be rather embarrassing if he insisted on staying.

'There's very little left to do, I'll get on to it straight away.' And with a formal expression of sympathy for his mother's death, Grace rang off.

She set to at once, calmly and methodically sorting the books, pamphlets, samples of lace and illustrations into neat piles according to size, protecting the corners and carefully wrapping each item. A couple of days later Federal Express picked up the three large boxes. There was nothing further for Murray to do, no further need for him to come to the house, her life would be her own again. Grace, surprising herself, felt flat. Not for long. A couple of days later he turned up looking blue, claiming he was at a loose end. She regarded him silently.

'I need to keep busy,' was all he said and now it was a thoroughly frustrated Grace's turn to lend support. A day, she told herself, two at most, then he has to go.

They worked their way through the shelves, sorting her entire stock into possible foundations for future catalogues. When he started on the filing system, she began to feel besieged, wondering if he'd ever leave and hating herself for crabby suspicions of exploitation which, when she tried to pinpoint them, evaporated, leaving only a nasty sense of an unfocused rage with the world. And her own spinelessness.

The bookroom had never been so organized, but it wasn't long before Murray apologetically admitted that he was simply making work to keep occupied.

'I didn't think my mother's death would affect me so much. She's been ill for so long and . . . hell, we didn't even get on particularly well.'

Disarmed, she surprised herself by saying:

'I don't know why I ever found it congenial to work alone.'

As he smiled his gratitude and settled in for the day, she asked herself if she was taking advantage of his good nature, or he of hers?

Acknowledgement of the lace collection from Max Lindquist was accompanied by a whopping great cheque. Hartfield Regional Books was free from imminent bankruptcy, and it was while they were sitting at the library table with a celebratory Highland Park malt apiece that Murray tentatively asked if she would like to employ him for a few months. She looked at him thoughtfully, aware that his request might not be entirely motiveless. She no longer had any desire to lose her tenuous control of either her independence or her business, nor did she mention that, in the steady state, her income had difficulty supporting one, never mind two. He was an intelligent man; she imagined he would already have gleaned that.

'My stock is very low. Have you any ideas?'

'Yep, I think so. You've got quite a number of issues from small presses. We could pursue one or two of those.'

*We.* Her heart sank.

'Oh, do you think so? I've got rather mixed feelings about some of them, all style and no content.'

'Not all. What about the Daniel Press? You've already got a few of the early editions, they're kind of rare.'

Grace nodded. 'Yes, they are something of an exception. Actually I picked up most of those the same day as the lace.'

'In Oxford? Of course. That's where the press was. Henry Daniel was Provost of Worcester College,' Murray intoned lugubriously. 'He managed to combine both style and content.' He grinned. 'I prefer the more elaborate stuff myself,' he drawled, 'being a flamboyant sort of fellow.'

She laughed. 'What? Like Kelmscott? But surely

some of the really small commercial presses were much more interesting?'

'You see! Between us we might make something very exciting.'

*Us, we.* There he goes again, she thought resignedly.

'What about your job?'

'I could extend my leave. I may not return.' He paused and poured himself another whisky. 'I have nothing to return to.'

She waited while he refilled her glass.

'My wife took off a few months ago.'

'Took off?'

'Yeah. Left. We were together twelve years. Then pow!'

'Children?'

'Not with me, she had her career. She's a conference organizer. Vice-president of quite a big outfit. Didn't want kids.' He sipped his whisky. 'No time. Until a guy she worked with got her pregnant. It turned out they'd been having an affair for years.' The disbelief still sounded in his voice. 'God, I was so dumb. All those conferences abroad. Everyone else seemed to know.'

No wonder he'd homed in on her so sympathetically. Weren't they in the same boat? Reggie slithered into Grace's thoughts.

'I'm sorry,' she said.

'I'll get over it, I guess. But I don't want to go back for a while.'

Grace said carefully: 'I've never worked with anyone else. I didn't think I'd like it.' She smiled to take the sting away and added, 'It's been good, but only on a temporary basis.' There was an awkward

230

pause. 'I'd be worried about paying you.' She hesitated, then half caved in with the dawning realization that he might be able to keep things afloat for the time being while she got on with the Lacey business. 'Perhaps we could . . . perhaps we could work independently? On a co-operative basis . . . sort something out . . . try it for a few weeks? If it works, it works. Then we could talk about extending the arrangement. Would that suit?'

'Do you mean it? Really?' he asked eagerly.

She eyed him warily, wondering if he could possibly be as genuine as he seemed. Vague resentment seeped through her. Would she ever be able to trust anyone again? She hated what she was becoming; the erosion of her character, her carping search for hidden motives, her mistrust. But at the same time, she doubted his seeming amiability. Then she looked at Murray's open, attractive, lopsided smile and felt thoroughly ashamed.

'The pickings are pretty lean, you know that, Murray. Are you sure it's what you want?'

'It would save my life,' he said simply. 'I could start on this lot right away.' His hand touched hers as he indicated a pile of books. She moved away quickly but murmured her acceptance.

Well, she owed his kindness something. Yet she still couldn't help speculating on what she might have told him.

'I'm going to be busy for the next few days,' she said suddenly.

'Oh?' His face fell.

'I have some things to do. We can iron out some sort of agreement when I'm free. If that's OK?'

'Uh huh.' He picked up his mac with the air of

231

someone who has lost a tenner and found a pound. Barely suppressing a grin, Grace rummaged in her bag and, with a firm effort at trust, handed him a key. 'You can let yourself in and out. If you feel like getting started . . .' The invitation was left dangling. 'If it's easier you can stay. The spare room's made up.'

After Murray left, Grace rang Sarah Roberts and suggested lunch the following day. Then, on impulse, she decided to go to Clerkenwell. As she left the house, the Pepperstock's disgruntled au pair came staggering along the pavement laden down with two carrier bags of groceries. A comically reluctant Jamie trailed behind her. His face brightened when he saw Grace.

'Can I go and see Reggie? He said he'd take me fishing. Can I go and see him, Grace?' he asked breathlessly. He was like a great Labrador puppy, his overlarge chubby hands grabbed at her skirt.

'Reggie's still away, Jamie.' She smiled down at his eager upturned face.

'But he told me!' His lower lip began to quiver. 'He told me we could go fishing!'

'When did he tell you that, darling?' She hunkered down beside him, but he pulled away, flung himself down on the doorstep and covered his face with a sigh of terminal resignation. After a second or two he peeped slyly through his fingers:

'Could I come and stay in your house, Grace? Mum's away.' He scrunched his face up with the effort of trying to convey tragedy. 'I love your chips.'

She stifled a guffaw. 'I can't cook now, poppet, I have to go and see someone. You could come when

I get back. In a day or two. We'll have lots of chips then. And hot dogs if you like.'

He turned away disconsolately and shuffled around the side of the house, for all the world like a disappointed old man. Grace stood transfixed, watching him. The au pair, catching her eye, smiled awkwardly and shrugged her shoulders. Grace shut the gate thoughtfully. All of a sudden her vague resolutions had turned to steely determination. She headed off towards Ealing Broadway and a pensive hour later turned into Everard Street.

The house was smaller than it looked from the outside, and was divided into only two flats: one comprising the basement and first floor; the other the second floor and attic. The hallway had been altered to provide a cramped vestibule with two doors set at an angle. The one on the right had Bid Lacey's name over the bell. Grace turned the key, pushed open the door, and entered.

The stairway gave on to a spacious landing from which two further doors led. The kitchen door was slightly ajar. Passing it, Grace went through the second. The living-room was a surprise: full of books, comfortable, and extremely neat. But having been closed up for the whole summer, it was now stale and slightly musty. Grace opened the windows, gathered the line of empty plant holders from the windowsill and took them to the kitchen. She threw open the windows here as well. She prowled restlessly opening and shutting cupboards, not yet sure where to start. A pile of mail lay neatly stacked on the kitchen table, most of it junk. A couple of empty milk bottles had grown an alarming fungus in the sink. She picked up a short olive green jacket from the back of a chair, absent-mindedly sniffed, then turned aside in distaste. A faint trace of stale human sweat mingled with the perfume it still retained. She hovered uncertainly, dumped the small amount of rubbish into a Sainsbury's plastic bag, then wandered upstairs peering briefly into the small bedroom and bathroom, not yet touching anything, trying to get a feel for the girl and how she'd lived; taking her bearings.

A light breeze began to waft through the dusty flat, clearing the air, stirring the curtains and bringing with it the rumble of traffic and the rarer cries of children playing in the city street. It was a cheering sound; Grace returned to the living-room to begin her search.

There were bookcases everywhere. Even at a glance she could tell the books were valued. Each was carefully in place, the shelves orderly. It was a surprisingly large collection for a young person. She reckoned that there must be about five or six hundred volumes. She began to pick them out at random and then, with quickening interest, more methodically. She jotted some names in her notebook.

'She knew what she was at,' Grace muttered to herself. 'If she brought all these she must have spent every spare penny on them.'

She ran her eye down the shelves. The greater proportion appeared to be twentieth-century Irish literature. Some odd buried memory niggled at the back of her mind: something vaguely familiar. As she pulled out a slim volume a faint smell of peat smoke was released from its flimsy discoloured pages and for a heart-stopping moment the buried memories of her own childhood threatened to overpower her.

She slipped the book back in place and moved to the two smaller bookcases on either side of what had once been a fireplace and which now sported a hideous gas contraption with a mock copper cowl. These contained a selection each of modern American and English novels which Grace could value at a glance. She was on shakier territory with the Irish books, nevertheless it was possible to hazard a guess and, as she began to take down and handle more of the volumes, she was intrigued to know how the girl had come by such a fine collection.

As if in answer to the question, the next, and almost every subsequent book she opened, disclosed that Fergus Lacey was the collector. On the inside cover of each was a neat little bookplate, handwritten in beautiful copperplate with his name, date of acquisition and underneath, in a more recent and less careful hand, BK Lacey. Four or five random exceptions, with more recent dates, were dedicated from an unidentified BM. Something about the signature set a tiny bell ringing, but for the moment she could not say why. She slipped the slimmest of these volumes into her jacket pocket for later examination. BM. There was the vaguest familiarity about the initials, too elusive, for the moment, for her to capture.

There was little else in the flat of much value except a couple of beautiful watercolours on the wall above the boarded-up fireplace. Brabazons, she noted with surprise when she peered at them more closely. Sarah Roberts had mentioned that the

Dutchman collected pictures – perhaps these were presents from him? She slipped them from their hooks and examined the backs but found no clue to their provenance. She replaced them and looked carefully at the other pictures. All except a small pencil drawing of a young woman, hanging on the side of the chimney breast at eye-level, were simply framed posters and prints. The drawing was faded and slightly foxed, signed JBY 1906. She turned it over. On the back in Fergus Lacey's copperplate was written: *For my dearest Bridget on her 21st birthday from Dad*. Underneath, in pencil, an earlier spidery hand had written: *Sketch of unidentified Abbey actress by John Butler Yeats (father of the poet)*. It was a charming study, simple and moving. The girl looked a little like Sarah. On impulse, Grace slipped it into her bag.

The drawer of the small table by the window yielded a large cache of letters. The first few she glanced at were all written on blue notepaper, signed *Mam*. Grace, swallowing her own violent feelings and hoping that they would contain some momentous disclosure, scanned the pages but they contained nothing more than inconsequential news only of interest to the correspondents. One thing struck her however: Eileen Lacey had quite a penchant for running into newly-married friends of her daughter; but whatever the sub-text of that was, wasn't immediately clear. There was certainly a campaign to get Bid back to Dublin. Away from her lover? Several of the later letters had obviously contained newspaper clippings of Dublin-based jobs because there were subsequent rather impatient enquiries as to why Bridget was not applying for

236

them. Grace rifled through to see if any remained but they did not.

The bundle from Fergus were of a different order, with all the warmth the letters from Eileen lacked, full of concerned enquiries about his daughter's health and happiness and interest in her activities. He had a real gift for small detail: the garden, the neighbours and the state of the weather all came in for droll comment, but his main interest was what he called his 'book-hunger' and triumphant announcements of his latest finds which he catalogued in detail. He clearly adored his only child and obviously believed she shared his interest; but even after a cursory glance Grace guessed she had not, at any rate not as literature. She had undoubtedly kept them in pristine condition in tribute to her dead father. They were lovingly preserved, but an experienced eye could tell how seldom they'd been opened or handled.

Bid Lacey must have kept every scrap of paper Cas Van Rijn ever wrote. They lay in chronological order in a cigar box underneath the letters from her parents. In truth they weren't much more than notes, but they were tender and loving and probably meant more to the recipient than to other prying eyes. There were neither dates nor addresses but someone, Bid presumably, had pencilled a date neatly on each one; silent witness to what he meant to her. He called her his treasure, his primavera, his bride, his love. The last moving little note from Holland spoke of their child and his great joy. It finished up:

*I have been too careless about the divorce, my*

*dearest one, too complacent about your trust.*
*Because you never said so until the other day, I*
*did not allow myself to think how you must have*
*hated the difficult position I put you in with your*
*mother and your friends. I have been stupid, my*
*precious. Now I will not let matters rest and*
*I promise it will be sorted out before the month*
*is over, before anyone but us realizes about*
*our baby, we'll be married. Joined as one,*
*for ever.*

It was dated just two months before she died. 6
February. Rereading it, Grace wondered, with a
snort, how he could possibly have been so disin-
genuous. Had Bid delayed putting on the pressure
until she was sure about the pregnancy? Until she
was sure of her man? What sort of relationship was
that?

She sat on the sofa and tried to conjure up the
lovers but the mother's image kept intruding. She
checked Eileen's letters more thoroughly, looking
for references to Van Rijn but there were none. Nor
to her daughter's pregnancy. Nothing except an
endless harping about a return to Dublin. There
was an eerie relentlessness about her lack of
comment on Bid's life in London. It was plain,
reading the letters, that there was little intimacy
between them.

Grace tried to imagine the girl in the flat, walking
about, reading. There was something vaguely
familiar about the place. Two heavy thirties-style
armchairs had brilliant red and yellow Indian
bedspreads covering them loosely – like Sarah's she
remembered suddenly – and surmised they dated

from her time at the flat. The floor was covered with fairly new rush matting. An ugly imitation bergère sofa in advanced need of repair stood against one wall. In front of it, a rather handsome glass coffee table. Lying open, with a dried coffee cup beside it, lay Mary Wesley's *Harnessing Peacocks* and a selection of *Diva* magazines, the most recent six months old. Then, as her eye travelled around, it came to rest on something lying on the floor by the window, almost obscured by the curtains.

The pictures must have fallen in the breeze because the glass of both had smashed. Grace carefully pulled the shards away from the small snapshots, one of the abominable Alice and another of a couple – a plump tweedy man and a slim dark woman. Eileen. Her heart pumping painfully, Grace picked it up gingerly and brought it close to the window to examine it more closely. A neat caption in the familiar copperplate read: *Mam and Dad at Kilduff 1979*. Her sister. So like herself that Grace closed her eyes in horror. Photographed eleven years before, when she was, what? Forty-one. Almost precisely the same age as she, Grace, was now. Dead. She stared at the smiling, enigmatic face and knew at once that, had they bumped into each other, she would certainly have known they were sisters.

But Eileen had known Grace was alive. How could someone so ordinary-looking, so familiar, be capable of such calculated malevolence? Impossible. Surely she couldn't have intended it? Yet, why then had she chosen to cut herself off?

'For what?' Grace spat the words through

clenched teeth. 'What did you do it for?' And without warning her head began to swim. She dashed up to the bathroom and was comprehensively sick.

The cistern held only enough water for one flush and there was no sound of it refilling. Her stomach swirling ferociously, she opened the small cabinet above the washbasin, looking for something to settle it. It contained little. Aspirin, mouthwash, soap, toothpaste and a small flat tortoisehell box, inside which were three full strips of a contraceptive pill in an unopened packet which still had the prescription date on the outside: September 1989. There were no others. Was this when she decided to stop taking the pill, to try for a child? Was it her own, unilateral decision? Grace turned over the box and on its base found a prescription label stuck on the inside of the box which neatly recorded that she'd started taking the pill in October 1988. The date was encircled in red ink beside which was written the word 'start'. Grace looked at it thoughtfully and wondered for the umpteenth time why Sarah had described Bid as scatty, which Grace had privately translated as light-hearted, being partisan. The carefully annotated label and the order of the books described something rather different. ED Hampshire had also given the impression that Bid was someone who needed looking after. Grace was more inclined to the opinion that her niece was both organized and very determined, yet somehow she played for sympathy, allowed herself to be patronized right and left. It was all rather sad. Even the abbreviation of her name sat oddly on that mixed-up personality. She was certainly less biddable, more interesting, and very much more complicated, than either had given her credit for. And probably a good deal more devious.

Or had the neatness, the secrecy, been assumed with the new image? Had she sloughed her scattiness as she sloughed her weight? Could anyone transform themselves that much? That quickly? And why would they want to, if not to impress the maker of the new image? Sugar daddy. The thought chilled.

A loud banging on the flat door disturbed her thoughts. She ran quickly downstairs. A slim, dapper man of about sixty stood beside the open door of the ground floor flat, eyeing her with undisguised interest and ill-disguised suspicion.

'Excuse me. Have you a right to be here? I heard the sound of running water. It gave me quite a turn.'

'I'm sorry if I disturbed you,' Grace said politely. 'I should have told you I was here. I am, er, sorting through the flat. I'm a relative of Bid's.'

'Yes. I can see that now,' he returned with frank curiosity. 'Sorry to be abrupt, I was afraid it might be squatters. Is there anything I can do? Perhaps you need some help?'

'There is actually, if you'd be so kind. Do you know how to turn on the water supply?'

He nodded briskly, slipped the latch on his own door, followed her upstairs and with admirable efficiency turned the stopcock in a small cupboard at the back of the kitchen. As he straightened up he held out his hand and smiled.

'I'm Roy Angel. I live downstairs.' He looked

around and said sadly, 'I miss dear Bid very, very much.'

Grace warmed to him at once. Dear Bid. No qualifying fat, thin or scatty. No reservation. Just a simple kind statement of affection. Dear Bid. Grace shook his hand. He looked startled when she began to offer him sympathy then, covering her own confusion, she said:

'I'm Grace Hartfield.'

'Oh?' He waited for her to continue and when she did not, he asked:

'Did you say you were a relative? Close? You're not a Lacey though, are you?' he added shrewdly. She shook her head wondering how she might avoid the incredible rigmarole yet hang on to him long enough to get him talking about the girl.

'No, not close.'

He looked as if he was about to comment but paused, inviting her to continue. His sharp eyes were everywhere. Grace had the uncanny feeling that he had made himself guardian of her niece's privacy and was waiting for her to justify her intrusion.

'I never met her,' she repeated. 'Sadly, I didn't know of her existence until she died. I last met her mother when I was a child. She's also dead, did you know?' He nodded.

'You knew her well? Bid, I mean? How long did she live here?'

To her embarrassment, his eyes filled with tears and it was several moments before he replied.

'Oh, for about seven or eight years I think, maybe a little more. She took this flat very shortly after she came to London, an Irish pal of hers let

242

her take over the lease. But I really got to know her after her flatmate, Sarah, moved out, four or five years ago. Bid and I became great chums. I was devastated by her death. We both were. She did a very dreadful thing.' He sighed and looked at her gloomily. 'It's very dark here, electricity still off?'

'Afraid so.'

'Would you like me to give you a hand or would you prefer a drink?'

'There's little I can do with the light gone. A drink would be welcome,' she said gratefully. 'I'll just close the windows and follow you down.'

He'd left the door to his flat open, and hailed Grace from the drawing-room at the front of the house. It had been done up with a great deal more flair and money than the flat above and retained its original fine moulded ceiling and a beautiful marble fireplace. Tall, glass-fronted bookcases rose on either side of the chimney breast. As she ran her eye over them she was startled to recognize some of her own books. Over the mantle there was a striking portrait of a stern balding academic.

'That's Bradley. My partner.' Roy swung around. 'We've been together for over thirty years.' There was a challenge in his precise voice.

Grace's jaw dropped. 'Not Bradley Moffat? From Queen Mary College? How extraordinary!' As her fingers closed on the little book in her pocket she sat down abruptly. BM.

'Do you know him?' The challenge was replaced by interest.

'We've never met, but we've corresponded for years. He sometimes buys books from me.'

'Hartfield. Of course that's why the name was so

243

familiar. You're the bookseller. Good heavens, how very odd. You know he sometimes bought things for Bid?' His eyes darted over her, he was almost hopping with curiosity, or was it mistrust?

Parallel thoughts raced through their heads. Grace Hartfield related to Bid. Hartfield catalogues in the same house. Why had she never sent books to Moffat's home, always to the college? She might have called, might have . . . might have . . . *Oh Bid, dear child.*

'What will you drink?'

'Scotch. With ice, if you have it,' she replied shakily.

He poured from a decanter. 'No ice, it's malt,' he said brusquely. 'Will water do?' He held out the jug and sat opposite her while Grace allowed herself to outline the events of the past months. When she got to her relationship to Bid's mother he simply nodded in affirmation.

'Yes, of course.'

'You knew?'

'Oh yes, immediately. The likeness is uncanny. You're a good deal younger of course.'

'Did you know her well?'

'Not terribly,' he said drily and was silent for a few minutes before adding provocatively: 'She was something of a homophobe I'm afraid.' When Grace didn't respond he said, 'I rather kept out of her way. I last saw her in, when was it? January, she stayed with Bid for Christmas. It was, as I recall, the last time she stayed here.'

He stared gloomily into the middle distance, rubbing his hand back and forth over his lips. One leg swinging against the leg of his chair made a dull clicking sound. He looked lonely – not as if he were habitually so, more like a gregarious man in need of company. He stared gloomily at Grace, then sighed and settled back into his chair.

'There was the most ghastly row, I thought the ceiling would fall in. When she left, Bid was in shreds.'

'Oh. Did they often row?'

'Not like that. They bickered a bit, specially in the last year. Odd, now that I think about it, it must have started when she began to lose her grip on Bid.'

'As soon as Cas Van Rijn came on the scene you mean?' Grace prompted him. He slowly nodded his head.

'Em, no. I rather think it was later than that. Perhaps when he became a sort of permanent fixture?'

'You mean once she got to know him? Or of him?'

'I suppose. Yes, how very perceptive of you. But,' he pounced, 'you say you didn't know Mrs Lacey?'

Grace surprised herself by blurting: 'She was an awful bully. She sulked.' Her jaw dropped open at her own disclosure. Roy Angel nodded slowly in agreement.

'Precisely,' he said with obvious satisfaction, 'precisely.'

'Mr Angel.' Grace swallowed. 'Mr Angel, could you tell me about her? Please?' She watched as he sipped his drink slowly, obviously relishing her invitation to gossip.

'She was very striking-looking. Those extraordinary pale grey eyes you both share. That's how I knew you were closely related. She was always very reserved and could be quite charming but my, she ruled both Bid and Fergus with the most fearsome regime of silence I've ever come across. Everything had to be done her way. If not, she could remain silent for days. Some might call it sulking.' Roy Angel left no doubt that he included himself in that number. 'Even at this remove she unnerved Brad and me. If her parents were coming to visit, the dear girl would be anxious for weeks, and it was infectious. That sort of anxiety usually is, no matter how much you try to ignore it. Both Bid and her father were quite craven with her, doing anything to appease. In a sense of course it cemented their alliance but poor Fergus was utterly under his wife's thumb and,' he added fiercely, 'I know I'm partisan but I'm perfectly certain that she left Bid utterly incapable of responding to anything other than domination.'

'Oh God.'

'Quite. She seemed to gravitate towards it like a druggie. Even Sarah, who's a very nice girl, if a little high-handed – though I care greatly for her – even Sarah was forever organizing her. Needlessly, in my view. As for that old schoolmistress she worked for! I do not know why dear Bid had so little self-confidence. She was very talented at her job, you know. But she realized early on that it was something of a dead end so she was always terrified someone would, as she said, rumble her. It was ridiculous but it kept her – well it's hard to say really – *menial* in outlook, if you grasp my meaning? No amount of bullying or cajoling on my part shifted that silly notion.' He drew a deep long sigh. 'Not silly, sad. Do you know that even the porter at that wretched magazine had her rushing to the hospital to see his horrid old wife . . .' Roy Angel didn't pull his punches in the excitement of discovery. 'That same curmudgeon who couldn't be bothered to give her a message if by chance you were foolish enough to ask him. As I was on several occasions.' He sat back.

Grace remembered her anxious wait for Bid's property and was about to remark on it, but Roy Angel had no need of encouragement now that he'd got started.

'Then there was that truly unspeakable Colin, the Dutchman's predecessor. Once or twice I wondered if that unpleasant young man was offering her physical violence. She always denied it but, you know, the sound-proofing in this building isn't all it might be and I sometimes noticed unexplained bruises on her arms. Once on her face. She spent a lot of time here, crying on my shoulder, after his departure. He left her utterly demoralized.'

He poured himself a sly refill, ignoring Grace's empty glass.

'Then for a brief interlude there was a nice chap called Richard. Rather good-looking too, in a dull sort of way. Reliable. We had great hopes of him. But,' he shrugged his shoulders and turned out his palms, 'it was, alas, not to be. So sad. She couldn't seem to cope with being treated as an equal. She admitted as much herself. A great pity. But of course she'd already met her Dutch chum by then.'

Had Bid confided everything? Angel's prim concerned voice seemed to indicate she had.

'And he . . . ?' she prompted.

'Oh yes. He too dominated her, but he must have been more subtle about it. In any event she was resplendent under his regime; absolutely blossomed, looked ravishing. Of course she moulded herself to suit him, but somehow it seemed to work. I suppose he loved her. She claimed to be ecstatic; she certainly looked very happy for a time.'

'But you're not too sure?'

'Well, I wondered you know,' his voice grew harsh, 'if it wasn't all a little one-sided. There wasn't any sign of a divorce. He dragged his feet over it and that put her in a very difficult position, especially with her mother, and of course, her background. She may not have been a very ardent Catholic but she certainly believed and, though she didn't say so, she would have minded. Very much. You, of course, will understand all that. Very difficult. I'm not sure that fellow was quite straightforward. And I did think he was much too old for her.'

'You knew him well?'

'No, hardly at all. They were very circumspect. As I recall, we only met socially once, if you could call it that.' Some memory caused a momentary lapse and a snort of merriment, but he didn't expand.

'And his wife? Was she there on that occasion?'

'Lord no. That sort of chap travels light.' He leaned towards her earnestly. 'You know, come to think of it, I would dearly like to talk to his wife. Of course it might mean a trip to Holland. She lives there I believe, at least Bid said she did.' He poured another drink for himself and, reluctantly, a much smaller one for her. For a reflective moment or two he swirled the pale malt around his glass. 'Had you thought of doing so?'

'Yes. I had it in mind.'

'Good. I have a bad feeling about that business.' He paced silently about and for a short time stood staring out the window, gathering his thoughts.

'You knew she was expecting a baby? That week, before her mother died, Bid came over for supper one night. I was terribly thrilled – she asked me to be the godfather you know. She was rather hyper I thought. Full of plans and excitement but terribly thin and drawn. Quite worn out, poor lamb. Her mother had cancer. Did you know that? It was diagnosed rather too late I fear, and spread very rapidly. At that stage Bid was flying over to see her two or three times a month. It was a great strain, she looked awfully tired.'

'How on earth could she afford it?'

'Old moneybags looked after that. Her Dutch-man. Rich as Croesus apparently. Opened an account with the airline.'

'Did you know him any better by then?'

'Not really.' Roy Angel looked uncomfortable. 'She rather kept him out of the way.' He shrugged. 'But I'm a bit of a curtain twitcher so I saw him a few times. Coming and going. Awfully good-look-ing. Really. For his age. He was pushing on, you know.'

'Yes, Sarah said about forty-five.'

'I should say!' he replied waspishly. 'At least. Whoever his tailor was, he ought to get a medal. Those shoulders. My, my.' He rolled his eyes heavenwards before falling into moody silence. Since there seemed little further point in continuing a discussion about a man neither of them knew, Grace returned to her own obsession.

'I take it she hadn't told her mother about the baby?'

'No. That's another thing. She kept avoiding it. Of course she'd grown so slim she hardly showed, and she dressed to disguise it, but when I last saw her, well, I'd have known. I did know. I didn't let on of course. Let her tell me herself. She said she planned to tell her mother that weekend, but I wonder? Heaven only knows why she delayed so long.' He looked at her speculatively.

'Mr Angel. Do you have any idea why she killed herself?'

'None,' he said sadly. 'No idea at all. After it happened I went to see Sarah. She was quite distraught and she talked a lot of nonsense about Bid being responsible for Tom's business going bust. Well, I ask you! You've only to look at the awful buildings these trendy young architects foist on us . . . I mean to say . . . who's surprised? But I held my tongue. Sarah can be a little righteous. To be truthful, I found it a bit rich, considering it was she who introduced them. I expect that's partly why she's feeling so bloody.' He looked as if he were going to weep again. 'She showed me Bid's last letter. I've gone over and over it in my mind, but no. I really don't. Something catastrophic seems to have happened in Dublin, I'm certain of that. Must have. Unless her chum was threatening to leave her?' Angel rubbed his forehead; his voice had become tired and discouraged. He spoke as if he were dragging information from himself that he could hardly face.

'The strangest thing . . . Bid rang from Dublin the night her mother died. Wednesday, was it? To tell me about it I thought, but no, she was looking for her man. She thought he might have turned up here to look for her. She rabbitted on about breaking a lunch date with him because she'd been called away. She hardly mentioned her mother. I must tell you, I was a little shocked. I mean she sounded more concerned about the missed lunch than about her mother's demise.

'Tom Roberts came looking for him next day and then, on the Friday after the funeral, Bid rang again. Several times. I got a bit narked, I'm afraid I was slightly short with her. Brad was down with a dreadful cold and was fussing something awful and I wasn't feeling too brilliant myself. I have since regretted it bitterly because of course I never spoke to her again.' He gave a dry little sob. 'Grief doesn't make heroes of any of us, does it? Poor Bid. She must have come home here on the Sunday night, the day before she died, but we heard nothing, not a sound; our bedroom is in the basement. By then we both had the flu and had gone to bed early, dosed up to the eyeballs with aspirin. And this stuff.' He looked at his glass, and gulped thirstily at his drink; his voice had become slightly slurred.

'It's very dreadful to me that she didn't ask for help, or call. I can't rid myself of the loneliness of that fearful act. In a strange city without a friend to talk her out of it. I was her friend, but I failed her you know. Utterly.' He closed his eyes. 'It was devastating.'

Grace wished she could evaporate or slip away without disturbing him further but when she moved his eyes shot open and he stood up.

'I beg your pardon, Mrs Hartfield, I'm forgetting my manners,' he said courteously.

'You've been very patient, Mr Angel, and helpful. I'll do as you suggest. I'll try to see Mrs Van Rijn.' As they walked towards the hall he took her elbow.

'We're going on holiday tomorrow,' he said. 'Flying to Venice for ten days early in the morning. Perhaps you'll call again when we get back?'

'Yes, of course.'

'Have you finished upstairs?'

'Till tomorrow.' She smiled and held out her hand.

'One last thing, Mr Angel. Something puzzles me. It probably means nothing but both Sarah and the people at Bid's office implied that Bid was scatty . . . disorganized. But her room . . .'

'They didn't know her very well, did they?' he interrupted briskly. 'All that was just a silly pose. Of course, Sarah was the stronger character and for a long time much the prettier. She was quite adept at making Bid her foil. It was not at all to her liking when Bid outstripped her. The dear girl was so over-anxious, desperately wanted to be loved and tried much, much too hard to please. It could appear as scattiness I suppose. Whatever that means. But when she was comfortable with you, as she was with me and Brad, then she was a most agreeable companion. And I mean companion. Good company and always interested in what you were doing. She had lovely manners. A dear friend, I miss her very much.'

Grace held out her hand and Roy Angel took it in both of his, slightly drawing her towards him. His face was a picture of sadness and indecision as he gathered himself to say what was troubling him.

'This may not make sense to you, Mrs Hartfield, but I've spent a lot of time thinking about poor Bid since she died. I never felt she was at home in London, not really. Her mother's instincts may have been right after all. Bid was not very sophisticated. Even with the fancy wardrobe, she was a simple girl with simple tastes and, well, she could sometimes be a little gullible. She was rather a bruised character. She gave out very conflicting signals and she was not understood. In many ways she was rather like a foreigner who never quite learns the nuances of the language – are you with me? She never learned to obfuscate. She was too open, too vulnerable. She was not quite at home here. We were discussing it once and she confessed that, besides us, her Dutchman was the only person who made her feel completely at ease. And though she kindly included us, I knew at once that she felt that he alone understood her. It crossed my mind then, though I cannot exactly say why, that it was probably because they were both strangers. When I remarked as much to her she took it quite seriously. So perhaps her mother was right to think she'd have been happier amongst her own?'

He loosened his hold on her hand and Grace drew away.

'I wonder. Poor girl. It's usually more complicated than one thinks, isn't it? I wish I'd known her. You make her sound very attractive, with all the contradictions. She was lucky to have known you.'

He watched her down the steps and as she turned to make a final farewell, he suddenly called:

'I'll tell Bradley I met you, shall I? He'll be so jealous!' She waved and then he added, 'and Mrs Hartfield, I've changed my mind. You're not in the least like your sister.'

**ABSENTEES & EMIGRATION:** *The Guilt and Baseness of Absentees fully displayed, or Strictures on Emigration, Milliken, 1798, shabby boards, scarce.*

## CHAPTER SEVENTEEN

The house was deserted when she got home. Apparently Murray had not taken up her invitation to stay though judging from the neat pile of work on the library table, he must have worked all day. She felt a twinge of disappointment at his absence.

That night, Grace lay awake for hours, her mind doing hula-hoops trying to link the sequence of events, as she understood them, which led up to Bid Lacey's death.

The mother died on a Wednesday, April 4th, of natural causes by all accounts. By the following Tuesday her pregnant daughter was also dead, by her own hand. Some time between those two events the lover died.

Van Rijn died in Dublin. When exactly had he gone there and why? To lend his fiancée support in her bereavement? If this was the case, why was she still looking for him on Friday? Or was there some other more sinister reason? Why was the missed lunch so important to her? Perhaps they had quarrelled in the preceding days? Had he threatened to abandon her just before she was called away? Before there was time or opportunity for a reconciliation? For that would surely have been the most obvious catastrophe for the girl: the defection of her lover, the father of her child. If this was the case, then Bid might have had something to do with his death.

He had drowned in the very canal which ran past her house, yet she convinced both the Roberts and Roy Angel that she hadn't seen him in Dublin. Sarah first, then Roy Angel confirmed that the last time Bid was in touch, on the Friday night, she'd still been looking for him. Frantically. And Tom Roberts had said that Van Rijn couldn't identify her body because he was also dead. So when did he die? More importantly, how? Did he jump or was he pushed? Had the lovers had their last confrontation on the canal bank? Why had she been so insistent that she had not met him? Had Bid been providing herself with an alibi by lying to her friends? This insidious thought began to take hold of Grace's imagination. A heated or violent argument could have resulted in her pushing him. But then he might just as easily have accidentally slipped.

Accident or suicide? Van Rijn's wife must have identified him; she would know. She might even know why. Pray God she spoke English. As she tried to script a conversation with the bereaved widow, Grace realized how unlikely it was that Mevrouw Van Rijn would want to discuss her wayward husband with the aunt of his late and pregnant mistress. She balked at the thought of even suggesting it.

Round and round Grace's thoughts whirled but, no matter how hard she tried to block her out, the image of her sister intruded. Was it her own

256

neurotic fear which made her distrust the neat solution of the lovers being responsible for each other's death? For her, Eileen Lacey still remained the bogey.

She'd died rather unexpectedly on the afternoon of Wednesday April 4th.

Bartley Quinlan had described it in detail. 'When the maid brought her lunch tray, she was gasping her last breath. They sent for her daughter at once,' he had announced dramatically and added that though Bid had flown over immediately she was too late. Eileen Lacey was already dead when she arrived.

Roy Angel said Bid had rung him that evening which confirmed Sarah's claim. The obvious solution was that somehow he'd heard of her mother's death and followed her to Dublin. Yet if that was the case why was she still looking for him after the funeral on Friday? And was there something out of the ordinary about that lunch date? Roy Angel reported she rang on Friday evening. So that left Saturday. Or late Friday night for the putative estrangement and her lover's death.

What about Eileen? Grace's last muddled thought as she finally dropped off to sleep was that she'd allowed the tragic death of the lovers to divert her from her own much deeper preoccupation with her dead sister and her curious disappearance all those years before.

Her nightmare recurred. She woke sweating and terrified at three, huddled against the bedhead, certain there was a man in the room. She edged her hand out to switch on the bedside light and found nothing but a horrible certainty that she, as well as her sister, was somehow implicated in Bid's death. There was a link, she was sure. Somewhere there was a link. She rocked to and fro, not pushing memory away as she had hitherto, but willing herself to remember, willing the images to clarify, willing herself back to that grim night, when she was a small terrified child. Throughout the night the dream played over and over like a broken record, until at last she fell into a deep sleep.

She woke at ten next morning, still wedged against the headboard, cramped, cold and ravenous. She hadn't bothered to eat the night before and had gone to bed with only a large scotch, topping up Roy Angel's supply, to sustain her. Grace showered quickly and rang Sarah to confirm lunch.

Sarah's first remark was that Cas Van Rijn's widow wanted Bid's stuff cleared from his flat. She was apparently on a flying visit to London. Sarah sounded a bit overawed by this turn of events.

'I told her we could do it today. I hope you don't mind?'

Grace was somewhat nonplussed at being volunteered for demolition duty until another thought occurred to her.

'Will Mrs Van Rijn be there?' she asked.

'Hanning Van Rijn,' Sarah corrected. 'She kept her own name, actually she prefers just plain Hanning.'

It appeared that indeed the widow herself would let them into Weymouth Mews at noon and, if they skipped lunch, Sarah said breathlessly, she'd be able to collect Alice from playschool at two. More interestingly, she added that baby Laurence would be along for the ride. From all of which Grace inferred that the Roberts family was getting back to normal. They arranged a meeting place convenient to the flat and rang off.

Since there was little to tempt her in the fridge, Grace gulped down a cup of coffee and left early, caught the tube and slipped into the Russell hotel for breakfast, and whether it was the comfort of the food, or the feeling that fate was interesting itself in her affairs at last, she walked into Queen's Square at noon with a good deal more confidence in the future than she'd had for some little time.

Sarah's gunmetal grey Volvo was parked beside the Craftworkers' Guild. She looked well, if keyed up, as she leaned across to open the passenger door. The baby was sleeping peacefully in a carry-cot on the back seat. On the journey to the flat the girl hardly drew breath, chattering non-stop about his feed, the number of hours he slept, Alice's exploits at playschool, Tom's new contracts. Bid wasn't mentioned. Even had she wanted to, it would have been impossible for Grace to get a word in edgeways. She found it hard to know what to make of young Sarah's frantic energy. The weeks since their first meeting had wrought a remarkable change in her and she'd resumed young mother-hood as if determined that her rejection of it had been a mere chimera.

Now, as they turned into the Euston Road, she spoke earnestly about how helpful that meeting had been along with their subsequent chats on the phone. She had, she suggested, been through a sort of catharsis that had provoked her and Tom into communication. They'd stopped blaming each other and now she could think of Bid again without hating her for the mess that Tom's business had fetched up in. Wasn't it amazing how these things worked? Now, suddenly, the partnership was beginning to get contracts again, not big, but steady. Stephen Rawlings claimed that Livy Hanning was responsible for the upturn, though she, Sarah, had some doubts about that. After all the wretched woman had pulled out of the main development.

Sincere though the little speech was, it was apparent to Grace that Sarah, quite rightly, was longing to put the whole sorry business of Bid's death out of her mind. Without actually saying so, she implied a resistance to any future contact. On both counts Grace was relieved; Sarah was rather too intense for comfort.

The child slept on. They'd fallen silent as the car turned right out of Portland Place and pulled up at a pair of high wooden gates. As they did so a woman got out of a green Daimler which was parked alongside and came to speak to Sarah.

'If you could let me go in first? Then follow. I'll see you inside.' She spoke curtly. They watched as she strode back to her car.

'That's her.'

She was petite and dressed with great elegance and formality in a severely tailored dark chestnut suit with her dark hair arranged in a large smooth coil at the nape of her neck. She looked rather like a ballet dancer and was a good deal older than

Grace had expected. As they parked she remarked upon it.

'Oh yes, she is, isn't she? Much older than him, of course. Over fifty I should say, wouldn't you? I expect that was why she wouldn't divorce him.' Sarah's voice dropped to a whisper as the Dutch-woman strolled over to be introduced.

'Livy Hanning,' she said and held out her hand.

The two older women walked ahead to the flat while Sarah fussed over the sleeping baby.

'You are the girl's aunt?' Mrs Hanning's English was excellent, her voice low-pitched and pleasing with only the slightest accent.

'Yes. I'm afraid this must be very difficult for you.'

'I think it's difficult all round.' Mrs Hanning stretched her fingers in a despairing gesture. 'The violence of suicide touches everyone, haven't you found? And when there are two . . .'

There it was. So simply stated. Grace was surprised at the depth of her relief.

'The office has arranged for a charity shop to collect whatever you don't want,' Livy Hanning said briskly when Sarah joined them. 'Will an hour and a half be enough? I have a business meeting now. I'll come back to lock up if you'd be so kind as to wait?' She directed her remarks vaguely in Grace's direction and exited abruptly.

'Phew,' said Sarah succinctly. 'Thank goodness she's gone.'

The flat was pristine and freshly aired. It had the careful appearance of having been done up by interior designers. There were two large light rooms with ceilings mitred into the roof space for added height, a gleaming unused kitchen and a sinfully luxuriant bathroom. The soft furnishings were all in pale colours. Expensively pale, Grace thought, concluding that whatever the unfortunate couple lacked, it hadn't been money. The only disorder was a stack of pictures against the wall of the living-room, otherwise the place might have been an illustration for a magazine, so impersonal did it seem. An elaborate hi-fi system squatted neatly against the side of the chimney breast, beside it a tall slim contraption designed for compact discs which was full. There must have been at least a hundred or so all neatly arranged in alphabetical order according to composer. Berlioz was obviously top favourite. There was not a single book in sight. They silently made their way to the bedroom.

The flat had been stripped of his effects. One side of the double wardrobe was ajar and empty, the other half-full of women's clothing: suits, dresses, a coat, a dozen blouses, several shrouded cashmere sweaters, slacks. They all looked new and scarcely worn. As Sarah ran her hand along the line of neatly hanging garments, she released the same faint perfume as had been in the jacket in Bid's own flat. They laid the clothes sadly on the bed, like so many corpses, beside the roll of macabre black waste bags which had been thoughtfully provided. Without comment they folded and packed each item.

'I've seen very few of these.' Sarah's voice was husky with emotion. 'I can't bear it. I'll check the baby.' She hurried off again.

Clothes and a box of Dior cosmetics apart, there

was little to throw any light on the couple who had, by Sarah's account, spent most of their time here. Then Grace pulled open the drawer of one of the bedside tables and came across a small bundle of airline tickets made out to BK Lacey. They were held in an elastic band and documented eight months of return journeys to Dublin: irregularly until October '89, then with increasing frequency except for January. In the last five weeks of her life Bid had flown to Dublin three times. All had been paid on her lover's account.

Sarah came in silently and stood looking over her shoulder.

'She didn't go over in January?' Grace mused aloud.

'I'm not sure, but no, I don't think so.'

'Was there some reason?' Grace persisted. Sarah reflected for a second or two.

'January. Yes. I remember now. She had a row with her mother. She didn't go for nearly a month after that.'

The row Roy Angel had described as cataclysmic?

'When was that?' Grace asked casually, neatly folding three or four sweaters into one of the bags.

'Just after Christmas. The last time Mrs Lacey came to London,' Sarah said promptly and sat down on the bed. 'We went to the zoo, it was an amazingly beautiful day. Surprisingly mild. Alice was being a pain. You know what they're like after Christmas. I was at my wits' end with her. I rang Bid on the spur of the moment.'

'Any idea what the row was all about?'

'Haven't a clue. Apparently about a bunch of flowers. Or at least that's how it started. Those bloody flowers.' She sat down on the bed. 'I know it wasn't really about the flowers. I know that, but I really couldn't make out what the hell was going on.'

'Perhaps she'd told her mother she was pregnant?'

'Lord no, she'd have barely known herself for sure, would she? Anyway I'm pretty certain she never told her mother. I mean she was still dithering about that a week before she died.'

'Who were the flowers from?' Grace asked.

Sarah looked at her strangely, as if some thought had half-formed, then evaporated.

'Cas, of course. He'd kept away while Mrs Lacey was staying. In Everard Street, of course, not here. I hadn't really twigged till then that she hadn't met him or that Bid was still fibbing about the relationship.' She bit her lip, then burst out: 'They should have had it out then, got it over with, but I guess Bid must have said she'd given him up or something. Typical really. If she could avoid trouble, she would. Anyway he must have been getting restive.' She giggled and blushed faintly. 'It was a jolly explicit message!'

'Perhaps that was what . . . ?'

'Maybe. That's what you'd think. But no. I remember how surprised I was that it didn't seem to be what bothered her.' She shrugged. 'But I'm damned if I know what did. Honestly, with Bid's mother it was hard to judge. One minute all smiles, then clunk, down with the shutters. She was completely unnerving.' She stared at

Grace in horror. 'Oh dear, I'm sorry, I keep forgetting.'

'No need. I knew neither of them, remember?'

After some further prompting the futility of retracing the same ground became obvious. So the incident joined all the other seemingly unrelated facts waiting to click into the scattered jigsaw. By now Sarah was obviously anxious to get away.

'I'm afraid the baby won't sleep much longer. Can we do the other rooms?'

Neither the bathroom nor kitchen yielded anything of the slightest interest and, other than a couple of cases of champagne in a cupboard, gave no clue as to how the couple lived.

'*Bijou* res. Isn't it awful?' Sarah voiced their disquiet. 'It's so unlike Bid. I thought coming here would bring it all back, but somehow it doesn't seem to have much to do with her. Or me.' Through the open window came the faint sound of the infant whimpering. Relief flooded into Sarah's face.

'I'll go now, Mrs Hartfield, if you don't mind. I have to collect Alice. If there's anything . . .'

'Yes. There is one thing.' Grace took the John Yeats picture from her bag and held it out tentatively. 'I'd like you to have this.'

For a moment Sarah's chin wobbled and for the first time that day she looked Grace straight in the eye and smiled her charming smile.

'I've always loved it. Thank you. That's so thoughtful. It'll remind me of the best times. And Bid's Dad. I liked him so much. None of this was worthy of her, was it?' Her lip curled with distaste and she shook her head. 'It's all so tacky. The bastard.' She almost spat the word then, with a swift change of mood, shyly took hold of Grace's hand.

'Goodbye, Mrs Hartfield, Grace.' A warm smile lit up her pretty young face.

'You've been through a terrible time, my dear. You must try to put it all behind you, stop feeling that it is in any way your fault. Will you try to do that? And Sarah, thank you so much for your help.' Grace leaned forward and kissed her cheek.

Sarah blushed, bit her lip, then smiled again. She was obviously on tenterhooks to get going.

'Excuse me to Mrs Hanning, will you please? I really couldn't face her again.'

They walked downstairs together and Grace watched as the car turned out of the gateway. As it gathered speed, Sarah leaned out the window and mouthed thank you, almost carefree for a moment, like any young mother going about her daily chores. Grace walked slowly back across the yard thinking how pretty it all looked in the late Summer sunshine but how much tragedy had been contained here. This was where the baby should have been born. The cobbled courtyard might have been cluttered with the paraphernalia of babyhood. But even the notion of it seemed unlikely. This was a flat for adults; a hideaway, a love-nest. Totally remote from everyday life. The only remaining clue to recent occupation were a couple of large terracotta pots at the doorway which still contained traces of their Summer planting.

'The flowers, those bloody flowers.' From nowhere came the echo of Sarah's stark phrase. As she climbed the stairs Grace pondered the mysteries of the Van Rijn household and how uncomfortably close they were to her own situation. About time she faced Reggie. She had a hunch that she would find him thus, well set-up, unget-at-able, a no-longer knowable Reggie. She could see them circling around each other, tearing away the tender adhesive that had bonded them for so long, that had, for almost a lifetime, withstood the evasions and half truths, the unadmitted cheating and the bruising hopeless longing for children.

She would have to arrange their meeting on neutral ground where they could better face each other and a grim partnerless future. Or was that reserved only for her? She could not bear to find him in a place like this with a young helpmeet easing his anxieties about middle age. Stirring his virility? Giving him the child that had been so cruelly withheld from them? She looked around at the understated, soulless, mind-blowing expensive luxury and almost laughed at the notion of Reggie shambling about, dropping pipe or book or slipper, with a young *poule-de-luxe* in swansdown draped around his bulk. Surely she would be spared that? His inclinations had a hint of humanity; he usually went for something more mature. Thirty-five at least. Mater familias. Bitch.

# Bid

*January 1990*

*Dear Confused: I am not surprised. Are you sure you know what you're doing? I know marriage is a compromise but surely this is going a bit far? You should have it all out with him. Now. Before it's too late to change your mind . . .*

## CHAPTER EIGHTEEN

The flowers. Those bloody flowers. Why on earth had he felt compelled to send that enormous bouquet with a card whose too explicit endearments left no room for doubt as to the nature of their attachment? It lay discarded on the coffee table. Bid, tossing and turning restlessly on the sofa, caught sight of it as she rolled over and thought how like a funeral wreath it looked, eerily lit by the yellow sodium street light. She glared at it malevolently. Having kept safely out of sight for a week, why couldn't he have waited for just two more days until she'd sorted things out with her mother? All her careful work was now destroyed; her plans in ruins. She groaned. Still, if not the flowers, surely something else would have set off the crisis. Such a romantic thought, too. Darling Cas. But, oh God, just look at what he'd let her in for. Her mood softened as she passed her hand gently across her queasy stomach. She turned gingerly onto her back and lay quite still, willing the nausea to pass and, for the umpteenth time during that restless night, tried to push away the memory of the pain and hurt she and her mother had inflicted on each other the

271

day before, then shuddered as it all came flooding back.

Mrs Lacey had been sitting rigid and grim-faced on the sofa when Sarah, anticipating the quarrel, had crept away with a bewildered Alice, just as it furiously erupted. Bid had managed to calm the first outburst but the storm followed inevitably as they all knew it would. So much for all her evasive efforts.

Bid had intended going home, as usual, for Christmas but at the last minute Edy Hampshire, finally wearied of her increasingly haphazard attendance at the office, had deftly slotted her in for the last three days of the old year.

'It'll only mean two or three hours each day, dearie. Surely you can manage that?' she'd said blithely, leaving Bid no option but to agree. For once, her mother seemed quite pleased to be asked to spend the holiday in London.

Walking home from church on Christmas morning, Bid, with a combination of seasonal goodwill and guilt brought on by anxiety over her mother's deteriorating health, suggested she prolong her visit over the New Year and was only mildly put out when Mrs Lacey agreed. In a surreptitious pre-dawn phone call next morning she pleaded with Cas to steer clear.

'Just for another few days, darling, promise?'

'Ten days.' He muttered something about some business in America, fussed a little about her pregnancy and suggested, once again, that it was high time she gave up her job. Then to the accompaniment of her stifled giggles, he outlined

272

how he would expect her to restore his deprived libido.

Freed from the anxiety that he might breeze in unexpectedly, Bid gave herself entirely to caring for her mother, fussing and cajoling and working herself up to the main purpose of the visit: coming clean about her relationship with Cas – well not exactly clean – rather a more, er, simplified version. She rehearsed her lines carefully with crossed fingers. Cas was waiting for the divorce to be finalized. As soon as it was they would be married. A matter of weeks. Whether her mother was told about the pregnancy would depend on how she took the first blast.

This at least was the resolution but, fearful that the mere mention of marriage would have her mother demanding when and where, she held back. While Cas still gave no clear word when the divorce might be granted, the possibility of satisfying Mrs Lacey's ecclesiastical ambitions seemed remote. So Bid did what she always did in such circumstances; she dissembled. Each day she promised herself she would come clean, tell her mother about Cas, her pregnancy and their plans, but each day passed without her saying anything to disturb the *status quo*.

The weather had been unexpectedly mild all through Christmas but it was particularly beautiful those first days of January with the early frost disappearing by eleven, leaving the air crisp in the brilliant sunshine. The day before Mrs Lacey was due to go home, Sarah rang to suggest an outing to the Zoo in Regent's Park. Alice had been clamouring to go all through Christmas but Sarah, now in

273

the seventh month of her pregnancy, was reluctant to go alone. Bid agreed for both of them, it seemed a nice harmless end to the holiday and, with Sarah and Alice around, would give her mother no opportunity for close questioning.

The day started happily enough, all of them in good spirits. Mrs Lacey looked pale but insisted she was well enough. If Bid had flunked the true confession, she had at least safely negotiated the ten days without conflict and as a result was feeling more at ease with her mother. Alice was in seventh heaven to have her 'Bideee' to boss about and, with the glint of the utterly ruthless in her eye, she loudly intoned a long list of demands in the firm expectation of having them fulfilled.

And indeed the day continued successful, not even the holiday crowd of marauding children could dampen their spirits. Eventually in mid-afternoon, as they sat in the warmth of the café watching the penguins careering in and out of their pond, Alice fell asleep.

'Want me to get the car?' Bid whispered. Sarah nodded and lazily handed over her keys.

The carpark was quite a long way off and so it was a good twenty minutes before Bid was back to find Sarah and Alice fast asleep and her mother fretful. Somehow they staggered to the car but by then the traffic was bumper to bumper so of course they got stuck, inching along for the next half hour or so. Mrs Lacey seemed to take it all personally and got more and more fidgety and soon Bid began to snap. Sarah tried vainly and tiredly to keep everyone's spirits up, fervently wishing both Laceys to kingdom come. She succeeded for a time until the child, fractious with hunger, began to howl.

'We'll go to my place, it's nearest,' Bid said with surprising firmness, determined to keep her buffer zone in place.

'Oh no, really. I must get Alice home, she's tired,' Sarah protested.

'But I've prepared tea and loads of bangers for you, Alice,' Bid retorted with surprisingly fast footwork. That did it. Sarah was furious at being out-manoeuvred, knowing that Alice, now fully steamed up was going to be a handful.

Bid has developed a genius for stirring up tension, she thought resentfully, before resigning herself to the inevitable.

The flowers were lying resplendently on the doormat and, had Bid not been carrying the little girl, she would have got to them first. Mrs Lacey reached out and casually read the attached card. It was signed C with a flourish. Bid, glimpsing it over her mother's shoulder, blushed scarlet and kept up a relentless patter to divert her attention, but she dropped the key. In the ensuing moment's silence her mother said accusingly:

'I thought you told me you'd given that Colin fellow up?'

Bid pretended not to hear. Alice's spirits had recovered on the promise of sausages and she was irritatingly counting how many she could stuff into her face. Sarah, bringing up the rear, wondered how quickly she might, without causing ructions, make her escape. Enough was enough. All her instincts screamed that there was going to be an almighty row, for the thunder clouds were already gathering on Mrs Lacey's face, who, with the belligerence of a bull terrier in possession of a particularly meaty bone, clung to the flowers, waving them about, ready to throw them once she'd got her target in sight. Sarah prepared to duck.

'I must go to the loo,' she said and fled.

Bid, much more experienced at deflecting her mother, marched blithely kitchen-wards and started slinging the sausages under the grill, at the same time keeping up an incessant sing-song with her demanding goddaughter.

'Don't you dare move, Alice-of-my-heart,' she hissed between breaths and broke into a raucous chorus of Frère Jacques. They both ding-donged feverishly.

Meantime Mrs Lacey stood frozen to the spot. Sarah, creeping from the bathroom, was so startled by her look of pure misery she couldn't simply ignore it. Resignedly, she tiptoed over towards the kitchen and closed the door. Then she went to her friend's mother, took her arm and led her gently to the sofa.

'What's the matter, Mrs Lacey? It's only an old bunch of flowers. Why is it so important?'

'I thought she'd given that fellow up.' She sounded flat and defeated.

'Oh no, I don't think she'll do that. She loves him too much. Besides, she's . . .' She paused uncertainly not knowing what rigmarole Bid had spun, since Mrs Lacey obviously thought Colin was back on the scene.

'What did you say?' Mrs Lacey broke in wildly.

276

'I said, er, Bid loves Cas.'

'Cas?' Mrs Lacey repeated. 'Who's he?'

'Cas Van Rijn,' Sarah repeated shortly. She pronounced the surname with fair approximation of authenticity – Rijn rhyming with rein. Now that Tom's company was getting involved with Dutch projects, Sarah was essaying an earnest course in Dutch language and culture.

Mrs Lacey went even paler. 'What sort of name is that?' Her voice shook. Sarah couldn't make out if it was anger or fury.

'It's Dutch, didn't she tell you?' Sarah cajoled, despising herself.

'Bridget tells me nothing,' Mrs Lacey said shortly. 'What is he?'

'You mean what does he work at? He owns a big development company in Holland. They've a branch here. He's the boss.'

Mrs Lacey said nothing for a moment or two. They both looked at the card. Oh Lord, thought Sarah re-reading it, did he have to be so explicit? So that's what he and Bid were up to! She suppressed a giggle.

Mrs Lacey put the flowers down and clutched Sarah's hand.

'Dutch is he? Do you know him?' she pleaded urgently. 'Is he a Catholic?'

Sarah choked back a nervous titter. 'Good heavens, Mrs Lacey, how would I know?' Observing the woman's misery, she softened her tone. 'He's OK. Nice. Really,' Sarah embroidered, 'you'd like him. Honestly. They're very happy.' She tried to get up but Mrs Lacey tightened her grip.

'Where does he live?'

'London, he goes back and forth to Holland, of course, but he lives in London. Quite near Regent's Park actually. Of course he travels a lot – with his work you know.'

Any minute now she's going to demand to see him.

'Tom works with him. His partner, Stephen, has known him for years.' Sarah stopped short, realizing she'd made a big mistake by drawing attention to Tom's much older partner. Then, without giving Mrs Lacey an opportunity to collect herself, she babbled on: 'He's very attractive. Really nice. Terribly kind to Bid. Very attentive.' What more could she say? She hardly knew the wretched man she was defending. She just didn't want a prolonged discussion of his shaky marital status, or his religion – whatever that might be. Nor had she any idea what form Bid's evasions had taken. Ten to one she was going to drop her in it whatever she said. There was a mad glint of determination in Mrs Lacey's eye. How ridiculous it all was. Sarah fumed with impatience that Bid, who was quite prepared to live with her undivorced lover, hadn't the courage to come clean with her mother.

By now the crescendo from the kitchen had reached fever pitch. Above the noise Mrs Lacey pounced, her voice deceptively calm.

'Tell me, Sarah, how old is he?'

Now what? Was this some trap for Bid? The convolutions of Mrs Lacey's thought processes were difficult to anticipate.

'Er, I've never really thought about it. I really couldn't say. Fortyish?' Sarah kept her tone insouciant.

'Fortyish? Is that more than forty? Or less?'

'A bit more probably. Not much though. I don't really know.'

Sarah suddenly felt very, very tired. Too late, she realized that Mrs Lacey, not unnaturally, had worked out that an attractive man of forty-plus would almost certainly be married. Sarah got clumsily to her feet. Time to collect her daughter and get the hell out. Let them sort this out for themselves, she thought angrily, perhaps they can make sense of all the carry-on. Let them get on with it. She smiled tightly at her friend's mother.

'I've really no idea how old he is. Why not ask Bid?' As Sarah went towards the kitchen Mrs Lacey fired the question she'd wanted to avoid.

'I know why she's been telling lies. He's married, isn't he?' The soft and lethal voice arrested her.

'No!' Sarah swung around in defence of her friend. 'Not any more.'

'Aah. So I was right. I suppose he has a family?' The woman's control was total. Without answering, Sarah turned on her heel and marched into the kitchen.

Alice was sitting contentedly on the counter while Bid scraped tomato ketchup from her face. Sarah grabbed the child and hissed:

'Phew. Your ma's on the frigging warpath. I think I dropped you in it, I'm sorry. She wants to know if he's married. For heaven's sake, Bid, you're so weak-kneed, why on earth didn't you tell her? You're not a child.'

Bid drew in her breath.

'Oh hell.' She looked at Sarah and shrugged. 'I'm an awful coward. I meant to tell her, I really did.'

She shrugged ruefully. 'Look, I'm sorry I got you involved, Sal, I guess it was bound to come sooner or later.' She took Alice by the hand. 'Come and say goodbye to my mother.'

'Will that woman shout?' Two round black eyes looked up at her.

'Certainly not! Come on, darling.'

They smiled their goodbyes nervously and Bid walked them down to the street then, with sinking heart, she climbed the stairs to have it out with her mother.

Mrs Lacey was still sitting on the sofa, pale, strained and lost in thought. Bid steeled herself, but the explosion, when it came, was vicious.

'Are you involved with a married man? Answer me that.'

'No! He's separated, he's getting a divorce.' Bid said sulkily, moving restlessly about the room.

'Getting? Getting? You're interfering in a marriage? My daughter? Ruining some poor woman's life?'

'No! Oh for God's sake, Mam! It's not like that.'

'No? What's it like then? Go on, tell me.'

'Oh what's the point? You wouldn't understand. You wouldn't even try.'

'Whore!' She spat the word. Bid shrank back. 'Slut. Have you forgotten your religion? Forgotten who you are?' her mother screamed.

'No. No. No. Please, Mam, listen to me. We're getting married. You'll be able to come and live with us. I'll be able to look after you. You're not well.' Bid's voice was a pathetic whine. She turned away but was suddenly yanked back by the hair, her mother's contorted face looming over her.

'Us? Us, is it?' she screeched. 'Are you planning to break up a family? God in heaven, Bridget Lacey, get wise to yourself. You think I'd lower myself to live with a blackguard who's cheating on his wife? You can't marry him. You're a Catholic. You can't marry a divorced man. And you're telling me he isn't even divorced. You wouldn't be allowed inside a church. You disgust me. You haven't the sense God gave you. He's playing with you. How can you be so stupid? You're a disgrace, girl.'

'It's not like that! For pity's sake listen to me . . .'

'Does that fella come here? Whoring? Answer me! Does that . . . does that fancy man come here?'

Bid closed her eyes as the tears poured down her face.

'I've been living with Cas for almost a year,' she whispered. 'I love him. Do you hear me? I love him.'

It was the bravest thing she'd ever done. She stood shaking as her mother drew back and, with demonic force, slapped her outstretched hand across her daughter's face. Bid rubbed her stinging cheek and stared at her mother in shocked disbelief.

I'm dreaming this, she thought, I'll wake up in a minute and everything will have calmed down. But it was far from a dream.

'I'm packing my bags. I won't stay here another minute.' Mrs Lacey's tone was glacial. 'I'm ashamed of you, do you hear me? I'm disgusted. You're a lying, scheming, dirty little bitch. Old enough to know better. Love? Love? What would you know about love, you fool? Falling for an adulterous cheat and a liar. Is it because he has money? Look at you. He's got you up like a tart.

I've been wondering where all those expensive clothes came from. You've been allowing him to buy them for you, haven't you? Living off him. Answer me. Haven't you?'

'He loves me.'

'Loves you?' her mother jeered. 'Sure you've never been able to keep a man five minutes. There's been a string of them for years, one worse than the last. You can't hold them. He'll soon be running off with someone else. You mark my words. A year you say? You think he'll leave his family now? For you?' She laughed harshly. 'You've made yourself too cheap. You're a fool, girl. A year you say? Whatever chance you had a year ago, let me tell you, you've none now.'

'Shut up! Shut up!' Bid screamed, stung by her own fear. 'Shut up! Stop it.'

It was her mother's turn to shrink back as Bid, goaded just too far, roused herself to her own defence.

'I'm thirty years of age. Thirty. I'm not a child. I know what I'm doing. You've a goddamn cheek coming in here treating me like a ... like a ... You know nothing whatever about Cas. You're living in the past. We'll get married, don't you worry. And there's nothing, absolutely nothing, you can do to stop it. You've no right. No right to talk to me like that. Do you hear me? I'm not harming anyone.'

'No?' Mrs Lacey suddenly looked old and ill. 'No, no-one but yourself maybe. By the time your man has had enough of you, he'll be on to something younger and you'll be left. Take care you're not left holding the ...' Her hand flew to her mouth. 'Oh Bridget,' she whispered. 'Oh Bridget please, not that. Not you?'

*Touché*. Bid smiled sourly. What a poor sap she was. Tell her ma about the baby? Have a nice cosy chat? She snorted in derision at her own *naïveté*.

'Oh for God's sake, Mam . . .' she skirted the issue tiredly, 'this is the twentieth century. I can take care of myself.'

They glared at each other in unforgiving silence. Mrs Lacey ran her hand through her hair, she looked distraught. By comparison Bid was deathly calm.

'Let me be perfectly clear about one thing. We are getting married. Whether you like it or not. I am quite aware we can't get married in church. We never intended to. A register office will suit us fine,' Bid said firmly, then, relenting slightly, she held out a pleading hand.

'I want you to come. You'll really like him when you meet him. Give us a chance.'

Her mother drew away. 'Bridget Lacey listen to me. You stop all this nonsense. I'll not meet another woman's husband with my daughter, be very sure of that. You take care what you're at. Take care I say, take care someone doesn't do the same to you some day.'

The slanging revived and continued for another exhausting hour. On and on it went, round and round. One vituperative claim begging another, they spat out the pent-up frustration of years. They appalled each other with the range and quality of the hurt they inflicted, realizing as they spoke that there was no going back. This was not a minor quarrel between mother and loving daughter, easy

283

words of regret would not take this pain away, nor the memory of bitterness so wounding that each recoiled from the recollection of it. The endurance of their relationship had depended on their skill at avoiding confrontation; holding back; papering the cracks; keeping things nice. Now, as they stood exposed and crushed, they realized that quarrelling too was a skill and they were no good at it. They had not practised on the nursery slopes and so did not know when to stop, put out a healing hand, soften the blows, share a peace-pipe. So it ended, inevitably, in tears. They retired hurt and silent. Mrs Lacey went off to bed, grim, pale and angry, leaving Bid to toss and turn on the sofa, with an oppressive burden of guilt which sat like a sick load on her stomach. She might have felt better had she realized how overwhelmed her mother was by the hurt she'd done, but Eileen Lacey could neither find the consoling words nor unbend enough to say them. She had spent too many years depending on Fergus's conciliatory skills in her dealings with Bid. And besides, she had her own demons; she was too afraid.

# Grace

MENTEUR, LE: *INTERIOR (with figure) THE COLLECTOR, chiaroscuro wood engraving – 1821 copy of sixteenth-century study, discoloured, edges charred (to falsify age?). Interesting.*

## CHAPTER NINETEEN

Grace was staring impatiently into the tiny enclosed yard below her when she became aware of Livy Hanning watching her from the hallway. As she turned, they appraised each other solemnly. Once again Grace was struck by her appearance. Their eyes met. Nemesis.

'Sarah couldn't stay I'm afraid.'

'Yes. I know. I waited for her to leave.' The mevrouw was quite unabashed. 'She makes me feel ashamed somehow. All this,' the sweep of her arm took in the entire flat, 'all this has left a dreadful trail. I feel so sorry for the poor Roberts, but the young can be so judgemental – don't you think?' Again the despairing gesture with her hands. She threw herself on the sofa and said: 'That dockland development has gone bust of course. It was all quite predictable, but I'm pretty sure the Rawlings-Roberts partnership didn't expect it; they've taken rather a dive. Foolish of them to have put all their eggs into that particular basket.'

Her next remark took Grace by surprise.

'Sarah mentioned that you are trying to find out why the girl killed herself?'

'Yes.'

'She told me something of your,' she searched for the *mot juste*, 'er, estrangement with your family. It was all a little confused, I'm afraid I make her rather nervous. Do I gather you never actually met your niece?' She enunciated with great precision and an almost too perfect command of English. It was this which subtly marked her as foreign. Save for a thickening of her s's, her accent was almost undetectable. She looked around the room with distaste and added half to herself, 'There are many things about all this that I, too, would like, er, cleared up.'

Then Livy Hanning spoke the words Grace had been working herself up to say.

'Mrs Hartfield, I wonder if you and I might not talk together?' She held out a small package she was carrying. 'I took the liberty of picking up a couple of sandwiches. You must be hungry.' Her calm impassive features were completely transformed by her smile.

'Thanks, a sandwich would be welcome,' Grace said. 'And it would be a great relief to talk.'

The older woman put the sandwiches on the coffee table and held out her hand.

'Call me Livy,' she said and pointed to the stack of pictures on the floor. 'I see you haven't sorted the paintings.' She sounded surprised. 'Will you do so while I find something to drink? Tell me what you think of them.' And, without waiting for an answer, she disappeared into the kitchen, leaving Grace preoccupied with the problem of how to tackle this unpredictable, if unexpectedly likeable woman about why she had delayed so long over the divorce. Why she had held out, unyielding, for the year her husband was shacked up with Bid? While he got her pregnant? And most of all why, if she'd hung on so hard, did she appear so detached, in control? Unresentful?

Grace turned the pictures one by one. There were six small and one large watercolour and each was signed by a name so famous that she could only gasp: female studies by Kokoschka and Nicholson, a tiny Matisse of a charming plump reclining figure, landscapes from Brabazon, Nolde, Van de Velde and Mauve. This last was a deceptively simple study of a flock of sheep, but more than any of the others, it held her enraptured. No sentiment, just a chubby group, hell-bent on squeezing through a farmyard gate, yet so alive did it seem that she could almost see the shepherd and dogs edging their charges to safety.

'Anton Mauve, he taught Van Gogh. Where do you think the shepherd's standing?' Livy's amused question fitted Grace's thoughts so exactly that she laughed and pointed to a spot well beyond the picture frame.

'Splendid, isn't it? I never tire of looking at it.' She was carrying a couple of glasses and a bottle of Bollinger. 'It's tepid I'm afraid, but there's nothing else. This place is quite unbelievable.'

'You know it then?' Grace touched the painting lightly.

'Oh indeed,' she said casually. 'We've had it for years.' With a stroke she re-aligned herself with her husband, then laughed as if to ease the sting. 'If you knew him you'd say that sheep would be the last thing to appeal to him.'

'Why is it here?'

'Ah that. When he took that away I knew he was serious about, er, about . . .'

'Bridget. Bid, if you like,' Grace said firmly. 'I think it will be easier if we name her.'

'Bridget, then.' Livy poured the champagne and passed the sandwiches. 'But I don't have to like her,' she added emphatically. 'She destroyed the equilibrium of my life. All that nonsense about divorce.'

'It was deadly earnest to her,' Grace said drily. 'And you didn't give in.'

'That is not true.' Livy almost threw away the words, and so casually that Grace thought she'd misheard but, before she could question her, Livy slid a folded sheet of paper across the coffee table.

On the headed notepaper of Hanning-Van Rijn b.v. was a signed deed of gift for seven small watercolours, dated December 17th 1989, to Bridget Kate Lacey from her lover. Grace looked up and met Livy's eyes.

'*Hanning*-Van Rijn? You are the senior partner?'

'In a sense, yes. My grandfather founded the firm.'

The significance of that piece of information was not lost on Grace, but she stored it away without comment and turned her attention back to the deed of gift. It was marked 'copy' on the top left hand corner. The sheep were not included. Grace sipped her wine while she contemplated the generosity of the gift and its significance.

'Two are missing, I'm afraid.' Livy's finger ran up the page to Brabazon, HH.

'They're in her flat,' Grace said promptly, 'in Everard Street. I'll return them, of course.'

'Why on earth should you? They don't belong to me. As you can see, he gave them to her. When her pregnancy was confirmed,' she added drily. 'I thought it might convince you how much he wanted the child. It certainly seems to have convinced her.'

'You knew about the pregnancy? He told you?'

'Yes. He told me most things. He was overjoyed about the child.' A slight touch of sarcasm, carefully controlled.

'But he didn't intend to marry her?' Grace asked slowly.

'I understood that by that stage he was utterly determined upon it.'

'As soon as the divorce came through?'

'Ye-es.'

'Yes? Then forgive my asking, but what stage had you got to?'

'With the divorce?'

'Yes.' Grace could barely keep the impatience from her voice. Livy Hanning kept her preoccupied gaze on the middle distance for some moments before facing Grace.

'The divorce had nothing to do with me, Mrs Hartfield,' she said calmly. 'Cas and I were not formally married.' As she lobbed her bombshell she smiled ruefully and shrugged with that elegant gesture Grace was becoming familiar with. 'But when you live in a society as rigid as ours you learn to practise subterfuge. People make their own assumptions.' She sat back and pursed her lips.

'You mean he was not married at all?' Christ, she thought, what was the man playing at?

'No, I don't mean that.'

'Then what?' She gasped, almost submerged.

Livy sighed. 'I said formally. He was once briefly married but was already separated when we met; I was a widow. We were together eighteen years and we certainly considered ourselves partners – married if you like – and not just in business.' She left the words hanging and watched Grace with interest but offered no help as she grappled with the implication of the revelation.

'Separated but not divorced?'

'That's right. She walked out on him.'

'Did she not want a divorce?'

'How would I know? We didn't discuss it. It was in the past and I certainly didn't feel it was relevant. I'm just telling you – he did not need a divorce from me.'

'So he could have married Bid?'

'I assume so. Unless there were some, ah, legal difficulties. Though I cannot see how, after all this time, can you? She disappeared so long ago.'

'So he was stalling? How cruel.' The words tumbled out unchecked. Livy held up her hand.

'Cruel to her?' She neatly sidestepped the issue and Grace intuitively felt that she had missed something, that her question was being skilfully deflected. She only half listened as Livy continued. 'Forgive me, but I feel limited sympathy for your niece. I was more concerned for my family and our business. It was a great upset.'

'But if you and he were not married, why the delay?' Grace persisted.

'Ah that.' Livy looked as if she might say more but did not. After another contemplative pause she took a different tack and Grace felt that she had laid candour aside and was now merely repeating a well-rehearsed line.

'Until the baby, he could procrastinate with impunity. I would not have willingly separated from him. Perhaps he used my intransigence to explain his inertia to your niece?' A certain relish crept into her voice. 'I wonder if she realized how very important the business was to him – to both of us? And how long it would take to dismantle?'

For some moments Grace contemplated the havoc the relationship had caused. She set the Dutch family and business against the predicament Bid had found herself in. No matter how she felt about the girl, the child, and the crass desire of a middle-aged man to flex his virility, all her instincts cried out in sympathy for Livy, her own mirror image – except for the family of course – and she found it salutary that not even the sons or the business had weighed against the vagaries of the male menopause. Looking at the mature beauty of the other woman, she recognized that they were kindred spirits and knew for certain that she'd lost Reggie for good.

'Did he tell Bid about your, er, arrangement?' It was a foolish question but Grace had suddenly lost her appetite for sleuthing. The similarities between this marital – or non-marital – tangle and her own were altogether too uncomfortable.

'I have no idea. I assume so, eventually. I was in the States for almost a month before he died. We

293

talked on the phone but we didn't meet,' Livy said sadly. 'He seemed preoccupied.'

'Poor Bid. She killed herself for a philanderer. Your rules were too sophisticated for her.'

'Oh come now. She wasn't a child, you know,' Livy answered blandly. 'I think she knew very well what she was doing. He was a very rich man, besides being very charming.' She hesitated. 'I find all this very awkward, none of it is very attractive and some things sound rather more shameful when one is asked to explain them. Don't you find?'

'The things you aren't telling me?'

'Probably. Yes. I don't believe they're relevant.' Another long silence. 'We were together a long time. It was not, perhaps, a conventional relationship. Cas needed certain, ah, freedoms. As did I.' Livy chose each word with care. 'I miss him. He had many fine qualities. He had exceptional talent in business. He was loyal. He was kind – don't look so sceptical – and very thoughtful.' She emphasized the words, then shrugged and added drily: 'There were some, er, personal difficulties . . . but our life suited us, suited Cas.'

'Someone should have told her.'

'I expect they should. But what makes you so sure she didn't know all about him?' Livy's voice was sharp with impatience. 'Could she have been that naïve?'

Grace gestured despairingly, knowing she'd made blinder assumptions herself. Her answer was tight-lipped.

'Yes, she could. How do I know? Because I'm in a not dissimilar position myself and I do not consider myself either stupid or naïve. You see what you want to see.' She looked straight at Livy. 'Don't you find?' They eyed each other warily.

'Yes. Yes, I'm afraid I do. I thought I knew everything, but clearly I did not.'

'What about your children?' Grace spoke more gently.

'Hardly children. They are in their early twenties. They both study in America. I live alone now. But then I have done ever since Cas set up the office here. And on and off before that. As I said, we are, were, both rather independent. I've been involved with the business all my life.'

'When did you begin to feel threatened by the affair with my niece?'

'At first I wasn't, I didn't think it would last. I expected it to run its course and end. That is what usually happened. He was not notably a one-girl man. You must understand, Cas and I were friends. We had an understanding that worked. Within limits, that is. Her pregnancy was the limit. He became obsessed with the idea of the child. That's when he first talked seriously about separation. It was a shock. The middle-aged man charmed with the idea of a second chance? Such a cliché. But at the last moment he seems to have lacked courage.'

'To leave you?'

'Yes, that too,' Livy Hanning answered evasively. 'What one has, one tends to hold on to. We had a good life. There was joint property and of course the company. It was complicated.'

'To put it mildly,' Grace said laconically. The irritating feeling persisted that she had missed something, that she hadn't quite grasped the significance of one, or perhaps several, clues the other woman had almost but not quite laid down. She felt thoroughly confused, not least because her instinctive rapport with Livy Hanning made her feel disloyal to Bid.

Lies lies lies. The girl's last cry began to make horrible sense. Had he, at the last, told her he could not go through with it? Had he told her that it was not Livy who was holding things up? Or had he, Grace wondered guiltily, thinking of her own marital turmoil, had he simply let things drift, strung her along, unconsciously feeding her his usual line until it was impossible to unravel what would, when he tried to explain it, look like a pack of deliberate lies? When had she found out that the divorce was a red herring?

'I wonder when she found out? About the earlier marriage? And if it's important?' Grace voiced her thoughts. For a long moment there was no reaction from the Dutch woman, except that she stood up and brushed imaginary crumbs from her skirt.

'I wonder? I'm not sure if it was at all relevant, or even if he intended doing anything about it. It was so long ago.' She spoke carefully. 'Cas was not a vicious man, whatever you think. He loved your niece, he would avoid hurting her. When he died I was angry with her, furious at the frightful waste of it. I did not resent him living with the girl, but I must tell you I very much resented him throwing away his life for her.'

'It was suicide, then?'

'Pretty certainly it seems. There were witnesses. Two little boys – seven- or eight-year-olds – saw him go into the water. The police let me talk to them. The way they told it, it rang true somehow.

They said he'd been drinking and the autopsy confirmed that. That surprised me but I think we must accept it.'

'You knew she lived nearby?'

'Yes. But the children insisted he was quite alone. She was not with him. They did not mention her. And the police were punctilious about not prompting them.' Livy looked up at Grace's relieved sigh but she continued talking. 'It's all so very strange. You see I wasn't surprised he'd gone to Dublin. We had recently bought a slice of the old docklands there. Our Amsterdam team was dealing with it, but a couple of weeks before I'd asked Cas to look into one or two irregularities for me. I had not known your niece was Irish. Ironic.'

It was not clear what she found ironic – the coincidence of the business branching out to Ireland, the irregularities she'd referred to, or the nationality of her rival.

'But when I was there I discovered that he had not contacted anyone about the docks. So I have to believe he went over for some other reason. Perhaps to see her, to be with her after her mother died. That would be like him,' she finished.

'There seems to be a large question mark over that.' Grace hesitated. 'It appears he did not contact her either. Several of her friends claim she was still looking for him the day before she killed herself. Had he threatened to leave her, do you know?'

'No, he wouldn't do that. I believe at the end he had fallen in love with your niece. She was giving him what he most wanted. He took the child very seriously.' She watched Grace closely.

'Why was that, particularly?' Grace asked softly.

'You don't have children?'

'No.' Grace's face flamed.

'Forgive me, from choice?'

'No.'

'Then perhaps you will not find it hard to understand how much he wanted one. Cas and I didn't have children together. My sons are from my first marriage.'

'Ah. So this child was very important to him.'

'Yes. Poor Cas worried about his virility rather a lot.' She delivered the shaft gently but it felt like a slap in the face. Grace closed her eyes against it for an instant and when she opened them Livy's expression was witness to the unconsciousness of the barb.

'I beg your pardon, that was quite unforgivable. I am overwrought.'

'Perhaps we both are.' Grace held out her hand. It was time to leave.

Livy Hanning grasped it for a moment, then said earnestly:

'Mrs Hartfield, Grace. I really want to know why my partner died. I care about what happened to him. Tell me, have you any idea why the girl killed herself?'

'No, I'm afraid I do not. Not yet at any rate,' Grace answered dubiously. 'No one thing seems important enough, you know? It may have been a concatenation of things: depression about Cas dawdling over marrying her and the uncertainty of her position. Guilt about her lousy relationship with her mother which, of course, would have been magnified by her sudden death. And if, as I suspect, she hadn't found courage to tell her mother about the baby . . . Well,' Grace sighed, 'that seems plenty to be going on with.'

'Were there also problems within your own family which might have been a contributing factor?' Livy countered quietly. Grace held her glance for a moment. Their mutual suspicion had softened to concern.

'*Touché*. I honestly don't know, but yes, I'm afraid there might. Which is why I'm trying to unravel that end of things. It's not easy.' She hesitated in the face of Livy's expectation before deciding not to elaborate. Because she was certain that the other woman was also holding back, she felt she needed to work out, privately, what was relevant and what she might share.

They fell silent then. Since neither seemed able to unbend any further, it was clear that the conversation had come to an end. Almost in unison they stood and began to make their farewells. As Livy opened the door Grace touched her arm.

'Forgive me for being so persistent,' she asked hesitantly, 'but can you tell me why he delayed so long about marrying her? Somehow I have a feeling that that is, at least partly, at the root of it.'

'I'm not sure I understand your meaning. You seem to have the idea that he kept her waiting for months? A year? She may have thought that, she may even have told her friends that, but I'd be very surprised if Cas had promised any such thing. It wasn't really all that long you know, not if you consider that he only made up his mind around December. I allow that he seems to have delayed at the end. We had pretty well sorted everything out between us, business-wise, by the beginning of

March. That left over a month. Perhaps it was simply that they had no time? She was going back and forth to her mother . . .'

'Yes. But from what her friends say, if asked, she would have found the time. The general impression seems to be that it was Cas who delayed.'

Livy shook her head in apparent perplexity. 'I need to think. I understood they were to be married at the beginning of April.' She grimaced ruefully and bit her lip. 'It might help if I find out exactly when and why he went to Dublin. I am going back to the office now. I'll have a search through his papers. There may be something to throw some light on the problem. And I'll talk to his secretary, though there's a slight difficulty there; she was down with flu when he disappeared.'

As they left the flat, Livy Hanning glanced about. 'I hate this sordid flat,' she said.

Grace had a last thought. 'Was Cas short for something?'

Livy threw back her head and laughed for the first time that afternoon. 'Oh yes indeed. It was my nickname for him.' She cocked an eyebrow and laughed again. 'But I don't need to explain it, do I? I guess you'll be able to work it out for yourself.'

After they parted, Grace set out for Everard Square again.

300

## CHAPTER TWENTY

No wonder the girl caved in, Grace reflected, as she turned the key to Bid Lacey's door. Rows, lies, pregnant, unmarried, no sign of a divorce and no doubt a whole host of nasty skeletons in the Dutch cupboard. And perhaps a couple in the Irish cupboard as well. Every time someone imparted information it only added to the picture of pervading gloom. If she had been truly so ignorant of her lover's background, then she was either entirely stupid or, because she was besotted, completely trusting. Whichever it was had the effect of isolating her from friends and contemporaries. Then there was the added oppression of her difficult, sulky mother, made more demanding by deteriorating health, just at the point when Bid had, by all accounts, finally worked herself up to coming clean about her pregnancy. And having funked it, her mother's death must have left the girl totally isolated in her guilt.

When had she begun to have doubts about her shadowy lover, on whom it was impossible to get a fix? With his tangled domestic life, his evasions. What exactly had held her? At best he was a pretty sordid involvement for a young woman, at worst downright dangerous. To put it brutally, there seemed as much reason for her to kill herself as not.

He remained an enigma. What had first attracted him to Bid? On the face of it that seemed the most mysterious thing of all: for she hardly seemed his type, being relatively unsophisticated and, when they first met, apparently not at all concerned with her appearance. And one look at the mews was enough to know that appearance counted for a great deal with Cas Van Rijn. The elegant Livy, too, was witness to that. Nor could it have been simply Bid's youth, for surely there must have been others, younger, more compliant? Bid, after all, was pushing thirty when they met. Had he just been flattered by her infatuation? On that score, at least, all were agreed: she was potty about him.

Rich, powerful, mysterious and sexy; he must have been extremely plausible or else Bid had been hopelessly credulous. Was she one of those women who are dazzled by a hint of danger? He certainly seemed to be able to haul the women in, yet Livy, who was nobody's fool, obviously liked and enjoyed him. She'd said he was kind. That description had almost scuppered Grace's preconceived notions of him. She wondered what other nuggets Livy had held back.

A note from Bradley Moffat had been pushed under Bid's door.

*Dear Grace Hartfield, I am sorry that the coincidence which brought you to our neck of the woods should have been such a sad one. I think Angel will already have assured you of our affection for your niece. I hope her death has not been too traumatic for you.*

The house was entirely empty and, apart from the buzz of traffic and the sharply creaking floorboards, the flat was morbidly silent. Pausing momentarily by the bookshelves, Grace was again struck by the homely pleasant room and thought how much more attractive it was than the mews. On impulse she wandered in and drew her hand idly along the worn spines, pausing every now and then – more from habit than anything else – to jot down a title. Perhaps it was then, as she stood surrounded by the girl's books, that Grace realized how similar they were and for an instant had a fleeting recognition of the anxieties which had forged that uncertain personality.

She might have been exasperated by her, but she would have loved her niece, she was sure of that. As she made her way up the flight of stairs to the bedroom she felt choked with rage at the wanton waste of her young life. To find out why Bid had done away with herself seemed the least tribute she could make. But even as she renewed her silent vow, the troublesome little voice in her head told her she was only doing it because the girl's death might hold the key to her own muddled emotional life.

Some time during that last visit Bid, too, must have climbed the stairs. Had she already made up her mind to kill herself then? Did every tread bring her nearer to that fateful decision? Suddenly Grace stopped short, asking herself why Bid had come here, like a wounded animal, back to her own private place and not to the flat she had shared with her lover? Somewhere within its confines she must have left some clue.

Had she known he was already dead? No! Unaccountably Grace clung to her instinct that she had not. Sarah claimed that Bid was still looking for him that Sunday. Odd that she assumed the telephone call was from Dublin. Had Bid said so? Was she giving herself an alibi? Surely there would have been no point in alibis if she was already intent on killing herself?

Sarah said Bid sounded frantic, as if she thought he'd had an accident. But wasn't that the sort of thing everyone thinks when a loved one is unaccountably absent? As a reaction it only gained significance in the light of their deaths. Normal enough for her to want him by her after her mother's death, even if they'd had a lover's tiff.

Assume then that she didn't know Van Rijn was dead. If she hadn't seen him, or quarrelled with him, or threatened him. Assume ... assume she didn't even know he was in Dublin.

Then who or what had caused his death? Why? And more to the point, what was the connection with Bid's subsequent suicide? Against all the odds, Grace believed that Bid was telling the truth when she'd told her friends that she hadn't seen him, but she couldn't explain that certainty even to herself.

Why hadn't someone talked her out of it? Why didn't she seek help? She could have tapped on the door of that motherly soul below, so aptly named and only too willing to be her guardian angel. Why hadn't she? She could have walked the short distance to her friend Sarah. What had happened to her during those vital days besides her mother's death? – an event which couldn't really have been that unexpected. Both Sarah and Roy Angel had claimed that Eileen Lacey had been ill for months and the airline tickets vouchsafed that Bid had watched the deterioration of her mother in the weeks before she died.

If not the knowledge of her lover's death, then what? What had happened to her in Dublin which propelled her on that strange journey north that Monday morning? And back to the empty flat the night before? Had she simply wanted to be alone to mourn? Or – the thought slowly formed and took shape – had something happened on that Sunday night, *when* she got back?

Grace walked deliberately towards the bedroom and stood at the doorway imagining her way into the girl's distracted mind, reworking her actions of that night. The room was papered in a busy blue and white Laura Ashley print. Small and sparsely furnished, it contained a roughly made-up bed, wardrobe, a small chest of drawers, a makeshift bedside table of planks and bricks. There were a couple of discoloured, dog-eared Giacometti posters on the walls. The room had an indefinable appearance of having seen too little human activity. Even granted that the flat had been empty for six months since its owner's death, it felt forlorn and neglected.

A skirt and blouse lay discarded on a wicker chair near the wardrobe. The skirt was the dark olive match of the jacket hanging in the kitchen and, when Grace picked it up, it gave off the same dulled perfume. Even before she touched the pale green blouse lying underneath, she could see it had been worn too long, along the edge of cuffs and neck ran a thin dark grease-mark. It was bunched with an expensive cream silk camisole and a laddered pair of tights obscuring a battered black leather handbag.

Grace opened it gingerly, releasing a musty scent of old face powder. The contents of a worn red wallet identified it as the property of EA Lacey. It was jam-packed with the usual inconsequentials of daily use which she ran through quickly: keys, wallet, bunch of receipts, cheque book. She laid each item on the bed as she removed it. An empty pale blue envelope with 'Bridget' scrawled across the front came next, scrunched together with a muddle of Kleenex and old bus tickets.

Grace held the envelope in her hand and cast about her. The bottom drawer of the chest had been shoved crookedly home and was now stuck slightly open on one side. She pulled at it but something solid had locked hard against the upper drawer. It yielded after a few minutes of alternate pushing and pulling.

It had been jammed by a large cardboard envelope with a Paris postmark dated April 1989, containing a proof sheet and a set of five colour photographs, each showing the girl from a different angle. The new made-over Bid. Arranging them in a line on the bed, Grace studied them greedily, and immediately the girl sprang to life, smiling up at her and she knew that if she'd come across them earlier she'd never have wondered why the Dutchman had fallen for her. One look was enough to understand why she'd appealed to the collector in him, for she was vibrant, with quite extraordinary marmalade eyes and flawless skin. Not conventionally lovely, the mouth was too wide and her teeth slightly crooked, but these only accentuated that wickedly sensual smile. She looked as if she was enjoying a joke – or about to fall into bed. Her hair was like glistening copper and cut short – the Paris hairdo? No wonder he prized her.

But then, as Grace absently rearranged the photos in a semicircle, she was startled by the memory of the little Matisse sketch in the Dutchman's flat and the sudden realization that, in attitude, Bid was its double. In two of the pictures she'd been similarly posed. Sickened, she slowly gathered up the pictures, crooning small consolations to the girl, scolding her softly for destroying herself, vowing to ... to ... what? Give her rest? Justify that dreadful end? To Grace's grief was now added the desolation of that lost beauty and humour and companionship. She slipped the pictures back in the envelope and set them aside.

The open drawer was stuffed full of typed and discoloured A4 sheets, held in disparate gatherings by rubber bands. A brief glance disclosed that each had at least one, and in some cases several, reject slips attached. None was dated later than 1986. Bid Lacey's trousseau of disappointments.

Working upwards, two of the three remaining drawers contained only small and discoloured remnants of underwear which looked as if they had lain undisturbed for a considerable time. The topmost drawer had not been pushed completely home and opened jerkily. It was full of worn tights and scarves and mismatched gloves. Grace ran her fingers through the jumble and dislodged an envelope lying vertically against the front panel, as if it had fallen unnoticed into the open drawer. Pale blue Basildon Bond with 'Bridget' scrawled across the front. It, too, was empty. Two envelopes, no letters. No letters. Grace's pulse quickened. She stood still, breathing rapidly, forcing herself to think calmly. Where were the letters?

She went to the door and mimicked Bid walking into the bedroom, the bag in her hand, sitting wearily on the bed, opening it, finding the letter, reading it. She looked around the room. Her eye fell on the skirt still rumpled up on the chair. At first her trembling fingers missed the semi-concealed pockets whose opening lay along the waistband, but, as she flung the skirt down, she felt the extra stiffness of the paper.

Trying to control the sickening lurch of her heart, she slowly read the mother's leave-taking of her daughter, apparently written the night before she went into hospital for the last time.

Her first thought was relief that the relationship between mother and daughter had been described so inaccurately. For if there had been difficulties, Eileen had taken her leave with dignity and affection on a single closely written sheet, both sides entirely covered by the cramped hand. As she read, Grace felt her first tinge of regret for her dead sister.

*Toronto Tce. March 14*

*Dearest Bridget,*
    *They've just telephoned from the hospital. I'm*

*to go in tomorrow. Until this moment I was frightened, now I feel calm. Please God everything will be all right and I'll get better . . .*

The letter was filled with praise of her daughter's care and support over the previous months. She told her how proud Fergus was of her and that it was the loss of him that had made her anxious and lonely.

*I know things haven't been so easy with us recently.* This was followed by a sort of apology: *I should have shown more confidence in you . . .*

She even gave her tacit blessing . . . *whatever you want to do, wherever you want to settle, I know you'll never do anything to be ashamed of . . .*

*Love, Mam.*

Grace slowly sat back on her heels absently stroking the paper. She re-read the lines wondering if it was just the fear of the operation which had made the endearments so stilted. Something felt wrong. She compared the two envelopes. They were identical. As she searched for the missing letter she jerked open the drawers again, going through them more methodically. Nothing. Then, more urgently, she pulled away the pillows and bed-cover, again nothing. Under the bed? She dropped on her hands and knees and tried to shift the heavy divan, but the legs had been sawn through to make it sit low on the floor and it was impossible to either shift or get her hand in under it.

Could it be in some other pocket? She tore open the wardrobe and one by one went through the stale and limp clothes. She scrambled among the dusty shoes thrown haphazardly at the bottom. As she did so, a large, loud bluebottle escaped and dambusted its way across her face. She swiped, missed, then chased it across the room. It landed on the rickety bedside table. She cautiously crept towards it and, grabbing a magazine from the undershelf, she pole-axed it in one, scattering bricks and planks both, then crept on her hands and knees to pick up the debris.

A rolled-up ball of blue notepaper lay against the skirting board; her hand brushed it as she leaned over to pick up a slim volume of poetry which lay beside it. She straightened, then still kneeling, smoothed out the torn sheets of writing paper, ironing them with the side of her hand. Neither was complete, one torn roughly across the middle, the other was just a scrap. With shaking hands she drew the first letter to her and compared the writing. Eerily, the opening of each letter was precisely the same.

*Toronto Tce. March 21*

*Dearest Bridget,*

*They've just telephoned from the hospital. I'm to go in tomorrow. Until this moment I was frightened, now I feel calm . . .*

She turned the page.

*. . . talked to Father Crowley and he said he would give you this and talk to you. We had to get away because there was terrible trouble when my father found out. I was never able to go back . . .*

Grace's head crashed, split, disintegrated; she

rocked to and fro. Father Crowley. The silence in the room was heart-stopping as she turned fearfully to the second page.

> . . . *expecting when I met Fergus. He was very good about it. We got married as soon as we could after you were born. No-one ever doubted*

There was nothing on the reverse, Grace read and re-read the last disjointed phrases. What came next? What had she gone on to say? It made no sense.

If Eileen had given an explanation of what they had not told their daughter long since, it had been expunged. By Bid? Conceived out of wedlock? A pathetic little phrase and of so little importance. Unless of course, Grace felt her way carefully, the girl already was consumed with fear at being in the same position? It all seemed pitifully old-fashioned.

So Eileen had known or guessed about Bid's pregnancy after all. Was it resentment or stupidity which led her to disclose her secret after being silent for so long? Time had magnified the distorted sense of the shame and guilt she comprehensively dumped on her daughter, pregnant, uncertain and at her most vulnerable. Mother and daughter with that one thing in common and all it brought was rancour and tragedy. Grace could picture the girl's fury as she tore the letter and flung it from her.

Both letters had that same date, the same opening. Had Eileen written them the same night and then suppressed one from fear or cowardice or indecision? Letting fate take its course? Had the second letter lain forgotten for Bid to find when she got back home, caught off-guard, as she went through the bits and pieces in her mother's bag?

Grace stared down at the crumpled remnants and knew beyond doubt that whatever had been disclosed on the missing pages had driven the girl out of her mind. She slowly sank back on her heels and began to count backwards. Had there been another child? Her revulsion for her dead sister almost choked her. Even in those truncated pages Eileen Lacey had not told the truth. The dates were wrong. She had missed out something. Bid was rising thirty-one when she died. Born in 1959. But Eileen had disappeared in '56 or '57. Grace rocked to and fro trying to put form to her own, connected, elusive dread and at last, sobbing with frustration and grief, she bent over the bed with her head in her arms and in the silence her own fears metastasized.

*Dada? Dada, don't kill her. Dada. The lashing rain. Someone at the window. Banging, banging. Not Dada! Someone else. Coming in! Who's that?*

This time it wasn't a dream. Grace buried her head deeper into the bedclothes as a sudden downpour beat against the window, matching the sound of her nightmare. She stared into the past, willing herself back. She could almost make out the shadowy figures.

*The child stands silently in the middle of the room watching. In the far corner of the room, on the bed, the great black thing eerily writhes. She has seen it before. It comes at night, just as she goes to sleep. She can hear the catch on the window clicking back. Then a sound, a stifled giggle, creaking springs. The rain is pelting down. The wet curtain flaps against the window. The sound of rushing water. The child creeps forward and begins* to *whimper. A face turns slowly towards her. Her sister's face! Something looms over her. It rises and, oh horror . . . The child screams. It crashes down on top of her, pressing on her mouth. Suddenly there is noise everywhere.*

*'For God's sake . . . she'll tell . . . she'll get us kilt. Stop her! Stop her!'*

*'Pull him off! Pull. Dada! I can't breathe. Don't, Dada, don't kill . . . Dadaaa!'*

Grace rocked back and forth, her eyes scrooged up tight, willing herself not to shut the images out. She re-rolls the grainy film of her memory until at last she began to understand: she was not a participant, she was the spectator. They said they'd kill her if she told Dada. Grace pressed her head to the crumpled counterpane, forcing the swirling, terrifying images to clarify. Her sister and a boy. Eileen and . . . and . . . No-name. Eileen pinched her arm, laughed and said he was called No-name. He'd been there before. Coming in the window. Whispering and laughing in the dark. She'd been moved to Eileen's room when Grandma Nonie came to nurse their sick mother. Eileen furiously shouting, calling her a little brat. But what of Dada?

*Nonie dragging her towards the bed, holding her. Hush hush alannah. Nobody touched you. Dada with the torch leaning out the window shouting. His face wet, his grey hair dripping with the rain pouring off the gutter.*

*Where was Eileen? Between them! Standing between them, her nightie torn away from her shoulders, screaming. What? Screaming 'no, Dada, no he didn't touch her . . .' Dada on the floor . . .*

*blood in his white hair . . . Nonie's hand over her eyes . . .*

Grace squeezed her eyes shut, forcing her memory where it would not go, until at last the mirage faded, almost, but not quite resolved. She lay whimpering softly in the gloom until at last her fear was obliterated by a deep sense of waste and loss. She rose wearily, wishing fervently that she had kept out of the Lacey affairs, left things severely alone, as her sister had clearly intended for all those years. Now she too was being eaten up; no longer able to push her own memories aside. Her recurring terror was growing with the realization that understanding was just within her grasp.

The rain cleared but the light was failing, and without electricity she could do no more in the flat, even if she could bear to stay. She picked up the bag and compulsively went through it once again. This time from among the jumbled Kleenex and bus tickets she found a scrunched up scrap of newspaper she had previously missed. As she opened it out, a vaguely familiar image was disclosed. It was a poor reproduction in black and white, the caption: *Today London, Tomorrow Dublin?* The hair on the back of her neck bristled. She leaned against the cool pane and forced herself to breathe slowly. She had seen that photograph before, in colour. The Dutchman, his faintly ridiculous helmet askew, his eyes squinting from the strong sunlight, smiled jauntily up at her. She stared at him for a long time until at last she began to pick up the things she'd scattered on the floor.

She walked to the door, turned and glanced back.

The room, in the soft fading light, looked appealing, the calm repository of Bid's despair and now her own catharsis. Their lives were like strands of the same rope, played out by each generation. Hoist by half-truths, told or perceived, both so pathetically similar in their fear of confrontation. For Bid it had meant tragedy. But Grace had been luckier: it wasn't yet too late for a reprieve.

Her questions about Bid's untimely death had so far yielded more answers to her own life, to the puzzles that had so benighted her marriage to Reggie, than to the causes of the girl's own suicide. To them, as to so much else, Eileen's story was the key and the person who knew most about that was the person whose name filtered through at every turn: the priest.

She could no longer put off seeing him. She stood quietly in the half-light gathering courage to go those final steps towards her own recovery.

**MY LADY:** *A TALE OF MODERN LIFE. A new edition. 1862 Smith Elder. Binding semi-detached, some childish scribbling.*

## CHAPTER TWENTY-ONE

King's Cross was closed by a bomb scare, and it was well after nine by the time Grace walked the distance to the tube station at Russell Square. As she trudged along, she wearily turned over each little bit of information the day had yielded, conceding that her questions about Bid were only other versions of the questions she had at last begun to ask about herself. And, having framed the questions, it only needed a determined burst of courage to stretch towards the answers. It was time to stop dithering, time to cut loose.

She sat in the almost deserted carriage planning her next move, ironically marvelling at her new-found skill in compartmentalizing the two main preoccupations of her life. She determined, for the next twenty hours or so, to keep the Lacey file firmly shut while she faced her own future and released Reginald Staveley Hartfield to live his semi-detached life with another.

It only struck her as she left the tube station at Ealing Broadway that her anger at Reggie had eased. She no longer wondered what he was up to; she knew. It was as if all the time she was concentrating on Bid, Eileen and her own night-terrors, her part in the break-up of her marriage had been subliminally admitted.

The aching hurt of Reggie's betrayal remained, informing her every familiar move. Her own obstinate unwillingness to perceive the obvious burnt through her with a pain that did not lessen with reminder. He had accused her of being wrapped up in a cocoon. Had he wanted to console himself or her with that carefully chosen harmless-sounding word? Why had he not shocked her into reality with more brutal, more truthful, descriptions of the travesty their life had become?

Each time she walked the familiar leafy suburban streets she saw him, in every park, hailing her across every street. After he left, in the beginning, she expected him at every turn. Each day she'd hoped he would shamble in, take her in his bear-like embrace and soothe away her fears. She couldn't tell now what day or hour she had begun to accept that their life hadn't been a life together but a fragmentation of hope and love. The sexual comfort which had been such a revelation at the beginning only temporarily disguised the monstrous demands she made on his unswerving loyalty and affection. She had closed her eyes and shut out reality, then forced him to do the same in a complicity which blindly destroyed both past and future.

How many nights had he listened to her crying silently after attempted coupling which grew more painful as their desperation grew? When headache, miscarriage, cold or fever was not enough to dull his despair at not being able to move her? When had love became submerged in that ill-fated, repeated urge for procreation?

Desperation had driven their sexuality. When they could not work out their difficulties, she had taken comfort once, briefly and disastrously, where she deemed it would do least harm and knew, or thought she knew, he did the same, so wrapped up in her own self-protection she had not noticed that Reggie was still driven by his need for children; he had not stopped at one or two.

For twenty-two years they had been together. How had they managed, through the increasing pain, to present so united a front? Their public act had, from practice, been honed to a perfection which in the end had almost fooled themselves. Reggie and Grace: the great social success. What party, what outing, what rave-up would have been complete without them? How many dinners had they sat through in best bib and tucker? Smiling and nodding their portrayal of the perfectly matched couple? Hinting at a sexual satisfaction with casual touch? Their seemingly contented child-lessness, enviable proof of their happiness? Never running out of things to say. Companions to the last, they had interred their marriage with a fanfare of style.

Subdued, Grace walked swiftly homewards, head down, the rustling leaves beneath her feet making the only sound on the silent streets. It was almost ten forty-five when she finally pushed open the front door. She was keyed up and ravenous. The house was in darkness. Dropping her bag in the sitting-room, she poured herself a gigantic Scotch before going through to the kitchen.

The fridge had been topped up, neat packages of cheese and salami lay on the top shelf and a small bowl of soup below. Murray Magraw must have been about in the afternoon. She had almost forgotten she'd given him a key. She dipped her finger in the soup and had just identified canned mushroom when a hand grasped her shoulder.

'Who the hell? . . . Murray? Do you mind?' She pressed the light switch above the stove, swung around too suddenly, tripped and slid to the floor.

'Grace! Oh my goodness. I didn't mean to frighten you.'

Grace rubbed her head crossly then stopped short at the sight of Murray, clad only in scarlet and white striped boxer shorts – the comic touch. Amusement momentarily overcame her anger that he should have so swiftly settled in. She eyed him with her head on one side. Broad shoulders, chest not too hairy. He still carried a little weight around the middle.

'Great outfit.' Her tone was measured and cool. 'I hadn't realized you'd moved in.'

Looking sheepish he put out his hands to help her rise, then with admirable dexterity gathered her to him.

'I've been wanting to do that,' he drawled, 'since the first day. You look tired.'

'Oh.'

He smoothed her hair gently with the flat of his hand.

'I, er, didn't expect you to be here,' she said, vainly trying to keep control.

'Nor I. I only stayed on because the john got

blocked. I was waiting for a plumber. He didn't show up till nearly eight-thirty.'

He held her close. His skin was smooth. He smelt clean and delicious and faintly of her bath oil.

'The john, eh?' She didn't quite believe him but, oh, how heavenly it would be to forget everything else.

'I like the way you kiss,' she said.

'You do, huh? Good. I improve with time. Soon you'll love it.' He smiled his lopsided smile.

'Soon?' He felt so safe. Marvellous to feel safe and excited both. Nice to stop thinking.

'Oh yes. It'll take assiduous practice, but soon you'll be insatiable. You wait and see if I'm right.'

'You intend to, er . . . hang about for a while?' *Hold me please.*

'Oh yes. Quite a while.'

'Mmm. You're so comforting,' she sighed. He held her face in both hands and looked at her intently.

'I don't want to comfort you, Grace, I want to make love to you.'

She eased herself away and said over-brightly, 'If I don't have something to eat, I'll faint. I've got a busy day tomorrow.'

He watched silently as she reopened the fridge and busied herself with heating the soup and cutting bread. When she turned he'd left the kitchen. She took some ice-cubes from the fridge and reached for the whisky.

'There's a bottle of Burgundy open. Why don't we try that instead?' He'd put on a shirt and slacks. 'I'm sorry for startling you, are you OK?' She nodded.

'I'm also sorry for rushing you,' he said slowly, 'I had no right.'

She didn't reply, concentrating on her food. He leaned backwards in his chair and silently considered the sudden change and the way she avoided his eye. It didn't exactly surprise him, he'd been through it all a couple of times already.

The same come-on, then wham. This time she'd really responded to his tentative advance, hadn't she? Surely he wasn't mistaken? She'd wanted him near her. Until his kiss had demanded a little more than passivity. And then suddenly she looked . . . shy? embarrassed? Not just that, for a split second he fancied she looked frightened.

Neither spoke until they'd finished eating and he refilled their glasses. As he put down the bottle he took her hand.

'We made love, Grace, when you were ill.'

The colour slowly rose from her neck until the bent face was suffused, she didn't respond.

'Grace,' he said gently, 'Grace?' Her hand gripped his, she looked stricken. He had the uncomfortable feeling that he was comforting a child, while fighting his desire for the woman.

Yet in bed that night, after she'd woken from the nightmare, after he had calmed her, her love-making had been as hungry and as urgent as his. He recalled sadly how neither of them had spoken and the humour and gentleness which so attracted him to her had been entirely missing. When she'd anxiously asked him for the third time if she'd pleased him he'd held her close and almost wept with disappointment and shame that it was not pleasure, but some more complicated need, which had inspired her response.

Afterwards, she'd curled herself up and fallen into a deep sleep, still clinging to him, until some time in the night, disturbed by the heat of her feverish body, he had slipped away to shower and catch a few hours' sleep on the sofa. He woke next morning stricken at how he could have taken advantage of her so opportunistically. Yet when he shuffled uneasily in with her breakfast tray, she smiled and put out her hand as casually as if nothing had happened between them, had asked if he would attend to some book business or other.

Well, he'd thought, if that's the way she wants it . . .

But during the following days, as they worked side by side, he wondered if she remembered because she didn't once refer to that night; and when he tried to get her to repeat the litany of fear she had poured out in her half-sleep, she had turned away, not just ignoring his invitation to talk, but as if she simply hadn't heard. It was so uncanny that he felt ashamed, as though he had taken advantage of her grief. Yet he could have sworn it hadn't been like that.

They'd chatted in the desultory way people do while they work together and by the time they'd packed the lace collection off, he'd laid a great deal of his own personal history before her; yet she remained guarded, adding little to what she'd let slip that one night.

Intrigued, he sifted and re-sifted through her words, fleshing out the meagre clues until the stark history of a terrified child emerged. But Murray was rather less interested in the child than in the woman. Watching her now, he was certain that once again she hadn't allowed herself to accept his claim that they'd made love.

'Did anyone call?' She confirmed his thought.

'There are a few messages on the machine. And Deirdre dropped by this afternoon.'

'Oh.'

'She seemed anxious to talk to you.'

'Oh yes?' Her tone was non-committal. 'I expect she wanted to know what you were up to.'

'Got it in one!' He laughed. 'But I made it quite plain that I was working on a project with you. Temporarily. Besides, she knows you've been out and about,' he said stiffly and pushed his chair back. 'I'm sorry if I've upset you. I'll call a cab.'

'Don't do that, you can stay. I'll be starting out early in the morning. I didn't mean to be rude. My head is splitting. There's so much . . .'

Her voice drifted off and as her mood suddenly changed, she smiled. 'By the way, I found some books today. I may need some help with them. A small library.'

'Oh?'

'Mmm. Some American, I'm not sure how good . . . Irish stuff mostly. That's what I need help with. Quite interesting I think, but I know very little about Irish literature.'

'But . . . Aren't you Irish?'

She whirled around. 'What do you . . .' she asked then stopped, her thoughtful eyes on his. 'Oh. The nightmare? Did I talk?'

'Ye . . . ees.' He blinked slowly. 'So you remember?'

Grace pushed back her chair, paced about then stood gazing sightlessly through the dark window.

'It's difficult. I've got this huge puzzle in my head that I can't quite work out . . .'

She turned and smiled sheepishly.

'I remember you . . . er . . . comforted me.'

'We made love, Grace,' he said flatly. 'I thought you wanted it as much as I did.'

He watched as she grappled with her unseen demons. Her next remark stunned him.

'It was the first time for a couple of years.' She spoke as if to herself.

'What a damn waste.' He tried to keep his voice neutral.

'For years I blamed all the trouble I had . . . on the miscarriages . . . or on Reggie. Mostly I blamed Reggie. I suppose it was easier than . . .'

She reached out and drained her glass, then refilled it with water and took a long draught. She looked resigned. Murray bit back the questions he wanted to ask, the comforting words, the useless awful desire to hold her tight which came, he knew, as much from a need to be consoled, as to console. Serene Grace, so pale and still, the dim light underscoring the delicate structure of her face. She had a new strength about her, as of solitude embraced?

Murray quietly began to clear the table and after a little time she helped him, then, too embarrassed to precede her upstairs, he poured a last nightcap. She bade him good night and crossed the room to check the bolt of the back door.

'I may have to go away soon,' she said, her back to him. 'I can't say how long for. But first, tomorrow, I'm going to see my husband. Clear things up.'

He knew she was trying to tell him to go but allowed himself a bit of character-retrieving perversity:

'Yes?'

'And then to Ireland.'

'I don't suppose you'd like some company?' he asked lightly. She considered him silently, then smiled ruefully.

'I'm not ready for company. I'm sorry, Murray.'

'Will you?' He tried nonchalance, it didn't work.

'Will I what?'

'Be ready some time?' More pressing, this time. She looked at him questioningly.

'For me,' he added lightly. There she had it, dammit, she excited the hell out of him.

'I don't know.' She looked at him at last. 'I could keep in touch,' she said hesitantly, 'if you like.'

'That's all right then,' he said and grinned his lopsided grin.

'Thank you,' she said softly, 'you've been very patient.'

'You're welcome.' He made a mock bow.

He heard her going to check the front door and switch off the porch light, then she put her head around the kitchen door again.

'Did she say anything else?'

'Who?'

'Deirdre,' she asked impatiently.

He considered her for a very long time before he replied:

'Yep. Quite a bit. I guess I got something like the whole picture.'

They stood silently looking at each other and she seemed relieved that he offered neither sympathy nor advice.

*L'AVENTURIER HOLLANDAIS ou La vie et Les Aventures divertissantes et extraordinaires d'un Hollandais. Avec gravures. Nouvelle edition. Worn.*

## CHAPTER TWENTY-TWO

The phone began ringing as Grace came downstairs just after seven next morning.

'It's Livy, Livy Hanning. I'm sorry to call so early. I was afraid I'd miss you, Mrs Hartfield.' She sounded agitated.

'I wish you'd call me Grace. Don't worry, I was up. I have to go to Bath this morning. Was there something . . . ?'

'I think so.' Livy gave a slight cough. 'Grace. I'm afraid I was less than frank with you yesterday. I've been thinking it over and now, well, I think you and I better have another talk.' Pause. 'Did you say you were going to Bath?'

'Yes, I'm having lunch there.' She didn't sound over-enthusiastic.

'So you have no time today? That's difficult, I'm afraid I must fly to the States this afternoon.'

Grace pulled open her diary. 'I could catch a later train. There's a fast one from Paddington at eleven-fifteen that might do or, at a pinch, there's one an hour later.'

They arranged to meet at nine in a small French croissanterie, which Grace hoped was still in business, just opposite the station. At the rate such places were folding, it was hard to be sure.

There was no sign of Murray. Assuming he was keeping out of her way, Grace brewed some coffee and while she gulped it wrote him a short note, leaving it propped up against the coffee pot.

The tube was packed with commuters, the journey slow and uncomfortable. It was hardly the way she would have chosen to start her day of confrontation with Reggie. Livy Hanning was waiting anxiously when she arrived. Gone was the groomed, impeccably dressed woman of the day before. She looked older, almost haggard, as if she hadn't slept and this she confirmed as soon as Grace sat down. The sympathy between them held and it was clear that both understood, without lengthy explanations, how involved they had become in trying to discover some possible reasons for the two suicides.

They ordered coffee and rolls and made small-talk while they waited to be served. Livy was obviously reluctant to get to what was troubling her and spent the first few fidgety minutes explaining that she was closing the London office and moving the staff either back to Amsterdam or to their new American operation. She implied that the difficulties of continuing without the blessed Cas were manifold. She seemed at pains to show her dead partner in the best possible light. As she continued to paint in the backdrop, Grace, on her way to bury her own marriage, understood the impulse driving her. After all, were they not, both of them, simply justifying all that time and exertion they had spent on their men and steadfastly resisting all attempts to rubbish their efforts?

Then, the long preamble over, Livy began describing their early life together, explaining with her first sentence why her English was so good.

'I was living in London when I met him. I was a student at the LSE and trying to cope with two infants alone. It wasn't so easy in those days. My husband had been killed in a car crash a couple of years before; he drove into a central reservation on the way back from Newmarket. Drunk. He was a diplomat. And a gambler on a heroic scale. The embassy wanted to ship us straight back home but I had already started my course and opted to stay. In any case I felt compelled to settle his debts.

'I'd married very young against my parents' wishes. They knew what Bau was like long before I did – our families were vaguely related and he was more their age than mine. His status as black sheep only increased his attraction for me. My parents were very bitter about it and I didn't feel able to crawl back to them for help. Perhaps I was just too proud. I knew I would have to eventually, to get work and so on, but I wanted to go with some semblance of self-respect. I was selling the contents of our flat to keep alive. That's how I met Cas. At Sotheby's. The third time I put some pictures in, he bought the lot. Every damn one, including the Mauve. Then he took me out to lunch. After that he sort of adopted us. He liked having a family, even – maybe mostly – part-time. And I loved having him around. He saved my life, or at the least my sanity.'

The waitress arrived with a loaded tray and the women remained silent while she laid the table.

'After a couple of years, we got into some, er,

difficulties and it seemed wisest to get out of the country. By then there'd been a bit of *rapprochement* with my parents. My father's health was poor and they were anxious that I return to Holland so we packed up one night and skipped over to Amsterdam.'

Livy busied herself pouring the coffee and did not continue until both of them were settled with a croissant apiece. 'Everything happened very quickly.' Livy looked straight at Grace. 'There wasn't time for legalities, even if we'd been so inclined, but in any case he couldn't get a divorce; his wife had long since disappeared. He had tried but failed to find her. I knew my family would cut me off completely if they found out. They'd already had the scandal of Bau. They wouldn't countenance us just living together, we had to be married. Respectability was everything to my people. So I'm afraid we just presented them with a *fait accompli*. We said we'd been married quietly in London. To my amazement my father accepted Cas, got on with him like a house on fire, treated him like a son. Not only that, he took him into the family business. He'd already learned some Dutch from me.' She paused expectantly.

'Hang on a second.' Grace was on to it at once. 'Did you say *learned* Dutch?'

'Yes.' Livy nodded slowly.

'Cas Van Rijn? Learned Dutch?' Grace repeated incredulously.

'The Van was an addition, I'll explain in a moment.' Livy plunged on quickly, blocking any further comment.

'My father wanted to settle the business on us jointly. Remember, he assumed us to be married. It never occurred to him to ask for proof.'

'So,' interjected Grace niftily, 'what was his real name?'

'I told you. That was his name – more or less. We, er, just changed the spelling.' Livy smiled sheepishly, she did not seem to be able to meet Grace's eye nor did she sound entirely convinced.

'How?'

'It was originally spelt with a y, we just changed that to an i-j and added the Van. As it happened, our offices were on the banks of the Rhine anyway and it seemed rather a nice, er, coincidence.'

'Van Rijn.' Grace repeated incredulously but she was less interested in the name than in Livy's more electrifying disclosure. 'Tell me, do you know how long he was in London?'

'When?' The insouciance was wearing a little thin.

'When you first met him,' Grace said impatiently.

'Oh, he lived there.'

'Are you,' Grace's eyes narrowed, 'are you telling me he was English?'

'You thought he was Dutch?' Livy answered evasively.

'Well, didn't everyone?'

'We always spoke Dutch.' Livy went off on another diversionary tangent. 'My father wouldn't speak English so Cas had to learn pretty damn quickly. It didn't take long; he was an extraordinary linguist. After he came back to London, people here just assumed he was Dutch, in Holland they

331

assumed he was German. His accent was slightly off and his colouring perhaps suggested it.' She broke off and spread out her hands despairingly.

'Oh really? You mean he let people think that, don't you? My, wasn't he the sly one.' Grace spoke *sotto voce*. Livy didn't respond.

'He changed his name and masqueraded as your husband *and* as a Dutchman. Why?' Grace persisted.

'Ah.'

'There's a mystery about that too?' Grace's eyebrows shot into her hairline. She put down her cup. 'Livy, I'm sorry to keep battering you but hadn't you better tell me the worst? Isn't that what we're here for?'

'The worst is probably what I held back yesterday. You were curious about the money he spent on pictures, his wealth. I think you'd decided there was something crooked about the dock development, about our company?' She looked at Grace questioningly, holding her head slightly to one side. Grace inclined hers.

'There is absolutely nothing crooked about Hanning-Van Rijn and within the company Cas never did worse than cut corners – though perhaps he was more opportunistic than most, less sentimental about what happened to those who travelled in his wake. That bloody mews, for instance, he picked up when some poor fool went bust. But on paper it was all quite legal and it made us a great deal of money. But not as much as his original line of business. That's what I held back. The reason why he had to, er, evaporate. The reason he came to Holland.' She sighed.

'Criminal business?'

'That's a moot point. It depends on how you look at these things. In the late sixties everyone was at it and he always said he just fell into it. In a small way at first but like everything he touched, it grew and grew.'

'Drugs.'

'Hash. He never ever had anything to do with hard drugs. He wasn't so foolish as to tangle with the big boys. But they kept an eye on him; watched him building up his network. He avoided trouble for several years, then they pounced. Things began to look pretty nasty, specially as the police started sniffing around as well. They never actually got anything on Cas, but that's when we skipped back to Holland and he . . . er . . . eventually re-emerged with a new identity. I was quite a useful person to know wasn't I? One way and another.' Livy spoke bitterly.

'But he was dealing when you met? Didn't you mind?'

'I drink and I smoke – tobacco now, I was a student then and most of us smoked pot at one time or another.' She spread her hands. 'The law on cannabis seemed to me,' she emphasized the word, 'to be idiotic. Besides, I was as culpable as he. As a student I provided useful contacts but, more importantly, a lot of the stuff came in through Rotterdam. I spoke the language, my family was in *dock* development for heaven's sake. In return Cas supported me and my sons.'

'A quid pro quo.'

'In a word.'

'Was his first wife also involved?'

'No.' Livy brushed the question aside impatiently. 'I told you. She'd left him years before.'

'You're certain?'

'You mean if she'd known she could have blackmailed him or something? No. I'm afraid the drug business only started after he met me.' She was a little shamefaced.

'Ah. Your contacts. I see.' *What opportunists.* 'Did you say the late sixties? How old was he when he died?'

'Fifty-two. A year younger than me.'

'Drug dealer? Not Dutch? Over fifty? Anything else?'

'No. I don't think so. Why does his age matter?'

'It probably doesn't, except that Bid lied about it so much it must have bothered her. I'm just trying to work out what exactly Bid knew about him. From what she told her friends, it doesn't appear to be much.'

'How can you tell? He would have insisted on discretion. She might have . . .'

'Learnt his mendacious skills? Maybe, but I somehow doubt it. From what I've discovered she wouldn't have the wit. She seems to have been remarkably gullible or else she just didn't want to know.'

'She was in love,' said Livy ruefully. 'If you look at it all in the cold light of morning, he does sound a complete stinker. One thing though, in personal matters he didn't usually lie. Not outright. He would avoid confidence, but if you asked, he always gave a straight answer.'

'But you had to have the wit to think of the appropriate question?'

'Exact rather than appropriate,' Livy rejoined drily. 'Yes, that about sums it up. When I look at it from her point of view, I can see why she might have despaired. As far as I know he never sorted out the divorce, she had every right to be angry about that. Perhaps, perhaps if she confronted him? But why did he kill himself? I keep going over and over it – none of what I've told you was news to Cas – so why did *he* kill himself?' she pleaded.

'You haven't speculated as to why he was dawdling about marrying her, have you? Do you know anything more about that?' Grace asked quietly. 'You're holding something back, aren't you?'

Livy stared silently at her for a moment, as if trying to make up her mind about something.

'No more than you, I think? You've said nothing about why there was such dissension in your family. Would that have some bearing on the girl's frame of mind do you think? You seem to be assuming that he is solely to blame.' Brief hostility flared between them and as quickly died away. Grace leaned earnestly towards her companion.

'The last thing I want is to apportion blame. That is not what I'm about. The past for me is just an increasingly horrible blur. I buried it so long ago I don't seem to be able to retrieve it. But yes, Bid is in there somewhere. I couldn't say why, but I feel there's a link to her death. But then I think all the nasty things that have happened lately are connected with my past so I don't quite trust myself; I'm a bit irrational on that subject.'

'What will you do?'

'I've more or less decided to go to Ireland. To do

some digging. If anything turns up to throw some light on all this, I will let you know, I promise. But there is something you might have some thoughts on. I've puzzled about why and I wonder if it had occurred to you – or indeed if it has any significance at all – they died *separately*. Alone. That's one of the saddest things about this. Alone. They were lovers and they died within hours of each other. Apart. It obviously wasn't a suicide pact. Was each responsible in some way for the other's death? I think so, though I couldn't give you a precise reason why. I also feel the girl's death has some bearing on why my life is such a mess. Which seems absurd, doesn't it? It hardly makes sense and it certainly explains nothing about Cas's death, does it?'

'Not really, but then you've said so little.' Livy looked at her thoughtfully, hesitated, then slowly bent down and drew a bulky briefcase from under the table from which she extracted a blue folder. She held her hand firmly over it as if reluctant to part with it.

'Since he came back to London, Cas was very, very careful to keep a low profile. He was always afraid that the drug syndicates would catch up with him. He completely shut out his past life here. My instinct is that self-preservation was the main inhibitor of dredging up his first marriage also. Recently, there was a magazine article about developers; a rehash of something the *Telegraph* published a couple of years ago. It identified Cas from an old photo. He was furious. And, I think, a little frightened,' Livy said slowly. 'He was right to be. They were on to him. Johannes, his assistant, and

336

his secretary, Mrs Petrie said that in the month or so before his death there were a series of strange phone calls. They just mentioned it in passing, as something odd and out of the ordinary. They thought it was a mix-up, a mistake. The name the caller asked for meant nothing to them. But it did to me. That's really what I wanted to tell you. I'm certain it had something to do with the past and Cas must have been afraid because he hired a detective. It worries me. It opens up the whole circumstances of his death. But I can't get the police involved, can I, without implicating myself? The past is the past. Or at least I thought it was.' She grimaced and passed her hand wearily over her eyes. 'I've gathered his passport and some other papers you may find helpful. I don't want them found. Will you take them with you? They may give you some leads. Then return them please.' She spoke rapidly and kept her voice so low that Grace had some difficulty following what she said.

'I feel I can trust you, Grace. I hope I'm right. I'd prefer if you don't open this until you're at home, in private. Will you promise me that? I've written my private telephone numbers, in Boston and at home, where you can reach me any time of day or night. If you find out anything more about Cas's death, or who was after him, will you tell me? Grace, please? I feel very vulnerable. I worry about my sons.'

'Yes, I will.' Grace was businesslike. 'Do you have a good photograph of him?'

'There's one in the passport but I've also put in another more recent one. Oh and one last thing, will you take the paintings? He wanted her to have them. If you give me your address I'll have them sent around.'

'No, Livy. Thank you, but if you don't mind, I prefer not. I've already benefited too much from Bid's death. They'd make me uncomfortable. Keep them, they're yours by right anyway. I'm moving house soon, everything will have to be stored,' Grace said unhappily. She stood up and held out her hand. 'Livy, I'm sorry for the pain all this has caused you. I promise I'll ring if anything turns up. Or write.'

'I hope you will also come to see me some time soon. It would help to talk it all over. In Amsterdam. I'm afraid I'm finished with London. I don't feel safe.'

They shook hands warmly. Grace crossed the road to the station, then turned and waved to Livy who stood outlined in the doorway, her hand raised as if in benediction. She looked forlorn and tiny. Grace walked swiftly towards the ticket office, her heart in her mouth at the prospect of her next encounter.

# Eileen

*20 March – 4 April 1990*

*Dear Confused: You'll have to work harder at your relationship. Suspicion and misunderstanding are almost inevitable when you live so far apart emotionally from your daughter ...*

## CHAPTER TWENTY-THREE

Mrs Lacey exited reluctantly from her house, pausing in the doorway with her face turned up to the sky, trying to determine if the galloping clouds augured more showers. She decided to chance it, banged the door shut and descended the five granite steps onto the patch of scrubby green in front.

Instantly her greying hair lifted and played around her face. She pulled a printed headscarf from her pocket and, turning her back to the wind, folded it into a triangle, wrapped it around her head and tied it firmly under her chin. Then she picked up her shopping basket and crossed the road to the canal bank. As she passed, two little boys moved their assortment of plastic containers and an open tin of worms, but she neither greeted nor appeared to notice them. They kept their heads down, having no wish to be questioned on their absence from school, but also because they were a little afraid of her.

Her tense pale face, which appeared so stern to them, would certainly have been described by other, more sophisticated taste as striking – beautiful even. Lined and sallow she might be, but the pale grey eyes, so deep in their dark sockets, still had the power to arrest. She walked erect, neatly dressed in a well-tailored, timeless, tweed coat which outlined her over-slender body. The patterned silk headscarf tied under her chin added to her slightly dated appearance so that she might easily have stepped straight out of fifties. Her attitudes too were those of an older generation. She had been the child of an invalid mother and elderly father and many of her values derived, though she would have been appalled to acknowledge it, from them.

Few ever called her by her Christian name. Eileen Lacey was definitely a Mrs and she clung to her title as a drowning man might to a lifebuoy; somehow it defined her position and her reality.

Over the bridge she strode, grim with effort, the vigour of her step now and then faltering as she covered the quarter mile past the derelict sites of Charlemont Street until she came to Camden Street where the morning market was already in full swing. She removed her gloves and pausing at one stall and another, chose each of a small number of items carefully, placing them one by one in her basket: a couple of tomatoes, an onion, half a pound of beans (past their best), a Jaffa orange and a lettuce.

'There y'are now, Missis.' The stallholder wrapped the lettuce in a sheet of newspaper. 'How'ya holdin' up at all?'

Mrs Lacey smiled fleetingly and muttered something inaudible. She moved more slowly now, pausing every couple of yards as if to examine the windows of the shops lining the street; in reality to rest. The crowd grew and the level of banter rose as she made her way to the bus queue where she caught sight of her reflection in one of the plate-glass windows and, arrested by her spectral appearance, she stared in horror at what she had become. Thus shattered, she climbed into the bus and settled just inside the entrance for the short two-stop ride to the bridge.

The pain was back, gnawing away at her distended stomach, and getting worse as the effect of the painkillers wore off. Since the brief remission over Christmas, she'd been in agony or knocked out with drugs, but today the discomfort was worse, had changed in some way. She felt exhausted. As soon as she got off the bus, she crossed the street and sank wearily down on the bench in front of the pub overlooking the canal. Leaning back, she held up her face to the weak sun. Shielded as she was from the wind, there was some warmth in it. She closed her eyes and allowed herself to drift backwards to her sun-dappled youth. Life as it might have been. Her daydreaming had always sustained her, now it completely dominated her and had a reality which each new disappointment merely strengthened.

The sun shining through the still bare trees made the dingy sluggish green water of the canal sparkle and dance.

'Afternoon, Mrs – how are y'feeling?' The gruff voice startled her. It was the old man who came each day to feed the bedraggled ducks which by some miracle survived the attentions of the more sinister inhabitants of the canal bank.

'Hello, Mr Burke.' She smiled weakly. 'Not too bad, the fine weather helps. Isn't it a grand day? I see you're keeping the ducks up to scratch.'

He muttered something unintelligible and grumbled away on down the bank, the ducks honking and scolding in his wake. Now and then he scattered some crumbs of bread on the filthy water. She watched idly, suddenly recollecting Bridget as a child stomping along after Fergus with that moth-eaten old dog they used to take swimming. She couldn't now recall its name.

She sighed and felt in her pocket for a peppermint and hauled out an unopened letter. She stared, wondering how long it had been there, then remembered the postman thrusting it into her hand the day before. Bridget's scrawl, she thought irritably, wondering what had she forgotten this time? The girl had a head like a sieve. She'd only just gone back after yet another weekend of jumping about, hauling her all over the place for meals neither of them wanted to eat, then fussing and alerting the unwanted attention of both Maureen Lenehan and Father Crowley. Bridget was definitely getting on her nerves. She tore open the envelope impatiently and was instantly alert.

*. . . I don't understand what the problem is unless there was some mistake about my date of birth. They just don't seem to be able to find any sign of the registration. They're so unhelpful. I hate to bother you Mam with you feeling so unwell but do you think you could see if you can sort it out? I'm sure it's something very simple . . .*

So that was that. Bridget was going to marry that man and all the lies and stratagems had done no good. Because she hadn't mentioned him since their quarrel, Mrs Lacey had allowed herself to believe he'd been given the boot. It never occurred to her that Bid would simply send off for her birth certificate herself. She sighed. If only she had brought it with her after Christmas when there was time to explain, instead of letting the whole thing get out of hand by clinging to the wild hope that, if she did nothing, it would go away. Now she knew that it was fear of exposure that had driven her anger, not concern that her child was involved with a married man. She shivered. She would not upset herself thinking about it.

A fine mess the girl had got herself into. A family man. If he couldn't hold on to one lot, what hope was there for poor infatuated Bridget? Sometimes she wondered whether the girl had a brain in her head. Marriage? If you could call it that. Skulking in a registry office among strangers. If only she'd seen sense and given him up. Mrs Lacey closed her eyes again.

Why had it all come out so wrong? Everything was so muddled. Mismanaged. Reasonable objections nullified by her own cringing self-pity, she had left her daughter exposed and unprotected against a philanderer and cheat.

Mess, mess, mess! She silently railed against fate and the worries she wasn't well enough to deal with – these days decisions were beyond her, all she craved was peace and sleep. She pulled her coat collar close around her cold cheeks.

She should have told her long ago, after Fergus died. That would have been the time. Now it was too late. Her vain hope that Bridget would one day walk up the aisle of St Stephen's in shimmering white was over. Gone. It would have been simplicity itself – just produce the baptism certificate and no-one the wiser. Hadn't she done the same for the passport, all those years ago? She smiled in soul triumph.

If only she had gone to the doctor immediately, when the ulcers first started. When was that? Some time in the winter after Fergus's death. Only the local chemist remarking on the increasing number of antacid pills she was buying made her acknowledge how filthy she was feeling, but even then the stomach ulcers had masked the cancer, allowing it to spread undetected. But now the euphemisms had stopped. The day before, the consultant Mr McFadden had been chillingly matter-of-fact.

'Though God knows,' she muttered, 'he's taken long enough.'

It somehow escaped her mind that, in spite of constant urging from her daughter and from her GP, she'd first consulted him just before Christmas. The appointment for the hospital had been waiting for her when she got back from that disastrous visit to London.

Between barium meals and biopsies, during those awful weeks her moods had swung from deep despair to unrealistic optimism. How could she, at fifty-two, have come to the end? She'd hardly had a day's illness in her life. That thought was quickly followed by the chilling remembrance of Fergus's sudden collapse and death four years earlier, when he was only sixty-three.

Poor old Fergus. Where was he when she needed him and his common sense? In her fear, Mrs Lacey forgot how seldom she had listened to her husband in those last few years before he died. Or indeed ever.

'Why can't you tell her, Eily? What the hell's stopping you? If anyone should mind it's me – you're not being fair on any of us.'

She gripped the bench as she remembered that bitter fight just before he died. He'd roared at her – Fergus, whom she used to think derisively wouldn't say boo to a goose – had stood over her at the kitchen table and shouted.

'Mark my words, Eileen, if you don't tell her, then I will, and I'll waste no more time about it either. A week is all. After that I'll go and see her myself.'

He put his hand on her shoulder.

'I don't understand what you're so afraid of. You were only a child. Why can't you forgive yourself?' he pleaded. 'For pity's sake, what does it matter now? This is the twentieth century. You're being ridiculous.'

'I'm afraid of losing her respect,' she whispered, lying, and he'd laughed in her face.

He couldn't know that her fear was also to do with him learning, after twenty-five years of marriage, the full extent of her treachery. Even Fergus did not know the whole truth.

'We've been lying to the girl too long,' he shouted. 'It's got to stop.'

'I've never lied,' she started.

'No,' he snorted. 'But you've never told her the truth either, have you?'

The colour faded from her face. He took it for fury when she slammed out of the room. If only she could have told him then, begged his forgiveness, shared the burden. But the habit of injured silence was too strong and Fergus didn't realize that her bottled anxiety had become obsessive self-preservation.

Bridget had been on holiday with Sarah in Scotland when Fergus had dropped down dead, two days later, on the way home from work. A massive stroke killed him before the ambulance had even arrived. Eileen went into shock and was kept sedated by her doctor. They buried Fergus in a complete daze, her white face contrasting starkly with the tanned good health of her daughter's. She feared that in those last days after their quarrel he might have written to Bridget. But she couldn't bring herself to ask or even to speak of it.

It was astonishing how comprehensively their relationship deteriorated in those few short weeks while she remained frozen, waiting for the accusations to be hurled at her. Nothing happened, but by that time she'd stopped worrying, they were so uncomfortable together that there seemed no way they could ever be easy again. They became distant and resentful, each nourishing their grief in solitude. And as the days passed, Mrs Lacey took account at last of how deeply attached to Fergus Bridget had been. It still outraged her for she had always discounted that relationship, assuming herself to be the central figure in her daughter's life. But in the months following Fergus's death, her jealousy became virulent and barely controllable as she realized how profoundly the girl was missing him. At times she'd wanted to scream – for God's sake he wasn't even your father – love me, love me.

You owe it to me – I sacrificed my life for you. Instead of consoling the girl, she turned in on herself, unable to confide her secret or ask for help, and resentment of Bridget's unquestioning love of Fergus began to eat her up.

When, at last, it became clear that he had died without betraying her, Eileen valiantly tried to rebuild her relationship with her daughter and, because Bridget assumed their partial estrangement to be a manifestation of grief, she responded warmly. But they had never really lost the wariness which grew from that vital failure of affection.

The sun went in, but still Mrs Lacey sat disconsolately staring into space. She hadn't yet spoken to her daughter of the doctor's prognosis. Nor told her she was selling the house. Her face lightened fleetingly as she thought how Fergus would have split his sides if he'd known how much their house would fetch. He'd always claimed it would be an investment when she demanded somewhere modern and easy to keep. She looked across at the crumbling brickwork, at the paintwork peeling in the sunshine. Only a couple of the houses on the terrace still remained in private hands. The whole area around the canal, just a mile or so from the city centre, was gradually being converted to offices. As a result the value of property had climbed steeply, regardless of condition. Only two or three months before, unasked, she'd been offered a sum which had nearly made her faint until she gleefully calculated that, with careful management, she'd been handed her financial independence; she could do what she liked for the first time in her life.

Despite Bridget's pious noises, or even because of

them, Eileen Lacey had no intention of uprooting herself to London for her daughter's convenience. She loathed London. Better to be alone. Solitary she'd become, and solitary she intended to remain. Several months back she'd instructed Bartley Quinlan to open negotiations to sell and after a persistent hunt she found a quiet flat overlooking the sea in Sandymount, viewing it so many times she knew each wrinkle in the wallpaper. The young couple who'd been trying to buy a bigger place had just written to ask impatiently if she was still interested in completing the sale.

'And if the operation is a success,' she muttered and crossed her fingers superstitiously, 'I will.'

She hadn't told her daughter anything about that either. She would talk to her once she knew where she stood. Then and only then, she would have to have it all out.

Mrs Lacey stood up stiffly and walked slowly across the bridge. The morning had turned chilly and she stamped her cold feet as she waited for a break in the traffic to cross the road. In the distance she glimpsed the stocky figure of Father Crowley rounding the corner from the church. She watched him thoughtfully until an impatient motorist asked her roughly whether she was coming or going.

She glared at him and crossed the road, slowing her pace as, out of the corner of her eye, she watched the priest draw nearer. He had his head down and did not notice her. She turned towards the house as if she too was unaware of him. They all but collided.

'I beg your pardon. Oh, Mrs Lacey!' The priest drew back, shocked at her thin ill face. He raised his hat formally and blurted:

'How are you?' The ruddy face crinkled in a smile as he held out his hand.

'Not too bad today, Father.' She spoke stiffly. 'Thank you.' He waited for her to invite him in and when she did not he said:

'I was just passing. I was talking to Bridget when she was over last weekend. She said you weren't too good.' There was an awkward pause.

'Perhaps you could drop around tomorrow?' she said remotely and nodded goodbye. He watched while she mounted the steps and took her door key from her pocket and without turning walked stiffly into the house.

*Dear Confused: I'm not sure I agree with all this business of The Right To Know. I cannot see what's to be gained at this stage . . .*

## CHAPTER TWENTY-FOUR

All through the afternoon Mrs Lacey sat at the old roll-top desk, methodically sorting through each small compartment and drawer. The fire flared up each time a bundle of paper was fed into the huge grate, then died down as she read, tore up or retained this document or that. Now and then she pushed back the chair impatiently and paced up and down the shabby room, gesticulating in agitation or clenching her fists against her temples. Several times an involuntary, strangulated cry of despair escaped her. After a while she moved back to the desk to read and tear and burn, the cycle repeating and repeating in the fading afternoon.

Once, the phone sounded faintly through the closed door but, if she heard it, she did not respond as she bent in concentration over a small pad of blue paper and began to write. Page after page was torn out half-finished, rolled up and flung into the fireplace until at last the only sound was made by the scratching of the pen as the pages were filled and pushed to one side with the side of her hand. When she finished, she laid her head on her folded arms and dozed for a little time. Afterwards, sighing, she sat up and read back what she'd written, folded the pages, slipped them into an envelope and scrawled 'Bridget' across the front. Setting it aside, she opened a small flat box and extracted a photograph of her daughter. She stared at it for a long time. Bridget's haircut had brought out the unnerving likeness, a daily reminder of what she'd thrown away. The same inviting smile, dredging up the past with a clarity that awoke her dampened senses. The same sensual knowing look that only came from the excitement of constant and satisfying sex. Every time she looked at her daughter it embarrassed her.

'You should never have cut your hair,' she admonished softly. 'Now I cannot look at you without seeing him, and I cannot endure it.'

She deliberately tore the photograph in two and then with more urgency into tiny bits. These, too, were gathered up and thrown impatiently into the fire. She picked up the letter and a scrap of newspaper, pocketed them, closed the desk and climbed the stairs to the top of the house.

The two rooms on the third floor of the house were no longer used. Bridget's childhood bedroom was at the back, but she had long since moved to the bigger room below on her visits home. The front room was almost empty, containing only a small writing table and a large old-fashioned wardrobe, but the walls still retained the outline of the bookcases which had been there when Fergus had used it as his escape.

Mrs Lacey ran her hand over the surface of the old table and the faint trace of his tobacco which clung to it made her shudder at the memory of all those years when she submitted herself to his hopeless attempts at love-making, his mouth moving like a mollusc across her clamped lips. His sexual advances had never made her feel anything but revulsion and eventually he had wordlessly agreed to his imposed celibacy. It had not been much of a sacrifice, she thought sourly. He had as little interest as ability and he never really wanted another child. From the first Bridget had been enough for him. She had given him that at least.

If, at that moment, Eileen Lacey had been asked to sum up her life she would have said that it had been a series of grievous disappointments. Everyone she ever trusted had, without reason, betrayed her and let her down. Because nothing had turned out as she'd expected or wanted – neither people nor events – her responses were governed by an inability to forgive. Her suppressed rage was fed by a consuming sense of betrayal and loss.

She opened the wardrobe and after much fumbling brought out an old black handbag, which she turned upside down on the little table. A small pile of papers and photographs tipped out, the detritus of thirty-odd years. She slid a photo from a tattered envelope and examined the old-fashioned couple who gazed sternly out and she shuddered as she looked again at the faces of her parents. Even now, they looked old to her; Victorian in attitude and dress. Thus they had looked that night when the brat's squalling had brought the old man in on top of them, screaming his threats and his obscenities.

Abandoning the table, she went to the window and stood looking moodily down on the canal. Her attention was caught by a young girl as she climbed over the fence of the corporation flats opposite and began to run along the canal bank. A minute or two later a young man clad in jeans and thin white shirt vaulted over the railings. He was shivering with cold. He stood indecisively, looking to right and left, before sprinting after the girl. He called, she half-turned, then stood and laughed and, as if in slow motion, his stride lengthened and he held out his arms, catching her to him as she opened hers.

High above them, unseen, Eileen closed her eyes and drew his arms around her, feeling again the blood race through her, their shapes blending as they melted away into the shadows, making for that secret place where they had created their own world, rolling through the long grass until their flesh was etched by outlines of meadowsweet and pale blue flax. Could anything ever tear them apart? They drove into each other, hands and tongues in a frenzy of exploration, pushing their ecstasy ever beyond the boundaries that each day were redefined, greedily rising again and again to new heights of the passion which had exploded in them that very first time.

*He stands at the edge of the bridge, his eyes turned away in apparent contemplation of something more notable than a gawky schoolgirl. He looks dangerous. Dangerous but exciting as he turns to stare at her, taunting her with a half smile. She follows the cue, arranged and rearranged in his daily notes to her, slyly left in the crack of the bridge pier each morning. Today then is the day.*

*She slows her step, eyeing him brazenly as she passes. With an imperceptible movement, he puts out his hand and draws it knowingly down her face. They look at each other and she smiles in amazement at the breathless pleasure his touch releases. Then he smiles back and the finger lingering on her chin moves slowly down her childish blouse towards her unchildish breast. Flushed with pleasure, she plays at brushing it aside but he catches her fingers in his as they silently glide over the bridge towards the bank below.*

Had they made love that first time? Or had it been another move in their slow fandango? Had they crept towards it or had it swept them up? Had there ever been a moment when they didn't know there was no choice, or if there was, it wouldn't matter? They made love as naturally as breathing. Half-spoken threats of what happened to girls who surrendered themselves evaporated that first rapturous time. All the pious beliefs of punishment, appliquéd by home and church, floated away as they merged into the landscape and each other.

Neither had ever had the slightest fear that satisfaction would lead to disillusion. Satisfaction made them insatiable. At first they met decorously each day as she walked home after school. He would pass without a flicker of recognition and she would shed her friends and tear along the bank to the place beyond the encampment they had made their own. They planned each tryst carefully for fear of being discovered, for she had been warned against him as the no-good son of the bookie they also described as a tinker, a wife-beater and a drunk. Once, in the early days, when her father had caught them talking he had railed against her for belittling herself and when she'd shouted back at him, he had taken his strap to her. After that she began to mitch school but they were careful never to be seen together.

Their meetings became more frequent and more unrestrained. He came provided with condoms nicked from the cartons of twenty gross his old man obligingly smuggled from England or Belfast, with a nudge and a wink, for the upstanding citizens of the town. They were so dazzled by their own *savoir-faire* that, as the winter closed in, he began to climb in over the shed up to her room almost every night. They had it all worked out.

They would never have been discovered if it hadn't been for The Brat. They had already planned to run away as soon as they had enough money saved. And everything would have been all right if Mammy hadn't got so sick that Nonie had to come to look after her. The Brat was shifted into her room.

How could the old man understand, or have ever understood, what it was like when you wanted someone so much that even the sleeping Brat didn't matter. But he never stopped to ask, just shouted his accusations of corruption and damnation and disgrace while The Brat yowled like a banshee.

'You hoor! Watching that tinker molesting the child!'

'He didn't do anything to her! Tell him, you little bitch, tell him! He was only trying . . .'

Repugnance and fury contorted her father's face.

'*Get out of my sight before I have ye arrested! Bad cess to ye! The pair of ye'll never have a minute's luck!*' It was the last thing he roared before he succumbed to that fearsome blow, his blood flying all over the room.

They grabbed their clothes and ran into the dark night and kept running. They didn't care, they were together and happy. But their happiness lasted barely two years and her father's curse had followed her all her life.

They could never go back. Her father meant it when he said he'd have them arrested and his old man would have killed them with his bare hands for relieving him of every penny he'd hidden under the floorboards, and for setting the house on fire. They moved from place to place those first few weeks, checking into small and out-of-the-way guest houses, first in Dublin, then in Liverpool, and Birmingham, until the money ran out after they'd fetched up in that filthy kip in Kilburn. What had such a place to do with their fine hopes?

But nothing could dampen the relief of getting away with their dream intact. She got a job clerking and he picked up what he could, sometimes on the building sites, sometimes at other unspecified grafting. The days weren't dappled in sunlight then, at least not until her lover started coming home with ever thickening wads of notes. Poker, he said, claiming he'd learned a few tricks from his old man. He threw back his head and laughed and touched the side of his nose with his finger.

But oh the romance of their wedding! The romance of him arranging it secretly took her breath away. He pulled a huge box from under the bed one fine spring morning and took out the beautiful pale blue dress.

'*We're getting married*,' he said masterfully. '*I've arranged it all.*' She never asked how, just drifted in his wake, luxuriating in the Austin Princess he had waiting at the door. She hadn't quite believed in it. Weddings were in church after all, until then she'd never heard of registry offices, much less understood their legality. It was all such a lark.

He insisted she give up work, to be always ready for him. Whenever he came home they were fused to each other in the bed, his body so imprinting itself on hers that there could never, ever be a substitute. As a lover he could never again have an equal; sex was their *raison d'être*. Until he too turned on her. The day she found him at it like a dog with that huge pale lump of a one. She was barely twenty. The day she found out she was pregnant. The day she thought would be the beginning of the future. The day her world caved in.

Eileen Lacey turned in the shadows of the empty room, her body shaking with the memory of his calamitous perfidy. Angrily, she took the letter and newspaper cutting from her pocket and stuffed them, along with the rest of its contents, into the black bag. Then she made her way unsteadily and wearily downstairs.

*Dear Confused: You're not serious! I cannot believe that you could contemplate such a course of action, but since you ask for my advice I'll give it. DON'T EVEN THINK ABOUT IT!*

## CHAPTER TWENTY-FIVE

Father Crowley returned next afternoon. Mrs Lacey kept him waiting on the step so long that he was just about to retreat when the door opened. He was almost unnerved by her silent preoccupied stare. Her face was unnaturally flushed and her normally neat hair untidy and unwashed; she looked as though she'd woken from a deep sleep. Flustered, he muttered an apology for disturbing her but she remained silent as she led him down the hall into the warmth of the kitchen. He stood aside awkwardly while she filled a kettle and set it to boil. It was a good five minutes before she asked him to sit down.

'When you first came here, did you recognize me?' she asked abruptly, startling him.

'Yes, of course, at once.'

She flinched as if he'd struck her. 'You never said anything.'

'No.' He shook his head sadly. 'All those years, you were afraid I would?'

'No,' she replied stiffly. 'I hoped I could trust a priest.'

He was moved by how wretched she looked. So different from the bright youngster she had once

360

been, when he was a young curate in her native parish, the summer she'd run away, leaving havoc in her wake. How could he possibly forget her?

When, twelve years afterwards, he was appointed parish priest at St Stephen's, he recognized her immediately. He spotted her walking down the aisle, the sturdy little carrot-top at her side, as he stood at the back of his church greeting his parishioners after his first Sunday Mass. Their eyes met and instantly he saw terror dart across her face and her half-formed name died on his lips. She'd stared at him without the slightest flicker, challenging his trust. His only other attempt was to mention, as if in passing, their home town, suggesting a slight acquaintance but she stopped him in his tracks by telling him curtly he'd made a mistake, they'd never met. Through the years she kept her distance, attending weekly Mass but rarely lingering to chat afterwards. And never to him. She appeared to have few friends. Over time he had grown to know Fergus and Bridget well, but not Eileen Lacey.

Which meant it was hard to know how to begin. Trying to loosen the atmosphere he made small talk, remarking that Bridget seemed to be over very often. Was she coming back to Ireland or had she completely settled over beyond? Wasn't she looking grand? Time for her to be getting a husband for herself, and a family, he added jovially.

'Yes. It's about Bridget that I want to talk to you and,' she looked straight at him, 'and what happened back then.' She stopped and looked at him brazenly. 'In Ballymahon.' When there was no reaction she continued in a low flat tone:

'I need to clear up a few things before I go into hospital. In case anything happens to me.'

Normally he might have cajoled her with easy phrases of encouragement, but the isolation she conveyed moved him more deeply than her distress. She looked older than her years and as he studied her he wondered if it was only the emaciation of her face that made her look so bitter.

He could remember vividly the first time he saw her. Hair flying, as she ran along the bank of the Blackwater, slipping away into the overgrowth with the lad at her heels. The local gossip had nudged him and with much wagging and tut-tutting had opined that Schoolmaster Sullivan would skin her alive for consorting with the likes of the bookie's son.

'Do you remember the boy, Father?' She startled him into speaking this thought.

'The bookie's son? Good Lord, I've not seen hide or hair of any of that brigade for more than ... thirty years it must be.' He looked at her thoughtfully. 'What was his name?' He shook his head slowly from side to side. 'It's on the tip of my tongue. Ah yes. Con, wasn't it?' She stared at him blankly but didn't reply.

'I don't suppose I'd know him if I ran into him,' he murmured.

'You knew me.'

'But that was after a break of only ten years or so.'

She drew a scrap of paper from her hangbag and held it out to him. It was crumpled and yellowed and obviously torn from one of the Dublin Sunday papers. Part of the familiar *Tribune* banner still identifiable on the upper left hand corner. Most of the surrounding article and half the caption were missing but the photograph was more or less intact. He stared at it dubiously and then at her expectant face.

'It was wrapped around the lettuce,' she said inconsequentially. 'Yesterday. I got it in the market.' She touched the paper with an unsteady finger. 'I think it's him.'

If it wasn't so pathetic, he'd have laughed out loud – or wept. The contrast between the youthful health of the man and the sickly pallor of the woman's face was so far-fetched that he could only assume she was no longer able to see herself properly – for how could anyone her age look like this lad?

The priest concluded that her illness had turned her brain soft. He peered more closely at the picture. Something about the smile. Alarmed at finding himself caught up in her fantasy, he dropped the scrap of paper into her outstretched hand. He looked at her sadly, wondering at the power of romantic love which made a grievously sick woman keep her first love's image so clearly in her mind that a chance likeness was enough to clothe him in youthful flesh and blood, giving some sort of imprimatur to her regrets.

'Surely not.' He said it as gently as he could. 'You've made a mistake but that's not surprising, is it? After all this time, I'd barely recognize myself.' He could not quite succeed in keeping the derision from his voice and the cold stare of her eyes chided him silently for not playing along.

'I don't know what to do.' Her voice was feverish

but resolute. 'The operation is serious. I have to be prepared. Bridget has no-one left. She needs someone to keep an eye on her. I should tell him.'

'Tell who what, woman dear?' He peered closely at the picture again. 'Don't be foolish. You can't really think that's young Con? Do you?' he asked weakly and was at once disgusted with himself, knowing he was only raising hopes where there were none.

'Yes, yes,' she said eagerly, then almost simultaneously shook her head. 'But it's so old. I wonder how old it is? I only found it yesterday. There's no date.'

'Could be years old. It's all yellow. I don't understand what the excitement is about?' he said pityingly.

'Bridget,' she whispered.

'Yes?' A chill came over him.

'Fergus wasn't her father.'

'What? What are you telling me?' he asked sarcastically then looked at her earnest face and sighed. 'Oh Lord above. You mean it. Does Bridget know?'

Eileen Lacey drew her lips together nervously but said nothing.

'You didn't tell her? Fergus?' he asked sharply. She shook her head.

God Almighty. What was Fergus thinking about all those years? The priest moaned. The subtlety of people's self-delusion sometimes staggered him. He leaned towards her.

'Mrs Lacey. The truth now. I can't help you unless I know the truth. No prevaricating. Does

364

Bridget know that Fergus was not her father? She must. Fergus would never let her think that.'

'I wouldn't let him tell her. I couldn't tell her myself.'

'May God forgive you both,' he whispered.

She didn't look up. Lord Jesus, he thought, there's something else.

'And Con?' His voice sharpened. 'Did he know he had a child?'

'No. He doesn't.'

'Doesn't?' he repeated stupidly. 'You mean he doesn't know to this day? Why did you do that to him?'

'He was like a dog after other women,' she spat the words venomously. 'I wasn't going to stand for that. I packed my bags and left him to it.' There was an unpleasant note of triumph in her voice.

'Didn't he . . . ?'

'Oh no,' she snarled. 'He couldn't take the trouble to find me. I had that child all on my own.'

'But wasn't . . . didn't Fergus?'

'Oh yes. Good, kind Fergus,' she snapped, 'fussing like an old woman until the child was born, then all he wanted was the child this and the child that. It was the child Fergus wanted, not me. Couldn't wait to take her over.'

'Did Fergus know who the father was?' he asked quietly.

'No. I never said. It was nothing to do with him. I made up some story. I forget,' she said impatiently.

The priest closed his eyes and choked back his sick fury. Poor Bridget, entirely oblivious that Fergus, whom she worshipped, was not her father.

How was she going to cope with the fact that they'd kept her paternity a secret? How could they? Staring at his parishioner in wonderment, the priest suddenly realized she was waiting for his sympathy, her injured bitterness and self-pity plain upon her features. She was entirely oblivious of his distaste, and, what was infinitely worse, she had apparently subtracted the feelings of her daughter from her reckoning.

*Poor Bridget.* How could such a straightforward man as Fergus collude in this? Surely he didn't think it would do the girl any good to come by such information by accident? On a birth certificate for instance . . .

'What about her birth certificate?' he voiced the thought.

'That's the problem.' Her matter-of-fact tone was startling. 'She's been asking for it. She wants to get married. Over there. In a registry office.' The moral outrage was extraordinary. 'She needs it. Up to now I always managed to keep it from her. I wanted her to get married here, in St Stephen's . . .'

'. . . where the baptism cert would do instead,' he finished her sentence slowly. 'I've heard of better reasons for getting married in the church.' His lip curled in outrage. 'She wouldn't need either for the registrar, you know,' he added briskly and a shade triumphantly. 'As far as I know a passport would do just as well for that.'

Her jaw opened as she grappled with the import of his news.

'Then why is she asking for it?' she asked hoarsely.

'Perhaps she's just going on hearsay, it's a

common enough misconception, I believe.' His colour deepened at the unintended pun but she didn't comment. He shrugged. 'Or has she not got a passport?'

'Of course she has,' she said impatiently. 'I got it for her myself, years ago when she was a child.'

When she was too young to ask any questions, he supposed, and renewal would be a mere formality. Oh clever, clever Eileen Lacey.

'I needn't have worried then,' she said resentfully.

'I would say,' the priest said evenly, 'I would say you had much more to worry about than birth certificates.' Somehow he had to get her back to thinking about her daughter's welfare.

'Why is she not marrying in a church? Is he not a Catholic then?'

'I don't suppose so.'

'But they could still get married in a church. Not Mass maybe, but still . . .'

She gesticulated impatiently as if at some troublesome gnat.

'Father. He's divorced, or about to be. I don't know. I know nothing about him,' she said with pride.

Under his furiously beetling brows, Seamus Crowley's fierce blue eyes lasered into her.

'Well, all I can say is that if you don't, you should, Mrs Lacey,' he exploded. 'I cannot bring myself to believe that you are sitting here telling me that your only daughter is marrying a divorcé,' his voice rose, 'and all you're concerned about is yourself and what she'll think of you? Don't you care about the girl at all?'

'I sacrificed my happiness for her, staying with

that . . . that stick-in-the-mud to provide for her. How could I love someone like him? After what I had?'

'After what you had?' he mocked. 'And what was that, pray? Trouble for your family? Setting houses on fire? 'Tis a wonder the bookie didn't catch up with ye for robbing him blind. He'd have murdered the pair of ye. Your betrayal? Have you forgotten what really happened?'

'Oh no,' she sneered unpleasantly.

'Then for God's sake, woman, why do you want to get in touch with him? It's too late for reconciliations now. It's Bridget you have to think about. You must tell her as simply as possible, now, before the operation. Forget the past. It's absolute madness to bring all that back.'

'If I don't come through, she'll have no-one else. No relations. She'll be alone.'

'But you know that's not true. You just said she's getting married. And what about your sister? What about Gráinne? Doesn't she live in England? She must have a family by now.'

'I know nothing about that one. I never saw her since I left . . . it was all her fault.'

After thirty years. The priest drew in his breath and buried his head in his hands. He was appalled by the tortured bitterness she conveyed, aghast at the spite pulsating out of her. He prayed silently and, with a supreme effort at control, said quietly:

'I think you've forgotten your little sister was the injured party, not you. Your father was afraid, claimed, she'd been molested.'

'Con never touched the lying little bitch. Never. He jumped on her to shut her up, that's all.' Her

voice was chillingly uninterested. 'She was screaming her head off, making trouble as usual.'

'No,' he said slowly, 'that's what she kept saying.
But your father was afraid, believed, she'd been
abused. The child was sick with fear, traumatized.
Have you any idea what she went through?'

'And what had she to be frightened of? It was me
they threw out.'

'For God's sake, woman, have you no forgiveness? Whatever she said or did, she was only a
child. What would she know about such things?'

'She knew enough to cause trouble. She dragged
him in on us. The old man screaming blue bloody
murder and us half dead with fright. No-one to give
us shelter.'

The priest closed his eyes. What use trying to
reason with such convenient distortion? Did she
think he did not know what Gráinne had seen and
must have seen many times?

'She was a child,' he said sternly. 'She was
terrified out of her wits by the goings-on of the pair
of ye.'

But Eileen Lacey didn't want to hear, she rocked
to and fro, her face frozen with misery.

'What about your parents? Did they know about
your child?'

'Them? I told them nothing. What did they care
about me? They threw me out,' she said sullenly.

'They cared.' His hands itched to strike her.
'They destroyed themselves caring. Did they not
follow you? All over England searching for you? He
gave up his job to look for you. Moving to
Birmingham at his time of life and your poor
mother so ill.'

'No. No. It was not for me. Afraid of what the neighbours would say more like. He never lifted a hand except to strike me.' Her white face distorted in anger.

*Sweet Jesus she's going to faint.* Father Crowley went to the sideboard and pulled it open, searching for something to revive her. He poured two large brandies and pushed one into her hand, drained his own glass and refilled it.

'Father.' She looked wretched, leeched of colour. 'That isn't everything. There's something else. Something much worse.'

He put his head in his hands and waited.

'We were married. Not properly. In a registry office. Over there.' She spoke primly and so quietly that he thought he'd misheard. 'I married them both. I never told Fergus. I couldn't. I was afraid he wouldn't marry me if he knew. He was such a stickler for the right thing. I told myself it didn't count, being Catholics. After Bridget was born, Fergus and I got married, in Dundalk. Fergus had a friend there. It always worried me,' she finished righteously.

The priest silently began to count, trying to quieten the painful pumping of his heart and his disgust. He told himself she'd been a child, frightened, alone, afraid for her infant.

He wondered how it might be possible to wean the woman away from her guilt-ridden destructive course of total disclosure and save her daughter from anxieties with which she could never cope. She appeared to be utterly bereft of any maternal instinct or feeling but told her story with little regard for its effect on the girl. Whatever happened it was a poor look-out for Bridget, but maybe, just maybe, he could prevent her wretched mother from taking away everything she believed in.

'Have you eaten? Answer me, girl?'

'I have no appetite.'

Only an appetite for self-pity and universal bloody destruction, he thought savagely. He lumbered to his feet and unhooked her apron from the back of the door.

'Sit there. Have you eggs? I'll make an omelette. You look as though you need it,' he said gruffly.

She made to stand up then sank back and closed her eyes. He moved from fridge to stove with a surprising efficiency, neatly assembling his ingredients. Then, before heating the pan, he laid the table and buttered a couple of slices of brown bread and tossed a small salad. He divided the omelette neatly in two before he said anything.

'There, now. Eat up while it's hot, it'll do you good.' He tried to keep his dislike from his voice as he leaned towards her.

'Listen to me now, girl. Forget about that old newspaper. It must be years old. You've made a mistake. That fellow's much too young. He's been on your mind, that's all. In any case it's all too late. There's no way you could walk in on someone after thirty years and say, by the way, I forgot to tell you about your child? You'd be lucky to walk out alive, that's all I can say.' His voice became more urgent. 'Your priority is Bridget. Your daughter. And don't you forget it. Are you listening to me?'

'Yes, Father.' She looked at him hopefully.

'You love her, don't you?' Silence.

'I did my best. I found it hard.'

'Then fake it!' he roared. 'Or you'll set her on a course that'll destroy her. Fake it. You have no option.'

'I've made such a mess.'

'Spare me the regrets, Mrs Lacey.' He held up his hand. 'You sit down tomorrow and write a letter and explain as much and as lovingly as you can, without sending her on a wild goose chase looking for someone who doesn't even know of her existence.' He brought his face close to hers and added fiercely: 'Better if she thought he was dead.'

'But . . .'

'No buts. Hear me out. Why balk at one small white lie? For all you know he's dead anyway. Have you ever laid eyes on him? Has he been in touch? Made any attempt to find you? Tell her he's dead, for pity's sake. Write to her from your heart. If she's found a man she loves, be happy for her. Pity he's divorced but it's too late for worrying about that now. I would trust her. She's a good girl; she won't go astray. Look how devoted to you she's always been. And please, please remember how much she loved Fergus.' His voice was tense with effort. 'And how much Fergus loved her. Don't take that from her. Keep your feelings about Fergus out of it. He was her father for God's sake. Leave the biology out of it, he was a good and loving father to her. Don't destroy that.'

After a long time she said:

'Would you, would you talk to her?'

'Yes, of course I'll talk to her. Mrs Lacey, listen to me,' he pleaded urgently, 'if she's thinking of marriage she'll have too much on her mind to be skiddering around looking for the past. Don't worry. It'll be easier than you think, her mind is on the future.'

May God forgive my presumption, he thought piously, for he hardly believed what he was saying. It took another long hour of persuasion before she promised to write or talk to Bridget in the terms he suggested. That accomplished, he slipped into a more familiar role and encouraged her to talk then about her illness, her fear of hospital and of dying but all the time he wondered if she would heed anything he'd said, or whether in the end he had done any good. He did not feel any great confidence when he left her.

As he walked home, he thought wretchedly about his old friend Fergus, their frequent companionable walks, the poetry and songs, the occasional murdered bottle of malt, without ever a word about his private worries. Small wonder the poor man had spent so much time hiding away in bookshops. If anyone had asked him, Seamus Crowley would have said that Fergus was the closest he ever got to friendship. Now he wondered how close that was.

Forever on the sidelines, he thought tiredly, and suddenly felt very, very old.

It was well past midnight when his housekeeper heard his heavy footsteps climbing slowly towards his bedroom. At much the same time, Eileen was picking up the phone and dialling directory enquiries.

# Grace

*Late October 1990*

THE OLD MAN YOUNG AGAIN or AGE-REJUVENESCENCE in POWER of CONCUPIS-CENCE *literally translated from the Arabic by an English Bohemian. 1898. Unnumbered copy, limited edition, plain paper wrappers, uncut.*
THE WOMAN TURN'D BULLY: *A Play, acted at the Theatre at Bath October 1675. Slightly defective, misbound.*

## CHAPTER TWENTY-SIX

Grace stood for a few moments watching the tail-lights of the taxi disappear with Murray inside and what felt like the last connection to her old life. He'd popped out of nowhere just as she was leaving for Heathrow and sort of edged himself into the taxi.

'I've decided to go back to St Paul for a while,' he announced abruptly.

'But I thought you were going to stay in London?' She felt unaccountably disappointed.

'There are some things to sort out. No use running away – they just catch up,' he drawled.

Ever ready to bristle, she looked at his face to see if he was needling her, but no, he seemed preoccupied with his own thoughts.

'I'll say,' she agreed fervently.

The taxi climbed the ramp to the M4.

'Will you stay in Dublin long?' he asked diffidently.

'No more than a few days. Then I'll go to the

377

west, there's someone I need to talk to. Probably a week or two.'

'And then?'

'Then sell the house. Look for somewhere to live. Sort things out. My life.' She grinned.

'Snap,' he said and took her hand. They lapsed into silence, then, as the taxi entered the tunnel under the runway, Murray leaned towards her and kissed her cheek.

'Goodbye, Grace. I'll ride back with the taxi.' He pressed an envelope into her hand. 'Write to me.'

When the taxi stopped, Murray hugged her briefly then held her face between his hands.

'I'll be in touch, Grace. Remember what Bogart said.' He whistled and his face creased into its loopy grin. She kissed him lightly on the mouth. As the taxi pulled away, he yelled out the window:

'Max asked me to tell you that there's a job waiting whenever you want a change.' He waved, she could barely hear his last words.

'Accommodation includes . . .' He cupped his hands to his mouth.

'Includes?' she yelled.

'Includes me.' He kissed his hand to her and passed out of sight.

'Cast adrift,' she muttered turning to enter the airport.

It was like stepping out of time and space. As if at the doorway a giant vacuum stretched out its hose and guzzled personality, feeling and will. Once over the threshold, people assumed the same bland look of resignation. Anaesthetized from involvement, they floated about in apparent aimlessness as if

378

divested of past or future. Or at any rate that was how she felt, if felt wasn't too strong a word.

The flight was delayed. The check-in girl waved her hands loftily when asked for how long, then smiled charmingly and suggested that the departure lounge might be a tad quieter. So Grace, armed with a large container of freshly-squeezed orange juice, joined the flow drifting vaguely towards the departure gate.

The fact that she was setting out on the journey she'd so assiduously avoided for months did not alarm her as it might previously have done. The priest no longer presented the same threat. She didn't yet fully understand how or why he was so strong a part of her story, but the malignancy she had visited on him had slowly faded as fantasy and nightmare were replaced by something approximating the truth. So much of her fear had been of the unknown, of the imagination. Half truths and whole deceptions had woven an intricate cocoon which had almost stifled every natural feeling out of her.

Reggie had used the word cocoon the night he left but then she'd heard it, and perhaps he had meant it, as self-protection. She'd been able to disillusion him on that at least. In Bath, over lunch, he said she'd changed and she could see, with some satisfaction, he'd grown just a little afraid of her.

If she hadn't been sitting in the window of the bloody restaurant she wouldn't have spied Deirdre clinging to him as he shambled towards her, and she might have stuck to her resolve and remained her old passive self. As it was, he had barely time to remark on her extravagant choice of Mersault before she'd swung into the attack, pouring her pent-up rage at the cruelty of his departure until at last he'd buried his head in his hands.

'Christ, Grace, you know we were overdrawn. It was the sodding bank, not me,' he wheedled.

'You bloody instructed them.'

'No,' he roared. 'I bloody well didn't. Shut up and listen for a minute. The frigging clerk got my instructions wrong. I didn't realize there was that postal strike.'

'Where were you? Mars? On second thoughts, don't answer that.' Her eyes narrowed. 'Nearly five weeks. Bills coming in like confetti and no way to contact you. The service till swallowed my card. You did it on purpose, Reggie.'

'Honestly, Grace, how could you believe such a thing? Of me?' He was all injured pride. She snorted.

'I was waiting for my redundancy settlement. It would have got sorted.'

'Eventually. Don't worry, I'll make my own arrangements from now on.'

'How?'

She ignored his question and sipped her wine, eyeing him over the glass.

'I notice Deirdre's in the club again,' she remarked sweetly. 'Or has she just put on weight?'

'Jesus, Grace have you any more weapons in your arsenal?'

'Oh yes, quite a few. Jamie was looking for you . . . Daddy,' she said pleasantly and watched him deflate like a burst balloon.

'You knew?'

'No. I'm too much of a sap. It didn't dawn on me until the other day. Bastard,' she hissed.

'You were having it away with George,' he retorted tentatively. She was about to scream an outraged denial, then decided not to confirm or deny his self-justification. Better to leave him something to worry about.

'George,' she said levelly, 'usually bats for the other team. As you well know.'

'Nasty.'

'Well for God's sake! You sit there and admit you were bonking Dee Pepperstock for years. Years. It's outrageous. And expect me to defend myself against your random suppositions? How could you? Unmitigated bastard. I depended on you. Our next door neighbour for God's sake. You disgust me.'

The waiter, his eyes popping with interest, put paid to any further vituperation and somehow, after a sullen and silent hiatus, they managed to begin to talk.

With an urgency which almost convinced her of his residual feeling for her, but even more of his desperation for his child, he carefully took her through the long slide that had led him, the previous January, as Jamie had emerged from sickly babyhood into the tall lumbering child he'd suddenly become, to recognize the boy as his. So, alas, had Dee's husband, Jason. But despite appearances it hadn't been a long ongoing affair, he protested, more a stop-go type of thing. He clearly expected another outburst then but she held back. Even through her anger she could see that he, above anyone, would understand how wounded she would feel at her failure to give him and herself what each had so longed for. For a wild moment she wanted to cry out – share him with me – but instead she put out her hand and clinging to his, had wept her regret.

She looked at him covertly as she dried her eyes and wondered suddenly if he'd always looked so insubstantial. Good-looking, amusing, fun he certainly was but his strength was her illusion. They'd been hanging on to their semblance of a marriage for a long time. Too long.

'I'll move out of the house,' she said at last. 'You can have it. I can't bear it anymore. I'm going away for a bit. I'll let you know where to send my stuff. I don't want to fight you, Reggie.'

'How'll you manage?' His concern was genuine. 'How'll you?'

'I've got a job lined up. Jason has gone to the States.'

'You'll have quite a houseful,' she shafted spitefully. His answering grin was an uncomfortable mixture of apprehension and pleasure. She made herself very busy, spilling some wine. When he'd mopped it up, he said slyly:

'I hear you've a new partner.'

She grimaced. 'Neither for work nor pleasure,' she squeezed the words through tightened lips. 'That would suit you, wouldn't it? But you may tell your skinny friend she got that wrong.'

'We better talk about money,' he side-tracked with admirable understatement.

'I don't want your money,' she replied stiffly.

'You'd better hang on to it, with your commitments.'

'Don't be ridiculous. You can't live on the pittance you make. You couldn't possibly make a living out of the books.'

'You'd be surprised what you can do when you have to. I'll manage.' She sniffed loftily.

'Ah! So you do have someone else. That American?' he countered.

'You're pathetic,' she huffed, drawing in her breath. 'I told you. There isn't any bloody boyfriend, American or otherwise. I'll manage, that's all.'

'You've toughened up, Grace.' He sounded almost crushed, as if he couldn't imagine her existing without him, or some strong man, as if everything she said was shaking the foundation of their fiction and he clearly didn't like it very much.

'Yes,' she said. 'I've learnt a lot in the past six months. A lot about myself.'

And, regretting her spikiness, she told him then why she didn't need his money. She outlined what she knew of her sister's resurrection and demise, and of Bid's dramatic death, and how the fears that had driven such a wedge through their marriage had not been quite as she'd believed.

Reggie put down his glass and drew his hand over his eyes.

'I think,' he said more gently, 'I think, you'd better explain, Bird.'

She waited, gathering her thoughts while the waiter cleared the half-eaten food and poured coffee. She fiddled nervously with the milk, decided against it, poured a few gains of brown sugar onto her spoon and slowly stirred the steaming cup. All the while Reggie, who knew her delaying tactics well, watched her without blinking. He was clearly anticipating some major unpleasantness. She stared at the tablecloth.

'You should never have married me. I wasn't programmed for marriage or stability.' Her voice was barely audible. 'I made myself the heroine of our story. Blamed you for going walkabout. But now I know that you hadn't a chance. It was all make-believe. With the baggage I was carrying, we hadn't a chance.' She sighed and sat very still for a few moments. She stared straight past him, unseeing. Her unfocused eyes fixed on the past.

'For a long time I forgot. I put it out of my head. I thought my sister was dead and with my parents dead, there were no reminders of the past. The nightmares suddenly stopped. Those first years, when we were putting off having children, I never thought about my childhood. We were happy; I felt safe. Then as soon as we decided to start a family the terrors were back. Do you remember? You got that job in Partridges and we moved to Ealing and everything looked fine. But as soon as I started doing up the baby's room, before I miscarried, the nightmare started again. It was like a grainy old film, all shadowy, rolling round and round in my head. People moving about, screaming, then this awful fear would take me over. At first it was just the nightmares but then it began to happen when we made love. I was afraid to tell you. I kept trying to get it out of my head, but I couldn't. Sometimes something would click and I'd remember another

384

tiny detail. But that only seemed to make matters worse because what I couldn't remember, I speculated about.' Grace bit her lip and looked at her husband.

'Did your father abuse you? Rape you? Do you know?' Reggie gently put the question he had asked her many times over the years. When she replied her voice was flat and lifeless.

'I'm still not sure. I hope not. I'm sure not. Now, I know there were others in the room that night: my sister and a man I can't identify, my grandmother. There was violence. A fight? It's there just at the edge of my memory but, Oh God! I still can't work it out. Something dreadful happened and it's all mixed up with her, my sister. Somehow she's to blame. I feel it, so strongly. And I will find out. I will,' she cried fiercely and broke down. 'I'm so sorry Reggie.'

'What have you got to be sorry for?' he asked, tight-lipped. 'You were the bloody victim. We both were. Oh poor Grace, what a bloody futile waste.' He shook his head in disbelief and took her hand. 'We should have got you help. We might have got through. I should have insisted.'

'I didn't give you any option, I see that now. I was so busy trying to act sane neither of us realized how unhinged I was. I should have carried a bell or something.' She leaned forward earnestly. 'What I was afraid of was that my sister had seen my father abuse me and he killed her. That was my secret horror. All these years that's what I was terrified of. I kept burying it, but it was there at the back of my mind and what I couldn't explain or understand was that all the time I felt furiously angry with *her*,

385

not him. It just didn't make sense. But my instinct was right, because it turns out she wasn't dead after all. Whatever happened, she knew about it. I wronged him all those years. He didn't murder her and now I'm pretty sure, hope, he didn't abuse me either. But what could make her disappear like that? Something worse? Jesus. I just don't know. She certainly blighted my life, our lives,' she finished lamely, all the steam had gone out of her.

'Mine too,' he added fervently. 'Aren't you furious with her?'

'With Eileen? Oh, I am. I am. Worse than furious; murderous. Believe it. If she wasn't dead, I'd kill the bitch with my bare hands.'

Reggie looked away, trying to attract the waiter and neatly avoiding any more discussion. He was silent while he paid the bill and shuffled off to the toilet. He returned with a couple of glasses of brandy, leaned across the table and took her hands in his.

'Between us, we've made a right cock-up,' he announced succinctly. 'We might have made it, mightn't we, without all that?' He avoided her eye. 'I've always loved you, Bird, I still do.' She flinched but he continued as if unaware of her withdrawal. 'We could make it still, but for . . .'

'But for Jamie? And the baby,' she finished for him. 'Or are you not sure about the baby?'

'Of course,' he protested stoutly, then deflated again. 'No, not absolutely sure. But Jason's gone. Look, Grace. Deirdre and I had a fling, that's all. She got pregnant. It happens.'

'Twice?' Grace said tersely. 'Twice. And Jamie's three years old. So it must have started,' she looked at him shrewdly, 'practically the day the Pepper-stocks moved in.'

'If you remember, we hadn't had sex for months and months at that stage,' he trumped.

'We did. After . . .' her hand flew to her mouth. 'You're not, don't you dare suggest that Dee helped our sex life? God.'

'Well, in a way,' he started. Grace stumbled to her feet.

'I'm getting out of here,' she hissed. 'You've humiliated me too long.'

She stormed out of the restaurant, red-faced and angry. He slammed some notes on the table and ran after her. He eventually caught up with her, standing by the Jacob's ladder in front of the Abbey, tears pouring down her face. He took her arm. They walked about the city for hours and somehow managed to calm down enough to work through the minutiae of the dissolution of their marriage, disentangling themselves from each other, trying to ease the pain of dissociation. As they parted, they muttered pious hopes of future friendship, keenly aware that if that were achieved it would be a minor miracle – or because their childlessness had already set them in the habit. But she knew in her heart that now he would be constrained by roles unknown to her: parent, carer, provider. He would be no longer free to come and go. She knew that whatever they had in common would soon be obliterated by experiences she could not share; as time passed it would be as if she'd never existed in his life. She would have to seek her salvation elsewhere, because the reality of their marriage was that they had spent almost the whole of it propping each other up, each with the delusion that the other was the stronger character. Confronting him in unfamiliar surroundings, she had viewed him with new eyes. Yes, she still loved him. And yes, he could still hurt her. He was charming and, in his inimitable way, very attractive. But he was, and always had been, weak, she admitted harshly. In that at least they were a match. Neither of them could ever quite manage to confront problems. The line of least resistance was their stock-in-trade. In the end, when trouble loomed they simply walked away.

The flight call interrupted her reverie. As she plodded down the tunnel which linked terminal with aircraft she was momentarily gripped with apprehension. Was this obsessional dredging through the past yet another sign of her unhingement?

More like blue funk, she thought. Too late now . . .

## 20 March 1990

Dear Madam,
   The article you enquired about was published on the 15/10/88 and was reprinted from The Telegraph of 24/03/85. We trust this information may be of value to you.

# CHAPTER TWENTY-SEVEN

An ancient taxi swung neatly around and stopped within a couple of paces of the main entrance of the hospital. Directly facing it, safe in the shelter of his little snug, Giacomo Scanlan, guardian of B Wing, looked up from his racing form and watched with satisfaction as, on cue, the sky opened and the fourth shower of the morning cascaded down. The car door opened with a squeak and then was hurriedly shut again as driver and passenger sat back and waited for the downpour to pass.

As soon as the rain eased a little, the cabbie got out and sprinted to the building opposite through the doors marked *Reception*. He emerged a moment or two later with the head porter, who directed him with a flourish towards B Wing. At this point, the passenger emerged from the car and all three stood some moments longer while the fare was passed to the driver. He must have got a huge tip because his whole demeanour changed and, to Giacomo's disgust, he practically carried the man forward, so obsequious did he become.

With a brief and unprintable reflection on the power of ready cash, he admiringly noted the skill with which the passenger extracted himself from the clutches of the taxi-man. Giacomo sized him up as he approached. He wore a light suede jacket, beige twill slacks and carried a Burberry. Money was written all over him. A racing man very likely. Not the kind who grubs together a few miserable shillings for his daily flutter, more the sort who struts about enclosures with a bundle of tags hanging from his binoculars and a Jag in the carpark.

Giacomo drew himself up to his full five foot one and three quarters and prepared to exert his authority as soon as the automatic glass doors swung back to admit him.

'Yeah?' he challenged with satisfaction. 'Visiting hours as posted. Y'll have to come back. Doctors doing their rounds.'

The man eyed him steadily. He was tall and well preserved but looked as if he'd had a hard night. His eyes were bloodshot. Giacomo studiously resumed his perusal of the newspaper.

'St Luke's ward,' the man spoke impatiently. 'Which floor?'

On hearing this the porter looked up, contrite. 'Ah. Sorry sir, that's different. Third floor, see the sister first. What was the name? D'you have the room number?' He leaned out of the glass cubicle but the man strode away as if he owned the place and was quickly out of earshot. Giacomo shrugged and went back to his racing sheet.

There were few visitors. The staff padded quietly about their business. Nobody stopped to ask where he was going, or paid any attention to him. As he tiptoed silently past the ward sister's office he reached up and checked his tie and sleeked back his hair, wishing he'd had some sleep. Numb with fatigue, he walked the silent corridor.

Rooms one to four were followed by adjoining

doors marked discreetly *Ladies, Gents*. After a slight hesitation he slipped inside the second door and pulled an envelope from his pocket and checked the single sheet of notepaper for the room number he sought. The written message was terse.

*There's something important we need to discuss. A letter addressed care of the above will reach me for the next three weeks or so.*

*Room 7* was scrawled in as an afterthought.

The note was dated 22 March but the postal strike had delayed its delivery for nearly two weeks. She had cannily held back her home address and gave no indication of where she might be found after the allotted time. Preserving her own anonymity, she had thrown down her gauntlet without thought of his convenience. He smiled sardonically. It couldn't have mattered less. As it happened, she had timed her entry entirely satisfactorily. For him. Her pathetic conspirational note achieving at a stroke what his own half-hearted efforts and the inept searching of a private detective could not. He stuffed the letter back into his pocket, splashed cold water on his face, ran a comb through his hair and, checking that the corridor was empty, resumed his prowl.

Number five: Thomas Q Mulvey. Q? Quintin? Quasimodo? Ten paces then number six: A P Purcell, sex undesignated. One, two, five paces then he drew in his breath and paused to collect himself. At that moment the door to the next room swung open and a tall, slim, young medic came out. She glanced at him appreciatively.

'Seven?' he asked politely.

'Yes.' She smiled and stood with her back to the

door holding it open for him, obscuring the label. As he passed into the room, the young woman tripped away, her heels making a faint tip-tap on the polished floor.

He stood just inside the door and stared at the bed.

A woman was lying back against the white pillows and, though her hair had gone almost completely grey, he would still have recognized her. She was painfully thin, the skin stretched across the fine bone structure. She said nothing, following his movement with her eyes as he hesitantly approached the bed. There was not a flicker of expression on her face but the jumping pulse at her temple gave her away: she was as nervous as he was.

'Who put you on to me?'

'Ah. Newspaper. Photograph.' Her voice was low and tired. 'I was right then. I recognized you straightaway. You haven't changed much.'

'You found me yourself? Nobody put you up to it?'

'Who would know anything about us?'

There was a hint of triumph in her voice. She fumbled at the drawer of her bedside cabinet and held out a crumpled bit of newspaper.

He cleared his throat. 'I'm sorry you're so ill.'

She noticed how his voice had lost all trace of accent. It was neutral and hard to place, but it sounded educated. She wondered sourly where he'd picked up an education. He looked well set up. Good clothes. Very, very attractive. He still had the power to move her. Ashamed, she tried vainly to push away the demeaning thought.

'I'm mending,' she said drily. She struggled upwards and put one hand under her pillow but did not draw her hand out. Whatever it was she sought was not revealed. For a wild moment he wondered if she was going to pull a gun.

'There was something . . . I thought you should know . . . something I wanted to say to you.' She struggled with the words but he broke in before she tried again:

'Just as well you got in touch.' He didn't quite manage to sound casual. 'I've been trying to find you for some time.' His eyes slid from her face and she knew she was a mere object to him – a lump of clay. He had not the remotest interest in her, this man, who had dominated her emotional life for over thirty years. She waited, anger making a thin line of her mouth, as she watched him pace the room.

'I wonder if you'd sign some papers. We should arrange a divorce. It's about time we dealt with it.'

'We? Divorce? Now?' she cackled raucously and burst into a fit of coughing. 'Surely,' her breath came in gasps, 'you arranged that long ago. I thought you could fix anything.' As her hostility grew, he cut across her.

'No, I didn't, there was no need. But it would be convenient now,' he stated coldly.

'For who? You?' she drawled sarcastically. 'Been protecting yourself, have you? That doesn't surprise me.' Whatever she'd wanted to tell him was lost in her anxiety to score. 'You've left it a bit late in the day, haven't you?'

He came swiftly towards the bed and stood looking down on her, visibly controlling himself.

'Yes, I should have done it years ago. Stupid of me,' he said tersely. 'But if that's how you feel I can get one without your help. It doesn't matter. Might have sped things up, that's all,' he bluffed.

'So why the hurry? Your age?'

'No particular hurry. I want to get married.' He paused for effect. 'Properly this time.'

'Is there any other way?' she goaded, relishing her moment of power. His eyes bored into her.

'Oh yes. As I imagine you know. But this time,' he watched her reaction with mild interest, 'it's important that I do it right.'

The casual cruelty stung her. The insult caught her breath, then they both started talking at once, ignoring the other, using the same words:

'I want . . .' Her weak voice was drowned out by his.

'I want everything right,' he said. 'It's important to my fiancée. She's a Catholic.'

She started to speak again as if she had not heard him.

'There's something I need to tell you.' She tried vainly to interrupt him, but could make no impact. 'Listen to me, it's important. Listen!' Her interruptions became more urgent but now he affected not to hear. He moved over to the window and stood with his back to her, gazing out.

'. . . important, you see, my first child,' he continued softly as the rain began to lash against the windowpane.

'No,' she whispered roughly. 'No. No.'

He didn't stir, just stood watching the busy carpark below, then he turned and said tiredly:

'No? I see. In that case I shall make other

arrangements. Good day to you.' He started towards the door.

'No. Wait.' She hauled herself up on one arm. 'Please,' she gasped. 'It's not your first child. That's what I've been trying to tell you. You have a child already. We had a child.' She sank back exhausted. He glared at her, disdain fighting disbelief.

'We?' His voice was brittle with fury. She closed her eyes against it.

'Yes. A daughter. She was born six-and-a-half months after I left you.' She waited for another explosion but he just remarked with deadly quietness:

'You knew you were pregnant when you left.'

A brief jubilant flicker of hope rose in her. She looked into his eyes.

'Yes,' she said contritely.

'You walked out, knowing that, and never said a word?' He was so lethally controlled, she could not read his reaction.

'I never had another.' She smiled faintly, as if in expectation of his indulgence.

'You'll sign the release then,' he concluded softly.

It took a moment for the impact of his remark to reach her and suddenly she was shaking with furious indignation. Thirty years of lying and evasions and destroying the only two relationships that could have brought her happiness and he just stood there! He didn't even turn around. He didn't care, he didn't damn well care. Selfish bastard. Self-centred, destroying cur. Her heart began to thump painfully as at last he turned and looked at her curiously:

'Why are you telling me this now? It's really no

concern of mine. Did you think I'd come running to look after you?'

He could read the shamed assent in her eyes and laughed in her face.

'What the hell could I do for you? Or for an adult child I've never even heard of? Why the hell should I believe you? What do you want? Money? Is that your game? How much? You can have it but I don't need to know anything about your child.'

'Nor care! You don't care either, do you?' She began to cry.

'No. I don't care. Why should I?'

'I've wasted years, destroying myself, fretting about this, afraid to tell her, afraid to talk about it to either of them.' The tears coursed down her cheeks. He approached the bed in one swift moment, his face full of disgust at her self-pity.

'It was your choice. Don't you get sentimental with me, madam. What do I care about some child I don't know, never saw? A child you denied me? If it was mine, which I doubt. You've waited long enough to tell me, haven't you? Why should I believe it's mine? What the hell would I have to say to it anyway? You're sick. Not just your body, your fucking mind is warped. You stupid bitch, dreaming up this filthy lie after thirty years. Whatever child you had, it has nothing to do with me. Do you hear me?' As he worked himself into self-righteous rage the words acted upon her like a drill.

'Not an it! A her! A daughter! You selfish unnatural bastard,' she spat. 'You never gave a thought to anyone but yourself.'

'Enough.' He spoke between clenched teeth. 'You seem to have conveniently forgotten that you walked out on me. If you were pregnant, why didn't you damn well tell me then? We might have patched things up. Why wait for thirty years? It's disgusting. Do you hear me? Too late. You kept your child to yourself all those years. So you listen to me, madam. I don't care about your child. Nor do I want anything to do with it. I do not believe it is mine.' He played out the words singly. 'Tell me, just tell me, what are you trying to achieve?'

She was ashen-faced and silent, staring sightlessly into the middle distance until at last she whispered.

'I have her birth certificate here. Look,' she drew her hand from beneath the pillow, 'I registered her in your name.'

'You had no right. No,' he commanded. 'Put it away, I don't want to see it. It's too late. Put it away I said, I want nothing to do with it.'

She lay back exhausted and beaten. She should have listened to Seamus Crowley and left things alone.

'I've been wrong keeping it to myself,' she whispered. 'I was so afraid. I lied to both of them.'

He didn't trouble to ask her what she meant. He looked wretchedly tired but listened impatiently to what she said.

'I never told him that you and I married. I just pretended it didn't happen. I made myself forget about it. I didn't ever let myself think about what I'd done. He died believing I was his real wife. That's when it started to trouble me. Isn't that strange? All those years and just when I was safe, it began to eat me up.'

She drew her thin hand across her eyes and suddenly, without warning, his anger died. The woman meant nothing to him, bore no resemblance to the beautiful, lively girl whom, for a time, he had loved so fiercely. The first of so many. On impulse he perched on the side of the bed and touched her arm gently.

'Why couldn't you just leave things alone?' he asked softly.

'He adopted her, of course, that at least was in order . . .' she rambled. 'He thought the world of her. And she, I only realized it when he died – how much she loved him, how close they were.' Her voice broke. 'I think she preferred him to me.'

'Then why destroy that? You've left it all too late, haven't you?'

'I'll have to think. I feel tired.' She closed her eyes for an instant then put out her hand. 'Give me your paper, I'll sign whatever you want. What does it matter?'

He took the paper from his pocket and watched as, with trembling fingers, she signed her name. He tried unobtrusively to read it but could not without turning it around. She folded it over, and as she handed it back to him, clutched at his hand. He slid the paper into his pocket just as the door opened a crack. A nurse's head nodded at them, muttered an apology and quickly withdrew.

He waited until she dropped off to sleep before extracting his hand. Another shower of rain was lashing against the window. He eased himself off the bed, padded across the room and stood staring gloomily down into the carpark, waiting for the downpour to stop. He should not have come. Without warning, his tension began to grow. The hair on the back of his neck seemed to rise, like an animal alerted to danger. Get out. Get out, an inner voice urged, you've got what you came for.

The rain still pelted down. He turned to the woman in the bed. She looked so pitiful, wretched. Whatever hopes she had of her dismal confession, hadn't worked. But oh how difficult it was to turn his back on her. She'd meant so much to him once. Without meaning to, he whispered:

'Does she look like you?'

Her eyes fluttered open, she smiled faintly.

'No.' She spoke slowly and sleepily. 'She's growing more like you. He wanted me to tell her she wasn't his, but I was afraid she'd go looking for you and then they'd both find out about the marriage. I couldn't let them know how I'd lied. I'd lose her. I knew I'd lose him. I didn't want her to go to London. She'll never come back now . . .' her voice trailed off to a whisper, '. . . spoilt her . . . she preferred him . . . she never hugged me like that.' She drifted off momentarily. 'I don't have to tell her now, do I?' she pleaded.

He did not answer and after a little while she dropped off again and this time appeared to fall asleep. The sweat was standing out on her forehead. He could see it glistening in the light. Time stood still. The rain eased, then stopped. A sudden burst of sunlight flooded the room, making a glaring wall of light behind him as he tiptoed silently towards the door. He paused at the end of her bed when her eyelids fluttered open. She blinked, blinded by the light, and smiled sleepily:

'Ah, Bridget, you got here then.'

The word dropped like melting ice into the

silence. A hoarse croak erupted from his throat as he leapt at her and shook her awake.

'Her name. What is her name? Show me that thing. For God's sake, tell me her name?'

She stared up at him, fear of him flooding into her face again.

'Bridget. I named her Bridget Kate. Why do you ask?'

He blanched. His hands tightened on her shoulders.

'And you? What name do you go by now? Answer me?' He shook her violently.

'Eileen Lacey. I married Fergus Lacey.'

'Bid Lacey.' The name sobbed out of him. His face was contorted with horror as he rocked to and fro.

'Oh no. No.' His hoarse croak was like a death rattle, his dry sobs echoing in the still room while the sunlight made a brilliant mockery of the scene. Her shaking hands clutched at his and gripped them.

'Con? You know her?' Her whisper was barely audible. 'You know my Bridget? Answer me, answer me. How could you know her?'

'Her friend Tom Roberts works for me.'

She looked up at him in puzzlement, shaking her head.

'I met her at his house,' he said flatly.

'I don't understand.' Her words were barely audible.

'We became . . .' He stopped and closed his eyes. 'I love her.'

'No. No. Her fiancé . . . Sarah said . . . foreign . . .' The words came in short gasps. 'Foreign.

402

The flowers ... flowers. I don't understand. She lied ... Bridget,' she whimpered hoarsely. 'You're ... Oh God no ... child ... you said you were ... Oh Oh Oh ... oh dear Mother of God ...' Her hand was at her mouth, her huge terrified eyes boring into him. He just kept nodding as the slow realization dawned, then her mouth opened and with a harsh intake of breath she gave a stifled scream.

'Your child. Your child,' she gasped, her hand at her throat. 'I wrote a letter ... Father ... don't let her get it. Keep it from her.'

He grabbed her by the shoulders and shook and shook her, his face contorted, teeth bared.

'What did you write? When?'

She clutched at her chest and their eyes met in despair as she slumped back against the pillow.

'Oh dear Mother of God,' she prayed, 'oh sweet Jesus help us. The priest. Oh Holy Mother, what have I done?' The wail strangled in her throat.

'What priest? What priest?' he repeated, between clenched teeth. 'What priest? Tell me?' But she had slipped from consciousness. He shook her until she gasped for breath and the spittle drooled from the side of her mouth.

Cas Van Rijn stood up and walked slowly from the room. At the door he stopped to read the name he had missed on the way in and slowly traced its outline with his trembling fingers. Then he passed silently through the hospital like a sleepwalker, his ears pounding to the raucous echo of her gasping breath.

# Bid

*4–9 April 1990*

# CHAPTER TWENTY-EIGHT

Mrs Lacey's body lay pale and still against the rough white sheets, the painfully thin shape barely making an impression on the bed. She had been removed to a small room, tucked away at the end of a long corridor. The dark blue blinds were half-drawn and, apart from the small wooden crucifix above the bed, contained only a white painted chair set close to it. She lay peaceful and serene but so unlike herself that Bid's first reaction was – this is not my mother, there is no life to her.

The incongruity of the thought did not strike her as she stood staring at the effigy, fully realizing for the first time that Eileen's hallmark had been her nervous vivacity; the quick impatient movements her most notable characteristic. Now she looked as numb as Bid felt, the closed face gave no clue to her state of mind when she died. The waxen image was doll-like. Private, independent and unyielding to the last.

As Bid followed the nurse to the room, gagging slightly from the smell of disinfectant, she almost cried out that there had been a mistake. But the nurse went embarrassingly down on her knees and bent her head over her hands. Bid mutely followed, but only out of courtesy, for she could not pray. The shock was too violent, she could barely keep hold of her rampaging thoughts.

After the nurse tiptoed noisily away on her

squeaking shoes, Bid sat for half an hour, silently attempting at last the confession she had so long postponed. Too long. It was so easy now to whisper the loving and soothing words, give the joyful news and receive in return the response she dictated. It was so simple. She wondered dreamily why they had made themselves wretched for so many months.

A life for a death. The stock little phrase repeated in her mind as she tried to block out the treacherous feeling of relief that the punishing silence, following the inevitable recriminations which would have greeted her news, wouldn't now happen. The bookend had slipped off the mantelpiece. She had stepped into the front line, neither child nor yet parent, without an uncomfortable voice to question her actions or motives. These relieved thoughts kept intruding even as she pushed them resolutely aside.

She touched her mother's hands: they were cool rather than cold. Remembering her dead father, she dreaded the waxen touch but Eileen had only been dead for a few short hours. The vestiges of life were not yet obliterated by her death. Bid shuddered and touched the forehead briefly with her lips then turned away and slipped into the corridor towards the room which, over the past weeks, she'd thought of as her mother's. The name was still on the door, the small white label in nun's copperplate: Mrs Eileen Anne Lacey.

The plump middle-aged nurse bustled in after her.

'Will I help you clear the locker?'

'What locker?' Bid, dazed with shock and grief, stood staring at the empty bed. 'Oh . . . I see . . . the bedside locker. No. Keep everything. Or get rid of it.'

'Oh no, I think you should check it out.' The woman spoke with strained patience. 'She was very particular about her personal things. Her handbag is there. Look it's stuffed full.'

Bid smiled wanly. 'Oh, that old one. I haven't seen it for years. A real grown-up bag. I used to long to have one like it when I was small. I always wanted to know what she kept in it.' She stopped short. 'I'm sorry I must go, I can't really do it, not now.' She turned very pale.

'If you like I can help, it'll only take a couple of minutes. We'll have it finished in no time. Anyway I think the doctor would like a few words,' her voice lowered stagily, 'about the post-mortem.'

'Post-mortem?' Bid stared, wondering what the gruesome woman was going on about. 'What do you mean? I don't know anything about a post-mortem.' Panic rose. 'Is that usual?'

'There now. I'm sorry. I thought . . . look I'll go and see if Dr O'Neill is free now, then I'll be back to help.' She bustled out, then paused at the doorway: 'Would you like a cup of tea, pet?'

She returned quickly with a cup of sweet, milky tea. Bid drank it thirstily, suddenly weary and hungry. Everything had happened so suddenly. A few hours before she had been feeling carefree and happy and, with just another week of her notice to work out, even less scrupulous than usual about time. She'd been late in and she fully intended a protracted lunch-time. The wedding day was fixed. Well, almost. Cas had been full of it over the phone from Rotterdam a couple of days before. He asked her how she'd like to live in New York. He had a plan, he said, the divorce was sorted out, they could fix the date, he promised. The champagne was cooling.

Then without warning, just as she was leaving to meet him, everything changed. Ingrid came calling after her as she left the building:

'The hospital just rang. They said you should go at once, your mother has had a bad turn.'

'What?' Bid tried to switch her mind away from thoughts of Cas and bed as she and Ingrid retraced their steps to the office to ring the airport.

She quickly rang the mews and then his office but Cas was at neither. Assuming him to be between the two, she scribbled both telephone numbers and asked Ingrid to explain, then she dashed to the airport.

By the time she'd got to the hospital at twenty past four, it was too late. Her mother had been dead before she'd even stepped on the plane. What was so devastating was that on the previous night, when she'd phoned, her mother had seemed unusually calm, relaxed even. The fact that both of them found it easier to maintain an illusion of closeness by phone was pushed aside, unacknowledged. It was simply something they had worked out since she'd gone into hospital; Bid cajoled and Eileen responded. The night before, they had talked about convalescence and then more vaguely about plans for a short holiday when she recovered.

As soon as the surgeon gave the word, Bid promised, she would go over and settle her in the nursing home in the Wicklow mountains for a couple of weeks. After which, Bid was determined, she would have to persuade her mother to London, at least for a while.

Time and the pregnancy were moving on. The constant travel was exhausting and the recognition that shortly her swelling belly would not conform to the most cunning camouflage was an added strain. If Eileen once brought herself to look at her daughter properly, she would know, but Eileen was mercifully completely preoccupied with her own condition.

Each time she flew to Dublin, Bid told herself that this time, this time for sure she'd spill the beans and each time she shied away, torn between jubilation at the thought of her baby and misery at her mother's probable reaction. When she was strong and safely in London, she knew she was being absurd. Surely her mother would withdraw her objections to Cas once she met him? Cas could charm anyone. And when she knew they were going to get married, surely her objections would be stilled? Specially, oh happy thought, if they could face her with a *fait accompli*. Somehow, she cheered herself, somehow, everything would work out.

Well, it worked out right enough, but it was too sudden, too tremendous to take in. Tears gathered as she recalled the previous grim months. Even while telling herself that pain was distorting Eileen's character, she hadn't responded well to what she saw as her mother's unreasonableness over Cas. That she herself was equally unfair and mendacious did not seem to occur to her. The strain of trying to shield him from the turmoil had become intolerable. Often, she longed to scream her rage

411

against her mother, and seek his consolation. But she always shied away, knowing that what she could forgive, he would not.

Then the cancer. She'd felt responsible for that too, as if her defiance had in some way caused it. But lately, dealing with the illness together, mother and daughter had mercifully managed a sort of truce. Perhaps her mother hoped that now, at last, Bid would come home permanently to look after her? In any event her attitude changed. She became more polite, skirting, but never directly mentioning, Bid's London life. Hardly realizing it, they reverted to their time-honoured practice of keeping unpleasantness at bay. A tactic Eileen had always used with such skill, now Bid too succumbed. Problems ignored ceased to exist. What did not exist required no response. Bid's fall from grace was not mentioned, her lapses dismissed as being of no importance to her Irish existence. London alone was responsible; it wasn't a fit place for a girl.

In this way they concentrated on getting Mrs Lacey through her illness. Frequently, during her visits, Bid felt that her private life was completely unreal; Cas a figment of her imagination. The years in London faded in the face of her mother's determination to excise them. This seemed to be the price of reinstatement in her good opinion. Even as Bid sighed and chided herself for being weak and vacillating, she felt powerless and unwilling to break whatever unspoken agreement they had. It was enough for the moment that they avoided confrontation. Not for the first time she realized that assuaging her mother's moods was, and had

412

always been, the determining dynamic of their small family.

So Bid concentrated on keeping the peace when she might have been wondering if Eileen had always reacted so badly to her boyfriends, or if her prejudice against Cas was especially virulent? In particular she would have done well to pinpoint the moment when marriage was first mooted as the contentious issue. Not sex, *marriage*. But that small quirk got lost somehow.

Part of the trouble was that Bid shared her mother's distaste for Cas's dubious marital status and was shamed by it. Divorce had always been a difficult concept for her. To Eileen it was alien and sordid and Bid's reaction wasn't much different. In many ways it was quite outside either's experience, but Bid's preferences were confused with the realization that, as she got older, the available men she met were, on the whole, quite likely to be divorced. Without consciously consulting her feelings about the issue, and overwhelmed with her consuming passion for her beloved, she accepted it. During their fight, Eileen voiced the repugnance that Bid innately felt but suppressed. If there had ever been a chance of confronting each other it was then, except the moment was lost as fears and insecurities were buried in layers of platitudes, half-truths and finally, stony silence. Their relationship moved to a different plane. They had, in past times, merely simulated closeness, now they found a level of duty and residual regard which perforce took the place of everything more intimate. In any case intimacy had never been Eileen's best suit, at least not with her daughter. For that, and for

413

affection, and for the expression of her loving nature, Bid had always turned to her father. Daddy's girl.

The doctor was tall, painfully thin and owl-eyed with fatigue.

'Miss Lacey? I'm Maire O'Neill, Mr McFadden's registrar.' She shook hands formally then dragged over a chair.

'I'm very sorry to have kept you waiting. We're rushed off our feet. This must be a great shock to you. I'm very sorry. So sudden too.'

'That is what I don't understand.' Bid's voice wobbled momentarily. 'When I spoke to Mr McFadden a couple of days ago he said she was doing well. I was coming to settle her in Mount Rose next weekend.'

'Yes. We were very pleased. The operation was a big hurdle but it went well.' She paused. 'We don't really think the cancer was directly responsible for her death, we think it may have been her heart. We'll be able to say more exactly after the post-mortem.'

'I don't understand . . .'

'It was so sudden.' Dr O'Neill spoke quietly, calming the eruption of emotion which threatened Bid. 'There is always fear of pulmonary embolism after such a major operation, but I examined her some time after eleven this morning and she gave no signs of distress. She was looking forward to seeing you and leaving hospital. Really, she was in good form. We chatted for a few minutes. She was well enough to see a vistitor. He arrived just as I was leaving her.

'Then at lunch-time, one of the nursing staff

414

found her collapsed and unconscious. It must have happened only minutes before.'

'Wasn't anything done to revive her?'

'We tried, of course. I'm very, very sorry.' She put her hand on Bid's. 'Will you be able to come in tomorrow? Mid-morning. I'm sure you'd like to talk to Mr McFadden and we should be able to tell you the exact cause of death.'

A young nurse put her head around the door.

'Oh, Dr O'Neill, Mr Murphy is roaring the place down in number eight.'

The doctor stood up. 'Tomorrow then? I'll be here. We can clear everything up and you can have the death certificate. You'll need it to make . . . er . . . arrangements. I can ask the chaplain to be here if you like.'

'No. Thank you.' Bid held out her hand. 'Father Crowley will probably . . . The visitor, I expect it was him, was it?' she asked abruptly.

'Oh?' The young doctor was about to remark that it seemed an unlikely profession for so handsomely dressed a man, but Bid had apparently lost interest and began to fiddle with the objects on the bed.

Dr O'Neill left quietly. Shortly afterwards the nurse returned and began taking things from the locker. Towels, nightdresses and books piled up on the bed.

'I'll just take the handbag, nurse,' Bid said firmly. 'Can you arrange disposal of the rest?'

'Certainly, dear, but let me just check the pockets.'

She pulled several bits of paper, a fiver and a couple of letters Bid recognized as her own from the dressing-gown pocket. These she popped into the bag and handed it to Bid.

'I think that's everything. If anything else of importance shows up, I'll give it to you tomorrow.' She smiled briefly, nodded and picked up the bundle from the bed.

'Is there somewhere I can make a phone call please?'

'There's a callbox at the end of the corridor.' The nurse glanced at Bid's desolated face. 'There's a much more private one in the office. Come, you can use that.'

Bid let the number ring twenty-five times before hanging up. It was now well after six and Cas was still not at home, nor was there any reply from his office. She tried her own flat on the off-chance and got her anwering machine. She rang Sarah and told her about her mother's death.

'Oh, Bid dear, I'm so sorry. Are you all right? Do you want me to come over?' Bid didn't answer. 'Bid? Are you still there? I can come, honest, I could be there by tomorrow evening . . .'

'Sal.' Bid sounded out of control. 'I can't get hold of Cas. He should be at the flat. That blasted Ingrid, I asked her specially, I bet she forgot. Can you ring him? I'm just leaving the hospital. I'll be at home, you know the number.'

'Oh, Bid, no. Not on your own. Isn't there anyone? Cas should be with you.'

'Sarah, just ring him will you? Please. He'll come.' Bid impatiently rose to his defence. 'I'll be fine . . .'

'Don't worry, I'll tell him. Bid, did you hear what I said? Shall I come over?'

'Thanks, Sal, but no. I think I'd prefer to do this alone. There's the church thing. You'd be lost. The neighbours will help. I'll ring if . . .'

Listening to her disembodied voice, Sarah could almost feel her disappear into her background, her grief, her church, the lot. Suddenly Bid sounded like a foreigner and hearing it, Sarah felt shy and anxious.

'Bid, if you change your mind, I'll come at once.'

'Thanks, Sarah, just be there when I get back, please. I can't believe she's dead.' She spoke almost to herself. 'I wish I could have convinced her everything will be all right.'

'Bid? I'll ring later on. Sure you're OK? Is there anyone to take care of you?'

'Yes. More than enough. Just find Cas will you, Sal? Please.'

# CHAPTER TWENTY-NINE

The taxi began its long slow crawl to the old house by the canal, held up at every intersection by the rush-hour traffic streaming out of the city. Sinking back, Bid tried to concentrate on the business of arranging her mother's burial. Where to start? As she worked through what she remembered of the ritual of her father's funeral, her anxious thoughts kept sliding to her failure to make contact with Cas. She needed him with her to help sort things out, to get through it, otherwise she'd panic and make a complete mess . . .

The taxi came to an abrupt halt a couple of hundred yards from Charlemont bridge. She got out wearily and was paying the driver when Maureen Lenehan's car pulled up behind her.

'Oh, Bridget, there you are!' A middle-aged thickset woman hoisted herself out of the car and enfolded Bid in her arms. 'I'm sorry for your trouble, lamb. I rang the hospital at five to ask after your mam. God save us, Bridgie, what happened to her at all? I couldn't believe it.'

Bid fumbled in her bag for her keys. Her dry throat made her voice croak.

'Neither could I. It happened so suddenly. She was getting on great. They rang me at lunch-time. It seems like an age. Oh, Maureen, I was too late.' She started blindly towards the house.

'For heaven's sake, girl, you're not thinking of

going inside that house on your own? You're coming straight back with me this minute. I wouldn't hear of anything else. No noes, darlin'. You'll have plenty to do tomorrow. You look all in, girl.' Her lilting Kerry voice rose with her agitation. 'You come straight back with me. 'Tis only Dinny and myself. A warm supper and straight to sleep with you.'

Maureen took her arm firmly and led her back to where her battered Rover was sitting four or five feet from the curb, causing chaos to the traffic rounding the corner. Bid pulled back.

'I'd better stay here, Maureen, really. There'll be people trying to get me at this number.' She nodded towards the house. 'I'll come to your place tomorrow,' she promised bleakly.

'Indeed and you won't do any such thing. Sure what's wrong with our phone? 'Twas working the last time I tried. You can ring who you like.'

Bid looked indecisively from car to house.

'Bridget, facing things in the day is a whole lot easier than in a dark empty house at night, all on your own. Come on now, child, let us look after you.' Her voice softened with concern. 'You need something to eat. You look exhausted.'

Bid shrugged, smiled her thanks and took Maureen's arm again. As they turned back towards the car she glanced across the canal. There were two little boys perched on the bar of the lock-gate, fishing, otherwise the bank was deserted.

'What is it?' Maureen asked. Bid pointed at the children.

'My dad and I used to sit there, feeding the ducks. I wish . . .' She sighed. 'They just reminded me.' She bit her lip and climbed into the car. At the same moment a short, portly priest came trotting around the corner, out of breath and red in the face.

'Mrs Lenehan. Bridget,' he puffed. 'Wait a minute!'

Bid went back to him. He caught her by the shoulders and held her to him. He smelt consolingly of tobacco, like Fergus: she leaned against him.

'My dear child,' he said. 'I am very, very sorry. Your poor mother. The Lord have mercy on her soul.'

'Oh Father,' she whispered. 'I got there too late, there was so much I wanted to . . . I was too late.'

'There, there child.' He patted her hand. 'You were over every five minutes. Sure no-one could have done more.' He held her around the shoulders as they walked to the car. 'You're going to the Lenehans' tonight? That's the best thing to do. In with you now.' He opened the car door. 'Bridget, there are some things to be gone through. Your mam asked me to give you a hand, before she went into hospital.' He spoke in a whisper, then leaned in the window. 'Mrs Lenehan, I'll come around tomorrow morning early and take her to the house.'

Maureen was astonished at his peremptory tone and then upset when her protests that she would come and help were unskilfully set aside.

'We need to have a bit of a chat first. In private. If you could take over a bit later, Mrs Lenehan, that would be grand. There'll be a lot to see to. Would you be able to manage breakfast for me if I come around at eight?' he wheedled.

Maureen regarded him speechlessly, affronted at the high-handed way he was muscling in. Was he suggesting she couldn't look after the girl she'd known since she was a schoolgirl? The cheek of him.

'Of course. We have it then ourselves. We'd be delighted.' She didn't sound overjoyed. 'Father.'

She turned the ignition and roared off, furious that she'd been outmanoeuvred in the caring stakes. Bid sat staring straight ahead, embarrassed.

'That Seamus Crowley has a very bossy way with him,' Maureen said peevishly. 'Breakfast indeed. He must think I came down in the last shower. Trying to avoid Mary Ann Finnerty's lumpy porridge is what he's up to. Those old priests are forever on the scrounge. Eight o'clock, how are you. What would you be getting up at eight for, pet? 'Tis the middle of the night,' she finished scornfully.

Bid blew her nose and, with the instinct that was second nature to her, poured oil on her troubled friend.

'Poor old thing spends his whole life trying to avoid meals at home. You should go around to his house on Miss Finnerty's day off and you'd find him fussing around the kitchen in his big red apron. Like an old woman. But he's a hell of a good cook.'

'You don't mean it?'

'Oh absolutely. A real pro.' She shot backwards as Maureen swerved into the pavement with a violent snort of laughter.

'Bridget Lacey. You're making it up.'

'No, I'm not. It's true.'

Maureen guffawed loudly.

'Well then, it must be a real purgatory for him living with the smell of Mary Ann Finnerty's messes. I nearly got sick the last time I called, you'd wonder what she does with it.' She laughed again, the priest temporarily restored to her good graces. Bid eased herself against the backrest and stared moodily out of the window.

The Lenehans had a lock-up garage a couple of streets from their house in Mount Pleasant. Maureen took Bid's arm as they walked home. Their mood had turned sombre, both of them filled with dread of the days ahead.

'Have a nice hot bath while I get the tea, pet. You look awful tired. You must try to put everything out of your mind tonight and rest. The next few days are going to be hard for you. And busy. You won't have time to bless yourself. The main thing to remember is that we're here, Dinny and me. Whatever you need, just ask, lamb. We'll be with you.' She squeezed Bid's arm and put the key in the door. As they entered the hall she put her finger to her lips.

'You go straight up to the phone in our bedroom and make whatever calls you like, then come and see Dinny. He's stretched out in front of the box. Snoring probably. I'll be in the kitchen. Off you go, I'll make up a bed for you in Mairead's old room.'

The phone was on a low table beside the gigantic bed. As she sat down Bid glimpsed herself in the dressing-table mirror. She was white as a sheet and, as she tried to dial, her fingers began to tremble.

'Please, oh please let him be there,' she prayed as the phone began to ring. Her longing for Cas's comforting arms was intense. Ten, twenty times and no reply. Where was he? Could he have gone back to Holland? She rang the office on the off-chance that, finding her away, he would work late, but the answering machine was on as it always was out of office hours. She left the Lenehans' number. Then she dialled directory enquiries for the code for Amsterdam. In answer to her stuttered enquiry, she was told that Mr Van Rijn had returned to London very early that morning, his present whereabouts were unknown.

Sarah must have been sitting beside the phone. 'Where are you, Bid? I've been ringing and ringing.'

'I didn't go home, I'm staying with the Lenehans.' She gave the number. 'I'll be at the house tomorrow I expect. So much to arrange . . .' Her voice trailed off. She was unaccountably frightened of asking if Sarah had found Cas.

'Bid, Mum said she'd have Alice if you needed me. Laurence would have to come because of the feeding.' Sarah sounded dubious but obviously anxious to help.

'No, Sarah. Please. It's not necessary. I'm very grateful, but honestly there's no need.'

'Are you sure?'

'Sure. Funerals happen very quickly here. Probably on Friday or Saturday, if her body is released from the hospital.'

'How do you mean, released?'

'There's to be a post-mortem.'

'Is that usual?'

'I don't know. Something about the death being so sudden.' Her voice broke. 'I suppose they want to be sure or something.'

'Won't it take ages?'

423

'I don't think so, tomorrow they said. I'll ring you when I know. Sarah? I'm coming back as soon as ever I can. I just want to get home. It's all very strange here. I feel as if I don't belong any more. I don't think I can stand it for long.' She fell silent.

'Bid, I didn't manage to get on to Cas yet. The secretary, what's-her-name, is off with flu, Mrs Petrie. I could get no sense out of the temp, finally I managed to get hold of Johannes. He said Cas got in from Amsterdam early this morning then left again about half an hour later.'

'Did he say where he was going?'

'Seems not. But he told Johannes to arrange some appointments for tomorrow, so I guess he's around. I tried the flat several times but no luck. I asked Roy Angel to stick a message on your door in case he turns up there.'

'That's OK then. As long as he knows where I am. I was supposed to meet him at lunch-time. I don't know what I'd do without him . . . or you,' she added hurriedly. 'Sal? Does he know my mother died?'

'Not unless someone from your office told him.'

Dinny's liberality with the Tullamore Dew sent an exhausted Bid into a long restless sleep. In the middle of the night, half-asleep half-awake, she was sure Cas had followed her and was waiting on the steps of her house. She came awake as she struggled with her clothes and whimpered with frustration and anxiety before crawling back to bed.

When she woke next morning she could not, for a few minutes, remember where she was or why.

The sun was streaming in the window but when she looked out she saw the sky was already filling with dark clouds and surmised that the day's ration of sunlight was about to be cut off.

'And here's me without a raincoat,' she murmured distractedly as memories of the previous day came flooding back, with the accompanying regrets for opportunities missed.

If only. The refrain had become her theme song. If only the hospital had rung earlier. If only she'd taken time off. She lamented not staying in Dublin for the duration of her mother's illness while admitting that she couldn't have borne separation from Cas for so long. Her guilt welled up, obliterating for the moment her mother's contribution to the tensions of their relationship. She could feel a huge blank in her emotions. All that futile energy wasted on evasions and half-truths, when the air might so easily have been cleared. She should have come straight out and presented with conviction the fact of her love for Cas. She should have insisted that, at thirty, she was capable of choosing for herself.

Then, with a slight flush of anger, she suddenly recalled her mother's reply when, as a little girl, she had asked why she didn't have grandparents like everyone else.

'Your daddy's parents are dead.'

'But what about my other grandmother and grandfather? Mairead Lenehan has two whole sets!'

Her mother's face had been suffused with anger as she looked away.

'They didn't like me running off to get married,' she said roughly and banged the saucepan down on the stove. 'Go out and play.'

And that apparently was that. No other information required, at least not by a curious eight-year-old. No amount of sly questioning had yielded anything further.

Shivering, she got out of bed. The memory of the abandoned parents underlined just how unrealistic her fantasy had been. Her mother had a relentless, unforgiving streak. But then, as suddenly, she was assailed by happier memories of her childhood: Fergus's arms wrapped around her when nightmares terrified her into her parents' bed. The three of them by the sea in Kilduff, huddled behind the brightly coloured windshield, Mam rubbing warmth into her sea-chilled arms. Consoled, she discounted the bitterness she felt at more recent difficulties. They would have resolved them. They cared too much about each other not to. Didn't they? Well, didn't they?

A wave of nausea hit her as she stepped into the shower. She leaned back against the wall and waited for it to pass, then bent over the loo as she began to retch. She lay prone against it until the light-headedness was gone, then let the scalding shower ease her aching muscles. As she soaped herself she felt a flutter of movement in her belly. She closed her eyes and let the pleasure embrace her.

'Breakfast in ten minutes, Bridgie.' Maureen banged on the door. 'Himself will be here any minute with his knife and fork.' Father Seamus Crowley PP was obviously back in the dog-house. Bid wrapped the huge bath towel around her and came out of the bathroom drying her hair.

'I'll just get dressed, can I use Mairead's dryer?'

'Of course you can, what are you asking for?' Maureen looked at her closely. 'Did you sleep well, darlin'? You're still looking awful pale.'

'I think Dinny slipped me a Mickey Finn,' Bid said, avoiding her eye. 'I was out like a light.'

# CHAPTER THIRTY

Father Crowley was like a hen on a hot griddle all through breakfast, endlessly repeating an overlong explanation of the details of the requiem service. When he ran out of things to say, he sat hunched and silent before asking awkwardly when she'd last heard from her mother and if there was anything she wanted to discuss. This insistence startled Bid whose thoughts leapt guiltily to what was uppermost in her mind and the cause of the nausea which her plate of bacon and eggs revived; her baby. She was too busy trying to hold on to her breakfast to grasp the fact that the priest was referring to her mother. Nor did it occur to her that he might know how strained relations between them had become, since she persisted in the mistaken opinion that they had achieved such skill in the art of dissembling that nobody guessed they were not quite as close as mother and only child might be expected to be. Without articulating the thought, she was fearful that their failure to find happiness in each other – the only living relation either had – marked a fatal flaw in both their characters and she was ashamed lest anyone – the priest for instance – would perceive that failure and blame her. To keep him from more personal questions, she asked him to repeat the order of service again.

Maureen, hovering between kitchen and dining-room, watched the interaction with interest. It dawned on her that the priest was talking simply for the sake of it, rambling from one thing to another as he tried in vain to get Bid's full attention. He had clearly something specific on his mind but couldn't manage to get to the point, specially since every time the phone rang Bid jumped sky-high and rushed to answer it. But whoever she was waiting for didn't call, as was evident from the way she drooped each time she put down the receiver, becoming ever more distracted. Whatever it was Father Crowley had intended to say, was postponed for the time being.

After he left, Maureen and Bid went to call on the undertaker to discuss the funeral and removal. They were ushered into a waiting-room stagily designed in deep mournful red and black and so full of overstuffed chairs and drapes that sounds were also suitably muted. Avoiding each other's eyes, they sat in silence until an unseen hand switched on funereal muzak and Bid began to shake, at first with suppressed nervous giggles, then catching Maureen's eye, with great gasps of uncontrolled laughter. They were wiping the tears of mirth from their eyes when the undertaker glided into the room and stood sombrely at the door waiting for their attention.

After they'd calmed sufficiently, he explained what he was pleased to call the Arrangements. He gave the word a rather particular significance, an implied capital A. Imperceptibly he dispelled Bid's rising hysteria, describing his ceremonial duties impersonally and never once using emotive words like body or burial or dead. He had the stance and voice of an ageing actor. His voice was beautifully modulated and entirely compelling.

The deceased, he intoned piously, had to be taken to the church overnight or, if she preferred, he proffered his invitation in hushed tones, he could keep Mother in their own, private, chapel-of-rest. The two women were led forth, both unnerved and inclined to giggle again at the extraordinary decor. After a brief look at the inner sanctum, which matched the waiting-room, and which they afterwards described as Black Magic kitsch, Bid politely opted for St Stephen's.

By the time they drove to the hospital, the post-mortem had been completed; now, there was just the question of the release. Bid couldn't quite bring herself to talk about The Body either. She felt, if she felt at all, like an automaton. She listened, but at some remove. Maureen stood beside her, consolingly holding her arm, while the consultant explained to Bid that her mother had had a pulmonary embolus. It was not unusual, he said evenly, it sometimes happened after surgery. He rolled the smooth sentences like balm, quietly and without emphasis. The staff had been aware of the danger, he said. She had been monitored carefully but there had been no symptoms. Then Dr O'Neill confirmed she had seen Eileen an hour or so before it happened and she'd appeared normal, still a slight fever but recovering well. As a matter of fact she'd been talking about going to the Mount Rose convalescent home and was obviously looking forward to it.

There could have been no warning because she

didn't call the staff, nor indeed had her visitor, who was still with her at twelve when sister last checked. They could explain what had caused Eileen's death, but offered no explanation as to why it had happened so suddenly, so unexpectedly. Bid was relieved they did not try.

As if he had been waiting in the wings for his cue, the undertaker arrived to take charge just as the interview came to an end, bringing with him his weird hint of theatricality. Reality bowed out and Bid watched helplessly as, addressing himself to Maureen, he eased her gently through the well-practised routine. It was like stepping onto a conveyor belt requiring little but a flaccid acceptance that, as the hours rolled by, the arrangements would slot into place. Curiously, it proved a solace rather than the ordeal she'd anticipated. Almost without noticing, she became immersed in the ancient ritual augmented through practice and time. In this way, inexorably, she was drawn back into her native community and to her own people.

Some time during that long day she stopped hoping Cas would call, because she knew if he had, she probably would have urged him to stay away and let her get on with things alone. Deliberately, she set aside her adult self, for it was in a sense the last time she would be a child. She wanted about her only those who knew her mother and the little family in happier times. She became encapsulated in solitude and memory; unwilling to explain and unable to share.

And so, with the discreet help of the undertaker, Eileen Lacey's final journey to church and graveyard was arranged. By six o'clock that Thursday evening, Father Crowley was in his sombre vestments greeting the mourners who gathered outside the church. Faces from Bid's past stepped up and held her hand. Acquaintances mainly, for the eight years since her departure had thinned her circle to those who had not themselves emigrated. Her mother had few friends, being little given to socializing. 'Sorry for your trouble' was repeated again and again. Kindly half-remembered faces of her father's colleagues. The staff from the shoe shop where Eileen had worked. The priest's ancient housekeeper, the redoubtable Mary Ann. Bartley Quinlan. A surprising number of neighbours past and present. Old Matt Burke who fed the canal ducks. Two or three stall-holders from the market. A few of Bid's school-friends. She felt embraced, consoled. But where had they all come from?

'Dinny took care of the death notice in the newspapers,' Maureen whispered.

'When?' asked Bid, bewildered.

'While we were at the undertakers, lamb. People like to pay their respects.'

With the Lenehans on either side, Bid led the congregation into the church and the relentless ceremonial proceeded. Afterwards, Dinny or someone must have relayed the message that they should come back to the house and they had, bringing with them plates of sandwiches, or cake, or brown-bagged bottles. Everyone seemed to have an anecdote to tell. A small kindness remembered or more likely, invented. A word about Eileen's courage as the cancer took hold. Fergus was conjured up, the memory of his quiet thoughtfulness recollected by an old workmate. She was reminded consolingly of

432

her parents' pride in her and, mistaking the well-intentioned platitudes for knowledge, assumed Eileen must have spoken of her often, and was pleased. People smiled and nodded and asked if it wasn't time she was getting married? Had they heard a little hint from Mammy? A little rumour? Would she ever come back or was she settled beyond?

Beyond. It wasn't even named. It could have been anywhere or nowhere so little meaning did it have. Even the way England was pronounced had a special almost sinister emphasis suggesting a dreary landscape of belching factories or council wastelands. The years of living and loving in London floated away, reduced to an anonymity which might have shocked her had she been able to feel anything at all.

She wasn't alone for a second. She could think of nothing or no-one but her mother's absence, and the awful solitude of her own situation. At some point in the proceedings she found herself staring at her own image in the bathroom mirror and addressing the small blob within her which represented her only hope of a living, blood relative. Suddenly, with a force that amazed her, long-suppressed disappointment with Cas for his procrastination over the divorce turned to resentment. He should be with her, helping her. She needed a husband by her side, not strangers. He would have known what to do.

Or would he? How do they arrange funerals in Holland? she asked the mirror. What are the words? How do they arrange weddings? Or divorce? Or the frigging evening meal? How do they live and die? Who cares?

Cas cared. She laid her face against the cool glass and memories of his passion and gentleness swept over and submerged her doubts. But in that momentary terrifying loss of confidence, before she pushed that uncomfortable doubt aside, she had a stark glimpse of how little she knew about the father of her child. And the frailty of her trust.

She pulled herself together, ran a comb through her hair, and stared moodily at her image. She climbed the side of the bath to get a full-length view, turning precariously from side to side to see if she could detect the bulge. Only when she convinced herself she could not, did she force herself downstairs again. She hesitated in the hall, listening to the buzz of voices through the open doors then, unnoticed, slipped outside to walk the deserted streets in the cool and soothing evening air.

She was gone for something over half an hour and apparently had not been missed for, as soon as she returned, she was once more submerged in enquiry and consoling reminiscence and her melancholy thoughts were set aside for future contemplation. As the evening went on the party got livelier and it was well past midnight when, with yet another hot drink, she was tucked up in bed by Maureen.

'I can't believe she's gone. I don't feel anything. I haven't even cried.'

'Give yourself time, girl.' Maureen sat on the bed beside her. 'Just let yourself go with the arrangements. It gets you over those first few awful days. That's what it's all about. There'll be time enough to face reality. Just let it wash over you.' She sat quiet for a moment or two then took Bid's hand.

'Bid dear, you don't want to talk about anything do you? You're not, er ... blaming yourself for anything, are you? I've known you for a long time and I ... I.' Maureen sought the right words. 'I'm not interfering now, but I've seen you take too much on yourself. So don't be fretting about what might have been. If you need any help you always know where to find me. Or *anything* you need to talk about, I'll be here.' She smiled into Bid's eyes. 'You need to be strong now, lamb.' She bent and touched Bid's forehead with her lips and left the room quickly without glancing back at Bid's startled face.

The funeral was more difficult. The lessons were read and the hymns sung, then Father Crowley spoke about his old friend. Bid, sitting bolt upright in the front seat, wondered that he'd known her mother so long or so well. Or perhaps he didn't for she hardly recognized Eileen from his palliative description until she fathomed that actually he was talking about his friendship for her father, and it was with Fergus that he coloured his description of their family life. He made it sound idyllic. Yet, perversely, she resented her mother being set aside.

It was two forty-five when they set out on the long, sad journey to the grave. It was, by Dublin standards, a short procession: first the hearse, then a second sleek black undertaker's car with Father Crowley beside the driver. The Lenehans sat on the back seat with Bid wedged between them. Seven or eight private cars followed, each holding two or more friends or acquaintances. The cortège edged away from the church and looped slowly around through the side streets of Mount Pleasant until it

435

emerged by the traffic lights leading to Canal Road. Then, at a snail's pace, the line of cars turned left and paused for a few seconds on Toronto Terrace, outside the Lacey home, before gathering speed to the graveyard, several miles further to the west.

Bid, crushed uncomfortably between the bulky Lenehans, stared ahead, preoccupied and silent. As the car pulled away, Dinny, who was idly looking out the right-hand window, murmured to his wife:

'Those little gurriers have been glued to that lock for the past couple of weeks. They're a gas pair, they never give up. But I'd say any fish in that canal would be dead long ago. They ought to be at school.'

Maureen and Bid swivelled awkwardly to look out the back window. The scene looked much the same as the day before. The same two little boys. Bid glanced back, blinked, then peered intently into the receding view. Somewhere off at the very edge of her vision she saw, or imagined, a rising figure, hardly perceived before it faded. She shivered.

'Hello,' exclaimed Dinny a moment later. 'There seems to be a bit of excitement. They must have caught something – ah too late.' Bid, staring anxiously behind her, began to weep in great gasping sobs. Three hands reached out to hold hers but she rejected them and buried her face in her handkerchief and the rest of the journey was punctuated by her stifled whimpers.

The rain held off until after the coffin had been lowered into the grave, the decade of the Rosary recited and the mourners were ambling back towards the cars. A small group returned to the Lenehans'. This time it was more formal, a few

436

words, a cup of tea or drink and gradually they melted away. Bid was almost fainting with strain and fatigue by the time Maureen and Dinny escorted the last of the stragglers into the hall.

Father Crowley remained sitting beside her, as he had since their return from the cemetery. He'd said little but seemed unable to let her out of his sight and she was relieved by his undemanding presence. She had become disorientated and felt as though she were observing an illusory performance of strangers. She had not thought about her own life, or about Cas, all day except for that eerie moment on the way to the cemetery.

The phone had rung for her several times. She refused the calls saying she would return them later. London seemed a million miles away. She could no longer connect and, so isolated did she feel, that she could not imagine another place or time, except the experience she was floating through, swept along in the silence of her fermenting grief. Or was it terror that now, alone, she could no longer use her mother's opposition as justification for her actions?

'Will you stay here tonight, Bridget?' Father Crowley broke into her thoughts.

'No, Father, I think I must go to the house. There's all my mother's things to see to . . . I think I prefer to do it now.'

'Yes, lamb.' Maureen had come back. 'But you don't need to spend the night there, do you?'

'I think I must,' Bid said sadly. 'It may be the last time. I have to get back to London tomorrow or Sunday.' Her face was expressionless.

'Oh Lord,' said Maureen. 'I forgot all that. It's as if you never left – what with everything. Tell you what, Bridgie. I could come around with you for a bit. If you want, mind.'

'Please,' Bid said. 'I would, please.'

'And I'll drop around there after Mass tomorrow morning,' Father Crowley asserted firmly. 'Will that be all right?'

The house was cold, the blinds had been drawn and, after the weeks of Mrs Lacey's absence, was musty and dank. Maureen, clucking and scolding, set fires in the kitchen and front room.

'The place is like a morgue.' She started and her hand shot to her mouth. 'Oh God, Bridgie, I'm sorry.'

'It is like a morgue. It feels like nobody ever lived in it. Do you feel that?'

'I do, I do. It's a gloomy old place, never liked it myself. What'll you do with it? You know someone had approached her to buy it? Bartley Quinlan was telling me last night.'

'Yes. She told me last week. She was thinking of buying a flat in Sandymount. Poor Mam, she really liked that flat. I wish she hadn't waited so long. I asked Bartley to go ahead and sell. I could never bear to come back here after this,' she added fiercely. 'I don't ever want to see this house again.'

'I don't blame you. Tell me what you want to do now?'

'I suppose I should return some of those telephone calls.'

'Right. I've written the names and numbers. While you're doing that, I'll put on the kettle.'

Bid rang the magazine and spoke briefly to Edy Hampshire. Because of her mother's death, she explained, she would not be returning to work out

438

the last days of her notice. She felt relieved at her decision though still curiously divorced from her own life. The whole situation was so unfamiliar and unreal that she wasn't sure she could do much more talking without breaking down. She wished Maureen would go.

Neither Cas nor Sarah answered. Though part of her ached to talk, work things out, she welcomed the respite. Even Cas, beloved Cas, was retreating from her preoccupied mind. She knew he would be in touch eventually, meantime she would get on with what needed to be done. She rang Bartley Quinlan.

Then, drinking endless cups of tea, she and Maureen wandered the empty rooms, arranging the disposition of furniture and clothes. As they sorted and bagged the remains of Eileen Lacey's life, they hardly looked at each other and didn't speak much either. Until at ten o'clock Maureen said:

'I'm wilted. You're not going to go through that desk tonight are you, pet? Why not go to bed and give it an early start in the morning?'

Then, while Bid nervously tried the phone again, Maureen made up a bed and insisted on filling three hot-water bottles.

'The place will be freezing once the fires die down. You couldn't heat an old place like this. It'd give you your death of cold.' She groaned. 'Oh Lord, there I go again putting my big foot in it. I'll be back to take you away to lunch and we can close the place up after you see Bartley Quinlan – if you're ready that is . . .' She hugged Bid. 'I'm not happy about you being on your own. If you can't stand it, come around, or ring. I'll come anytime of the night. OK?'

The night was punctuated hourly with the results of the copious tea-drinking. At about five, Bid abandoned any hope of further sleep and, wrapping a blanket around herself, went down to the living-room. She revived the embers of the fire and opened the roll-top desk. Images of her mother immediately flooded into her mind: the slim hand turning the key. Her head turned, her hand covering whatever she was reading. The slight figure with the cloud of chestnut hair pounding at the piano while the child Bid marched around the sofa. Mam chasing her with a wet dishcloth, flailing the air when her rules had been broken. How young she must have been then. Bid wept as she recalled waking one day, after a painful visit to the dentist, to find her mother sitting at the edge of the bed with a great soft cream bun held out as a treat.

Other less comfortable images intruded: Bid and Fergus guiltily holding out a bunch of flowers, trying to make Eileen smile as she turned away and stared stonily out the bedroom window. Then Bid had a vivid recollection of walking to the church one Good Friday night with her cold hands stuck into the pockets of her mother's frightful moth-eaten fur coat. We were happy then, she thought. When did it all change? As if in answer, Fergus emerged from the background: the rock upon which they both depended. She could almost hear his gentle voice:

'Ah sweet Bridget, my *bonus bonorum bonarum*!'

Mrs Lacey's desk had a treble row of small drawers, a space in the centre for inkpots – missing – and a torn, black skiver writing-pad with space to hold pens. As a child, it had drawn Bid as would a magic box, the special treat for good girls to play at. It smelled faintly of lavender, the old oak darkened and polished almost black.

Starting at the top left hand corner, she began to slide open each drawer in turn: electricity, gas, insurance, telephone bills were set aside to be dealt with by the solicitor. There were bank statements, a deposit account with two thousand pounds, a current account holding one hundred and twenty-nine pounds, a half-used cheque book. Bid squinted sadly at the familiar writing. Some letters from Bartley Quinlan about the sale of the house. She felt outraged that Eileen wouldn't enjoy the benefit of her scrimping and saving. Then, touchingly, she came across a drawer full of her own letters and, in the one underneath, a thick bundle of her magazine columns, all neatly clipped and arranged chronologically. It was too much, Bid put her head down on the desk and wept bitterly.

Ten-year-old copies of her parents' wills were tied with magenta ribbon, everything to their beloved daughter, Bridget Kate Lacey. Notes on insurance policies were tucked neatly under the ribbon. Eileen had been so punctilious about her affairs that Bid concluded she must have realized how desperately ill she was.

The main drawers of the desk were not so neat. Bundles of old bills, all dated and marked paid and going back seven or eight years, letters, a box of old newspaper cuttings of no apparent interest, half-used note pads, labels, string. Bid used most of it to revive the smouldering fire. Then, as she gathered the last bits and pieces, she noticed the corner of a grubby manila envelope protruding from beneath the drawer lining. She pulled it open and spilled its contents on the desk top.

Four or five certificates: births, baptisms. Her parents' marriage, her father's death. She turned them over rapidly, searching for her own birth certificate which her mother had claimed, over and over, was mislaid.

*'I have them all safe somewhere, I just can't seem to lay my hands on them,'* she wrote long after Bid had already applied for the original, which was also inexplicably unavailable. But by then Bid realized that the Registrar would as easily accept her passport and hadn't pursued the matter. Now she wondered when she had last seen it? Or indeed if she had ever clapped eyes on it at all? Her first rough search did not reveal it. Perplexed, she went through the little pile again, more carefully.

Fergus Joseph Lacey and Eileen Ann Sullivan. Marriage. The scribbled signature of the witnesses and priest, names she had never heard. The date was blurred as if the writer had run out of the thick black ink in which it was written and had to go over it again, making it difficult to decipher. Church. Her parents had apparently been married in Dundalk, which puzzled her. As far as she knew they had no ties there.

Beneath it was her baptism certificate. Bridget Kate Lacey. Star of the Sea Church, Sandymount. 27 June 1959. Baptized on the day of birth? Strange. Of course, it was customary for sickly babies, as perhaps she might have been, though as far as she could recall such a thing had never been mentioned. Bid stared at it for a moment then, lining it up with the marriage certificate, compared the dates.

Well, well, well. Miss Bridget Kate Lacey was admitted to Holy Mother Church exactly nine weeks after her parents' wedding. The old frauds, was what she thought. Affectionately, even a little proudly.

She rubbed her stomach and grinned to herself. A second generation on the way. More of the same. Like mother like daughter. How very secretive they'd been. Suddenly it gave them a touch, a hint, of romance. An attractive sort of sinning. It humanized them. She went into the kitchen and made a cup of coffee. She hummed tunelessly. She returned to the desk and went through the other forms in more leisurely fashion.

Her parents' birth and baptisms recorded for posterity. She noted her mother's birthplace, Ballymahon, which she'd not known. Eileen had been very secretive about that too. Now of course Bid knew why. She checked the name against her old school atlas and found the village or small town straddling the border of Cork and Waterford. She vested Eileen in a warm glow of daring; thrown out of home because she was pregnant. No wonder she'd been so defensive about grandparents. Regret that she hadn't confided in her mother engulfed Bid. How easy it

443

would have made her predicament had she known her mother had gone through the same thing. Surely they would have been drawn closer, not riven apart?

A loud banging at the front door woke her from her abstraction. She glanced at her watch. It was only half-past seven.

'Did I wake you, Bridget?' Father Crowley stood on the doorstep. Behind him, to the left, two police cars blocked the bridge where a huge tarpaulin was being erected over the lock basin.

'Has there been an accident, Father?' she asked listlessly.

'There's a report that some drunk fell in the lock, God help us. I'm surprised you didn't hear the commotion. It's been going on since dawn. There's talk of pumping it out. I expect it's another false alarm. It happens from time to time.' He didn't seem unduly perturbed until he glanced at her swaddled form and looked shyly away. 'Would you prefer if I called back later?'

'No. Come in Father. I'll go and get dressed. There's a fire in the sitting-room and some coffee. I'll be down in a few minutes.'

He had drawn back the curtains and was standing at the desk with the two certificates in his hand when she returned.

'I see you've made a discovery,' he began cautiously.

'Yes. Did you know about it?' she asked chattily as she switched off the light. 'I'm sorry she never told me. It's rather romantic, isn't it?'

He gave a non-committal grunt.

'Have you found anything else of interest?' He spoke lightly, but his sharp blue eyes watched her so

444

intently she felt repelled by what she took to be prying. It was so unlike him. Unexpected. The way he'd been with Maureen. She wondered suddenly if she liked him at all.

'Nothing apart from the fact that my parents were married in Dundalk – I wonder why there? – only a couple of months before I was born. I wish they'd told me,' she said. 'I would have understood.'

'Would you, Bridget?'

'Of course.' She shrugged nonchalantly. 'It happens all the time, nobody takes the slightest notice.' She was dismissive, all woman-of-the-world.

'They do in small Irish villages,' he said quietly. 'Even now. If you've forgotten that, Bridget, you've been away too long.' She held his gaze for a second then blushed deeply. She nodded her head slowly.

'Yes, of course. I should have remembered,' she said contritely.

They sipped their coffee in silence while Father Crowley watched her moodily and she began to worry that she'd dressed too quickly. Was she showing? Had he noticed? She held her stomach muscles so tight they ached. Watching him, she again had the feeling that he was working himself up to something, but what she took to be overt nosiness made her so wary of him that she felt unable to put him at his ease. Suddenly he pulled his hand from his pocket and hesitantly held out a small blue envelope.

'The day she went into hospital your mother asked me to give you this, it's about all that.' He indicated the certificate which she still held on her lap. Barely glancing at the letter, Bid stuffed it, unread, into her pocket, then looked up inquiringly.

'She also asked me to talk to you . . . er, about . . . she had a lot on her mind, she was greatly troubled.'

Damn, thought Bid furiously. She's been discussing me and Cas with him. I hate that. Hate. Hate it. She'd no business. Now comes the lecture on faith and morals.

'She wanted me to see you before you . . .' He waved his hand in the direction of the desk. 'That's why I came so early. Not early enough though.' He smiled ruefully at her white, resentful face and patted her hand.

'Bridget, my child, you're a sophisticated young woman. I don't think you worry about these things as much as your poor mother did. I suppose your job would help with that . . .' A great rumbling noise from the street drowned his words. '. . . come across all sorts of strange situations.'

She glanced impatiently towards the window and listened sullenly, with only half an ear, until she realized that what he said referred, not to her own transgressions but to her mother's. He gave no indication, nor was she at any point aware, of how carefully he was laundering his stilted narrative.

'I first met your mother in the mid fifties when she was about seventeen. I was a young curate in her home town. She was walking out with a young man at the time but her parents were very much against it. His family was the problem; they were very irregular altogether and nobody knew much about them. Very rough and ready and worst of all, not from those parts. Your grandfather was the schoolmaster. He married late in life and was rather old-fashioned in his ways and very, very strict. He had great hopes for Eileen, she was a clever youngster . . .'

Blast, thought Bid mutinously, why is he treating me like a half-witted child? *Are you sitting comfortably? Then I'll begin* ... She strolled over to the window and stood with her back to him, watching the strange activity at the canal.

'When he found out what she was up to, there was the most almighty row. I was away at the time, I had to help out in another parish for a few weeks. When I got back to the village she'd run off with the lad. It was a nine-day wonder for a time. All sorts of queer stories were circulated but no-one seemed to know where they were and her parents wouldn't speak about it. His people cleared off soon after and a few months later your grandparents, too, left the place. After that the hullabaloo died down.

'As time went by I forgot about it all. Then, ten or so years later, I came to this parish. It was an odd coincidence that we found ourselves in the same place. It's a small world indeed. I recognized your mother immediately, but she cut me dead. Without saying anything, she made it plain that she didn't want me to refer to the past. Well, you know your mother. She made herself very clear. If I wanted anything to do with the Laceys, it would be on her terms. I was to ask no questions. I didn't. I was always a little nervous of your mother.' Father Crowley pulled out his handkerchief and mopped his forehead. 'She never mentioned her past again, until about a month ago when I called to see her. She was looking terrible, waiting to go into hospital, you remember? What an anxious time it's been for you, poor child.'

Seemingly mesmerized by the flashing blue lights on the street outside, Bid did not respond.

'She asked then if I would talk to you. The past was preying on her mind. Fergus had been at her for years to tell you, but she hadn't quite managed to tell the truth to poor Fergus either.'

At the mention of her father's name Bid swirled around so violently she all but toppled over.

'Look,' she spat the words out. 'I was conceived out of wedlock. So what? What's all the fuss about? It happens all the time. And why did *she* have to tell me? My father could have, himself. Why did she have to be the one? Oh, I see. The woman's shame. Is that what this is all about?' The agony aunt surfaced aggressively. 'Almost thirty per cent of children born in Britain are born to single parents and God knows what proportion of those are Irish. Or what the statistic is here. If they allow themselves such statistics. Not everyone chooses to be married, you know. Not any more. My parents,' she added loftily, 'were a little before their time. That's all.'

He bit back his anger and a strong urge to flee.

'I am not making judgements here, Bridget, I am simply telling you what your mother asked me to. It certainly wasn't something she flaunted, it bothered her a great deal.' And that's putting it mildly, he thought.

'I'm sorry,' she replied contritely. 'I shouldn't have spoken like that. But there's no need for all this. Really. I've seen the evidence. You don't have to tell me any more. Please, Father, just leave it alone.'

'Fine. That's probably best. I'm sorry for upsetting you, Bridget, but your mother made me promise. I really didn't want to. We'll leave it so?'

She came towards him and said shamefacedly:

'I am being very rude to you, Father. Sorry. I suppose you'd better tell me what she said.'

Now it was his turn to hesitate. Every instinct warned him to withdraw, offer some mild placebo or ask for the letter back.

'I don't know. We'll leave it. It's best. You're quite right, Bridget.'

She wished he would stop calling her Bridget. It added to her feeling of disconnection.

'Please.'

'If you're sure?' What foolishness was this? How could she be?

'I'm sure.' She turned to face him with a smile. 'Tell me, why did they go to Dundalk?'

'Who?' Her question took him aback.

'Mam and Dad.'

The priest sighed deeply and resignedly.

'Eileen didn't run away to Dundalk, not at first. She went to England.' The priest skirted the issue. He spoke rapidly, as if wanting what unpleasantness he had to impart out of the way as quickly as possible. 'Not with Fergus, with the other lad. They were no more than seventeen or eighteen, perhaps not even quite that. Children is all they were.' He stared moodily at Bid who stood with her hands clasped across her stomach. He drew himself up; now for it:

'From what she said, it wasn't till a couple of years after,' he cleared his throat, 'that she became pregnant. By then the relationship was deteriorating. She found him . . . with someone else.' He couldn't quite bring himself to say bed. 'Some other girl. Together. She walked out.' They appraised each other silently. Bid had gone as white as a sheet. The noise outside abated.

'But what about my father? What about Fergus?' she asked hoarsely.

'She met him soon after. He took care of her, saw her through the pregnancy. As soon as you were born they came back to Ireland. Dundalk. To a friend apparently, and lived there quietly for the six weeks till they could get married. Then they came on to Dublin.'

The priest's tone became emphatic. 'Fergus was your father in every sense but the biological one, Bridget. He never left her side. He was devoted to both of you. You cannot doubt it. I don't have to tell you how much he loved you.'

She stared past him and almost to herself intoned:

'*Bonus bonorum bonarum.* Why didn't they tell me? It doesn't make sense does it, Seamus?' He was startled by her use of his name. She was crushed and deathly pale, as if she'd been clouted.

'I don't suppose it does, child, until you remember her background and the fact she wouldn't go back to her people.' He drew himself up. 'There was something else.'

'Why didn't my dad tell me?' she interrupted. 'He should have. Why didn't he?' She sounded exhausted and far away. And far too calm, almost unbalanced. Looking at her the old priest became alarmed, afraid suddenly of what she might do. He felt threatened and old and sick, sick, sick to his stomach.

'Why didn't my dad tell me, Seamus?' Her tone was flat and conversational and only mildly puzzled.

'Because,' he trod carefully, 'because being an honourable man, I suppose he felt it was your mother's story, that he had no real right. Besides, she wouldn't let him and he never liked upsetting her, did he? And always, he was afraid of losing you. I'm only surmising, of course.'

'You said there was something else?'

'Uh?'

'Seamus? What else?' she said sharply.

'She allowed Fergus to make arrangements to, er, marry her. Here in Ireland. But she didn't tell him she was already married. She and the other boy had been married in London. Registry office.'

'Register Office,' corrected Bid *sotto voce*.

'She tried to convince herself it didn't count. Because they were both Catholics. Of course, deep down, she knew it was legal but she didn't tell Fergus about it. I suppose they might have been able to winkle out a priest somewhere who would have been able to convince himself that a civil marriage between two Catholics was invalid. But I would guess, as did she, that Fergus would have none of that Mickey Mouse business. So she took the line of least resistance and kept silent. She didn't bargain on her conscience. Poor soul, she was in quite a tricky position, one way and another. Times were different then, remember. Benefits were not so easily come by and she had a child to support. Poor foolish woman. One lie followed another. She spent the whole of her life covering up, trying to prevent him finding out.'

'But that doesn't excuse him not telling me. The two things were separate, weren't they?' Bid asked shakily.

'To you, perhaps. Not to her. Don't you understand, my child?' he said softly, 'Bigamy is an ugly word. All the covering up grew out of fear. For her the two things were inextricably linked. Fear took her over and dictated how she dealt with the problem of your birth – or didn't deal with it. Every time Fergus wanted to tell you she stopped him because she was afraid you'd go off looking for your biological father and then the whole story would be out – Fergus would discover that her marriage to him was bigamous. *That* was what she feared most. So stupid.' He sighed deeply. 'What a mess it was,' he mumbled, waiting for her to ask her father's name.

The crackling of the fire and the low rumble of traffic made the only sound in the room. Bid lay back in her chair with her eyes half-closed, almost asleep. Seamus Crowley, waiting patiently for her to react, prepared careful phrases of consolation. The minutes ticked by, yet she gave not the slightest indication of having taken in what he'd said.

She's in shock, he thought, she hasn't heard a word. Doesn't want to. How like her mother she is, after all.

He had often experienced similar reactions when trying to console the bereaved, when the suddenness of the death added shock to the unreality. And Bridget was already in that dangerous position. Would she remember anything of what he'd said?

He wondered uncertainly if he should repeat the whole rigmarole again and dismissed the idea. Had he not done his disagreeable duty? Against his own better judgement? If the merciful God chose to let her deal with it in that way then no good whatever would come of butting in again, he concluded robustly. But a nagging doubt twitched away at him all the same.

'Just read your mother's letter, Bridget,' he urged softly. 'I'm sure she's explained it better than I.'

She smiled at him calmly.

'Oh Seamus, I'm not much company I'm afraid.'

Her unfocused eyes darted back and forth unnerv-ingly. 'I've been up most of the night. It's lovely to see you but I feel very tired. I think I'll go and lie down for a bit.' She held out her hand. 'You've been very kind about everything. You gave Mam a lovely send-off. I don't know how to thank you.' She bent over and pecked him lightly on the cheek like a hostess dismissing a dinner guest. Then she walked serenely from the room as the phone in the hall began to ring. She ignored it, but paused at the door to say:

'I expect you'll be moving to Lahinch soon.' It was more statement than question and he did not reply. Her next remark stunned him: 'I'll come and see you after we get married. I told you about that, didn't I? I want you to meet my fiancé.'

She smiled remotely and closed the door, paying no further heed to him. The phone went on ringing even after he could hear her footsteps in the room above. It stopped momentarily then started to peal again. He hesitantly went to answer it.

'Oh Father Crowley! It's Maureen Lenehan. How is the poor creature this morning?'

'She just went to lie down,' he said breathlessly.

'Ah Father,' she broke in hotly, 'you haven't been tiring her out with business? There's no need you know, I can look after her.'

The priest had had enough for one morning. He felt old and tired and utterly drained.

'There were some things Mrs Lacey asked me to do.' He stopped, almost overwhelmed with longing to unburden himself. But he held his tongue, reflect-ing ruefully that the Lacey woman might have done better to let a motherly soul like Maureen Lenehan talk to the girl.

453

'Are you there, Father? Are you there?' Maureen toned down the aggression. 'Is she taking all this too calmly, do you think? She looks wretched, poor girl. Father? I mean it was all so sudden, wasn't it?'

'Yes,' he replied. 'Everything has been much too sudden.'

'And she's talking of going back to England tomorrow.' Maureen made it sound as though the dark satanic mills were threatening her lamb. 'Don't you think it's too soon?'

'No, I do not. Not at all,' he said fervently. 'I hope you'll encourage her. It's where her life is and she's probably better off with her friends at this point. Maureen? Did you know she's getting married?'

'No!' Her protest almost took his ear off. 'Did she tell you that? She never said a word to me. Mind you, I've an idea she . . . Are you sure, Father?'

'No. Not sure at all. Just something she said. I wondered, that's all.'

'I expect you're right.' Maureen belatedly assumed that Bridget was merely protecting herself and cut him short. 'Tell her I'll be with her in an hour or so, will you?'

Seamus Crowley cradled the phone and glanced up the stairs. All was quiet. He closed the sitting-room door and walked heavily along the hallway wishing he was retiring now, at once. A deep sense of failure settled on him. He felt a hundred years old as he lumbered slowly down the front steps. Behind him the phone started to ring again.

He was hailed from the canal bank by a tall ruddy-faced policeman. Bending his head against the wind, he walked slowly across the road.

# CHAPTER THIRTY-TWO

The shrilling of the phone eventually penetrated Bid's sleep, but by the time she worked out where she was it had stopped. Her watch read twelve-twenty. She splashed her face with water and ran a comb roughly through her hair. She was still too exhausted to take any trouble with herself. She re-dressed in the same dark green suit and pale blouse she'd worn since the day her mother died. As she went downstairs the phone rang again. This time she picked it up.

'Oh Bid, it's me.' Sarah's harassed voice. 'I've been ringing all morning. Are you OK?'

Bid's brain glazed over again.

'Fine. I'm fine, Sarah. Have you heard from Cas?'

'Me?' Sarah sounded surprised. 'No, Bid, haven't you?'

'No.' Bid didn't sound the least bit put out, just remote. They chatted for no more than a minute or so before she said: 'I'll probably come home in a day or two. I'll be in touch.' She hung up abruptly.

She shuffled distractedly into the sitting-room. The desk was still open, with papers strewn all over it. Automaton-like, she heaped the greater part of the debris into the dead fireplace and set a light to it, continuing to add to the flames at an ever more frantic rate for half an hour or so. She rolled down the desk top with a clatter just as the doorbell rang.

It was Maureen, laden down with a picnic lunch.

After they'd eaten, they blitzed through the house in a further attempt at clearing up. Bid went off to see her solicitor, Bartley Quinlan, some time after four, promising to be no more than an hour or so.

She didn't show up again until nearly eight. The Lenehans were waiting impatiently in their car outside the house. They watched her walking swiftly along the far bank of the canal from the direction of Quinlan's flat in Leeson Street. She slowed down to exchange a greeting with the guard who was standing near the tarpaulin covering the lock, before crossing Canal Road. She almost bumped into the old Rover before she recognized it.

Dinny leaned backwards to open the rear door and was so struck by her total lack of colour that he leapt out and suggested they repair at once to Jurys Hotel for a meal. Maureen lumbered out of the front seat and joined them on the pavement. To their relief, Bid excused herself, saying she was tired and that she'd already had a bite with Bartley Quinlan. She neither referred to her business with the solicitor nor offered any explanation as to how she'd spent the previous four hours.

'Maureen dear, I'm flying to London early tomorrow,' Bid said softly. 'There's really nothing to keep me here now. I've arranged for a car to take me to the airport.'

Maureen's jaw dropped. Bid didn't, she thought, look capable of arranging anything. She badly wanted to ask the girl what she'd been up to all afternoon. Surely Quinlan's business hadn't taken so long? Or had she been with Father Crowley? She didn't say. Sly or just preoccupied? Somehow it stuck in Maureen's craw that the girl was being so unaccountably secretive. Vague hurt welled up.

'Are you sure? I can easily drive you,' Dinny offered.

'Quite sure. It's all arranged, honestly.' Bid smiled apologetically, then held out her hands in a curiously supplicating gesture which etched itself on both their minds as silent witness to her sorrow.

'I'm so unhappy here, I can't tell you. I miss . . . It's all so grim. I don't really know how to thank you and Dinny.' Her eyes filled with tears. 'You know I couldn't have got through this nightmare without you.' And with a touching return of her old warmth and simplicity, she put an arm around each of their solid frames and hugged herself to them.

'Thank you,' she whispered, brokenly. 'You've been marvellous to me, always.' She gave a watery smile.

'I'll be back in a few months. I'm getting married. I was going to tell Mam this weekend,' she announced sadly, if inaccurately. 'We'll go ahead with it now as soon as we can, quietly, but I want you both to meet him.'

As Maureen walked her to the house she spoke briefly about Cas and their plans, which in truth sounded ill-defined. She didn't mention the baby. Or the divorce. One thing at least had penetrated Bid's consciousness since the morning: Ireland was still Ireland and she couldn't be sure how even such good friends as the Lenehans would feel about her predicament.

But in this she did Maureen an injustice and hurt her deeply. For the older woman had been aware of the girl's condition from the first. She had observed her morning sickness and was saddened that Bid hadn't trusted her enough to speak of it. Not everyone, she mumbled to Dinny as she hoisted herself back into the car, was as old-fashioned and judgmental as Eileen Lacey. As they drove off, she turned to look back as the solitary figure, poised in the act of entering the house, glanced over her shoulder at something behind her. It was Maureen's last glimpse of the girl she almost regarded as a second daughter and Bid's isolation filled her with an unbearable sadness.

'I don't know, Dinny.' She shook her head. 'I just don't know. I think poor Bridget's lost her centre somehow. I mean quite apart from Eileen's death. I feel very uneasy about her. I think she's in some sort of mess. But not a word did she say. Not a syllable. She doesn't seem to trust anyone any more. Does she think I haven't eyes in my head? She's at least four months gone. I bet she made up all that marriage nonsense for Father Crowley's benefit. It's the first I've heard of it. She has a poor opinion of our intelligence, is all I can say.'

As she entered the house, Bid absently put her hand in her pocket and pulled out the blue envelope Father Crowley had given her. Her name was on the front, scrawled in her mother's writing. She sat down moodily on the stairs and turned the letter over several times before opening it.

The priest might have spared himself the trouble, because to the very last Eileen had funked it. She died as she lived, nursing her secret.

\* \* \*

*Dearest Bridget,*

*They've just telephoned from the hospital. I'm to go in tomorrow. Until this moment I was frightened, now I feel calm. Please God everything will be all right and I'll get better, we'll just have to hope.*

*I know things haven't been so easy with us recently. I never thanked you for all the care and support you've been giving me, coming over so often. You know I only ever wanted the best for you. I've realized for some time that you're going to get married and what I wanted to say is – I should have shown more confidence in you. I always worry that you're too trusting and allow people to take advantage, but I know in my heart you won't ever do anything you think is wrong.*

*I won't pretend that I wouldn't prefer you to marry one of your own, at home. But if you feel that this man is right and will be good to you then I won't make any more fuss.*

*If things don't go right for me then please, please know that whatever you want to do, wherever you want to settle, I know you'll never do anything to be ashamed of.*

*Love, Mam.*

Bid drew the letter to her lips and, clutching it to her, climbed the stairs to bed.

Father Crowley dropped around to the house early the following morning after Sunday Mass. He was still troubled, having spent a sleepless night reviling the hapless Miss Finnerty's cuisine for his heartburn and Eileen Lacey for his heartache. His head was splitting. He was struck by Bid's appearance as she opened the door. Still deathly pale, her skin made such a marked contrast to the dark green suit that her beauty was almost ethereal.

'Oh, Seamus. You've come to say goodbye?' she smiled at him beatifically and stood back. 'The taxi will be here in a few minutes, but there's something I want to show you. Come in for a moment.'

Having expected the cold shoulder he was astonished. She drew the hateful blue envelope from her pocket and handed it to him.

'Mam left me such a nice letter. Read it. Go on, I want you to, please,' she urged.

He held back. Why was her face so wreathed in smiles? She waited while he, first in mounting disbelief, then in amazed anger, read what Eileen Lacey had written.

The woman had made a complete fool of him. Worse, she had both taken his advice and then inverted it by not warning him off telling the poor girl all that . . . that . . . Words failed him. Was this why she'd refused to let him visit her in hospital? Had what she confessed been a pack of lies after all?

He was appalled at the damage he might have done the girl. Would she ever get over it? Or forgive him? He hardly dared look her in the face, yet when he did so he realized that, if she remembered anything he said the day before, she'd already dismissed it. She wore a fixed smile.

'Isn't it a beautiful letter?' she gushed. 'I knew everything would be fine, she was only worried because I'm marrying a divorcé, a non-Catholic. I expect she told you? Oh yes, very soon now. You'll really like him. I'll be bringing him to see you in a couple of months. You're sort of family now, aren't you, Seamus?'

She hunched her shoulders and smiled her over-bright smile. Her cheeks grew very flushed.

'All I've got really. You and Maureen. I don't really count Dinny or Mairead. I like them of course, but. You'd like to meet him, wouldn't you? We'll be married by then. Respectable.' She spoke impetuously. Now it was Father Crowley's turn to look confused. He was casting about for some carefully considered reply when he was saved by the taxi-man banging at the door.

'I'll help you with your things, Bridget,' was all he could muster. His heart was thumping fearfully.

'There isn't much. I'll just go and check in case I've forgotten anything.'

She pointed to a small leather satchel and ran upstairs. Father Crowley cocked his head and followed her footsteps moving through the rooms above. There was a short pause before she reappeared. She was carrying an old black handbag and still wearing that eerie fixed smile. She held out a bunch of keys and asked politely if he'd kindly give them to Bartley Quinlan. Then she put the old handbag and another small bundle into a plastic carrier.

Seamus returned the letter and took the plastic carrier from her.

'I'll see to that, child. Ring me if there's anything else you'd like me to do, will you? And please come and see me. I'll be at the cottage in Lahinch from the end of the month – an old retired man.' He smiled dolefully at her and helped her into the taxi.

'Bring your young man. I would be very happy to see him – and you.' He patted her cheek and straightened with a grunt of pain. 'Take care of yourself, Bridget. God bless you, child.' He stood waving as the car pulled away.

'God bless us all,' he muttered piously, half to himself. 'For between us we've made an unholy mess.'

The taxi suddenly screeched to a halt and reversed. Bid leapt out and ran back towards him. She held something in her hand.

'Seamus. I found this last night.' Her cheeks had two livid red spots just below the brilliant sienna eyes. 'Look. My magic pad,' she sounded almost deranged.

The small flat rectangle of carbon was covered with stiff cellophane, held in place by a yellow metal band. She scribbled her name on it with her finger nail: *Bridget Kate* and on the line below *Lacey*.

'That's how my dad taught me to write my name. Look.' She drew the metal bar up over *Lacey* and it disappeared. She stared at the priest and, dropping the pad on the ground, turned and jumped back into the taxi. He stood open-mouthed as it sped away. He felt like sitting on the side of the road and screaming aloud his fear and confusion.

Oh dear sweet Holy Mother, he prayed, forgive me. I didn't mean it, I only did what I was asked.

What could Eileen have been about, he moaned, with her pious claptrap? Blethering on about coming clean, then sweeping the muck neatly into his muddling, meddlesome, old hands. Had her ghastly saga been pure – or more exactly, impure –

fiction? Or had she made it up because she couldn't face the fact that the girl was pregnant, as anyone, even a doddery old priest with lousy eyesight, could see? She had harped instead on her dislike of her daughter marrying a divorcé. Stupid, stupid woman.

Why in blazes had she involved him? Insisting that he tell that damaging rigmarole to a bereaved young woman, half killing her with fright and traducing poor Fergus into the bargain. And what a downright utter fool he'd been to go along with it. As he trudged homewards he went over and over what he remembered of that weary night when Eileen had poured out her heart to him. It had sounded plausible then – could he possibly be mistaken?

Indeed he could, he admitted sourly, stranger things had happened in his long ministry. But this? This beat everything. Had confessing assuaged Eileen Lacey's guilt? Maybe the Lord had given her the strength not to be visiting the grisly tale on her daughter. But why, oh why, had she not warned him and spared them both the pain? Then he recalled how suddenly she had died and charitably concluded that she had, after all, tried to protect her daughter. Perhaps she'd been too ill and confused to remember her instructions to him?

He felt sick with worry that Bid would remember and fret later on, when there would be nobody on hand to unravel her convoluted history for her. He resolved to keep in touch, no matter how unwelcome he might be. It had not escaped him that Bid could no longer bring herself to address him as Father. Not normally so sensitive, he felt reduced by her use of his first name. Rejecting the message he brought, she had demoted the messenger.

The bitter taste of failure desolated him. He went into the church and knelt down, head in hands, and thought of Bid setting out, as Eileen had always dreaded, on the search for her father and he feared for her. Then, with a jolt it came to him that she hadn't asked her father's name. He wondered if his first instinct, that she hadn't taken in anything he said, had been right after all. It was a slim enough straw, but he clutched at it hopefully. But his feeling of foreboding persisted. He was certain of one thing. The girl needed someone to look after her.

It was then that the idea of trying to find Bridget's only other living relative, Eileen's younger sister, Gráinne, first came to him.

# CHAPTER THIRTY-THREE

Everything seemed strange and unreal. Bid moved like a sleepwalker, dazed and unable to concentrate, but instinctively headed for where she could be on her own. She took the tube from Heathrow to King's Cross. Exhaustion saturated her. The fustiness of her stale clothes was offensive and she longed more than anything for a bath and solitude. She couldn't bear to face anyone, or talk, or rehearse what had happened. She wanted no more questions and no more battering with unwanted, bewildering fabrications.

The days in Dublin had been too hectic, too full of people wanting more of her than she could give. Too full of advice. A little peace and quiet was all she needed to adjust to her bereavement. Forgetting the months of angst about Cas, and about the baby, she felt a pang of regret that she hadn't managed to come clean and make peace with her mother before she died. But on the other hand, hadn't Eileen been spared long months, perhaps years, of suffering? When all was said and done, the cancer was well advanced and the operation would probably have only delayed rather than stopped the inevitable spread of the disease. Guilty relief slyly tinged her grief.

Before she turned up Percy Street she stopped at the corner mini-market and bought some oranges, a couple of bread rolls and coffee before continuing the short walk to the flat. She let herself in quietly and, taking off her shoes at the foot of the stairs, climbed them silently.

Someone had been there before her; her letters were gathered in a neat pile on the kitchen table. 'Cas?' she called softly. 'Oh my darling? Where are you?' She padded through to the sitting-room and up to the bedroom half expecting to see him but was curiously relieved to find he wasn't there. She played back her answering machine. Several blanks, followed by Sarah instructing her to come around whenever she got back. Ingrid. Edy. Roy Angel. Then a couple more blanks. Nothing from Cas. She pressed the review to see what message had been left. Roy Angel's voice, muffled by a heavy cold, directed callers to her Dublin number or to Sarah's, saying that Ms Lacey had been called away for a few days.

Bid started dialling Cas but stopped midway, knowing that the moment she announced her arrival he would come around before she had time to bathe or collect herself. She turned on the immersion heater and thought of his loving arms about her. Then she glanced down at her grubby clothes and decided to hold off the luxury for a couple of revitalizing hours. He liked her to look smart. First a bath, then a nap and a change of clothes. Then she would go to him.

While she waited for the bath water to heat, she put the rolls in the oven, made coffee and squeezed the oranges. The phone rang but she didn't notice and after four double peals the machine switched it off. While she sipped her coffee, she glanced

466

through the mail. A bank statement, a letter of condolence from her editor, a postcard from Alice sent with love in large smudgy Xs. The rest were circulars. An invitation to buy *Which?* magazine. A flyer for a half-price short stay in Edinburgh. Why Edinburgh? She glanced at the enclosed brochure idly and noticed that a forthcoming book fair was featured. The train timetable from King's Cross was thoughtfully enclosed. The colour illustrations of the castle and the town held her attention for some time before she dropped them languidly and sat staring into space.

She felt a curious reluctance to release herself from her numbed state. She nibbled at one of the rolls, drank more coffee and went upstairs to draw her bath.

It was now mid-afternoon. She lay soaking for a long time thinking about Dublin and her mother's death and the speed with which everything had happened. The previous week she'd been on a seesaw of elation about the baby and anxiety about telling her mother. Again she lamented that she hadn't had the courage. Too late, too late, she thought sadly. Odd how certain she'd been that her mam would have been horrified. Well. She couldn't have been more wrong could she? Her mother would have understood better than anyone.

As though the priest's disclosure had not imprinted itself upon her memory, Bid now conjured up a vision of her young parents – in love and fugitive. The delusion went comfortingly round and round her in her head. Bid smiled fondly at the thought of young Eileen and Fergus flaunting the rigid conventions of their upbringing.

How brave. How fine. How much in love they must have been. It didn't occur to her to wonder what scars resulted from their 'bravery'. Instead, Bid lay back in the warm scented water and conformed to the time-honoured process of visiting the dead with all the virtues. Such a fine romance. A link with her own beautiful baby. She closed her eyes and let the steamy moisture relax her tense muscles and jagged nerves.

Death was strange, odd. She wished she could feel sad or cry and start being sorry. She wished she could feel something – pain, loss, distress – anything, but there was only a big deadly blank. Nothing. She couldn't connect and felt much too tired to try. Her scalp felt curiously as if it was lifting off her head. Her mind was not at home. If someone rang or called, even Cas, she'd pretend she wasn't there. She knew she wasn't really there, most of her had gone somewhere else. Feelings eluded her – how could she describe them? And how could she explain the speed with which her experience had eroded her sense of belonging anywhere? She had lost contact with herself and with her life.

Her years in London had changed her, she knew. In England the rituals of death were taken at a slower pace. Time elapsed before burial – service private, no flowers by request – and more time before memorial services. So different from Ireland. And she needed time. Time to absorb the finality of her loss and her feelings – if she could ever touch them again.

But perhaps after all, the way things had been arranged in Dublin was the right way for her? Maureen had said it would get her through those first few awful days, and it had. Now was her time for reflection, if she could only think, concentrate, feel. If only her heart didn't ache so. Dullness paralysed her mind, one part of which observed her effort to crawl into a corner to lick her wounds. The only way she could cope, at least for the moment, was to do so alone. She needed to fix her images of her family firmly in her wandering mind.

She climbed out of the bath and wrapped a towel around herself and wandered down into the kitchen again. She picked up the Edinburgh flyer and read it more thoughtfully. She sat dreamily tapping the table with the coloured sheet, turning it over and over in her fingers. She could go north where no-one knew about her mother's death or her baby. Go on retreat in an effort to get back to normality and ordinariness; prepare herself for her wedding. She pulled the towel closely around her, absent-mindedly dropped the leaflet on the table and wandered aimlessly upstairs.

The stuff from her journey was where she'd dumped it. She looked into the wardrobe for something suitable to wear. She ran her eye dreamily along the straggled remnants of her once exuberant wardrobe and picked out a flowery number long past its best. Its fullness pleased her, she was tired of squeezing her swollen belly into neatly tailored togs. Shoes? Nightie? Bit by bit she assembled herself. Then she changed her mind and left the little pile sitting on the floor.

She went to the phone and dialled Cas's flat. Still no reply. Her reaction was muted: a slight shrug, no more. She rang Sarah but she too was out. Tom told her they hadn't yet managed to track Cas down. He promised to try again later and ring her back. If she wasn't going to be at her mother's house, Tom stumbled over the words, could she let them know where she was likely to be? Bid rang off, leaving him with the impression that she was still in Dublin. She did not feel like company. The house was entirely silent, she swept everything off the bed, climbed in and within seconds was fast asleep.

At about nine o'clock a distant ringing disturbed her. Bid turned over sluggishly, wondering what had awakened her, but the only sound was her alarm clock, ticking creakily. She lay for some time trying to remember her dream. Something menacing hammered at her head. She shuddered, drawing the blankets up to her chin, and dozed off again but the vague feeling of threat recurred. She sat on the side of the bed and rubbed her stomach, then smiled to herself; the gesture was becoming a habit. Her eye fell on her mother's old black bag. As she picked it up, the catch gave and a whole jumble of stuff spilled out. Stepping over it, she went to the kitchen to investigate her tiny freezer. Year-old lasagne was the best on offer. She bunged it in the oven and went back to the bedroom, trying to decide whether or not to get dressed. It seemed a monumental decision, well beyond her powers. She sat on the bed and looked absently down at the bag. It was so redolent of her mother. The faint trace of her perfume rose from the spilt powder. As long as Bid could remember, it was a smell she'd always associated with being grown-up. As a child she'd determined that one day, when she was big, she would have a bag like that.

She slid to the floor and, one by one, lined the items on the bed: a small red purse full of loose change; a wallet, split at the seams; a black plastic folder of photographs of herself and her parents, mostly out of focus, the figures too far from the box Brownie. There was an original of the photo used in Bid's column and a coloured one she'd never seen before of her parents arm in arm smiling radiantly at the camera. She held it close and examined it in the fading light. Eileen had been rather beautiful. Slowly the feeling of loss began to edge into Bid's heart.

A sheaf of papers lay half in, half out, of the bag. A blue envelope fell away as she trawled her catch. It had her name scrawled on the front. As she bent to pick it up, a piece of newspaper fluttered away from her. It was dirty and torn. As she leaned forward, Bid had a sudden vivid memory of the nurse picking it up from the hospital bed and stuffing it in the bag as she handed it over. Now Bid put out her hand idly and lifted it to the light.

Cas's beloved face smiled up at her. The original had been in the *Telegraph*, she had a hoarded copy in her desk at the office. This must have come from another version of the same story because it was a bad reproduction in black and white. It showed Cas standing on the scaffold of the huge building site in the Isle of Dogs. It was an excellent likeness except that the safety helmet hid the fine eyes. Most of the caption was missing, what was left simply identified the site.

She chewed on her hand. How very strange. Her mother had never met Cas so it couldn't have meant anything to her. She wondered where it had come from. Bid laid the clipping face down on the bed.

Someone had written something, in faint pencil, on the back. She put on the bedside light and to her astonishment read the phone number of Cas's London office. She stared at it for a long time, then carefully placed it on the bed.

A worm of doubt and fear began to burrow its way into her head. With a growing feeling of menace, she slit open the pale blue envelope.

> *Dearest Bridget,*
> *They've just telephoned from the hospital. I'm to go in tomorrow. Until this moment . . .*

Bid put the letter down, it was only a copy of the letter Father Crowley had given her. She drew in her breath, trying to block the weird story he'd tried to tell her. Pervert. She ran back down to the kitchen.

'Lies. Lies. Lies.' She clamped her hands over her ears. How dare he say those awful things? She mooched about the kitchen looking for knife, fork and plate. The phone rang.

'Shut up. Shut up,' she hissed. 'Can't you see we're eating?'

Again, her hand passed over her stomach.

From the other room came the sound of the answering machine clicking on. Bid took her spartan meal from the oven, sat at the table and switched on the radio. She gobbled at the food while desperately trying to concentrate on the Sunday play. They might have been talking Greek for all she understood. Being Radio 3, they probably were.

'Double Dutch,' she muttered, as she ran the hot water over the dishes. She didn't laugh, she felt sick. She went back her bedroom and set to tidying her mother's things.

*Dearest Bridget,*

*They've just telephoned from the hospital. I'm to go in tomorrow. Until this moment I was frightened, now I feel calm. Please God everything will be all right and I'll get better, we'll just have to hope.*

*Bridget, there's something I have to tell you. I should have done it long ago but I've been an awful coward. Now I'm afraid I'll never see you again, because if you're reading this it will be because I haven't been lucky and there won't be a chance for me to ask your forgiveness.*

Bid put the letter down and laid her head on the pillow. She felt like stone. The priest's presence hovered but she pushed him away, her face giving no sign of any reaction save exhaustion. She closed her eyes briefly then sat up again.

*I was seventeen when I ran away from home. With a young lad. Con Rynne he was called. We were mad about each other. My parents were against it. And him. I should have told you long ago. I talked to Father Crowley and he said he'd give you this and talk to you. We had to get away because there was terrible trouble when my father found out. I was never able to go back. His family wasn't thought much of in the town. Because they were incomers people didn't trust them. There was an awful fight and all sorts of*

473

*terrible things were said. That's why we ran.
London we ended up in. I hated it. I worried
about living with a man I wasn't married to, but
he wouldn't have a church at any price because
the parish in London would be asking questions
of the parish at home and the families would
come after us. I don't know how he got to
organizing everything but we had our wedding,
in a registry office. Con was always good at
fixing things.*

*A couple of years later I became very unwell. I
was that innocent I didn't realize what it was. By
then things were going wrong between us. He
was making a lot of money on the lump and he
was high on the pig's back. He was always out
before I woke in the morning and wasn't too hot
at getting home in the evening. When I went to
the doctor he told me I was two months gone.*

Bid rubbed her stomach. Her face wore no
expression but the paper in her hand quivered as
she read.

*I ran all the way home. It was about six
o'clock, I remember it as if it were yesterday.
When I walked into the room he was on the
settee on top of a great blonde one. Neither of
them had a stitch on and they were at it like a
pair of dogs. I just packed my bags and walked
out. So you see, I was already expecting when I
met Fergus. He was very good about it. We got
married as soon as we could after you were born.
No-one ever doubted he was your dad.*

*I never told him about the other marriage
because I was afraid I'd lose him and have no-*

*one to look after us. From the minute you were born he was mad about you. By then I'd convinced myself that first marriage didn't count. I think I believed it, at least for a long time. But I was always afraid Fergus would find out. I never saw hide or hair of the other fellow again. I hope . . .*

Bid's heart thumped painfully. Slowly and unconsciously she tore the letter without finishing it. She sat rocking to and fro while the information slowly filtered through her confused brain. The priest was right then, about Fergus. Think slowly. Fergus loved me. They both said so. Thirty years could not be cancelled out. How could this weird confession shift all that love and care?

She played absently with the scraps of paper, humming a high unearthly note, until her rising anger took possession of her. Her face flushed scarlet and she started to shake violently. Words rushed out of her in high-pitched fury, echoing in the empty flat.

'How dare you! How dare you do this after making my life a misery? All that pious crap about "married men"! All that fucking cant about "losing self-respect". How dare you? And that bloody priest! What the hell was he up to, aiding and abetting? What was the point? What was the bloody fucking damn point?'

The sobs burst from her in racking gulps. She banged her fists again and again into the pillow. The phone shrilled, she crept downstairs and did not notice that it cut off as she picked up the receiver.

'Cas? Oh, Cas? Help me. Please Please. They're saying awful things.' But there was only the dialling tone to console her. With trembling fingers she dialled his number. Twenty, thirty rings. No reply, her panic grew.

Where was he? She banged her head against the armrest of the sofa. Where was he? She counted backwards, she hadn't heard from him for almost a week. He'd let her down. Why wasn't he with her?

'Why aren't you here, my darling? I need you. Please, my love, I need you,' she crooned into the receiver, cradling it in both hands. 'Help me. Oh someone help me. Please, please Cas.'

She sank to the floor and wept like a child, in great heaving gasps of despair, then on all fours, she crawled out of the room and, still sobbing, climbed the stairs to her bedroom.

The torn letter still lay scattered by the bed. She grabbed some of the fragments and stuffed them into her mouth. She chewed and chewed and then gagged and stumbled to the lavatory to retch the contents of her stomach into the bowl. Then on all fours again, she crawled back into the warmth of her bed.

It was almost light when she woke up and staggered to the bathroom. Her face was red and blotchy. She bent over the cold tap and scooped the running water against her tired eyes. The floor was scattered with the torn bits of paper. She flushed and flushed the cistern, dropping the scraps into the swirling water, then followed the trail back to the bedroom. She scrunched the remainder into a tight ball and flung it from her.

She still felt sick. She dipped a teabag into tepid

water and sipped it slowly, trying to remember why she was up so early. The jumble of papers was still on the table. She picked it up daintily and let out a long slow sigh. Aaah. Edinburgh.

There was something she had to do, wasn't there? A plan. A scheme. A goal. What was it? She stared at the leaflet again. The book fair. The book fair was where she had to be. She would go because she was meant to go. The whys or the wherefores were beyond her. There was no choice. Simple.

She went upstairs to dress. She stuffed the scattered jumble back into the bag and hid it under her soiled clothes. Then, with preternatural calm, she placed her wash things on top of the nightie in her satchel and carried it down to the bottom of the stairs.

Now she went into overdrive and followed her usual routine for leaving the flat. She made a cursory inspection of the sitting-room, slipped some letters into a drawer, brought two or three plants to the kitchen sink, tied the bits and pieces of garbage into a plastic bag and switched off the water heater. She climbed the stairs for the last time and went back into the bedroom to switch off the lights.

The bed was a mess, she leaned over to straighten the covers and noticed a slip of discoloured paper clinging to the rough cotton. In her mind's eye she could see it slipping out of the envelope which lay beside it. She pulled her hand away as if she'd been stung.

'No more. No more. Forget about all that. You'll miss your train. You'll miss your train.'

Using the tips of finger and thumb, she picked up the envelope and paper and, holding them from her, dropped them on top of the chest of drawers. The sheet of paper fluttered slowly down and landed on her shoe. She stared at it, her antennae of fear quivering as, in slow motion, she bent to pick it up.

She unfolded the small, innocuous, yellowing sheet. The print was red. She focused blearily on the lion and unicorn rampant, then her eye dropped to the pink outlined square below in which were five short, neatly typed lines:

*Bridget Kate Rynne.*
*Girl*
*7 May 1959*
*Maida Vale.*
*London.*

Her vision turned red as she stood stock still. Her face was deathly white. Hardly breathing, she refused to acknowledge what she read. Her mouth formed the words: Bridget Kate Rynne. Rynne? Rynne. She gagged. Then merciful silence enclosed her. She refolded the page neatly and dropped it, watching mesmerized as it fluttered to the floor. With the tip of her shoe she pushed it firmly into the narrow slit between bed and floor. She straightened and picked up her bag. Then she tiptoed downstairs, let herself out of the flat and walked briskly towards the station. Whistling. It didn't do her any good. Despite her best efforts, the tangled bits of information were already unravelling into coherence. In the quiet of the empty railway carriage she could no longer defend herself. Gradually the rhythm of the speeding train took up the fearful refrain:

Rynne. Rynne. Rynne. Rynne. Rynne.

# CHAPTER THIRTY-FOUR

By the time the train reached Waverley station, Bid was on the point of collapse. Exhaustion now veered towards elation, her perceptions heightened to fever pitch. She had never looked at the world in so much detail, nor seen it so clearly. Even the colours of the carriage upholstery leapt at her, pulsating wildly, as she struggled to catch her demented thoughts.

She disembarked slowly, watching the purposeful haste of the other passengers with a puzzled expression. The intercom system blared an incomprehensible message. She stepped onto the platform and allowed herself to be swept along, past the barrier and out the great entrance around which the crowded road formed a steep horseshoe. A steady stream of cabs rolled down to pick up fares.

'Where to? Miss, Miss. Where d'you want to go?' the driver asked impatiently. Bid thrust the crumbled brochure under his nose, climbed silently into the back and lay back with her eyes closed.

Rynne. Rynne. Rynne. The wheels of the taxi took up the refrain as it drove to the hotel. She tried, as she stepped through the huge mahogany doors, to recall what she had to do but the squeaking brushes of the revolve deafened and distracted her. She was thrust into a huge reception area and stood transfixed as the ragged and sponged bright yellow walls swirled into the confusion of her mind. The light from the huge chandelier hurt her eyes and she felt she was being sucked through the deep pile of the carpet, sinking, sinking . . . sinking.

'Reception, Miss? Are you looking for Reception?' The porter approached her looking concerned. Bid smiled crazily at him.

'Yes. Oh yes,' she replied fervently. He led her towards the desk. Three young women stood facing her, dressed in navy blue. She wondered why they were got up as sailors – or was she imagining things? One of the girls was watching her dubiously. Bid attempted a smile.

'Two nights? Would you mind a double room, Miss? All the singles are full.'

'Doesn't matter.' She handed the girl her credit card.

'Top floor. Any baggage?'

Bid leaned against the lift wall and closed her eyes as it climbed dizzily upwards. The long corridor was empty and still. She wandered uncertainly along it, trailing her hand against the wall, searching for the right number.

The room was blue-grey. Blue carpet, grey walls, high ceilings, and on the tall windows, pale grey curtains; she felt seasick. The small double bed had a pretty flower-strewn cover. Bid leaned over to pick a sprig and began to cry softly when she found she could not. There were two small dark bedside tables and a matching dressing-table and chair. No full-length mirror.

She took her inventory precisely, methodically. She knew it was important that she should, but did not pause to wonder why. The bathroom was also scrutinized. It was clean and functional but so small that it was impossible to get to the loo without first closing the door. This fascinated her. Such modesty. She tested her theory several times before moving dreamily on.

A second door in the wall opposite the bathroom opened into a large sitting-room papered in hectic grey dragons. Bid stood close against the wall with her head thrown back and inspected the huge surreal design, hypnotized. I am going mad, she thought feverishly and sat down heavily. Her back ached.

The furnishings were dark blue. Strangely, the high windows let in very little light. The whole suite had an indefinable stuffiness and gloominess about it. Outside the sky was grey and ominous.

She unpacked her wash things, bathed her face and examined her image. The light-brown eyes stared back at her, like a puzzled monkey.

'Hello, old Bid, old friend.'

There were dark smudges under her over-bright eyes and her cheeks were so sunken beneath the wide cheekbones that she looked as if she were sucking them in. Her hair needed trimming, the moist air had turned the rich hennaed cap into a frizz. She sleeked it back with her hairbrush and touched her face. She did not notice how the garish floral dress mocked her wretchedness. Its loose folds hung limply from her thin shoulders, and a section of the hem had come undone.

She put on her old raincoat again and went downstairs and asked directions to the book fair. The brightly painted receptionist who watched her leave the hotel was confirmed in her view that

481

grubbing about with old books led a person to neglect herself. Having been slotted into that neat category, neither Bid's rag-bag appearance nor her subsequent behaviour gave rise to the slightest comment.

The hotel comprised one side of a fine Georgian square. It reminded her of a grander version of home. Bid moved sluggishly, her hand trailing the wrought-iron railings. She followed the length of the square until she came to an archway, which gave way to a deserted cobbled laneway running along the back of the terrace. It was lined on one side by a row of boutiques built into the old mews. She sauntered aimlessly towards the nearest and wandered in.

The interior was dimly lit. Pinpoint shafts focused on a collection of jewellery, but the strong lights, designed to show glittering splendour, merely managed to make the display cheap and utterly fake in contrast to the simple and varied collection of small pieces of old china in an adjacent showcase.

A bit like me, she muttered, tawdry and spurious. My whole life is a fake. Built of lies. Who am I? Nothing but a sham. Everything I thought was fixed and sure has blown away. Why couldn't I be Fergus's daughter? Why didn't he tell me? How could he leave it to her? Leaving me with half-hints. He should have told me. He had no right, no right. She closed her eyes in grieving desolation and then quite clearly heard his whispered words:

'Oh childie, light of my heart, you were such a bonus. From the moment I saw you in your

482

mother's arms, I was yours for ever. My darling girl.'

Her hand went to her mouth. Your mother? Oh God, that must be it. He must have thought I knew. He must have thought she told me.

And in that instant, with such tremendous force that she had to lean against the wall for support, her attitude to her mother moved from resentful mutiny to incandescent rage.

Had Eileen lied, even in that? Had she led Fergus to think Bid had been told the truth? With every atom of her being, Bid willed that Fergus at least had been truthful. It was something to hang on to but her belief only lasted a moment.

They were such cowards. He should have made sure, he should have told her himself, instead of being intimidated by Eileen. Always afraid to make trouble. They were both responsible.

Bridget Lacey. She carried his name. They had no right to let her believe their lies. What had they been afraid of? She knew now of course. The pair of them had covered up for so long that each evasion had added to their burden of guilt and their fear that she might turn on them.

Well, she'd turned against them, right enough. They had waited to pick and choose the best moment to tell her. They had paralysed themselves over it, weaving their smothering tissue of deceit. They must have thought the whole issue safely avoided; the unpleasantness swept firmly under the carpet. Bid leaned dizzily against the wall, her eyes closed, fighting against the muddle she'd been bequeathed.

No! No such thing as babies except in the warm cosy bosom of the church-blessed marriage. No illegitimacy here, not in this good Catholic country. Export the inconvenience, she thought savagely, in the good old, time-honoured way. A suppressed growl of laughter escaped her. And she wasn't even Irish. Maida Vale for God's sake.

They had lied even about that. But much worse were the things they hadn't said to her, or to each other. Sins of omission. No such luxury for her, she had inherited the problem they hadn't the courage to tackle themselves. In spades.

Problem? It was too monstrous for that tame word. What they so neatly dumped had attached itself, vice-like, to her, gnawing at both gut and reason. Names. Something wrong with the names. Con. Cling to that. Con. Short for? Conor? Or . . . ? What?

No. Don't think. Con. Daddy. Con Rynne. She staggered into the fresh air and looked around at the unfamiliar street. Where was she? What was she doing in this absurd place? Killing time – killing time before her long farewell. Rynne. Rynne. Rynne. Rynne.

Where was Cas? Why had he not contacted her? Did he not know she needed him? He must. He always knew. Always. Someone please tell him. Tell him it's urgent. A matter of life and death, she whispered softly. Ring Cas. Ring me. Please. Ring. Rynne.

It began to drizzle as she walked along. She hardly noticed, forcing herself to concentrate on the buildings, adding the numbers of the houses, subtracting, comparing the colours, focusing on the detail of decoration. Gradually, in spite of the terrible consuming anxiety, she half understood that the town was beautiful, its elegant houses and broad streets enhanced by the majestic mountains against which they were built.

I will stay here, she thought, far away where nobody knows. I'll have my baby here. She will have blue eyes. She will not have my eyes. Blue-eyed Cornelia. I will push her through that park and nobody will tell. I could live or die here and nobody would connect me . . .

She passed a secret little restaurant, licensed to sell oysters, clams, etc. Her stomach growled hungrily but it was the masculinity of its decoration that prompted the sudden rushing sweet memory of that first meal with her love. Cas. Con, came the treacherous echo. She walked on blindly.

The rain got heavier. She rounded the corner and came upon a modest little Italian bistro all gaudy red and green. Pressing her face against the window she could see the gay checked tablecloths and the plastic flowers which festooned the ceiling and a waiter gesticulating to her to come inside. A sudden desperate need for the warmth of it came over her. But she had to do something. What?

Did she have to do anything? For one breathless moment she thought of Eileen getting away with her righteous evasions for over thirty years – could she not have just a few, only a few, years of happiness for herself? One? Even one? But her inner voice hammered out its implacable message: she'd have to tell Cas.

'Oh dear heaven, let him not turn on me. Why should I suffer? I'm innocent. We're innocent.'

She went inside and sat down. As the smiling waiter approached the table, her head drummed out her fears for her child and her suppressed mistrust of Cas crept insidiously to the surface.

Why hadn't he told her more about his life? Why hadn't she asked? came the taunting riposte. The passport. The passport. Why was she so afraid? Even then? About his past. What about his past? Who was he? Why had he never taken her to Holland? Had he ever said he was Dutch? Had he ever actually said – this is where I was born and this was my family and this is what I am. No. No. He had not. She was appalled at how little she knew. Not even the origin of his strange name. Cas Van Rijn.

'Oh my sweet love.'

She felt weak. The waiter's smile had turned to concern.

'The signorina is not well? Wait, I will bring some *acqua minerale* OK?' He poured the acidulated water for her; she looked up tearfully and increased his concern. He picked up the menu and tucked it under his arm.

'Permit me, signorina, I will give you something light, something small for you. Leave it to me, eh?' She nodded gratefully.

*Renzo's*, the box of matches said. It was like every comforting little Italian restaurant she'd ever been in, like the little place they had eaten at, she and Cas, near Florence, where the elderly waitress stood by the table and intoned the same tired litany each night:

'Spaghetti, puntarelle petto di pollo, fettucine, bistecca, cannelloni . . .' And Cas would imitate her exactly so that now, when they went out to eat, he would lean over and intone the litany . . . *Oh my love, my life. Ring me.* Rynne. Rijn. Rynne. Rynne.

The music was as old-fashioned as the decor. Mantovani was replaced by Simon and Garfunkel singing 'Scarborough Fair'. Close enough, she thought, parsley, sage, rosemary . . .

Rosemary for remembrance. Her mother's strained, ill face rose up before her, pleading. Poor, sad, disappointed, proud Eileen. Had she been loved too well that first time? She, who had never realized how much she depended on Fergus. Eileen. Punishing him for her betrayal. Eileen. What would be her exact relationship to the child?

Grandmother? Certainly. Stepmother? Was there some neat shorthand to describe this convoluted link? My father's child, his daughter's child.

Renzo returned. He fussed around her like a father – *Oh Cas Cas*. He bent over her, placed the napkin on her lap and a small plate of delicate creamy pasta in front of her. Bread and more mineral water appeared from nowhere. Bid smiled up at him.

'Thank you.' Her eyes watered again. He patted her hand and poured her a small glass of wine.

'You must drink this, beautiful signorina,' he coaxed stagily. 'It will be good for you. Things are never so bad as they look. You'll see, everything will be OK.' He beamed down at her and left to greet a group of four coming through the door, all smiles and *bonhomie*. Bid looked down at the pale coils on her plate. Like my mind, she thought, worms in my mind. I wish Sal was here, she'd know what to do.

The record changed, Ella Fitzgerald crooned softly: *Every time we say goodbye, I die . . .*

The words of the song startled her into certainty that she would not see Cas again. He would not telephone. She wouldn't talk to him. He was . . . WHAT? Her jangled nerves screamed.

He knew. How could he? What was that picture doing in her mother's bag? Rynne. Rijn. Now, with peculiar clarity, she remembered young Dr O'Neill saying:

'I left her just as a visitor arrived and when they came with her lunch she was dead.' The visitor was a man? She'd said that, hadn't she? Could it have been Cas? Was that why Eileen was dead?

Oh dear God in Heaven. Bid closed her eyes in horror and knew as certainly as she knew anything that Cas was wandering off somewhere in the same state of shock as herself. She rose unsteadily to her feet.

'Have you a telephone please?' Renzo led her off to a small hallway. She rang Cas's office. The line was engaged. Bid didn't seem to notice. She leaned against the wall and drummed her fingers against her cheek.

'Listen to me,' she sobbed hoarsely. 'Listen. Somebody please listen to me. He's gone, gone to Dublin. I know he has. Oh Cas, help . . . help . . .' She dropped the receiver and left it dangling.

## CHAPTER THIRTY-FIVE

She tore from the restaurant and rushed into the street, running awkwardly through unnoticed elegance. Eyes down, keeping guard on her feet, intent on avoiding the lines of the paving stones. Round and round the town she went, blindly staggering through squares and streets and she knew not where, until some hours later she found herself sitting desolately by a pond in the park below the castle.

Children played around her, feeding ducks. Mothers walked by with tiny babies in pushchairs. She could have her baby here. Who would notice them among so many? That is what she would do; she would not leave. Nobody would find her. How lucky she had not told them where she was going.

A girl joined her on the bench. She was fair and serene and carried a baby on her hip. The toddler trotting beside her held a fishing rod in her hand. The sight of their contentment agonized Bid and, when the young mother smiled in greeting, she rushed headlong out of the park, running along the teeming streets until at last she reached the hotel.

She slipped through the foyer like a wraith, unnoticed. The lift was open, waiting. She ran swiftly and silently along the corridor. Let him be safe, she prayed.

She snatched up the phone and dialled the office again. The phone was still engaged. She redialled and redialled compulsively. Each time the same frustrating high-pitched tone greeted her. Sometimes she mumbled incoherently, then wept, then prayed aloud. He was there. He was there. He'd come to help her. How could she have doubted him? He had raced to her side as soon as he heard. How could she have thought he would do otherwise? Oh Cas.

She dialled the number again. This time it was answered immediately.

'Cas?' she whispered.

Silence, then a rather shaky voice answered.

'Mr Van Rijn is not in the office.' The line went dead.

Bid's heart slid down an escalator, a half-formed memory of a figure rising by the water . . .

'Where is he?' she whispered and cradled the phone. She walked slowly to the mirror and studied her reflection for a long time. She licked her finger and dreamily traced her outline. The flowered dress mocked her ghostly appearance, distracted her. Someone she once knew wore clothes like that – gay, and bright, full of colour. Someone people loved because she was fat and jolly and did things to make them happy. She had to do something now. What was it again? She gazed intently at the glass and began to nod her head as her mind went into a different shift. She dialled room service.

'A bottle of gin, and ice please. And a couple of glasses,' she added brightly. Her friend would need a glass.

She unclasped the gold cross and chain she always wore and ran a comb through her hair. She sat at the table and wrote while she waited. The tray, complete with tonic and crisps, arrived ten minutes later. She paid the waiter and gave him the letter to post. When he left, she drew the curtains and rang reception.

'I'll be going out for the evening,' she said gaily. 'I shall probably be very late, I don't want to be disturbed in the morning. On no account. I shall probably sleep till lunch-time.'

'Have a nice evening, madame.'

She turned on the television and poured a straight gin. She flicked restlessly from channel to channel as she gulped her drink. She gagged, poured a second, then a third. The warmth flooded back into her stiff body but her mind refused to let go, she still felt sober, wound-up, alert. She half-watched a wildlife programme, about whales, the music was nice, she closed her eyes. Then a repeat of *Till Death Us Do Part* came on. She drank deep and raised her glass in mock salute.

Whom God had joined together let no man – or daughter – pull asunder.

Cas was dead. She was sure of that now. The invisible cord would bind them together for eternity. God will not be mocked. Not by me.

She poured another drink and walked carefully to the bathroom, and undressed laboriously as the bath filled. She took her nightdress from her bag.

'Decent to the last,' she giggled and turned off the taps. She stood, glass in hand, in front of the mirror. It cut her off at the shoulders and the knees and focused on her swollen belly. She rubbed her hand across it and then doubled over as fear and panic overwhelmed her. She put out her hand to take something from her bag as the television turned to raucous pop. As she tried to switch it off, she dropped what she held. The two bottles of pills she had taken from her mother's house rolled towards her bare right foot. She bent unsteadily to pick them up and her head began to spin.

'Ah my friends! You've arrived then.' She cradled the tiny bottles lovingly in either hand and spoke softly, as to a child. The gin was rapidly taking effect. She could not read the labels, or distinguish one from the other. She smiled confidently. She already knew what they contained. She needed time that was all. Time. She switched off the television and refilled the glass. Her head swam as she staggered to the door and opening it a squeak, slipped the *Do not disturb* sign on the handle.

She turned on the radio. Ah good, a concert. They would think her friends had arrived early. As indeed they had. Bid felt very, very clever and witty. She smiled her dazed smile.

She opened both bottles of pills and counted six or seven capsules from each onto her hand, then gulped them down with more gin. Then, with the deliberate care of the drunkard, she put both open bottles and her full glass on the bedside table and turned down the cover. Everything was prepared.

She stepped into the steaming water, lay back and closed her eyes. She awoke an hour or so later confused and cold and reached blearily for the towel. She was immediately overcome with nausea and had to sit on the loo to steady herself before essaying the long journey to the bed where she dropped the towel and struggled into the old pink nightie. She did not notice that she was beginning to bleed.

'Now what have I to do?' She looked perplexedly around the strange room. The gin stood gleaming under the bedside light beckoning to her. The little pill bottles sat dark and smug beside it. She reached out, tipped the contents of both onto her hand and without hesitation washed them down.

She lay back. The sheets were cold. She wished Cas would hurry up. Why was he taking so long? Was this another surprise? Ah there he was! Wasn't he clever floating in like that? Darling Cas. Now he would take her in his arms and explain everything. So clever. He would take care of her. Nobody knew how to love her like Cas . . .

Her mind floated in and out of consciousness, the warmth of the too-heavy blankets almost smothering her.

'Why are you so sad, my love?' he asked, as he took her in his arms. 'Do not cry my lovely primavera, my Botticelli girl. I'll take care of you. Oh Bid, my love, my child, do not leave me. Come, my treasure, my springtime. Come! Oh Bid . . . oh darling Bid . . .'

'Cas?' she whispered softly. 'Oh Cas.'

# Grace

*Late October 1990*

**CAOINEADH AIRT UI LAOGHAIRE:** *The most moving lament in the Irish language, written by his wife for her dead husband. Fine translation by Eilis Dillon. Printed from the Poems of the Dispossessed.* DOLMEN, *Ireland.*

## CHAPTER THIRTY-SIX

'She looked so pitiful,' Father Crowley said. 'Unbalanced almost, as she dropped the pad at my feet. That really frightened me. Then she went away and did that terrible thing. I feel foolish speaking premonitions but I felt strongly that she was at risk and needed looking after.'

His eyes met Grace's. 'And you were her only living relative – if you were alive and if I could find you.' He reflected briefly. 'You see, since Eileen had spoken to me, I couldn't get you out of my mind. I saw you as her other victim and I'm not sure now which of you I felt more anxious about at that time. You or Bridget.' He brushed his hand over his hair.

'As I watched her taxi drive off, I made up my mind to do what I should have done twenty years before. I went straight around to Bartley Quinlan and asked him to start looking for you. After that I just got in the car and hared off to Ballymahon.'

'Why, have I relatives there still?' Grace asked in surprise.

'No, but I felt I had to do something, and there was an old postmistress still living whom I thought might have some idea of your family's where-abouts.'

They stood on the pier looking out into the Atlantic where the wind whipped up huge waves and sent them crashing into the bay. The clouds were on the move as the sky began to darken. The seagulls swirled above them crying their mournful dirge. There were few people about. Even the most enthusiastic golfers had abandoned the famous links which stretched into the distance behind them.

Grace had slipped quietly into the town a few days before, checked into a small hotel on its outskirts, then lay low for a recuperative twenty-four hours before presenting herself, timidly, to the priest, who had immediately, albeit unobtrusively, taken charge.

The sale of the Dublin house and its contents had been completed by private treaty. One hundred and eighty-four thousand Irish punts had been deposited at six and three-quarters per cent. But Grace had not once entered the house or taken part in the sale; Bartley Quinlan had arranged both. This he did with minimum fuss and little comment but she was aware, when at last she asked directions to Father Crowley's cottage, that he'd discovered a good deal about her since their first meeting and was perhaps anxious to learn more, for he fairly bristled with curiosity. It was a relief to get away.

She hired a car for the last lap of her journey and headed south-west from Dublin with mixed feelings of relief and fear of what might emerge. It had taken a determined effort. The priest's name still filled her with disquiet, so she was completely unprepared when her ogre turned out to be a stocky, kind-eyed seventy-five-year-old with a gammy leg and a warm smile. With his brick-red complexion and shock of snow white hair, he reminded her of Spencer Tracy.

'Call me Seamus,' he laughed after she'd stumbled her greeting. His eyes crinkled in amusement at her discomfort. She could see he didn't miss much.

'I don't think you're too comfortable with "Father," are you, Gráinne?'

'Grace,' she replied stiffly. 'I haven't been called Gráinne since I was a child. I prefer Grace.' She met his piercing gaze uncomfortably. 'Seamus,' she added awkwardly.

They had stood appraising each other, then, struck by the absurdity of her stand, she laughed and held out a hand.

'You're a great family for changing identities,' he remarked obscurely as he led her through the front door.

He lived in a snug little cottage on the south-west edge of the small seaside town and the smell of fresh-baked bread was as welcoming as a mother's arms. He fussed over her like a lost child, clucking about the cold and the rain. Then he poured her a glass of hot spiced whiskey which he let her drink peacefully and alone by the fire.

One wall of his small living-room was book-lined. There were theological works on the bottom shelf and working upwards, the books were classified by subject and size, ascending from folio to octavo. He appeared to be bilingual because the two uppermost shelves were Irish language, mainly

499

printed in the uncial. Grace ran her eye over his considerable collection of Irish Renaissance literature, an interest he obviously shared with Fergus Lacey, and was amused to notice that small pink filing cards punctuated the neat rows, on each of which was written a title and, in the top left hand corner, the word: *desideratum*.

The priest disappeared into the kitchen. She could hear him whistling softly while he moved about. When at last he called her for supper, he presented the feast he'd prepared with a smirk of self-satisfaction so infectious she'd surrendered the last of her suspicions.

For a couple of days, having encouraged her to come and go at her own pace and without intrusion, he steered away from personal matters. It was as good as a rest cure. She explored the majestic coastline and allowed the calm of the place to seep into her.

On the third day, he must have judged she was ready because he came calling to her lodging after breakfast and suggested a stroll along the beach. The day was mild and sunny. They set out at ten, stopping and starting as his lameness demanded, and gradually let the talk drift towards those subjects which were uppermost in their minds.

'And did the postmistress know where my parents lived?' Grace asked.

'In a roundabout way only,' he replied. 'She knew they'd settled in Birmingham because a relation of hers was a doctor there.'

'Doctor Lawson?' she asked in surprise. The priest nodded.

'But he's dead.'

'Yes, but it was a lead of sorts. It gave Bartley something to go on, but unfortunately the postal strike held things up. Not that time mattered by then.'

He fell silent for a time as they stood watching the sea.

'It was so easy. All those years when I should have done something and didn't . . .' He sounded despairing. 'I pushed it all out of my mind and made a virtue of not interfering.' He clutched momentarily at her arm. 'You were part of my flock, my responsibility, and I let you down. A failure of charity. I cannot forgive myself.'

Flock? So innocuous a word, reminding her of early catechism drills. Pastoral or biblical, it had resonances of past guilt and threat. Then, bizarrely, the Anton Mauve painting from the mews flat flashed through her memory, unnerving her. She turned to him earnestly.

'How could you have done anything?'

'I could have spoken to your parents at the beginning, when I suspected what was happening. But I was younger then and intimidated by your father who was a rather formidable man. He was so much older – in attitude as well as age. He refused to discuss such delicate matters with me and it seemed an impertinence to insist. You were sacrificed to good manners, Grace,' he said sadly. 'Or maybe there was the same shyness in both of us about personal things. Either way, it was the worst we could have done.'

They walked slowly along the edge of the links, the springy grass soft and yielding beneath their feet. The old man obviously found the going easier because he increased his pace.

'Your grandmother came to me before she died,' he continued presently. 'Your father always insisted the boy had abused you. *Interfered* was the word he used. But Nonie said it wasn't so, and she was right, because Eileen confirmed that he only jumped on you to try to stop you screaming. That was when I realized she hadn't ever seen any of you again, or wanted to, even to the last. I was appalled at her bitterness. She'd manufactured demons even where there were none. Your sister had little capacity for happiness. Or forgiveness.'

He then described calmly, and in as much detail as he could, the story Eileen had told. Grace listened without comment. Her anxieties and her sister's hardly seemed to match in any particular, but she was touched and grateful for his determination to ease the burden of the past and make clear what had perplexed her for so long. That she had already worked through most of it she knew was due to Bid; to her the credit. She urgently wanted him to see how Bid had been victim of that same stupidity. She longed to rehabilitate the girl in his eyes because he hinted that her suicide had not only disturbed him at a personal level but had done violence to his faith. But while she was framing her plea he broke into her thoughts, drawing her backwards:

'All the time I let myself believe you'd just lost contact the way families do, or that your parents had refused to make it up. When she told me she'd done it deliberately, I couldn't credit it. I was shocked, then ashamed, at my own negligence.

After all, though I knew her as Fergus's wife for almost twenty years, I also knew her as Eileen Sullivan. Knew you both as children.'

Grace stared fixedly ahead, seeing again the child and feeling again the cold grip of her old terror. Hesitantly, she began to describe it in an almost childlike way and voice which chillingly recalled for Father Crowley his last encounter with Bid.

'Dada came in. The wind and rain were lashing at the window. It must have been banging against the drainpipe because I woke up and got out of bed to shut it . . . and then I saw this monstrous thing on my sister's bed. All black. I was terrified. I had seen it before, many times, but I would bury my head in the blankets and pretend it wasn't there. That night it turned its face and looked at me. I couldn't move with fear. I stood transfixed on the cold linoleum and screamed and screamed. The eyes were bloodshot, the hair plastered down on the face. He must have been soaked with the rain but it terrified me.'

'Poor Con,' he said but so softly that she did not hear.

'He jumped on top of me. I could smell him and feel the soft, damp skin on my face. He put his hands over my mouth and suddenly Nonie was there and Dada . . . dragging me away and holding me too tight and there was blood and, Oh God, Dada was lying on the floor and they were all shouting and screaming.'

'Nobody touched you, Grace do you hear me? You weren't raped,' he said sharply.

'They wouldn't listen to me. I was kept in bed. The doctor came and hurt me. Nobody explained

503

anything. Eileen was gone and I thought everyone was blaming me, looking at me as if I was dirty. Then Mammy and Dada disappeared and Nonie got sick and nobody would talk, or listen. I thought it was all my fault. *She'll get us kilt, he said.* I lost track of time ... It's all so confused.' Her voice had become flat, robbing her narrative of all emotion.

'I don't know when the nightmares started. I dreamt Dada would come into my room and put his hand over my mouth to stop me screaming. He sat on the bed and held me in his arms and told me not to disturb Mama. She was so sick. He said I'd have to forget and not tell a soul. It was wicked, he said. Then you started coming to the house and I thought you were trying to punish me, take me away ... that I'd go to hell.

'Eileen never came back. The house was full of people. They said she was taken from them and I thought she was dead and that Dada'd killed her. You see I thought it was my father who abused me and that he killed her to stop her telling. I don't know what I thought. The awful thing is that I didn't remember the boy for years and years. Not until Bid.'

He stopped short and when she turned he was looking at her in horrified disbelief, his hand to his mouth.

'You confused the two? You thought it was your father had touched you? And then killed her? You lived with that? My God, my God. I didn't try hard enough. I should have kept at it. May God forgive me, I abandoned you.'

He took her hand and held it tightly as they

walked along, as he might a child, and she felt comforted.

'They ran off. Poor children, they were terrified too. Your father threatened the lad with the police for molesting you, and his own da was after him for the money they stole before they went. It didn't help that they set fire to the house, though I don't think that was intentional. I don't even know if they were responsible. There were those who said it was the bookie set light to it himself, as an insurance scam.'

Grace barely heard him, now she'd started, she was unable to stop talking.

'After Nonie died . . . I can't remember when that was . . . We went away. My parents never, ever spoke about Eileen to me. My father died when I was fourteen. He was seventy-five then, but he looked a hundred. Long after, I tried to ask my mother but she said she couldn't bear to think of it. She was so frail and ill. She never got over her tuberculosis you know, she just faded away. Gothic, isn't it? Perhaps I was always a bit mad.

'I was doing my A levels when she died, I didn't finish them. Dr Lawson found me an au pair job in Richmond with some relations of his. That's how I met Reggie. What could the poor sap do but marry me? Orphaned, barely out of school and penniless.

'I was happy then. His parents were wonderful to me and Reggie was like brother and friend and husband all at once. He hadn't that awful burden of guilt which sat on our house like an uneruped volcano, waiting to belch out and smother you. Those first years were like summer. He tried to get me to study again but every time I tried, the

505

memory of my mother's last years got in the way. It was a dismal failure. Then one day I went out and sold all my textbooks and somehow I just went on from there. With the books I mean.

'Reggie and I were fine until we decided we'd like to start a family. Suddenly sex became a problem and the nightmares came back. I had one miscarriage after another. Nothing Reggie said would persuade me to talk about it. How could I tell anyone that I thought my father was either a rapist or a murderer or both? I couldn't talk and I wouldn't listen. I was much too afraid.

'It did for my marriage all right. It took a long, long time but then everything happened at once. Reggie left me in April, the week after Bid died. In May Bartley Quinlan resurrected my long-lost sister for me,' she said bitterly. 'I think I went mad in earnest then.'

The priest walked beside her in silence while she spoke about the break-up of her marriage. Describing the inevitability of it, the pain, the disappointments and Reggie's search for consolation which in the end became intolerable for both of them. All the time he held her hand between his rough paws, kneading her cold fingers in wordless consolation.

'I suppose when it comes down to it, I needed a parent and Reggie wanted a grown-up woman. He also wanted children. I needed him to be my tower of strength. I manufactured dependability for him, then blamed him when it turned out that he needed propping up as much as I did. Our incompatibility grew from such innocent beginnings. We both thought we wanted the same thing and it took me a very long time indeed to admit how terrified I was of parenthood. It brought the past crashing in on me.'

Seamus sat down heavily on the round grey stones and asked if she'd mind him catching his breath for a few minutes. She stood skimming flat pebbles over the water until he rose to his feet and took up the story once more.

'Bartley was already looking for you the week Bridget died, that's how we found you so soon afterwards. When I got back from Ballymahon on the Monday, I started ringing Bridget's flat. All day Tuesday as well. I rang the magazine but the young one I talked to knew nothing. It was too late of course and in my bones I knew I'd lost her. I should have hung on to her, not let her out of my sight, the state she was in.'

'Father Crowley,' Grace interrupted, 'do you remember a drowning in the canal about that time?'

'Oh yes, very well.' He looked puzzled at the *non sequitur* but answered promptly enough. 'As I recall, the comings and goings at the canal under-scored Eileen's funeral. A Dutchman, wasn't it? You can imagine what the local wags made out of that one – a Dutchman drowning in a canal.' He turned to her. 'Why do you ask?'

'Did Bid remark on it?' She evaded his question.

He stopped and scratched his head meditatively before replying.

'Yes, I believe she asked about it when I went around the morning after the funeral. Saturday. There were several police cars about. She didn't show much interest though.'

'Didn't you think that was a bit unusual?'

'No, not really. Her mother had just died. She

507

was overwrought. I'm not sure she was noticing anything very much. Specially after what I felt compelled to tell her.' He stopped dead and rubbed his jaw. 'But come to think of it,' he added pensively, 'there was another rather curious incident. It happened on the way to the cemetery for the burial. As we paused by the house, Dinny pointed at some youngsters fishing by the canal. I didn't catch what he said, but it seemed to upset Bridget because she began to cry.'

'Did she go near the canal? Meet anyone?' She perplexed him with her insistence.

'I've no idea. How could I have? You should ask Maureen Lenehan.'

'I did,' she said shortly and added: 'While you were with her did she ever go out alone?'

'Why yes. The Thursday night, after the removal. We were all round at the Lenehans'. Halfway through the evening I noticed she wasn't with the group. Maureen said she must have gone out for a breath of air. I was waiting for an opportunity to talk to her as Eileen had asked, and I was just working up to it when I realized she'd gone, for about half an hour I'd say. Didn't Maureen say?'

'Yes. I just wanted to be sure. I walked from the Lenehans' house to the canal and back, several times. At my fastest it took twenty-five minutes.' Grace spoke as if to herself. The priest shook his head and looked at her curiously.

'You think Bridget had something to do with the man's death?' His voice was tight. 'She couldn't. I was there when they dragged his body out and I talked to the sergeant in charge. He said the children who saw him drown insisted it happened just after the funeral passed. Bridget was with us in the car. Besides, the police . . .' He stopped short as Grace cried out in astonishment: 'Look, the peninsula is disappearing!'

A great ball of mist, like a giant white carpet, began to roll over the end of Liscannor point.

'It's no wonder we Irish crave excitement,' observed the priest drily. 'Nothing lives up to the dramatics of our weather.'

They watched, fascinated for a few minutes while the landscape disappeared.

'We'd better step lively,' he said. 'It'll be pouring down on us in a few minutes.'

Skirting the golf-links, she ran and he hobbled across to the small stone cottage nestling in a low incline. They could hardly see the rain it was so fine, but within seconds they were soaked.

'Dry yourself, Grace, or you'll get your death of cold. I'll stoke up the fire, then I think we both need a drink.' He brought her a fresh towel and, while she dried herself, made them each a hot whiskey.

'Do you know the man? Did Bridget?' he asked when they sat down.

'Yes,' she said quietly. 'He was her lover. The father of her child.'

He sat down heavily. 'Could you repeat that?'

It was as though she'd hit him, as if the air had been punched out of him. He slumped back and closed his eyes for so long that she thought he was asleep. She sipped her drink and watched the leaping flames, wishing she hadn't mentioned it. After a long silence he said:

'She looked terribly frail when she left. Maureen Lenehan said she hardly ate a thing all the time she

509

was there. She had traces of that strange mask some women get when they're expecting. Rather unearthly it was. Sadly, she didn't say anything to either of us about that. Didn't trust us. Poor child, she was very defensive. With reason. Perhaps she thought we hadn't noticed her condition.'

'But you had, of course?'

'Yes.'

'Did her mother know?'

'She never mentioned it, if she did. Grace, tell me, what has this to do with the drowning?' He eyed her suspiciously. 'What exactly are you implying?'

'I just wanted to be sure,' she mumbled.

'Sure that he committed suicide, or sure that Bridget didn't push him? That is a serious allegation to make.' He held her gaze for a long moment before softening his tone. 'There is something else, isn't there? Something you aren't telling me?'

She nodded miserably. 'I don't know for certain. There are so many things I'm not sure about. Really. There are things you know and things I think I know, but they don't yet match.' She looked at him sorrowfully. 'And perhaps things she would have wanted neither of us to know.'

He left the room abruptly and disappeared into what she presumed must be his bedroom. Silence fell, apart from the slight crackling of the fire, and for a time Grace lingered uncertainly. When he didn't return, she picked up her damp jacket and was tip-toeing towards the front door when the priest hailed her from the kitchen. He held a saucepan of steaming soup – tomato by the smell – and was absurdly got out in a huge red apron, as if he wanted to lighten the tension, make amends. He

510

directed her briskly to the table and ladled out the soup, then pushed a plate of pale brown soda cake towards her.

'I had just made up my mind to fly off to London to see her,' he said, 'when the Edinburgh police called . . .'

'You went there? How did they know who to contact?' A faint recollection of Sarah mentioning a clergyman came to her.

'She left a letter for me. In the hotel. I identified her body.'

'But I thought Sarah Roberts did that?'

'Ah yes, she got there just before I did. They had some difficulty finding me. I left for Ballymahon in such a rush I forgot to even tell my housekeeper.'

He pulled a letter from his pocket and made as if to give it to her then held it on the table. He pointed to what was written on the envelope:

Rev. Seamus Crowley
St Stephen's
Portobello.

Underneath in another hand was added:

Dublin, Rep. of Ireland.

'The letter was in her hotel room, stuffed in the envelope but not sealed. The address wasn't exactly informative. There is a Portobello just outside Edinburgh but the church there is called St Mary's. They started searching for other Portobellos but then a young sergeant – an Irishman as luck would have it – remembered noticing an Aer Lingus label on her bag and put two and two together. Knowing there was a Portobello in Dublin, he directed them to my parish. But by then her friend had got on to the police.'

'Bid wrote to her.'

'I didn't realize that. What did she say?'

'One sad thing stuck in my mind: *They destroyed us with their lies.*'

'Do you know what she meant?'

'Yes I think so, but it is one of the uncertainties.' She took the dishes to the sink and stood with her back to him staring out the window. The rain had stopped and the weak October sun tried timidly to break through the clouds. Stretching her neck she could see it glinting in small patches on the restless sea. Presently she turned to him and said:

'I found a fragment of a letter Eileen wrote before she died.'

'That wretched letter,' he broke in angrily. 'It didn't say a blessed thing. After she'd instructed me to talk to the girl. She wouldn't listen to me when I begged her to leave well enough alone. She said she had to tell her, write to her. She made me promise I'd talk to Bridget, if she died. Against my own better judgement I agreed. I thought I knew what she'd written, then it turned out she'd changed her mind and told her nothing. So I bulldozed in . . . I feel responsible for the poor girl's despair.' He shook his head from side to side in disbelief at how completely he'd been guyed.

'But she did,' Grace said quietly. 'I'm very much afraid she did.'

'What?' he roared.

'I found two envelopes. Same writing. One complete letter, but only a fragment of a second, both apparently written the night before she went into hospital.'

He began to say something then thought better of

it and held back, waiting for her to continue. A nerve in his right temple pulsated rapidly. He put down his spoon and took off the apron as if to draw attention to his clerical clothes. The letter from Bid was still lying beside his plate. Grace had a strong urge to put her hand out for it, to read it.

'Father,' she said at last. 'Father, it wasn't Fergus Eileen ran off with, was it?'

'No. Of course not,' he cried impatiently. 'I thought you knew that? Surely you remember the boy?'

She said urgently: 'I told you. For a long time I only remembered my father in the room. It was in Bid's flat that I finally remembered there was someone else – a boy – but no matter how I tried I had no recollection of his name.' She stopped, then asked carefully: 'Can you tell me who my sister ran off with? What was his name?'

'Con,' he replied without hesitation. 'Con, he was called. He was aptly named, and his ould fella before him.'

'Con. Yes. That rings a bell. Con.' She sounded anxious. 'Was that short for something?'

'Yes. Cornelius.'

'Ah.' Her breath expelled loudly. 'Isn't that unusual?'

'Not in Cork, where his mother was from, it's quite common there. His surname was less common, which is why I remembered it. Rynne.'

'Aaah.' She shrank into herself. 'He was from Cork?'

'No. His mother only, I believe. God only knows where his father came from. England, I think. Trouble he was and up to all sorts of mischief.

513

They'd only been in the town a year or so. Before that the Lord only knows. I seem to remember Con was also born in England, or so it was said. They came and went. Some of the townspeople called them travellers.'

'Cornelius Rynne,' she murmured softly and closed her eyes. 'Bid's father?'

'Yes. Read this.' He passed the letter across the table.

> You were right. I didn't want to believe you were right. I know now you were only trying to help. But you see I'd already found my father. He was going to give me back my name. Bridget Kate Rynne. I don't think I like it any more.
>
> I am doing this because he's dead. So, you see, now I have no name again. So many lies, there were so many lies that I did not believe you when you tried to tell the truth but you took my Dad away. Both of them. I've done so many bad things that I don't know what else to do. Pray for me.

Grace swallowed hard, treading carefully. 'Do you know what she meant by I'd already found my father?'

'No. I thought she must have been confused. At first I didn't take it in that she'd got the name right. Because I hadn't mentioned it. Then I thought she must have found the birth certificate in the house, but if she did, she didn't say. But then I can't really remember what she said that last day.'

Seamus Crowley suddenly looked old, without vigour, hunched over the table, his stubby fingers playing over the writing on the creased envelope.

The movement continued as Grace silently laid a scrap of newspaper beside it. His forefinger slid over the smiling face, paused; he looked up at her in surprise.

'Eileen showed me this. She thought it was . . .'

'Bid's father?'

'Yes.' Surprised. 'How did you know?'

Before replying she fetched the magazine clipping and a studio photo of Cas from her bag and brought them to the table.

'When I was in Dublin I went to the hospital and spoke to Dr O'Neill.' She picked up the photograph. 'I showed her this. She recognized him at once. She said he had visited my sister a couple of hours before she died. She remembered it perfectly because she'd met him as she was leaving the room. She said she held the door open to let him pass so she got a good look at him. She knew he was a relation because he looked so like Eileen's daughter.'

He laid the two pictures side by side and examined them minutely.

'That's Con all right.'

'Yes.'

'Where,' he asked carefully 'where did you get this?'

'The magazine clipping came from Bid's office,' she prevaricated. He raised his head slowly. She could almost see his thoughts ballooning above his head and she dreaded what was coming.

'Was there some particular reason why you showed the photographs to the doctor? Grace?' His eyes narrowed as he flicked the scrap of newspaper towards her. 'And this?'

'I found it in Bid's place, by the bed, when I found the letters. I think they may have come from her mother's bag which was there as well.'

'She must have got in touch with him after all.' Disbelief blanched his voice. 'Did the letter mention Con's name?'

'Not in the scrap I found.'

'Then how . . . Where did it come from?'

She shied from his persistence, hesitating before she turned the sheet to show him the telephone number scrawled on the other side.

'Did you write this?'

'No.'

'But it meant something to you?'

'Yes. I checked it out. It was Rynne's business number. In London.'

'But you said you'd never heard his name until I told you just now?' he accused.

'It's true! You must believe that. I did not know. He'd changed his name – adjusted it.' She scribbled Rynne. Then laboriously dotted both branches of the y and put a stroke through the second n and e. Rÿn. Then she wrote *Van Rijn* beside the telephone number and passed it to him. 'Different spelling.' Her finger jabbed at the words Van Rijn. The priest grabbed it.

'What does that mean?'

'It's a name.'

'Which means something to you?'

'Yes,' she mumbled not meeting his eye.

'Grace. Whose name?'

'The man who drowned in the canal.'

'Bridget's, er, lover? Was he some relation of Con?' his voice rose querulously.

'Yes,' she mumbled, eyes down.

'Look at me, Grace. Are you playing games or trying to protect my feelings? You're talking about the Dutchman?'

'So he claimed.' She couldn't meet his eye.

'Claimed?' He drew the word out in rising disbelief.

'He wasn't really Dutch. When Bid met him he was introduced to her as a Dutchman. Apparently he didn't correct that impression at the time. I suppose he didn't intend to get involved.'

'Being already married?' His voice had taken on a harsh edge.

'Well, yes.'

Almost too late, she pulled back, ashamed that she was repaying his concern with iconoclastic swipes at his beliefs.

'She said he was divorced. Was he?'

'No, it hadn't, er, quite come through,' she feebly echoed poor, sad Bid's hope.

'Poor foolish Bid.' Father Crowley looked thoughtfully at Grace, light dawning. 'Grace? What did he call himself?' he begged quietly.

'Cas Van Rijn,' she answered simply. 'He was the joint managing director of a firm called Hanning-Van Rijn. His partner suggested the adjustment of the name. It sounded more Dutch,' she extemporized, not meeting his eye.

'Cas? Did you say? What sort of name is that?'

She looked at him steadily but did not share Livy's little joke.

'Could be just short for Cornelius?' She emptied her voice of emotion and added softly, 'He didn't know about Bid. Neither of them knew anything

517

about the connection. It was a complete fluke that they met at all. They were innocent. If Eileen Lacey had told the poor girl her father's name, the penny might have dropped. But apparently she didn't. And Eileen is a common name, so he can't have made that connection either. Perhaps Bid never referred to her mother by her first name. Nobody else did either. Everyone I talked to called her Mrs Lacey. I noticed, because it's quite unusual these days.' She raised her eyes and spoke very deliberately: 'Father Cowley, I am certain that until the end, neither of them knew they were related. I'm so sorry.'

His mouth opened as the full import of what she said reached him, then he leaned on the table and rested his head in his hands. He began to rock to and fro.

## CHAPTER THIRTY-SEVEN

'What will you do now, Grace?' Father Crowley asked when she came to say goodbye a couple of days later.

'There are some things I have to see to at home. Sort out Bid's flat, find somewhere to live, move out of the house. Reggie will need it for his new family.'

'No family for you?'

She smiled and shook her head. 'I don't think I could manage that,' she said lightly, 'at least not for a long time.'

'What'll you do?' he repeated.

'I thought I might come back to Ireland for a while. A few months. Go to Ballymahon perhaps, see what I can do about Gráinne Sullivan.'

'You could do worse than help her grow into grace,' he quipped, and chuckled.

'I had it in mind.' She smiled and held out her hand. 'Goodbye, Seamus. Thank you.' She wanted to hug him but held back shyly.

'I hope you'll come back to see me, Grace? Soon?'

'I'd like that.'

He held the car door open while she adjusted her seat belt. She grinned up at him.

'Seamus? I believe I may be able to fill some of those gaps in your shelves.'

'Oh dear, oh dear, you've found me out. Greed is all it is,' he twinkled.

'I have a feeling there are many of your desiderata on Bid's bookshelves.'

'Fergus's books? Surely you won't break up such a fine collection?'

'I think so. Let other people have a bit of fun. Besides, I bet she'd be pleased for you to have what you need. I've taken note.'

'Have you now?' he said, then added sadly, 'I'm not sure Bid had much understanding of those lovely books, poor girl, she wasn't a scholar.'

'Perhaps not, but she certainly cherished them. Perhaps because they belonged to her father. They're in beautiful condition. I think she'd be pleased for you to take what you want. And so would I.'

As he beamed his pleasure, his already red face deepened alarmingly.

'Then you'd better come back soon with your benisons,' he grinned.

'There's a condition.'

'Well now, I wondered if there might be.'

'You choose what you want and then help me find homes for the rest?'

'Ah. The bookseller.'

'That's right.' She smiled. 'I may as well learn something while I bury the angst. What do you think?'

'You've persuaded me. I think it's a fine idea.' He touched her shoulder affectionately. 'I'll expect you then. Goodbye, Grace, dear child.'

'Goodbye, Father.'

As she drove away, she watched through her rear view mirror until his stocky figure was just a black speck on the horizon.

# ENVOI

*Dear Livy,*

*I promised I would write to you if I found out anything more about Cas's death. Over the past few weeks I've learned a good deal, but even now the exact circumstances remain a matter of conjecture. It is, I'm afraid, a long and sad story – mine and theirs – inextricably linked as you will see. There is no-one to blame. We each had our own agenda and fears, and though they overlapped, none coincided exactly with the fears of another.*

*One thing is quite certain: Cas was not in Dublin to see Bid and she was nowhere near him when he went into the canal. She was in the undertaker's car on her way to Mount Jerome cemetery. I'm not saying they did not meet – after all he died not a hundred yards from her house – but as the story unfolds I think you will come to believe, as I do, that they both took quite independent decisions to die, even though the culminating reason was the same in each case.*

*The first crucial element was the interview Eileen Lacey had with Father Crowley the night before she went into hospital – and the letters she subsequently wrote. Having, he thought, dis-*

suaded her from her determination to find Bid's father, he spent hours begging her to be gentle in her disclosures to Bid. He felt strongly, and tried to make her see that there was nothing to be gained from breast beating at that stage. He urged her to write simply and lovingly and just give Bid, at most, the bare bones of the story. And though he did not know it, he was successful on one point at least: the letter she gave him next day, to pass on to Bid, was entirely anodyne. The pity was that Eileen omitted to say so and entirely forgot to rescind her request that he explain things to Bid. Nor did she mention Con. But, though I have no way of checking it, I am convinced that far from abandoning her search, she was already on his track.

A further unfortunate complication was that Eileen also wrote a full confession that night and then suppressed, but alas, did not destroy it. Instead it either went with her to the hospital or was left somewhere in the house for Bid to find. I cannot believe she really intended this, it would be too cruel. She was mortally ill, in pain and probably much too confused to remember exactly what she was doing, much less to sort things out. Father Crowley had no further influence because he never saw her alone again. The only time she accepted his visits was when her daughter brought him to the hospital.

The second and probably the most important factor was the timing of my sister's death and Cas's connection with it – of which more anon – for I discovered he'd been to see her the morning of the day she died. The doctor I spoke to

*identified him from the photo you lent me. I
believe it was then he discovered that the woman
he had married as Eileen Ann Sullivan had for
thirty years been living as Eileen Lacey – my
sister and Bid's mother.*

*How that grotesque meeting was arranged I
cannot be sure. A chance sight of a press photo
seems likeliest because I don't think he would
have ever found her without her first getting in
touch. She must have used her maiden name
when she wrote. At what point the link was
made heaven only knows. But I believe that
when Cas walked from the hospital he knew that
he had fathered a child on his own daughter and
that Eileen was holding the evidence of their
relationship. After that, the whole tragedy was
unstoppable.*

*Some time during Wednesday afternoon he
may have tried to contact Bid and been told
she'd gone to Dublin. He waited, for the best
part of a couple of days, on the bench outside the
pub which looks directly across Canal Road to
the Lacey house on Toronto Terrace. If he was
hoping to talk to her before she saw her mother,
circumstances conspired against him. When Bid
arrived she was immediately carried off by her
friends. On Thursday too, she was constantly
chaperoned, except for a brief half-hour or so
late in the evening. It is just possible that they
might have met then but somehow I can't
convince myself they did – the timing seems all
wrong.*

*Then on Friday afternoon, the funeral cortège
stopped outside the house, as is the custom here.*

Cas had certainly enough local knowledge to realize that if Eileen was buried on Friday the chances were that she died on Wednesday. Perhaps he killed her – or thought he had? God knows. Or maybe the funeral procession may have given him the hope that with Eileen dead Bid need never know – if he was also out of the way. I now believe, perhaps foolishly, that slender thread of hope propelled him into the water. He must really have loved Bid.

Perhaps it was the drink that distorted the poor man's thinking, because the sad fact is, the evidence Eileen had shown him was still in the hospital and, with her death, passed into Bid's possession. But I suppose even if that occurred to him he would have known that the questions Bid should have asked earlier would now be asked – you said yourself that he could never resist a direct question – so whichever way, he was bound to lose. Poor Cas.

Poor devious Cas. You're probably wondering why I thought he had local knowledge? How had he come by it? I'm afraid, Livy, even with you he was not as straight as you thought. For one thing, he crucially failed to tell you of his Irish connection and Irish wife. But once I saw the name on his English passport something in my memory clicked and the pieces of the jigsaw began to fit into place. I did not recognize the name exactly, but something, somewhere stirred. It is a base thought I know, but I wonder if that unknown, unguessed at, connection added yet another frisson to his, as we now know, familial attraction to and for Bid.

*How much he told her or how much she guessed we can only speculate about. But enough, I believe, for her to work out their relationship once she'd found the letter Eileen meant to suppress, and then, for whatever blurred reasoning, did not. But to explain properly I think I'd better start at the beginning for it is there, I believe, that the first crucial misunderstanding took place which sowed the seed they were to reap so plentifully and so disastrously.*

*You see, Livy, if he had not been speaking Dutch . . .*

**THE END**

# A SELECTION OF CRIME NOVELS
# AVAILABLE FROM BANTAM BOOKS

| 50540 8 | KILLING FLOOR | Lee Child £5.99 |
| 50541 6 | DIE TRYING | Lee Child £5.99 |
| 17510 6 | A GREAT DELIVERANCE | Elizabeth George £5.99 |
| 40168 8 | A SUITABLE VENGEANCE | Elizabeth George £5.99 |
| 40237 4 | FOR THE SAKE OF ELENA | Elizabeth George £5.99 |
| 40846 1 | IN THE PRESENCE OF THE ENEMY | Elizabeth George £5.99 |
| 40238 2 | MISSING JOSEPH | Elizabeth George £5.99 |
| 17511 4 | PAYMENT IN BLOOD | Elizabeth George £5.99 |
| 40845 3 | PLAYING FOR THE ASHES | Elizabeth George £5.99 |
| 40167 X | WELL-SCHOOLED IN MURDER | Elizabeth George £5.99 |
| 50385 5 | A DRINK BEFORE THE WAR | Dennis Lehane £5.99 |
| 50584 X | DARKNESS, TAKE MY HAND | Dennis Lehane £5.99 |
| 50585 8 | SACRED | Dennis Lehane £5.99 |
| 81220 3 | GONE, BABY, GONE | Dennis Lehane £5.99 |
| 50586 6 | FAREWELL TO THE FLESH | Gemma O'Connor £5.99 |
| 50587 4 | TIME TO REMEMBER | Gemma O'Connor £5.99 |
| 81263 7 | SINS OF OMISSION | Gemma O'Connor £5.99 |
| 81262 9 | FALLS THE SHADOW | Gemma O'Connor £5.99 |
| 50542 4 | THE POISON TREE | Tony Strong £5.99 |

All Transworld titles are available by post from:

**Book Service by Post, PO Box 29, Douglas, Isle of Man IM99 1BQ.**

Credit cards accepted. Please telephone 01624 675137,

fax 01624 670923, Internet http://www.bookpost.co.uk or

e-mail: bookshop@enterprise.net for details.

**Free postage and packing in the UK.** Overseas customers

allow £1 per book (paperbacks) and £3 per book (hardbacks).